"You are a liar, Amara, and a bad one at that . . .

"Amara, I care little of what path we choose. The result will be the same. I can kiss you senseless or prod your cursed temper until neither of us sees reason. Either way, it will be my body covering yours, my name you cry out when the passion crests, making you wonder if a person could die from the shattering joy."

They stared at each other, both remembering the kisses they had shared and she forgot to be angry or afraid of him. He could make her feel that way again. She must have sensed his purpose because she asked, "This is your notion of courtship?"

"No, just a pleasurable means to end the madness. From my way of thinking, the last ten years or so have been a courtship of sorts. It is not my fault if you have not been paying attention."

TEMPTING
the Heiress

Barbara Pierce

St. Martin's Paperbacks

TEMPTING THE HEIRESS

Copyright © 2004 by Barbara Pierce.

ISBN: 0-312-98621-1

Printed in the United States of America

St. Martin's Paperbacks edition / May 2004

St. Martin's Paperbacks are published by St. Martin's Press, 175 Fifth Avenue, New York, NY 10010.

10 9 8 7 6 5 4 3 2 1

*I dedicate this book in memory of
my grandparents, Annabell and Homer Whitmore.*

TEMPTING
the *Heiress*

Phebe: *Good shepherd, tell this youth what 'tis to love.*

Silvius: *It is to be all made of sighs and tears . . .*
It is to be all made of fantasy,
All made of passion and all made of wishes,
All adoration, duty and observance,
All humbleness, all patience and impatience,
All purity, all trial, all observance . . .

—William Shakespeare, from
As You Like It, act 5, sc. 2, 1. 83–97.

CHAPTER ONE

London, 1810

It was a cunning ambush. Amara Claeg had certainly underestimated the gentleman's daring. As the tolling bell signaled the imminent commencement of Vauxhall Garden's eleven o'clock fireworks, Matteo Taldo, Conte Prola, took advantage of the situation. Anticipating their party's distracted eagerness to depart the dark avenue in search of a splendid viewing location, the Italian gallant culled her from the crowd and pushed her deeper into the shadowed elm grove. Her objections were promptly silenced by a ravishing kiss. Such intensity provided little opportunity for her to savor his impromptu display of clandestine passion. Amara's muffled protest only seemed to encourage her new suitor. Placing her palms on his chest, she tried shoving him away, but he shackled her wrists and pressed them to his heart.

Desperate for breath, Amara ended the kiss by turning her face away. "My lord, cease. The others will wonder about our absence." She did not mention that of late, her parents, the newly promoted Lord and Lady Keyworth, had had aspirations to marry her off to this specific Italian aristocrat. Being discovered in a passionate entanglement would only encourage the outcome.

His grip on her wrists allowed Conte Prola to effortlessly pull her back into his embrace. The shadows concealing them could not mask the subtle arcing of his mouth and glimpse of white teeth, nor the rebellious glitter blazing in his dark gaze. "Signorina Claeg, forgive me. Am I to forever admire and never stroke? Your beauty inspires boldness."

Sensing his mood was more teasing than predatory, she warily returned his smile. It was difficult to remain angry with the gentleman when he was trying to be so charming. Conte Prola was a dashing fellow. With his tall, lean build, his dark curling locks, expressive black eyes, and accented English he had entranced more than one lady since his arrival in London five months ago at the invitation of her father. She had assumed that once his business was concluded he would return to Genova. Since he never spoke of returning to his homeland, her suspicious nature forced her to conclude she had become part of his intriguing business venture.

"My lord, your flummery is wasted on the likes of me," Amara said, exasperated by his tenacity. "Confound it! Release my hands at once!" Relinquishing all thought of a graceful retreat, she struggled against his unrelenting grip. Twisting her wrists to and fro, she jerked one hand free and then the other.

"Such passion, my fire," he marveled. Gallantly, he ignored her inelegant snort of disbelief. "Think of the making of love between us."

She would entertain no such idiocy. Scowling, she

rubbed her abused wrists. "I have no intention of encouraging you." Disgusted at being expertly maneuvered, she marched down the dark avenue not bothering to glance back.

"Signorina Claeg, this endeavor is futile," he gently entreated, his long legs easily overtaking her. "These fireworks, they have begun. You will not find your friends and family—"

Several brilliant, sonorous explosions overhead caused them both to flinch. As they approached the bottom of the avenue, Amara realized the hopelessness of her search. The fireworks had lured thousands of spectators. With everyone's attention focused on the sky, it was impossible for her to thread her way through the crowd.

"This is your fault!" she charged over the thunderous explosions, the cheering and applause.

Woefully apologetic, he gestured at the heavens. "The blame is mine. Come now, we will be friends again and admire the sky together."

She pressed her lips together to cease their embarrassing tremor. "And how do you propose explaining our absence from the party?"

The conte's grin was full of masculine arrogance. "*Carina,* it is the way of new lovers. Your papa understands. He approves."

Amara closed her eyes at his admission. It was as she had feared. Conte Prola's presence in London was serving her family's interests in addition to his own. "You do not appear to be a man who openly seeks another man's approval."

He frowned. "I need no man's sanction." He drew himself up, a proud, alluring male specimen. "I speak only to ease your maidenly fears."

Amara laughed. Maidenly fears indeed. She blinked, holding a gloved hand as a shield over her eyes. The flashes of light blinded her vision, reminding her of lightning. It also reminded her of another night, another man. Without warning she felt the invisible hairs on the back of her neck prickle. It was an unpleasant sensation, a symptom of a greater humiliation she had thought she had overcome. "I have to leave this p-place." Dread washed over her, leaving her cold despite the temperate evening. Not certain of her destination, she turned, intending to return to the avenue.

Feeling more than capable of subduing a fractious female, Conte Prola circled his arms around her, effectively caging her within his embrace. His touch was her undoing. As she fought him in earnest, the top of her head collided with his chin. Surprised by the painful impact, he released her.

Wasting no time, Amara turned and pushed her way through the crowd, heedless of how her actions might be construed. She had to get away. It was too dark. There were too many people. Each explosion ricocheted in her head. Gasping for air, she felt her chest tighten so that it was difficult to draw a deep breath.

"Signorina!"

She could hear the conte shouting in the distance. Ignoring his plea to wait, she pushed her way beyond the crowd and reached for the nearest tree for support.

"Amara." A distant voice softly evoked her name.

Her eyes stinging from the drifting smoke, she shook her head. She tried closing her mind off to everything and concentrated on slowing her breathing. "There is nothing to fear," she whispered, although her frantic heartbeat contradicted the statement.

"Which one of us are you reassuring, Miss Claeg?"

His voice filtered through the buzzing noise in her ears and sank into the heart of her. She snapped open her eyes and only the tree she clutched kept her on her feet. The blond gentleman who stood several yards from her seemed as elusive as the smoke that drifted between them. Brock Bedegrayne. The merciless bolt of pain slicing through her chest surprised her. As she drew in a swift breath, all she could think was that he was such a beautiful man. As if sensing her desire, Brock removed his hat, which allowed her to study his face unhindered. Greedily, she accepted his unspoken offer. He still wore his blond hair unfashionably long, she noted, but kept its length secured at his nape. While the sun had lightened his hair, it had darkened his skin. The contrast enhanced the intensity of his pale green eyes. He seemed leaner, harsher, like a wild predator who had spent too much time surviving off the land. The differences did not diminish him. Nay, in truth, he appeared taller, stronger, and overwhelmingly virile. The look in his green gaze was mocking and disturbingly hungry. Digging her gloved fingers into the rough bark of the tree, she questioned whether the man before her was real or a mirage induced by her hysteria.

"Oh, I am real, little dove," he said, accurately reading her thoughts. Older and more handsome than the images from her meager memories, he opened his arms as if he meant to embrace her. "The man from your nightmares has returned." As he stepped closer, the light from the overhanging oil lamp bathed his face with wavering shadows. The slightly mocking smile he wore faded when he noticed that her pale skin glistened with sweat and her trembling lips were bloodless. "I see our years apart have not diminished your impression that my name and the devil are synonymous. I pray we are both ready for me to prove otherwise."

Instinctively, Amara took a step backward, keeping out of his reach.

"Signorina Claeg!"

She glanced back, realizing she had not escaped Conte Prola after all, and that he was not alone. Trailing behind him were her irritated mother and her cousin Miss Novell. The ramifications of her mother encountering Brock Bedegrayne cleared any lingering bewilderment from her mind.

"Sir, I think it best that you leave—" Amara's voice faded when she turned and noticed she was alone. She looked about but there was no sign that he had ever been there.

CHAPTER TWO

The warm stroke of a playful tongue over his lips pulled him from his slumber. *Amara.* Too cynical to believe his erotic fantasies had come to life, Brock warily opened his eyes. Black eyes gazed lovingly down at him.

"No offense, love," he said, "but the last bitch I took to bed cost me a gold bracelet and more skin than I could afford."

The white Maltese did not seem to take offense. Pleased to have his complete attention, she lavished his unshaven cheeks with friendly licks. "Enough!" Choking on laughter, he sat up and tried grasping her before her tiny, sharp claws carved furrows in his bare chest. He tucked her under his arm and grabbed a discarded blue silk dressing gown at the end of his bed. Grappling with the squirming dog, he worked his arms into the sleeves, giving him a more respectable appearance than his trousers alone provided. He would not have bothered if he were alone, but this was his brother-in-law's residence. If Rayne Wyman, Viscount Tipton, had taught him anything during their acquaintance, it was a grudging respect.

Tucking a flap of fluttering fabric into his left side, Brock stalked out of his chamber in search of Tipton's fey sibling and owner of the affectionate canine digging its tiny sharp nails into his ribs. "Madeleina!" The door to her room was open, but the girl was not within. He was tempted to shove the dog into the room, close the door, and be done with it.

"Brock, anything amiss? I vow, you almost sound as thunderous as Papa in a rage," his youngest sister, Devona, teased as she came down the hall. She was small in size, although age and the bearing of his nephew had ripened her slender figure. As she tilted her heart-shaped face upward, her blue eyes were already brimming with laughter at his predicament. The apple-green morning dress she wore complemented the copper tresses curling around her freshly scrubbed face. He tried reconciling this polished viscountess with the mischievous hoyden of his memories. So much had changed in his absence.

"I found *this* in my bed," he explained, holding up the Maltese. The dog wriggled, attempting to move closer. Brock's long hair tickled the animal's inquisitive nose, prompting a hearty wet sneeze. Appalled, he shoved the small dog into his laughing sister's hands. "Who would want such a creature? Nothing but a hank of hair and bones."

"Maddy does. And if you want to spare us all a scathing lecture, you will refrain from insulting her cater-cousin."

With his hands free, he secured the buttons on his dressing gown and removed several strands of long white dog hair. "Fine. As long as she can keep it from my bed."

"Come along, Mr. Crosspatch." She hooked her free hand through his arm and led him down the passageway. "Food will improve your disposition."

"I need to dress," he protested.

Her unladylike snort irritated him, as she had intended. "Such modesty. Dear brother, if your virtue is in jeopardy, I am certain Flora will protect you." The dog, reacting to her name, barked several times.

Brock seized Devona's neck. Instead of throttling her, he pulled her close and kissed her on the temple. "Mouthy imp."

Rayne Wyman, Viscount Tipton, was informally dressed and seated at the table when Devona and Brock entered the morning room. Even seated, the man was imposing. He was a gentleman of respectable proportions, but his strange eyes were what first captured an observer's attention. Of the lightest blue Brock had ever seen in a human, the odd eye color seemed to shift to pewter with heightened emotions. His hair, a mix of chestnut and honey, bore a shocking streak of white springing from his right temple. It had been shoulder-length once, but Tipton had cut it sometime during Brock's absence. As Tipton touched his manservant, Speck, on the sleeve, Brock noticed and briefly wondered about the long scar branching from the viscount's thumb to his wrist. It reminded Brock that there were some unsavory factors in the man's past. Although Tipton was warily accepted by the *ton* and a respectable surgeon by profession, his life before he married Devona had always troubled Brock. Nevertheless, he could see that his youngest sister was happy in her marriage.

Speck replied to something the viscount said, pulling Brock from his musings. As he stood poised at his lord's side, the servant had his attention fixed on the two-year-old boy chewing on the scrolled wood of a chair arm.

"Tipton, this diet of wax and wood cannot be good for our son." Handing the dog to a scowling Speck, she scooped up the giggling Lucien and examined the chair. "Every chair we own bears the scars of his teeth. Flora did not give us such trouble when she was a puppy."

"At least he has stopped biting people." Putting aside his morning paper, Tipton settled his son on his knee and accepted a kiss from his wife. "Speck, we are finished here." The manservant quietly slipped out of the room with the exuberant Flora.

Acknowledging Brock with a nod, his brother-in-law narrowed his shrewd light blue eyes. "Bedegrayne, traveling to India has suited you. Forgive me for missing your arrival yesterday. I had consults at the hospital and an evening lecture. I see you have attended to your comfort on your own."

The casual observation regarding his state of undress brought a slight sting of embarrassment to his unshaven face. Tipton had a manner about him that always made Brock feel like an arse. He shot a brotherly glare at his sister for dismissing his protests.

Unaffected, she watched the footman pour coffee into her cup. "Oh, Tipton, do not let him chew on that spoon—" She broke off her scolding at the sight of her housekeeper, Pearl Brown. "You are our salvation, Pearl. Lucien is eating the house down around us. Has he had his breakfast?"

"Yes, madam. Nurse fed him several hours ago. Shall I see if Cook has something in the kitchen that is less grinding on the young master's teeth?" Already knowing the answer, Pearl moved to collect her charge from Tipton.

Devona sent the woman a grateful smile. "You are an asset to this household, Pearl. How did I steal you away from Papa?"

Savoring the smell of his coffee, Brock murmured, "He probably thought Tipton needed help keeping you from casting yourself into the briars."

From the moment she took her first unaided steps, the family had been rescuing the youngest headstrong Bedegrayne from her wild mischief. Glancing at his howling nephew, he saw the boy had inherited his mother's temperament. There was justice, after all.

"Really, brother, you make me sound like a fidge," Devona protested, while blowing kisses to her departing son.

"A saucy fidge," her husband corrected.

More amused than outraged, Devona replied, "I must have been having a spell when I wished seeing you and Tipton together in the same room again. Still, it is good to have you home, Brock."

The affection in her voice warmed a part of him that had grown cold in his absence. He had missed his family. Discreetly, he studied his sister. If Devona suspected the reasons for his leaving England and his decision to return, she had not voiced them aloud. Not above doing his own needling, Brock said, "Marriage seems to have mellowed you both."

Shrugging, Devona poked at the food on her plate. "I would not presume to speak for Tipton—"

"Nothing has prevented you from doing so in the past," countered Tipton, earning himself a playful kick under the table.

"I, however, have been too busy with Lucien for any

hubble-bubble. So, beloved brother, if you have returned believing I need another jackanapes at my side, you will simply be disappointed."

Brock could not be more pleased, although he was prudent not to mention it. The months before he had departed England, danger and scandal clung to his youngest sister like a shadow. No one could have predicted that Devona's guilty devotion in saving a childhood friend from the gallows would have pulled her into a convoluted plot to murder the viscount. Brock absently rubbed the ridged scar on his left temple, recalling that it was Tipton's medical skills that saved his sister. In some ways he owed his liberation to the man as well.

"Thanks to my sire, I am inlaid with sisters. So who should I vex, Wynne or Irene? While I possess a knack for annoying Irene with my presence alone, I must confess there is not a more wondrous sight than our halcyon Wynne in a fury." Only half-serious about pestering his sisters, he observed the silent exchange between husband and wife with concern. "Has something happened?"

Devona cleared her throat and took her time fussing with the napery. "Not exactly. There was that business with Digaud and his ilk last season, but Keanan Milroy settled the matter for us all."

"Milroy?" Brock repeated, trying to place the name. "Reckless Milroy, the pugilist? What does he have to do with—" He stopped, pouncing on the subject his sister seemed intent on evading. "What matter?"

"Did you not receive our letters?" She frowned, considering the ramifications. "Then you do not know . . ." she said, trailing off.

Amused by his wife's hesitation, Tipton decided to help her out. "During your absence, there have been a few additions to the family. Wynne married Mr. Keanan Milroy last August."

If he had not been sitting, the shock of Tipton's casual announcement would have sunk him to his knees. Keanan Milroy. The man was unmatched in the ring. Brock had wagered once or twice on those formidable fists. His thoughts conjured Wynne's image. She had the look of their mother with her pale blond hair and green eyes that matched his own. Her beauty and a generous dowry should have allowed her the choice of any man she desired. How the devil had she ended up yoked to a low-born pugilist? Brock was about to voice the very question when Tipton's sister, Madeleina Wyman, burst into the room.

"Good morning. Forgive my tardiness. I fear Flora slipped her leash again," the girl said in a rush, not seeming particularly apologetic.

Mumbling a greeting, Brock stood and offered her the chair beside him. He had not recognized her the previous afternoon when they met. She had grown during his two-year absence and was slightly taller than Devona. Her light brown hair, damp from her hasty ablutions, was entwined into a practical braid down her back. Knowing she preferred gardens to *la mode,* Brock sensed his sisters' influence in the choice of her fashionable gown. When he had first met her, she had been fourteen and quite withdrawn from the world after the death of her mother. Obviously, the years living with her brother and sister-in-law had helped to heal her battered spirit because her light blue eyes sparkled with a joy that had been absent in the past.

"Your dog found her way into my chamber this morning," he gruffly admitted.

The allusion to his bedchamber brought a pretty blush to her cheeks. "She meant no harm, sir. I will see to it that she does not bother you again."

He felt a twinge of guilt that his tone had cooled the friendliness he had observed in her wary blue eyes. Apparently, she was not the first lady since his return he had frightened. To put her at ease, he said, "Since we are family, you will call me Brock and I shall call you Maddy. Is this agreeable?"

She nodded, flashing him a warmer smile. "I wanted to express my gratitude again for the Fairchild book. Wherever did you find such an old tome?"

He made a vague gesture with his hand. He had spent the last two years experiencing both the splendor and misery India had to offer an ambitious Englishman. It was not a tale for a young lady. Like Tipton, he was entitled to his secrets. "There was an estate auction outside Calcutta. I recalled your enthusiasm for gardens and thought you would enjoy possessing it." Anticipating Devona's sisterly complaint, he added, "I have gifts for everyone, once the cargo from the *Roost* has been unloaded."

"A praiseworthy act, Bedegrayne," his brother-in-law drawled.

"Plaudits from you, Tipton, can only be regarded with high suspicion." Glancing from his solemn younger sister to her husband, Brock rubbed the slight ache in his neck. "You both may find this disappointing, but Maddy's timely arrival has not diverted me from my questions. What dire circumstances placed our sister into the custody of Reckless Milroy?"

Uncertain of the mood, Maddy stared down at the hot chocolate she was idly stirring. "I rather like the man."

She pursed her lips in contemplation. "He cossets Aideen and Anna."

Brock strangled on a swallow of hot coffee. "Fiery Gehenna! Who are Aideen and Anna?" He glared at Tipton.

Puzzled by his anger, Maddy touched him lightly on his sleeve. "What offense is it for a man to love his wife and daughters?"

"Daughters?" The word burned his throat, while his agile mind counted the months. "Twins?"

Devona stood, bracing her palms on the table. He recognized the stubborn stance. She intended to dissuade him from his somber conclusions. He could not think of any tale that would absolve the bounder who had seduced his sister.

She slapped her hand on the table, commanding his attention. "Hear me, Brock Bedegrayne. The family has weathered enough scandal. I will not allow you to go charging off to challenge Wynne's Mr. Milroy to a duel!"

Brock rose to his feet, prepared to suggest the very notion. Tipton stepped in front of him, preventing him from putting his hands on Devona. Maddy slouched lower in her seat as the volume of the sibling argument increased, thereby summoning Tipton's manservant into the room. Flora was at his heels barking at the commotion. Chaos reigned.

CHAPTER THREE

Cradling two-month-old Aideen Rose in her arms, Amara moved about the drawing room using the infant's fussiness to conceal her own restlessness, while Wynne Milroy put her other daughter, Anna Faith, to her breast.

"Offer her your finger," Wynne suggested, needing to ease her child's distress. She leaned back into the chair and closed her eyes. "Keanan has a certain knack for calming the girls."

"So that was the reason he escaped from the house the moment I arrived," Amara teased, and was rewarded with a tired chuckle from Wynne. She tickled Aideen's quivering lower lip with her finger. It surprised her when the child latched on and fiercely suckled. In wonderment she glanced curiously at her friend. Despite their years of friendship, she did not have the courage to ask Wynne how she endured such enthusiasm at her breast. Such shameless queries were best left burning on her tongue.

At four and twenty, even exhaustion could not dim Wynne's beauty. She had dressed simply for her unexpected visitor and treated her with the negligence she would extend to any of her sisters. Her waist-length blond tresses had been coiled into an unsophisticated bun at the back of her head. Nevertheless, the results were striking. Hers was a face that needed no adornment. Animated with intelligence and kindness, her classical features would have inspired any army.

"I have missed you these months," Wynne said, her pale green eyes misty with joy.

The simple admission brought the sting of unexpected tears to Amara's eyes. "I, as well, my friend. Did you enjoy your confinement at Holinshead? Was the house in disrepair, as you had feared?"

In honor of their marriage, Keanan Milroy's half brother, Drake Fawks, the Duke of Reckester, had presented the couple with one of his northern estates. News of the generous gift and speculation swirled around London for months. This was hardly surprising since Milroy was the natural child of the old duke and an Irish actress, even though his claim to the Reckester clan had been refuted for years.

Milroy had equally despised his family. He had never forgiven his father for Aideen Milroy's ruination and her eventual death at the hands of a drunken patron. The old duke's assassination last summer and Keanan's capricious truce with his half brother, the former Lord Nevin, only increased the *ton*'s interest.

Wynne sighed. "The main house was astonishingly solid for its years of neglect. A few of the outer buildings were in need of repair. All in all, my time at Holinshead was restful. I sulked for a time when you were unable to accept my invitation."

Ashamed, Amara stared down at the infant in her arms. Little Aideen had fallen asleep, her tiny mouth still latched tightly onto her finger. "My mother—" she began. Her persistence in maintaining a friendship with the Bedegrayne women had created an acrimonious rift between her and her mother. The viscountess was quite vocal about her dislike and blamed Devona for her son's death in Newgate Prison. Amara was the only one in her family who knew Doran's true fate. With Tipton's assistance, Devona had saved Amara's brother from the hangman's noose. Unfortunately, Amara had promised to keep silent on the matter and the Bedegraynes were forced to deal with her mother's unfounded wrath.

"Stop scowling at my sweet Aideen. She will think you do not like her." The pale green depths of Wynne's eyes sparkled with affection and shrewdness. "I have always understood, Amara. I would never forgive myself if our friendship caused you pain."

It had, but she never voiced her complaints aloud. Disobedience in the Claeg household was always punished. She preferred not burdening Wynne with the humiliating details. "Nothing I cannot tolerate," she lied. Swaying to a faint piece of music in her head, Amara moved closer to her friend now that she had covered her breast and had adjusted the squirming baby onto her shoulder.

Rubbing Anna's back, Wynne appeared to hesitate over her next words. "I have received word my brother's ship has returned."

Feeling the weight of her friend's scrutiny, she tried not to show any reaction to the announcement. "Has the Bedegrayne changeling finally returned?" she asked, hoping her query sounded innocent. Wynne's father, Sir Thomas, had had two sons, though no one uttered the name of Nyle Bedegrayne. Father and son had had a falling-out years ago and then Nyle had vanished. It seemed he had ceased to be a member of the family. The fact she dared mention him bespoke her desperation to avoid the unsettling elder brother.

Grief flashed across Wynne's beautiful face. Whatever Nyle Bedegrayne's misdeeds, his sister had not forgotten him. "Nyle is lost to us. I doubt anyone has knowledge of his whereabouts. I speak of Brock."

Something in Amara's expression must have alerted her friend. Cocking her head slightly to the left, Wynne stared deliberatingly at Amara. "Then again, perhaps Brock's return is old news for you. What has happened?"

She blinked rapidly. "Nothing worthy of an inquisition." Wynne was not convinced. Amara tried again. "Truly, this visit was impulsive."

Wigget, the Milroys' butler, discreetly cleared his throat. Somewhere in his late forties, he was an imposing figure with his silvered hair and patched right eye. "Madam, there is a gentleman requesting an audience."

Wynne's brow lifted and she glanced askance in Amara's direction. "Unless he is family, please send him away, Wigget."

"I believe I qualify, Mrs. Milroy," Brock said, deftly avoiding the butler's attempt to block his entry. He spoke the words to his sister, but his inscrutable gaze was arrested on a startled Amara.

Her lips parted as if to speak, yet no words formed. When he had approached her last evening, he seemed an illusion. The boldness of daylight allowed her no such denials.

"Brock! The devil take you for not giving me any warning." The joy in her expression dispelled any chastisement.

Brother and sister slipped gracefully into a welcoming embrace with the child between them. "I must look horrid."

"Father always complained you were too pretty," he teased, grinning when she stepped on his toes. His hand almost hesitant, he lightly caressed the invisible blond hair on the baby's head. He looked thoughtful; his expression sobered. "You have led quite the adventurous life in my absence. And here I thought Devona was the one who would give the family trouble."

Separation had not dimmed Wynne's understanding of her brother. "I am in no mood to be scolded for second-hand innuendos, Brock. Keanan—"

"Should have been more of a gentleman and less the scoundrel he is purported to be," Brock said, ruthlessly slicing through his sister's defense.

Aghast, Wynne stepped back from him. "You do not know of what you speak."

His hand made a sweeping gesture from child to child. "A twinning duplicity on my sister's honor."

"That is quite enough!" Amara commanded. She had made a private vow not to involve herself in an argument that was strictly a family matter, but Wynne was her friend. She would not abandon her. "Neither your sister nor Mr. Milroy deserve your censure, Mr. Bedegrayne." She felt herself faltering, now that she had gained their attention.

"Amazing," he muttered, shaking his head. "She speaks. I should have anticipated that the first words from your succulent lips would be to take me to task over family business."

Amara felt the familiar weakness that stole into her limbs whenever Brock Bedegrayne was around, but she did not back down as he probably expected. His sisters were not the only women he knew who had changed. "This has nothing to do with your family. Or what Mr. Milroy should or should not have done." She met Wynne's reassuring gaze and felt her approval.

Denied a target for his anger, he focused on Amara. "And pray tell, Miss Claeg. In your most excellent experience of love and family, where do I place the blame?"

That cut, and the villain knew it. Brock had always found her family lacking, or at least possessing nothing comparable to his own. Fear and respect was what held the Claeg clan together. As for love, well, it was as stingy as warm weather in January.

A tiny mewling sound drew Amara's attention down to the baby in her arms. "I fear her patience has ended." She waited for Wynne to place Anna into the cradle before she handed over Aideen. Not trusting her trembling hands, she was grateful to give up her precious burden. Sensing Brock would not permit her to leave without a suitable reply, she met his candid perusal. "Direct your mockery inward, Mr. Bedegrayne. You are angry that Wynne muddled through her difficulties without your esteemed wisdom to guide her. Assuage your guilt elsewhere."

"Oh, I shall, Miss Claeg," he softly growled. "On my oath."

A cool wind of unease washed over her body. His promise sounded more like a threat and it was directed at her! A part of her knew she was being unfair when she accused him of feeling guilty about abandoning his sister. She had done her best not to react to the flash of anger her comment evoked.

What guilt Brock Bedegrayne felt was not all directed at his sister. His and Amara's past would always be a living entity between them. Some of her despair must have showed because his shoulder jerked as he began to unfold his arms from their stubborn stance. She held up her palm when he took a step in her direction. "I have remained longer than I should. I must leave."

Feeling the tension between her brother and her dear friend, Wynne tried easing the finality of Amara's departure. "You will come again?"

"Of course," she replied, not certain at the moment if she meant the words. With a fleeting glance at Brock, she left the room.

"Cabbage-head," Wynne said, her green eyes gleaming challengingly in the candlelight. Straightening her lithe form from a reclining position on the gold-and-hyacinth-striped chaise longue, she implored to the ceiling of her sitting room. "Widgeon!"

Keanan Milroy leaned back against the towel-padded wooden bath enjoying his wife's outburst. It was not too difficult since the lady was a tempting vision. Her waist-length blond hair was undone and flowed seductively over her shoulders. The rest of her captivating body was clad only in a sheet. "I am certain you made your feelings quite clear on the subject, Mrs. Milroy," he drawled, reaching for the glass of excellent Sauternes he had abandoned on a small fanciful stool shaped like a toadstool.

"Indeed," she replied, swishing the end of her sheet like a tail. "And pulled his ear for good measure." She did not bother keeping the satisfaction out of her tone.

Keanan regretted missing what must have been quite an interesting reconciliation. He had already arranged a meeting with his half brother, the Duke of Reckester, at

Tattersall's and later they had gone on to Fives Court to watch a sparring match between two lightweights. He might have retired from prizefighting, but the atmosphere still beckoned him from time to time.

"If your brother even remotely resembles your sire in temperament, my damson, I doubt demanding that he blindly accept our marriage without prejudice will hasten him to offer his blessing."

"I do not require his wretched blessing!" she vehemently declared.

Most of Keanan's twenty-nine years of life had been devoid of the kind of family Wynne had the privilege of claiming as her own. His mother, Aideen Milroy, had called herself an actress. In truth, she had been little more than a drunken whore when she had been murdered by one of her patrons, leaving her grieving and angry thirteen-year-old son to make his own way in the world. His sire, Wesley Fawks, the late Duke of Reckester, had renounced any connection to his son. Keanan had wasted too many years hating the Reckester family and craving revenge.

Oddly, it was the old duke's death last July that had allowed him and his half brother, Drake, to make headway in settling their differences. However, it was Wynne and his beautiful little daughters who had taught him the value of family. It was something precious, and even now he feared he might do something to lose them. He personally did not care what Bedegrayne thought of him, but he did not want to be responsible for the discord between brother and sister.

He reached out and caught the sheet to halt her pacing. "Tipton mentioned your brother was something of a firebrand. Give him time to accept me, accept us. If not . . ." He shrugged. "I will have to convince him."

"No duels."

"Why, Wynne, I have yet to fight one. Young Reckester is testament to my restraint." He grinned, hoping to cajole her out of her ill humor.

She sat on the lip of the tub. Stroking her back, he resisted the urge to lick the wet channels his fingers left on her skin.

Wynne sighed. "I know he will come about in his thinking. My upset goes beyond his outrage that I married a commoner." She gave him a small reassuring smile that always managed to strike him in the breadbasket. "I thought I understood Brock. His time away from the family has made him a stranger. The way he looked at Amara . . ." She let her words trail off.

"Is there something between them?"

"Something," she agreed, leaning into his touch. "I never told her, but Brock insisted I maintain our friendship in his absence."

Keanan drew a serpentine pattern down her spine, relishing her delicate shudder. "Did you consider his request strange?"

"Somewhat. I assumed at the time that he still felt guilty for his participation in unmasking her role in Devona's doomed plan to rescue Amara's brother from prison. He and Tipton caused quite a scene when they practically carried her out of the ball and frightened her into confessing all."

His fingers tensed on her back. "Hmm . . . I must have missed the retelling of this particular tale. What role did you play in your sister's ruse?"

Glancing back, she said, "I distracted the guards so Devona—" His expression silenced her confession.

Recovering quickly, she muttered, "Truly, Mr. Milroy, you can look quite intimidating when you set your mind to it."

"I can do more than just *look,* Mrs. Milroy." He closed his eyes, trying to banish the image of his Wynne plying her seductive skills on several cynical prison guards. The thought dried the very spittle from his mouth.

"Well, there is no need to be so vexed. Tipton arrived, ruining all our plans."

"A fact for which I shall be grateful till I cock up me toes," he countered, slipping into the coarser dialect of his youth. It was a vivid indicator of how upset he was about the matter.

Wynne was not impressed.

"Regardless, that was not the point I was making. Now pay attention," she commanded, her nose crinkling in an endearing manner that showed him she was serious. "I have spent two years watching Amara tense up every time my brother's name is uttered. There is something between them that goes beyond polite courtesies. Whatever my brother has done, Amara will not speak of it."

Wanting to soothe the concern he heard in her voice, Keanan slid his hand over her hip and gave her a comforting squeeze. "There, there. Whatever is betwixt them is private for now. They don't need you stepping between them."

"You do not—"

"Aye, Wynne, I do. It seems to me that if you have time to meddle in your brother's and Miss Claeg's business, then I've been dodging my duties." With a mischievous grin, he dragged her into the tub.

"Keanan!" she gasped, wrapping her arms around his

neck. Sitting on his lap, she needed mere seconds to grasp his intent. She enticingly bit his lower lip. "I can be quite persistent, you know."

"I am counting on it, my damson." Working the sodden sheet down, his hand possessively cupped her breast. She leaned closer, eager for his caress. A small sound rumbled in his throat as he nipped her shoulder. It would be hours before either gave young Bedegrayne and his curious attention to Miss Claeg another thought.

CHAPTER FOUR

"I must confess, I find your choice of amusements this afternoon odd even for you, Miss Claeg."

Amara sent an impatient glance at her cousin, Miss Pipere Novell. Bedecked in a flattering white cambric morning dress with a pelisse of primrose sarcenet and a bonnet of straw, her cousin, or Piper as her father had indulgently dubbed her, was fashionable. She certainly stood out from the dusty and tarnished arms and armor they had been observing for the past hour, she sourly thought, fingering one of the gilt drop buttons on her own pale blue pelisse.

"You did not find the Reverend Kendall's lecture on entomology fascinating?"

"No, I did not," her cousin crisply replied, her prodigious black curls bouncing with her irritation. "How could the man expect any enlightened person to heed his discourse while bugs were crawling up and down his limbs?"

Amara made a sympathetic noise. "I pray you are not

upset about that rather unfortunate incident with the cicadae. I doubt even the fine reverend could have predicted such an outcome."

"It was not your new bonnet upon which those hideous insects alighted!"

Turning away, Amara fixed her attention on a twelfth-century lance. She bit her tongue, hoping the pain would arrest the laughter burning her throat. Her dear cousin had indeed been a sight, flailing and screeching about the room trying to remove the curious insects. Perhaps it was horrid of her, but she could not think of another individual so deserving of an infestation.

"Although I find their evening chirr pleasant, they can be destructive little pests."

Aghast, Miss Novell said, "Only you would find something noteworthy about the unremarkable. Your mama believes your dabbling with that little charity—oh, what is it called? The Benevolent Sisterhood? She fears it has made you shamefully provincial. I have lost count of the numerous occasions upon which she has expressed her disappointment."

"I do not doubt it. I fear her condition is terminal," she said lightly, ignoring the tightening in her chest. Her mother was never one to suffer in martyred silence. Amara was all too aware of her numerous grievances. What she found nettlesome was that her mother considered this poor relation nonesuch. Miss Novell's father had sent her to London for the season in hopes that her beauty and connection to the Keyworth title would secure his daughter a respectable marriage. A sad tale, indeed, and Amara sympathized with the impoverished bookseller who had five daughters to marry off. It was regrettable that her young cousin was an opinionated, devious harpy. Their uncomfortable situation was becoming insufferable.

"What providence stumbling across my most devoted sister."

The amiable masculine voice reverberated about the large exhibition hall, commanding everyone's attention. Amara could not help admiring her brother's commanding presence, even when she dreaded being the focus of his attention. Bidding farewell to his male companions, Mallory Claeg strode purposefully toward them. She supposed most thought him a handsome gentleman, a tall imposing figure with eyes a blue hue lighter than her own. He wore his brown hair longer than most, and he had hastily tied it back as if he could not be troubled with it. Always the artist, he had his sketching journal tucked under his arm. She noticed his hands were bare.

"Amara!" Dropping his journal, he swept her into a crushing embrace and spun her as he had when she was a child. Distance and eight years stretched between them, so she assumed deviltry more than affection motivated her older sibling. Allowing Amara to regain her balance, Mallory shifted his gaze from her face and lingered on their cousin's. "And who is your companion?"

Wary of his interest, she declared, "Our cousin, Miss Pipere Novell. Miss Novell, this is my brother, Mr. Mallory Claeg."

Bowing, he said, "Miss Novell, pray ease my heart and tell me you are a distant relation. Very distant." Not diverting his focus, he retrieved his journal from the floor.

Amara was amazed. Mallory's flirtatious nature had actually flustered their beautiful cousin.

"M-my father is the son of your great-uncle through Lord Keyworth's lineage. That makes us—"

"Temptingly distant, it appears," he murmured. It was obvious to Amara he was silently contemplating the wicked possibilities.

She decided intervention was required or her mother would blame her for the paragon's ruination. "You are too young for her, brother. And she is too poor for you." She did not acknowledge her cousin's unintelligible protest. "Her papa has high hopes of matching her with a respectable gentleman."

"You wound me, sister. I turned thirty last month and Miss Novell—"

"Is far too old for you even at the tender age of twenty. Come, Miss Novell, allow me to rescue you from this bounder's clutches before he begs you to pose as his Helen."

Unrepentant, Mallory followed after them and said to Amara, "I am more inspired to paint you as Eris, my fractious goddess of discord." He hooked his arm through hers, thwarting her retreat. "You have the look of our mother when you set your face like that." He laughed at her horrified expression. "Come now, puss, permit me to make amends. Meandering through all of this dust has parched my throat. With your permission, I shall escort you and Miss Novell to Mivart's for refreshments."

Her cynical thoughts directed inward, Amara pondered his persistence. Mallory had kept his distance since their brother Doran's "death." His disinterest in her life had not concerned her. They had never been close. Years earlier, his callous opinions about Doran—which were devastatingly aligned with their father's cruelty—had driven a wedge between them. This made his sudden attention all the more suspicious.

"Miss Claeg?" her cousin queried, puzzled by her hesitation.

"I see no harm in it," Amara admitted.

"A chary declaration indeed." He guided both ladies down the hall to the doors. "Deservedly so, I confess. I have been a neglectful brother, Miss Novell."

"*Neglectful* implies loss. How can I lose something I have never had?" Amara wondered, feeling provoked.

Mallory moaned, acting as if her unsympathetic words had pierced his chest. She was unmoved by the drama.

"You were always an unyielding puss."

They both knew he was referring to Doran. She refused to be baited and remained silent. He sighed as if he were disappointed in her.

"The past is steeped in pain and recriminations so we shall look forward. Of late, the prattle-boxes have bantered your name about. Rumors have reached me that some Italian beau has tossed the handkerchief."

"Cousin, Conte Prola has declared himself?"

If her brother's announcement had not been so disconcerting, she might have found her cousin's disbelief downright insulting.

"Prola?" her brother snorted in derision. "His name sounds like a freckle cream. Confess, dear sister. Are the rumors true?"

Amara wordlessly walked through the door an attendant had opened for them. All her careful planning had been for naught. She had been avoiding the conte for days. Brock Bedegrayne's reappearance in London had only added to her misery. What did she care of lectures on entomology and rusty medieval armor? She had chosen amusements that would prevent either man from waylaying her and thereby fueling the *ton*'s interest. If word had reached even Mallory's apathetic ears, then she was truly in trouble. She glanced at her brother, seeing nothing but sympathy. She tried to swallow, but something was stuck in her throat.

"I believe you need a drink more than I, puss."

"Ladies, you missed tea," Lady Keyworth chastised, taking note of Amara's heightened coloring. "Again. Gentlemen find tardiness unappealing, daughter. It makes a lady look flighty." The viscountess returned her attention to the ledger the butler held out for her viewing. "Buckle, incompetence has cost me three pieces of creamware in two days. I assume the culprit has been sacked."

The butler closed the book with a crisp snap. "The scullery maid was discharged immediately."

The older woman sniffed. "Obviously, not soon enough. You are dismissed." She fixed her unforgiving gaze on Amara and Miss Novell.

The pair of them had lined up side by side like repentant children. Amara took several steps forward, severing any illusion that she and her cousin were collaborating in mischief.

"My apologies, madam. We encountered Mallory at one of the museums. He has fixed on the odd notion that I should model for him. Nothing I said dissuaded him." She refused to mention her brother's curiosity about the conte. If her mother learned of the gossip, it might provoke her into action.

"Miss Novell, there appears to be a lapse in my daughter's recollection. Did we or did we not agree on Miss Pettifoot's literary circle for this afternoon's amusements?

It was understood the acclaimed critic Mr. Dela Court would be in attendance."

Amara despised it when her mother spoke of her as if she were not present in the room. "*We* agreed at breakfast that Mr. Dela Court's honored presence at Miss Pettifoot's would not spare it from being an utter bore."

"Amara Claeg!"

Her mother's appalled exclamation always managed to ripple down her spine. She ruthlessly suppressed any outward reaction. This was the way between them. Madam was shocked. Amara was at fault. The tragic scene had played for years.

"It was regrettable that we did not attend the literary circle," her cousin said, clearly uncomfortable with Lady Keyworth's disapproval. "We did attend a fascinating lecture by . . ." She visibly struggled for the name.

Gracious, Miss Novell was pitiful at deceit. Observing the woman falter with half-truths was just too painful. "The Reverend Kendall," Amara supplied.

"Yes, his name had escaped me. The reverend presented a most interesting lecture on—on . . ." Her cousin glanced helplessly at her.

"Entomology. The subjects were rather taken with Miss Novell's bonnet."

The comment would have earned her a terse rebuttal from her cousin if her mother had not silenced them with a look.

"Your defiance shames not only you, Amara, but your family. Conte Prola was disappointed when you failed to make an appearance at Miss Pettifoot's. He has expressed concern that you are avoiding him. Naturally, I made the appropriate excuses."

"Naturally," she softly echoed.

Lady Keyworth abruptly stood. Instinctively, Amara knew the mockery in her tone had tested the boundaries of her mother's tolerance. She was at fault. Again. Within her imagination, her mother was always a tower of fury, but in truth, she was only three inches taller than Amara. What beauty she possessed was pinched by frustration and anger. With strength that always managed to surprise Amara, Lady Keyworth seized her by the nape. The bite of her mother's nails was enough to make her eyes water. Lady Keyworth pushed and dragged her daughter to the door.

"Miss Novell, open the door." She might have managed it herself if Amara had not begun struggling for her release.

"I tire of these lectures, daughter."

The servants they passed were not shocked by the commotion. Lady Keyworth's temper was legendary. With self-preservation foremost in their minds, they cleared the path for Amara's humiliating journey to her bedchamber.

"Release me!" Amara demanded, her teeth clenched from the pain. She twisted and turned to no avail. She could hear her cousin's footfalls behind them. Having Miss Novell as a witness to her punishment, once again, made Amara despise the woman all the more.

With one hand steadying her ascent, and the other easing the manacle at her nape, she cursed her mother. The last time she had dared to be so vocal, her mother had cut her waist-length hair to her chin. She would have cut her to the scalp if her father and a servant had not interfered. That had happened two years earlier.

The side of her face connected with wood as her mother fumbled with the door latch. It sprang open. Lady Keyworth shoved her into the room. Amara staggered, catching herself before she fell into an ignoble heap on the floor. Her neck was tender from the abuse. Reflexively, she curled her hand around her wounded flesh.

Panting from her exertion, her mother declared, "You shall remain here until I send for you. In my absence, it would be wise to contemplate the humble apologies you will bestow on Conte Prola and me this evening. He intends to claim the first dance. We will not disappoint him." She closed the door, effectively cutting off any heated vow of denial.

Hugging herself, Amara went to her window and stared blindly at the scene below. Absently, she slipped her hand into her bodice and withdrew a pendant. Blinking away the stinging grit in her eyes, she traced the plain oval bezel with her fingertip. The patina of the gold revealed its age. Against her palm, the agate intaglio felt hot. The scene depicted in the stone was of a Grecian maiden walking fearlessly alongside a lion. Her gown streamed about her as she embraced her fate. It was an image of strength and passion. The pendant had become her talisman, something tangible to draw upon when she found her own life so lacking. Amara longed for such courage as the maiden and her beast possessed. With her heart brimming with sadness, she curled her fingers into a fist. Her talisman brought her no comfort this day. She felt so alone, she thought she might die of it.

CHAPTER FIVE

Brock detested these functions. The area between his shoulders began itching the moment he sauntered into the ballroom. A certain amount of inquisitiveness was to be expected. His return to England would have garnered interest among the *ton*. The more bloodthirsty were probably anticipating a confrontation between him and Wynne's Milroy. He intended to disappoint them. Whatever his feelings about his sister's husband, he intended to keep them private.

No, the quarry he hunted this evening was cunning and elusive as smoke. It would be her choice whether their confrontation was public or private. He was beyond caring. Years of waiting had a way of fraying a man's patience.

"Young Brock," the matron approaching him said, her pleasure shining in her twinkling dark blue eyes. "I vow, age has improved upon your handsome visage."

So much so that most considered him beyond the nursery. However, Brock was stoic as he accepted the compliment. His companion was a friend of the family and would always see the unruly boy instead of the man. "You are too generous, Lady Dodd." Accepting her hand, he bowed. His keen gaze discreetly searched the crowded ballroom.

His inattentiveness had not gone unnoticed. Lady Dodd smiled. "She is not here."

Her declaration jarred him from his quest. "I beg your pardon."

With admirable grace she unfolded her fan with a flick of her wrist, and gently stirred the air near her face. "Your sister. Lady Tipton. I recall another fine evening before her marriage when you were her most devoted guardian."

She spoke of a masquerade she had held two years earlier. He was certain he would never forget that evening. It had been an unmitigated debacle. Devona had been missing so he and Tipton bullied and embarrassed Amara into divulging his sister's whereabouts. His teeth clenched at the memory. "Tipton has relieved me of my guardian duties."

"And Mr. Milroy has espoused your other sister. So which beauty has earned your chivalrous considerations?" she mused.

Brock hesitated. If he revealed the lady's name, his interest would be known throughout the ballroom within an hour. His pale green eyes gleamed with unholy mischief. He could not think of another, more public method of breaching the lady's battlements. "I was seeking Miss Claeg."

"M-Miss Claeg," the woman sputtered, not believing him until she met his steady gaze. The two-year-old memory of how he had half-carried Amara out of the Dodds' ballroom flashed silently between them. The matron smiled approvingly. "Miss Claeg, indeed. Why, young Brock, you always did enjoy a challenge."

Amara walked rigidly beside her mother while Lady Keyworth maneuvered their way through the ballroom in a brisk manner laudable of any colonel. She stopped occasionally, speaking to people she deemed worthy of her brief civility. Amara cast a bitter glance at Miss Novell, who seemed beyond the strife in the Claeg household. They had barely entered the room when a flirtatious gentleman had begged the viscountess for her cousin's participation in a set. Watching her competently execute the lively steps of a reel, Amara was grateful she would be spared Miss Novell's presence for what she had already deemed a miserable evening.

"Are you of the same opinion, Miss Claeg?"

"I do beg your pardon, Mrs. Sheers," Amara replied, feeling the air around them warm with each passing second. "My thoughts were directed—" She mentally castigated herself when she noticed her mother's lips had thinned to a disapproving line. "Elsewhere," she lamely finished.

Not offended, the woman gave her an indulgent smile. "It was always thus for me at the start of a new season. Each year brings the spring of new love yet to be discovered, and the autumn of despair. Three seasons passed before my shy ambassador unearthed the courage to propose. Since then we have enjoyed seven-and-twenty years together."

"It is a worthy aspiration, madam."

The sapphire and diamonds that adorned the older woman's hair, neck, and wrists winked with her every gesture. "Your mother has confided to me that your time for rejoicing spring is at hand, my dear."

"I confess I do not share my mother's confidence. Spring may bring a more temperate clime, but it also harbors whirlwinds, chilling rain, not to mention thunder and lightning."

Mrs. Sheers's eyes glimmered with delight. "Glenda, I believe your Italian count will need to sharpen his wits if he intends to possess your daughter's regard."

There was a soft amused smile on Lady Keyworth's face, but the look she fixed on her only daughter was pure cold determination. "No man changes at the whim of a woman. Why else would womankind be so amendable?"

There was a stilted silence between the two women. Amara sensed Mrs. Sheers was poised to disagree. There was a telling flash of temper in the woman's eyes, but she did not respond. Perhaps being married to an ambassador had taught her diplomacy. Such marvelous restraint was probably why their friendship had lasted twelve years.

Amara's gaze shifted, seeking some sort of distraction before she proved how gauche she had become in her two-and-twenty years. Her aimless search of the room halted on the two men who had entered. One was focused on the face of a matron she could not identify from her position. The other gentleman appeared to be as restless as she felt. He searched the crowd, his handsome mouth drawn tight into a saturnine pout. Physically and in temperament they were opposites. Yet she was involuntarily drawn to both of them on some level. Attempting to keep her breathing calm, she acknowledged that it was one of the reasons she feared them both.

"Miss Claeg, you have drifted *elsewhere* again," Mrs. Sheers teased. "What lures your thoughts from us?"

"Conte Prola," Lady Keyworth said, her satisfaction interwoven in her observation.

Amara knew the moment the conte noticed her. His sullen expression eased into an unappealingly smug grin and he started to make his way to them. There would be no avoiding him this evening. He and her mother had seen to it. Not wanting to encourage him further by gaping at him as if she were moonstruck, she shifted her gaze to the right, locking onto Brock Bedegrayne's.

She suspected he was not particularly shocked by this encounter. The woman beside him seemed oblivious to their silent exchange. Her gestures suggested that she was happily carrying on the conversation for them both. Brock smiled and said something to the woman. Perhaps it was vain, but Amara felt the intimate smile was directed at her instead of his companion. The wink confirmed it.

"Lady Keyworth and Miss Claeg, it is a pleasure," Conte Prola said, executing a formal bow. "Your presence alone has transformed a rather dull evening into something extraordinary."

"Conte Prola, may I present a good friend of mine, Mrs. Sheers."

"Madam," he said, acknowledging her with another bow. His attention turned to Amara. "Miss Claeg, you have led me on a merry chase. The hunt can be as stimulating as the surrender. What do you think, ladies? Should I demand a forfeit from the charming Miss Claeg for stealing my heart?"

The older women immediately concurred. He sounded sincere enough that Amara was almost convinced that what he claimed was true.

"I claim a dance. It is a small price, no, for a strong, beating heart?"

Neatly boxed between her mother and a reprisal if she disagreed, Amara lowered her gaze to the floor. "Yes, my lord."

"Eccellente." He offered his right hand. She rested her left on top of his. "If you will excuse us, ladies. Lady Keyworth, your daughter will be safe in my care."

"I do not doubt it, Conte Prola," her mother assured him.

Pivoting away from the older women, Amara risked a subtle glance at Brock. He stood alone. And he was not smiling.

Across the ballroom, Amara and Conte Prola joined three other couples to form a square for the cotillion. It was certainly an eclectic group of individuals. Fifty-year-old gout-ridden Lord Rodon was partnered with their host's youngest daughter, Lady Blythe.

Across from them, Lord Middlefell stood beside his current mistress, Lady Gribbin. Observing the blatant flirtation between them, Amara assumed Lord Gribbin had not attended the ball. She doubted a man of Lord Middlefell's notorious stamp would be deterred by the threat of a dawn appointment. She had always disliked the gambler, and if she had been alone would have given him a direct cut. Since doing so now would only force her into revealing confidences, she ignored the pair.

Turning her attention to the couple across from her, she noticed timid Miss Palmer had been paired with a gentleman who introduced himself as Mr. Maguire. Their stances were awkward while everyone waited for the music to commence.

Amara greeted her companions and made the appropriate introductions. Miss Palmer, when introduced to the conte, turned a very unflattering red and fumbled her fan. Amara could sympathize with the poor woman. The handsome Italian managed to turn almost any woman into a stuttering, clumsy goose.

"Dancing is required for a proper courtship, no?" Conte Prola murmured, his low, accented voice slipping under her skin. She resisted the urge to shudder.

"It can be, my lord. However, we are not engaged in a courtship."

The master of ceremonies called out a warning and the music began.

"You challenge me, Miss Claeg," he said over the music.

"No, I am discouraging you, Conte Prola."

He laughed and shook his head, clearly not dissuaded by her comment. The conversation ended as they concentrated on the figures of the dance. With regard to skill, they were fairly matched as partners. Her mother had employed a French dance master when she was eleven, and the years of instruction had not been wasted. Although Amara would not have employed the word *graceful* when describing a gentleman, there was a careless elegance in the conte's movements. They did not speak, but his expression was eloquent. It was brimming with joy and he was daring her to join him.

He was difficult to resist.

The conte coaxed a reluctant smile from her. When the dance ended, instead of bowing, he boldly tugged her into an embrace and spun her in a circle. The other couples applauded. By the time her slippers had touched the floor, she feared her face was as ruddy as Miss Palmer's had been.

"You are as agile as a bird taking flight, Miss Claeg.

I am loath to return you to your mama. It is my secret wish to carry you off into the night and keep you for myself."

"You are too presumptuous, my lord."

"Your beauty makes a man feel reckless," he confessed.

The combination of his intense gaze and his flattery was overwhelming for Amara. He was not the first man to court her. She had been betrothed once. Still, Amara was aware that even though most considered her fair in appearance, she was not the type of woman who inspired the devotion that gleamed in the conte's eyes. She had encountered his ilk in the past. Only last season, the Marquess of Lothbury had eloquently praised her beauty and intelligence. She had learned later the man had courted her because of her friendship with Wynne Milroy. Her heart had been slightly bruised from his cruel manipulation, but she was the wiser for it.

"I am too old for recklessness, my lord."

"What is this nonsense?" he demanded, the bitterness in her admission confusing him.

"Something I seem destined to repeat," she replied, wishing she could glimpse beyond her companion's expression. "Thank you for the dance. It was invigorating. I believe I shall retire upstairs for a few minutes. Would you be kind enough to tell my mother when you see her?"

Propriety demanded that he accept her dismissal without protest. As he bowed, his posture acquired a rigidity that reflected his displeaure. Meeting her gaze again, his expression softened. "I am your servant, Miss Claeg. I wish to be the man who grants all of your desires."

The manner in which he stressed *desire* had its own effect on her system. "Y-yes, that is an enterprising notion. Please tell my mother I will return to her soon." She stepped away from him and then paused. "I did thank you for the dance, did I not?"

He took her gloved hand and kissed above the knuckles. "Perhaps we shall dance again? Soon, I think."

She hastily nodded, backing away before she agreed to anything else. It would have been more prudent to allow the conte to escort her back to her mother. However, Amara needed a few minutes to herself. She headed out of the ballroom and up the stairs. She kept a leisurely pace. There was no reason to call unwarranted attention to her actions. So intent was she on deciding which room she should use, she did not notice that someone was following her until a firm hand closed over her mouth.

With thundering conversation and music vying for supremacy in the background, no one heard her muffled scream. She bit down on her captor's hand, but the white kid gloves buffered any damage her teeth could have inflicted. Dragging her backward, her assailant deftly opened a door with one hand while keeping her subdued with the other. He pulled her into the room. The bedchamber's oil lamps were lit and the smell of coal drifted from the grate.

A helpless sound vibrated in her throat when she heard the key turn in its lock. Warm lips brushed her ear, causing her to cringe.

"This is the second time I have carried you off from one of the Dodds' balls. It could become an interesting habit."

"Brock Bedegrayne, how dare you!" Amara demanded the moment he had removed his hand from her mouth.

Brock leaned against the door, letting her know that

she would not escape him until he was prepared to free her. "How could I resist?"

She shook her fist at him. "Next time, try." She whirled away from him, purposely distancing herself from the bed.

Amara had always been a tempting morsel when she was incensed. Two years had erased the girlish softness in her cheeks while rounding her delightfully in her hips and bosom. Her hair was longer, he noted with relief. She had it swept up into a sophisticated style. Plumed aigrettes of citrine and brilliants secured the fetching curls from her face. A matching necklace, earrings, and armlets completed the set. The jewelry complemented the pale topaz gossamer silk dress draping her curvaceous frame. The bodice of the dress was revealingly low and not exactly what he considered Amara's taste, but he was not foolish enough to object to such a generous view of her charms.

"Ah, little dove, with or without the fancy plumage, your beauty dims the image that burns in my memories." She was skittish from his touch and he wanted to reassure her that she was safe from harm. Standing close to the fireplace, he saw that his admission surprised her.

"Very poetic, Mr. Bedegrayne. If I did not know you so well, I might believe you had spoken with sincerity."

Stubborn, he thought. He expected nothing less from her. "Since you *know* me so well, then you can use my given name. You have uttered it before and have not been damned for it."

She gave him a sulky glare. "That is not a wager I would accept frivolously."

"I do not mind waiting here until you do. How long will it be before Lady Keyworth searches for you?"

"About as long as it would take my father to demand

satisfaction for your nefarious actions," was her smug retort. She smoothed the front of her dress and fussed with the long pale blue silk scarf that cascaded like a waterfall down her left shoulder and was pinned at her right hip. "I do not understand this mischief, sir. I have not conspired with any of your sisters for at least a fortnight. Your family is safe from my machinations, I can assure you."

"I have always regretted that business, dove," he said, purposely using the childhood nickname he had given her, forcing her to remember the perdurable bond between them. "Will you ever forgive me?"

"I do not know if it is about forgiveness, Brock."

It heartened him that she had uttered his name without fear. Perhaps, in time, he could do something to ease the sadness.

"Why the elaborate ruse?" She waved her hands in the air about her. "You could have approached me downstairs. If you had asked me to dance—"

"And have your mother refuse me," he countered. "I think not. Suffering the pangs of rejection would not suit me."

He approached her slowly, promising himself that he would halt if she backed away from him. Remaining near the warmth of the grate, Amara narrowed her almond-shaped eyes, clearly suspicious of his intentions. He could not blame the lady. No one had ever claimed that she lacked intelligence. Foolishly charmed by her ringlets, Brock reached out, testing their suppleness.

"How ever did you coax your straight mane into these clever coils?"

The wonder in his voice seemed to amuse her. The wariness and anger that had clouded her turbulent dark blue eyes faded. She fought back a smile.

"Paper and curling fluid."

He shook his head in amazement. "Bless me, you have never owned a dram of guile. Has no one ever told you that a lady should never divulge her beauty secrets to a gentleman?"

Perplexed, she frowned at his gentle teasing. "Whyever not?"

His gloved finger lightly trailed down her face, from her temple to her chin. "For the curious gentleman, seeking the answers is more fascinating than being given them." He leaned forward. Pressing his nose into her ringlets, he inhaled. "Mmm," he sighed with pleasure. "Jessamine. That sweet flower and you have always been tangled in my mind. How do you get the scent in your hair?"

His closeness made her tremble. Perhaps it was male conceit, but he was pleased her reaction had little to do with alarm.

"Well, I—" She hesitated. A sly womanly smile softened her lips. "I will leave you to discover that particular secret."

Her challenge cut through him like a broadsword. His lower body constricted with lust. With her sweet fragrance teasing his senses, he discovered that impulse overruled all his careful planning. "Never have I been offered a more enticing challenge."

Before she could fathom what he meant, he dragged her into his arms and covered her mouth with his. She emitted a muted sound, but he selfishly blocked out her reaction. The press of her lips to his staggered him. Clutching at her shoulders, he held her closer, to keep, he told himself, from falling on his arse. Amara's hands were at her sides, but she was not pulling away from him. A part of him wondered what he would have done if she tried. He was not feeling precisely honorable at the moment.

He pulled back long enough for them to take a breath. "Open your mouth," he ordered.

"I cannot think. I cannot breathe," she said, gasping for breath.

Brock hushed her with another kiss. Experimenting, he sucked ardently on her lower lip. She made an agreeable sound, which was almost his undoing. For her sake, and partly for his, he had ruthlessly buried his attraction to her. It had only taken one kiss to unleash the hungry beast within him.

The dark animal inside him demanded that he carry her to the bed. He imagined her fragile dress would tear easily, exposing a body he had long dreamed about. He groaned against her mouth. His cock pulsed with need despite the snug fit of his breeches. Instinctively, he rubbed himself against her. There would be other times for exploration, the sinister whisper in his head rationalized. All he wanted was to open his breeches and push himself deep inside her sultry sheath. Sweat beaded at his temples. He could make her want him. Her cries— He ruthlessly extinguished the lusty fantasy. Damn it, her cries would have been of pain, not pleasure.

Shaken, he tore his mouth from hers. Her lips were rosy and swollen from his kisses. Too full of his own guilty feelings, he could not interpret what he saw on her face.

Stepping away from her, he rubbed his hand over his face. "This was not what I wanted. Can you forgive me, Amara?"

Incensed, she said, "Mr. Bedegrayne, if you think apologizing for a kiss *you* instigated will elevate you in my regard, then you might as well drop into the nearest cargo hold with the other rats and sail back to India." She wiped her mouth with the back of her gloved hand.

That was the final insult. His eyes narrowed. "Heed my words, you cheeky malcontent. Nothing will rid you of the taste and feel of me. I will not have you confuse me with that bastard Cornley!"

Brock knew he had gone too far. No one spoke of the man Lord Keyworth had betrothed Amara to in her sixteenth year, especially not him. So focused was he on the pain in her dark haunted eyes, he never anticipated he could provoke her to violence. The prickling pain from her slap was the least he deserved for his behavior.

"I will not speak of Lord Cornley, not even to you." She marched over to the white lacquered dressing mirror and scrutinized her reflection. "Well, you have done a thorough job of it. There is no doubt everyone in the ballroom will know I have been kissed."

"I will not apologize again for the kiss, Amara. I do, nonetheless, regret the manner. I was not gentle," he admitted, still unsettled by how close he had come to acting on his carnal thoughts.

She stopped poking at her hair and turned to face him. The flare of emotion had burned itself into ash. Her demeanor was calm, too much so for Brock's liking. "And I am fragile," she mused, "not the kind of woman with whom a man can express his passionate nature."

Brock scowled. "It is just like a woman to twist a man's words until he cannot make sense of his own thoughts. You have passion, woman. Our kissing proved that well enough. I just do not want you running from me. Never from me, Amara!"

"I did not have to run. You distanced yourself from me long before you departed England." She gave her reflection a final glance and then moved to the door.

"First, Lothbury . . . and now this Italian. Neither man is worthy of you," he said. The truth of her words stung more than her slap.

Amara twisted the key, springing the lock. "Lothbury?" There was a hint of surprise in the question. "I heartily concur."

"I know of his interest, that your heart might have been engaged. Is it true?" He despised asking, but he needed to know whom he was fighting.

"How did you—" She dismissed the question with a shake of her head. "Wait. It was Wynne. She must have written you."

"Aye, she thought I might be interested." He had been in an inconsolable rage when he had read Wynne's letter, which hinted of Lothbury's attentions last season. He spent most of the homebound journey fearing he might be too late, that Amara had married during his absence. "So what happened? I thought your ambitious mother would have rejoiced over a bloody marquess," he sneered.

His attitude had put the temper back into her eyes. "She did. I did not. That is all I intend to say about the matter."

"And the Italian?"

With her chin tilted up, she said, "Not your concern." Amara opened the door. It took only several brisk strides to reach her and slam the door shut with the palm of his hand.

"I am not running anymore. It is time you dealt with it." His statement sounded like a threat. Perhaps it was.

She leaned against the door. Her regal bearing, the

dignity with which she tilted her chin, gave him the impression she was looking down on him even though he was taller by more than eight inches.

"Your pugnacity may appeal to some, but I am not as malleable as I once was. Your threat does not frighten me."

He was damned to live in perpetual discomfort if her uppishness alone made him hard. Since he longed to haul her back into his arms and kiss her senseless, Brock locked his hands behind his back.

"I am not your enemy, little dove."

Agitated by his informality, she retorted, "Nor my friend!"

"No, I am *more*."

CHAPTER SIX

The evening air chilled Amara as she and her cousin sat in the coach awaiting Lady Keyworth. Her father had departed the Dodds' ball hours earlier, preferring the risk of hazard to the silken intrigue of the ballroom. Her interest in the evening's revelry had ceased after she had left Brock, his parting words still ringing in her ears.

"No, I am more."

She sagged back into the seat with a heavy sigh. The man had inherited a noteworthy theatrical flair. It was bred in the Bedegraynes, like their good looks and intellect. Brock Bedegrayne had taken his natural gifts and honed them into a lethal combination of danger and charisma. While she spent the remaining hours of the night worrying that he might attempt a public confrontation which would alert her mother of his interest, a part of her kept reliving those minutes in his embrace. Amara bit her lower lip in contemplation. Whatever her feelings, the most dominant was not a maidenly terror.

The coach door opened, and a footman assisted her mother as she stepped into the compartment. She settled into the empty bench across from them. The footman shut the door and called out to the coachman.

"Cease chewing your lip, Amara. I thought we cured you of that nervous habit when you were ten."

"Yes, Mama." One brazen kiss, she lamented silently, and all her girlish eccentricities had reappeared. Next, she would be chewing on the fingertips of her kid gloves!

"Hold fast!" the coachman called out and the ladies dutifully braced themselves. The horses bounded forward, their harnesses jangling like music in the night. The sudden motion jostled the occupants within the compartment. Lady Keyworth placed a hand up to her turban, keeping it from sliding off. Appearances were everything, even if no one was watching.

"Piper," her mother said, "I expect you will write your mother and father about this event. Your beauty and graciousness have served you well."

Even in the dim lamp-lit interior her cousin's face glowed at the praise. "Everyone was so kind. It seemed there was an eternal fountainhead of partners. Why, my slippers are surely ruined."

"A worthy reason for a shopping jaunt. Amara will show you which shops we favor with our patronage. As I vowed to your dear father, you will have the proper polish when you leave us."

Much of the enthusiasm on her cousin's face withered. Either her mother's not-so-subtle reminder that Piper had arrived on their doorstep too countrified for the *ton* had induced the sudden mood, or it was her suggestion that the two ladies spend another afternoon together. Any commiserating that might have developed vanished at the venomous stare Piper delivered in Amara's direction. Perhaps it was rather unkind of her, but she returned the glare

in spades. They would never be confidantes. What veil of
civility they possessed had been wholly rended with her
mother's callous words. It was a loss she did not regret.
She preferred forthright hostility to false amity.

Any hope the rest of their journey would be made in
blessed silence was quashed by Lady Keyworth's next
words.

"Daughter, I pray you did not embarrass yourself with
the conte."

Quickly reviewing their encounter in her head, she
sounded guarded when she replied, "I presume, no worse
than any other occasion."

Piper brought her handkerchief up to her lips, and delicately coughed. She was staring out the window at the
passing street activity, but Amara would have wagered
her new amethyst sarcenet mantle that the woman was
relishing every minute of her discomfort.

"You really should not have run off after the set," her
mother chided. "The poor man thought you had taken
offense to something he said."

"I shall apologize at the next opportunity, Mama," she
promised, certain the gentleman and her family would
provide one.

"Really, Amara, such an insipid tone is rather off-
putting. It is not surprising gentlemen find your conduct
baffling."

She thought of Brock Bedegrayne. He seemed more
amused and challenged by her abrasiveness than offended.
"There is equality in that, since I find men and their ways
most mysterious."

"Nonsense," Lady Keyworth contradicted. "Gentlemen
are simple creatures. They prefer order in their household,
dutifulness in their women and offspring. Heed me,

daughter, all our efforts will be for naught if you persist in resisting my good counsel."

"Speaking of mysteries," Piper said, interrupting the silent testing of wills. "You were missing for some time, cousin. Where did you wander off? I recall that several others commented on your hasty departure from the conte."

"That is an intriguing question. Where did you go, Amara?"

Whether or not her cousin was exaggerating was inconsequential. It was clear from her mother's expression that she believed the worst. The word *scandal* vibrated in the air as if spoken. Any inclination for honesty died under the keen scrutiny of her mother. Her lie would have to be convincing, for speaking the truth would without doubt induce an apoplexy.

Instead of wasting hours searching the various balls, gaming hells, and exclusive clubs for his father, Brock decided an impromptu stop at the Bedegrayne town house was necessary to ascertain Sir Thomas's whereabouts. His quest took him to an unsavory lane off Upper Thames Street. Crammed between a steel yard and a brothel was the Red Crummy coffeehouse.

Armed only with a walking stick, Brock ignored the ribald invitation by two ambitious doxies from their open window and entered the shabby establishment. Searching the room, he could not imagine what had lured his father to such a place. It took him only seconds to find his father. Neither distance nor a smoke-filled room could diminish Sir Thomas Bedegrayne's presence.

At sixty, the Bedegrayne patriarch was a robust fellow, with a build that had once rivaled his son's. The passing years had widened his girth and face, but his large frame bore the weight better than most of his contemporaries. Even though his hair and side-whiskers had silvered, his intelligent blue-green eyes were as razor sharp as they had been in his youth.

Brock pushed his way to the side of the room where his father sat engaged in conversation with two gentlemen. At his approach, his father's fierce scowl for the unwary interloper gave way to pleasure.

"Brock, my boy! Join us," he said, waving him over. "Let me introduce my associates, Mr. Marsh and Mr. Smiles."

The two men stood, offering their salutations. Their worn attire and rough cadence disclosed their humble origins. Nevertheless, the men were not unnerved by his sudden appearance and directly met his curious gaze. Whatever their business with his father, the men stood as equals.

"Gentlemen." Brock politely returned their greeting. The coffeehouse was crowded and no vacant chair or bench was visible.

Sensing his dilemma, Mr. Marsh rose from the bench he shared with Mr. Smiles. "'Ere now, young Bedegrayne, squat yer bones an' sip some gin-punch wit' yer sire. We've done our business. An't that so, yer lordship?" He squinted at Sir Thomas, despite the dim lighting.

"Indeed, gentlemen. I will expect a weekly accounting of your efforts," Sir Thomas reminded them.

"We'll do it up right for ye, sir," Mr. Smiles promised, sidestepping his partner. "Leave it to us." Tugging on their hats, the pair departed.

Brock settled down on the vacated bench. Picking up the abandoned pint-pot, he sniffed the contents. "Well,

Father, if your choice of establishment was not enough to arouse my interest, your new business partners have succeeded. What are you about?"

Sir Thomas chuckled and signaled a barmaid. "Marsh spoke the truth. It was just business."

Checking in all directions to make certain they were not being overheard, Brock leaned closer before he said, "Your standards have lowered in my absence."

Sir Thomas quirked his brow. "Bilge. I am at heart a merchant. What better place to do business than an establishment that lures sailors, poets, laborers, statesmen, and noblemen?"

"Spare me the Jacobinic rhetoric. Do you want to incite a mob before I can get you out of this hovel?"

The barmaid slammed down two pint-pots in front of them, ending their conversation. He sent the barmaid an easy smile, but her dour features did not thaw. "That'll be two shillings an' eightpence, *gentlemen*," she said, stressing the last word as if she had her doubts.

Brock slipped the coins into her open palm. Clasping the coins, she gave them a dismissive sniff and flounced off.

"A man has spent too much time abroad when he cannot win over a simple English gel," Sir Thomas chided. He sampled his gin-punch.

Three drunken men in the corner started chanting her name. The harried barmaid changed directions. Confident the woman could handle the unruly summons, Brock returned his attention to his father.

"My ambition was somewhat higher than what lies betwixt her plump thighs." He picked up his pint-pot. "She would have had my enthusiastic gratitude for swill void of spittle and piss." Sir Thomas barked with laughter. Brock took a sip and grimaced. Setting down the punch he said, "So why are the Bedegraynes undertaking business with the criminal class?"

The older man cringed. "Have care, my boy. The wrong word spoken here brings unforeseen consequences."

"That is exactly my point."

Understanding lit his father's cutting stare. "Bugger me. You came charging in to rescue your dotty old sire. Is that it? I wasn't too senile for you when you ran off like your coldhearted brother and left the care of the business and family to me."

Brock closed his eyes, feeling the stirrings of a headache. Anger and scandal had impelled his brother Nyle to cut his ties with his family more than seven years ago. As far as anyone knew, the younger Bedegrayne had left England, leaving a wound within Sir Thomas that had never healed. Brock felt he had spent most of the time afterward paying for his brother's sins. "Christ, there is no reasoning with you when you throw Nyle's name down like a damned gauntlet. Come along, I will see you home."

His father pounded a fist on the table, knocking over several of the pint-pots. "I am not some old woman who needs a strong arm to walk a straight line. I can find my own way home, if it is all the same to you."

Temper matched temper. He stood, bracing his hands on the table. "It isn't. The punch has rotted your common sense if you think I will abandon you to a room of brigands. Get up." He reached out, intending to haul him to his feet. His fingers barely grazed his father's sleeve. Someone grabbed him from behind.

"Jus' a gang of cutthroats and whores, are we?" his captor jeered in his right ear. The crowd around them had become unfriendly yet rapt spectators.

Resigned, he muttered, "Brigands."

"Come again, mate?" another man demanded, moving so that Brock could recognize the men at least by profession. They were crimps, or press-gangers.

Brock glanced down at his father. Their gazes locked and a silent discourse was exchanged. Whatever their differences, blood defended blood.

He cleared his throat. "I believe the word I used was *brigands*," he said, adding enough disdain in his inflection to incite the mob that had concerned him earlier. The noise in the room rose to an annoying buzz of outrage and insults.

Brock did not hesitate. He drove his elbow into his captor's side, gaining his freedom. Pivoting, he punched the man in the jaw and sent him careening on top of the table behind him. Before he could advance, the second man rushed him and managed to catch him by the waist. They landed hard on the wooden floor, literally knocking the breath out of Brock. He clasped his ribs, and rolled away from his attacker, sending patrons scurrying out of his path.

Sir Thomas clouted the angry sailor with a chair. He lifted the chair high above his head and bellowed a challenge to the onlookers. No one seemed eager to accept. The surge of pride Brock felt was brief. Taking advantage of the distraction, the other sailor landed a ruthless kick in Brock's lower back. Hissing out the pain, he staggered onto his feet and leapt for his opponent.

Pandemonium ensued, reminding him of his wilder years. Brock could not think of a grander homecoming.

"Brawling?" Devona gave her brother an icy stare while she blotted the drying blood from a small cut near Sir

Thomas's left eye. She had repeated the word numerous times in as many minutes. Brock attributed her slowness to shock and the late hour.

Trying to keep his breathing shallow, Brock mumbled, "Hell, Devona, you act as if we started it." Summoning his brother-in-law for his indispensable medical skills had seemed like a stroke of brilliance at one in the morning. An hour later, his sister's pithy scolding and murderous glares had him regretting the decision. Tipton should have left Devona sleeping in her bed, he ungraciously thought. Women possessed no humor about these situations.

"What a fine evening," Sir Thomas confessed, still animated by all the excitement. He was relatively unscathed considering he had been in the thick of the mayhem. "Tipton, you missed a rousing scuffle. We could have used Milroy's fists a time or two."

"Our skills were more than adequate to handle a few drunken crimps," Brock countered, his pride pricking at him. "Were we not the ones who walked out of the Red Crummy before someone had the sense to alert the watch?"

The cloth-wrapped ice he pressed to his swollen cheek felt rapturous. He would have whimpered if his sister's presence had not demanded that he remain stoic. Tipton was contemplative as he examined the nasty bruise on Brock's back. "Have I broken the rib?"

The surgeon did not answer immediately. His touch was competent, but each poke sent branches of pain directly into Brock's stomach. He shifted away, worrying that he might be ill.

"How grievous are his injuries, Tipton?" Devona pressed, her concern overriding her anger at him for placing their father in danger.

"He will not require bleeding," he said, the muscle along his jaw tensing in sympathy to the pain his examination was causing his patient. His expression softened when he glanced up and noted her distress. "Come, love, no tears. The Bedegraynes can take a knock or two without permanent damage. I did not pack even one bone saw."

He and his father watched as the viscount drew his wife into a one-armed embrace and kissed her. The irony of the compassionate action made Brock grin. He could recall an occasion or two when the bruises mottling his flesh had been administered by Tipton's skillful hands. Although he would never admit it, he conceded that his brother-in-law had been justified. It was odd how age had a way of changing one's perspective.

"You can tup your wife later," Brock complained. Their kiss had reminded him what it felt like to have Amara in his arms. The fight and the pain had almost pushed her from his thoughts. In his present condition, he was not particularly grateful for the reminder. "How 'bout easing your patient's fears?"

Devona pushed away from her husband. Her pretty blush was almost as dark as her fiery tresses. Sneaking a peek at her chuckling father, she took his bruised hand and pushed it into a bowl of solution Tipton had prepared. She smiled a little too sweetly when Sir Thomas yelped because of the sting.

There was a gleam in the surgeon's light blue eyes as well, but he was too intelligent to let his wife see it. "To ease your fears, Bedegrayne, it is my professional opinion that you are suffering from severe bruising. The one on your back is painful, but I doubt the rib is cracked. You are in better condition than you deserve for taking on two men."

"Three," Brock corrected. "Including the barmaid. Of the three, I think she was the most vicious."

"And most likely would've cut your throat if I hadn't taken that broken bottle out of her hand," Sir Thomas added. "Your charm failed you this night, my boy."

Brock sucked in his breath while Tipton bound his sore ribs. The growing ache was spreading to all his limbs. He would pay dearly on the morrow for this evening's entertainment. The unbidden image of Amara Claeg rose in his mind. "I am endeavoring to improve myself, sir."

Amara's thoughts of Brock were less charitable. Tugging the jeweled aigrettes from her hair, she placed them in the velvet-lined box her maid, Elsie Corry, held out.

"It must have been some night," the enthusiastic servant said. With her carrot-colored curls and rusty freckles highlighting her cheeks and nose, she looked younger than seventeen and more suited to country life than life in London.

She added her armlets to the box, and reached behind to remove the necklace. "Oh? Gossiping with your footman again, Corry?"

"Here now, let me see to that clasp, else we'll be spending the rest of the night on our feet." Setting the box on the dressing table, she moved behind Amara and began working on the clasp. "I gave up on Brian last week. Handsome he is, but dense as dirt about a lady's interest." There was regret in her sigh. She placed the necklace in the box. Without permission, she set about removing Amara's earrings. "One of the grooms has offered to escort me to a play in Covent Garden. He's not as fine looking as Brian, mind you, but a lady could do worse."

"Perhaps seeing you with a new admirer is just the thing to jolt your Brian into action," Amara suggested, adjusting her position so the maid could free her from her gown.

"It might," Corry agreed, obviously cheered by the notion. "Aw, Miss Claeg, you are too kind letting me go on about my troubles when I'd rather hear about the dashing rake you kissed."

Good heavens, had he left marks on her? It took all her will to strap down her curiosity and not check her reflection in the dressing mirror. "Me? Kissed? You jest." She tried to sound shocked by the charge, but the nervous giggle ruined it all.

"I've been looking after you nigh eight months, and you aren't the sort to turn over to my care torn lace on your sleeves. Not like my last employer." She sniffed. "I repaired more than one torn bodice in that household."

Flabbergasted, Amara meekly stood still while Corry gathered the gown up and pulled it over her head. Shaking the fabric out, the maid expertly flipped the topaz gown over her arm and presented the sleeve. "Your gent must have had a fierce passion for you. His fingers caught in the lace and tore it here and here. A shame, that. It will have to be replaced."

Shame, indeed! She had wandered about after her encounter with Brock and had chatted with at least a dozen people. Had anyone noticed? More importantly, had her mother? Glancing down at her arms, she noticed it was not only the gown that bore the marks of Brock Bedegrayne's zeal. Several small, fingerlike bruises were already darkening on her arms. Shivering, she closed her eyes.

Misinterpreting her distress, Corry said, "There now, what's a bit of lace to a lady like yourself? I'll fix the sleeves and the gown will be like new again." Laying the gown aside, she put her nimble fingers to work on the strings of the corset. "So, madam, confess all to Corry. Who was the ardent gent? Considering my sad circumstances with men, I wouldn't mind feathering my dreams with a few saucy tales."

If it had been any other gentleman, Amara might have been tempted to regale the incorrigible Corry with the truth. Cursing Brock Bedegrayne and herself, she called upon the talent she had honed these past years. She lied.

CHAPTER SEVEN

Brock fought back a groan as he followed the Milroys' butler, Wigget, through the town garden to the stables. He wondered if his sister Wynne had already learned of last evening's activities and was exacting a bit of feminine revenge by forcing him to hunt for her. Despite the servant's casual pace, the exertion had Brock sweating. The design of the garden consisted of alternating keyhole and diamond patterns. Glancing longingly at a stone bench, he wondered if Maddie had created this tranquil sanctuary.

"Bedegrayne," a male voice called out, pulling him from his contemplation and pain. "I see two years has changed little about you."

His grimace curved into a grin at the droll observation. "Nevin!" Shaking his head at his blunder, he closed the remaining distance between them and bowed. "I beg your pardon, Your Grace."

"Spare me the formality," Drake Fawks, the sixth Duke of Reckester drawled, the dimple in his left cheek becoming prominent as he smiled. "You always did sound too insolent when you tried. The number of dawn appointments for which I acted as your second attested to that."

Dropping all pretense of formality, the men embraced. Extraordinarily tall, Brock felt inferior standing so close to someone who had a physique that even gentlemen venerated. Pulling back, he pressed his hand to his side in a futile attempt to ease the pain. "I heard about your father, Drake. You have my condolences."

His friend sobered, his aquamarine-colored eyes narrowed with concern. Only a year older than Brock, he had always seemed even older, more willing to accept the yoke of responsibility. "What the deuce have you done to yourself?"

The rebuke was not improving his disposition. "You speak as if I thrive on dissension," Brock grumbled.

The complaint was just the right thing to ease the sadness shadowing his friend's gaze. The young duke smirked. "And what of the colorful bruising on your cheek and crushed ribs? Were they delivered under the guise of friendship?"

Brock muttered an oath. "I do not start all the brawls, you know."

"Just enough," replied the man behind them. Even though he was dressed for the stable, his costly boots, if not his bearing, indicated to Brock that this man was no one's servant.

"Mr. Keanan Milroy?" He left the question in his inflection. Regardless, he had no doubts that the dark blond muscled giant was Drake's half brother and Wynne's husband.

"Aye," he admitted, mulling over the scene he had interrupted. "You must be one of the brothers. The eldest, would be my guess. You've got the look of my Wynne about the eyes."

Brock had imagined many exchanges with the retired pugilist, but the sentimental assessment was not one of them. Disarmed, he laughed. Drake, in the position of knowing both men's histories, visibly relaxed and sent a querying look in his direction. It would take too much breath to explain, so he just shook his head. He braced both hands against his side to buffer the punishment his laughter caused. "I would beg you to keep your voice down when you are making such comparisons."

"And why is that?" Milroy asked, a hint of a smile twitching his lips.

"What woman cares to be compared to her brother? She almost tore an ear from my head the last time someone mentioned it!"

As the man crossed his arms against his chest, his smile was not reassuring. "I'll bear that in mind, Mr. Bedegrayne."

Descending the stairs an hour and a half later than her usual time, Amara stifled a yawn. The late hours of town were never agreeable with her constitution. With her maid's assistance, she had donned a long-sleeved white muslin gown decorated with sprigs of blue forget-me-nots and heelless white kid shoes with blue bows. Corry had braided her shoulder-length tresses, neatly tucking them in to a fanciful lace cap adorned with blue flowers and beading.

She headed for the morning room, expecting she would be enjoying her tea and toast in solitude. It was rare for the family to break fast together. The late hours of town only encouraged individual schedules. If her mother or father required her attention, they would simply summon her. Recalling her mother's lecture last evening, Amara had every intention of spending the afternoon out of the house.

"A moment, Miss Claeg." Buckle, the butler, approached. He had traded his dark coat for a full-length apron. The dusty smudge on his left shoulder and the red leather notebook in his hand hinted that he had spent that past hour down in the cellar.

"Good morning, Buckle. Has Lady Keyworth arisen?"

"No, Miss Claeg." He opened his notebook and retrieved a sealed letter. "A boy delivered it early this morning. Two other deliveries were made in the past two hours."

Accepting the letter, she puzzled over the nondescript seal. "Really? From whom?"

"Can't say, miss. Shall I bring them to the morning room?"

"Yes, that will be fine," she said, distracted by the letter. Brock Bedegrayne's daring was boundless. He was breaking all their unspoken rules. Unable to resist, she broke the seal. The note was terse as well as enigmatic.

"Forget not the past."

It was unsigned. "So typical of a Bedegrayne," she muttered, folding and tucking the note into her bodice. She preferred to avoid explanations to her family until she had gained a few of them for herself.

Amara had barely settled down with her tea when Buckle entered, carrying two packages.

"Lord Keyworth has requested your presence when you have finished your repast, Miss Claeg."

"Thank you, Buckle." Excitement blossomed within her as she picked up a knife and sawed through the cord. Another two weeks would pass before it was her twenty-second birthday. It was too early for someone to be sending her gifts.

Removing the cerecloth covering, she peered inside. In wonderment, she removed an opaque glass bowl containing a bouquet of marzipan flowers. She delicately touched an unfurling petal of a red camellia. "It almost looks real. The confectioner is a master artist."

The butler discreetly cleared his throat. "Miss Claeg, shall I summon a footman for your reply?"

The question brought her head up. "What? Oh, no, I will send for one later. You can tell my father I will attend him shortly."

She waited until the servant had departed before she reached for the card. " 'For my incomparable bloom,' " she read aloud. The writing was different from that of the other note. There was no signature. "Well, my mysterious benefactor, I cannot fault your taste."

Amara set the bowl on to the table. Taking a sip of her cooling tea, she slid her fingers across the surface of coarse green baize used to wrap the other box. It was a large rectangular box with a depth no more than four inches. Putting her tea down, she seized the knife and efficiently cut through the cord.

Underneath the yards of baize, she uncovered a teak box. Carved into the yellowish-brown wood was an unusual circular pattern of lotus flowers, peacocks, and palm leaves. The box itself was a costly gift. Lifting the lid, she bit the tip of her finger as she studied the prize within. Laid out on red velvet was an opened fan. The sticks were made of pierced ivory. Near the head, replicas of a nude woman reached skyward toward panels of varying crisscrossing designs, each more intricate than the last. The leaf was silk and the color matched the ivory sticks. Scattered across the fabric were silver sequins, and thin silver ribbons scalloped the edge. Overcome, she pressed at the lump forming in her throat. It was the most beautiful fan she had ever beheld.

She allowed the lid to drop at the sound of the door opening. Relieved at the sight of the footman, she retrieved the discarded green baize and went about wrapping the box.

"Miss Claeg, pardon my intrusion, but your father is most insistent that you see him at once."

Her father. She had forgotten all about him. Returning the marzipan bouquet to its box, she stacked the two boxes. "Mundy, please take these packages to my room. Tell my maid to leave them to my care."

"Yes, miss."

Amara made a quick search of her surroundings, even lifting the tablecloth high so she could peek under the table. Like the sender of the note, whoever sent the gifts had chosen to remain anonymous. She released the tablecloth, allowing it to fall back in place. Perhaps one person had sent all three. She straightened, thinking over the possibilities. Donning her gloves, she abandoned her barely touched breakfast. The revelation of her mysterious benefactor would also have to wait. She quit the morning room in search of her father.

Instead of inviting Brock into the house, which would have added a certain formality to his visit, his new brother-in-law headed back into the stables. The building was new. The clean smell of new timber was still evident despite the more prominent odors of horse and hay. They walked down a narrow corridor past the stable office and tack room.

"Your patience is admirable, Mr. Bedegrayne," Milroy said, "and it will be taxed a few minutes more if you can bear it. A bee stung one of the bays three days ago and its right hock is swollen. I'd like to see if the poultice has helped."

Brock's mouth quirked. "I think I can find something here to amuse myself."

"I thought as much. I figure a man who has baked under India's sun for more than two years can handle some manure on his fine boots."

With that, they stepped out of the corridor. The connecting room was larger in height and breadth, accommodating wooden stalls and bales of hay. The head coachman raised a hand in greeting, and begged a moment to discuss the horse that had concerned Milroy. Excusing himself, Brock took advantage of the distraction. Moving from stall to stall, he admired the occupants. Whatever the man's faults, Milroy possessed an appreciation for excellent horseflesh.

His brother-in-law joined him at the fourth stall. "Impressive," Brock said, running his hand down the neck of the black roan stallion that had caught his attention. "Have you considered selling him?"

Genuine amusement crept into the indigo depths of the man's eyes. "No more than I would Wynne or my daughters."

"Do you race him?"

"For what? Money? Status? No, Mr. Bedegrayne, Fardoragh and I already know his worth."

The stallion blew out an answering breath, and swung his head toward his master's outstretched hand. Milroy at some time during their walk from the outdoors to the stables had lost his gloves. A glimpse of a thin white-silver scar across the finger pads of his left hand reminded Brock how greatly the fighter's rough life contrasted with his own.

"How is the bay?"

Giving the stallion a hearty pat on the shoulder, Milroy lifted his brows, perhaps surprised by the question. "It is too early to tell if the poultice Drake suggested will ease the animal's swelling."

The casual reference to the duke produced a strained silence between them. Keanan Milroy and the Duke of Reckester were half brothers. For years, it had been a public secret, although the Reckester family had denied the connection. Brock did not know the particulars, but he assumed the men had reconciled their differences when their father had perished by the hand of a footpad.

Milroy murmured a farewell to his stallion, and headed for the open side door. Brock easily matched his stride.

"There is little resemblance between you."

To his credit, the man did not profess confusion about the change of topic. "Aye. Each day before the shaving mirror, I imagine we both say a prayer or two for that small boon." He wiped the sweat from his forehead with his sleeve. "How long have you known?"

"From the start." Brock had first encountered the nine-year-old Drake, then bearing the title Lord Nevin, at Eton. A friendship had sprung up which continued even after university. There was a time when he had hoped the heir to a dukedom would marry one of his sisters. "I thought Drake would marry Wynne." He had not realized he had spoken the words aloud until Milroy suddenly halted.

"Her heart took another direction." Something akin to guilt shadowed his visage. "How long will you punish her for loving the wrong brother?"

"I am not—" Brock was taken aback by the cutting truth of the accusation. Rallying his thoughts, he acknowledged, "It has not been my intention to hurt her. I love Wynne. True, I feel Drake would have been a sensible choice for a husband. However, my bias is measured by years of friendship with one man and frightful rumors of another. Can you say you would have chosen a different course?"

"Perhaps not," Milroy conceded. He stared past Brock, surveying the changes the renovation over the past year had wrought. "I doubt any man fits a brother's expectation. I was told you and Tipton milled once or twice before he married his lady."

An undignified snort erupted from Brock. He had despised Tipton from the outset. His youngest sister had been too naïve and gentle to believe that the gossip about the notorious surgeon was quite factual. Quarrelsome and full of conceit, he had challenged the viscount on several occasions, but the cunning man had always managed to gain the upper hand. It had been humiliating at the time.

"Tipton can be persuasive."

A past encounter with the viscount had the blond bruiser nodding. "And he wields a rather nasty walking stick."

Brock made a concurring noise in his throat. It was rather comforting to learn that he was not the only one in the family acquainted with the lethal point of the surgeon's hidden blade. Even more interesting was what Milroy might have done to provoke Tipton to action.

They had reached the center of the garden. The heart of the design was a diamond-shaped brick pool lined with an impermeable render of pozzolana. Several buckets placed at its base suggested that the center not only provided sustenance for the eye, but was also a source of water for the multitude of flowers, trees, and hedges.

Milroy dipped his bare hands into the water. Scrubbing the grime from his hands and arms, he looked in Brock's direction, his eyes squinting against the sun. "Wynne is visiting your aunt Moll. It appears her dear friend Mr. Keel has worked up the courage to propose and she has accepted."

It grated a little that his brother-in-law knew more about the private details of his family than he did. He had yet to pay a visit to his elderly aunt, the widow of his father's older brother. This current news only reminded him how distracted he had become.

"Who is Mr. Keel?" He despised asking, but Wynne's husband was the only one who would not lecture him for his shameful neglect of his family.

Milroy rubbed the back of his neck with the tepid water, earning Brock's envy. Perched against the edge of the pool, he crossed his arms and considered the question. "Not the sort of man worthy of the challenge I see in your eyes. If I were you, I'd forget all about having a private visit with her betrothed. What's more, Aunt Moll would strike a birch whip across your hands for even considering it. Her Mr. Keel is sixty and too comfortable to be a fortune hunter. He is a well-mannered proprietor of a perfumery off Bond Street. If you insist on fighting someone, Wynne will not like it, but I can oblige you."

"You are protecting my aunt against me?" It was too outrageous to contemplate. "Why?"

The fighter shrugged, the agile movement drawing attention to the solid muscle concealed under his linen shirt. "I've a keen affection for the dear woman. Spending most of my life without a family has taught me to treasure the one I've been granted through Wynne. You are not the only male around who knows how to look after the ones he loves."

The message was clear. Keanan Milroy protected his own. Something shifted inside Brock, lessening the ache in his gut. He had felt responsible for protecting his family for so long that he was still uncomfortable with the notion that he had three brothers-in-law who would stand beside him if he asked. "My aunt must have adored you at first sight."

"Aye, she did. It was Wynne who needed charming." He nodded toward the house. "Come along. I promise to behave like a proper host since you've changed your mind about the milling."

He would be damned if the heat in his face was a blush. "I did not come here to fight. I might have a reputation for unruliness, but no one has ever accused me of lunacy."

Unconvinced, the man pressed, "What brought you here then?"

He hesitated. Clenching his teeth, he said, "Miss Claeg."

Milroy's easy stride faltered at the admission but he recovered quickly. To his credit, he did not laugh, for perhaps he understood all too well.

Lord Keyworth was not in his library managing his various interests as Amara had assumed. Closing the door, she realized how little she knew of her father's affairs. There had been little interest on her side, and having two older brothers had diminished the value in educating her. Doran had shared their father's pursuits, but was found lacking in talent. Mallory, the heir and reluctant prince, had chosen pursuits that continually vexed the family. Her mother was confident her firstborn would assume the mantle of responsibility when called upon. Amara thought it would take more than threats and bribery to sway her wayward brother.

Striding across the empty back parlor, Amara walked through the open doors onto the balcony. Potted bay and yellow jasmine added a welcoming warmth of color to the wrought-iron railing while the fragrance of the plants enticed the curious ambler down the broad stone steps that led to the garden.

On her descent, she spotted her father standing outside the aviary. The original owners of the house had built the ecclesiastical Gothic structure with the intention of using it as a conservatory. Its octagonal sides framed arched floor-length traceried glass windows. Her mother had declared it a madman's folly. She had hoped to replace it with an edifice that harmonized architecturally with the house and surrounding outbuildings, but her father had refused. Amara had been pleased by the decision. As a child, she had raced Doran round and round the two-story structure, which had always reminded them of an ornate campanile. When the game had grown tiring, they had pressed their faces to the glass and marveled at their father's predatory menagerie.

"Good morning, Papa," she said softly, not wanting to disturb the falcon perched on the padded buckskin gauntlet he wore over his left hand. The bird was about the size of a crow, and a slit hood covered its head, exposing its pale yellow cere and sharp beak. The back and head of the bird was slate blue in color, whereas its throat and breast were white with vertical markings. The direction of the dark slashes switched to horizontal farther down the breast, pannel, and legs. The peregrine falcon was a stunning predator and her father's particular favorite.

Turning his head, he acknowledged the affection laced in her salutation with an answering smile. Lord Keyworth was an athletic man for the estimable age of fifty-two. The blond hair of his youth had darkened to brown and was accented by white streaks at his temples. He was balding at the crown of his head, but he concealed the flaw by wearing hats or, if the occasion demanded, a peruke.

Years of enjoying the outdoors had scored lines around his eyes and mouth. Nevertheless, it had not extinguished completely the devastating handsomeness of his youth. At their country estate, a painting commissioned by his mother when he was twenty hung in the gallery. Walking beside him, she still saw the glimpses of the young ambitious lord who had secured her mother's heart.

"There you are, my dear. I had called for you earlier, but no one could find you."

Despite the jesses tethered to the falcon's legs, Amara kept her distance. The hood calmed the bird; however, she had witnessed on numerous occasions the natural pugnacious tendencies of her father's prized pets.

"I arose later than usual." Hanging back seemed cowardly so she edged closer to the servant assisting her father. She could not recall the young man's name, but she recognized him as one of the gamekeeper's sons. "I see I am in time for the entertainment."

The sardonic tone drew a bark of laughter from her father, unsettling his plumed companion. The bating falcon settled with an expert touch and a few soothing words.

"You never did have the heart for this sport. If you would rather wait for me in the library—"

"No, no," she declined, glancing down at the square wood and wirework cage that contained half a dozen grouse. "There is nothing quite like the display of the falcon when it stoops on its quarry." She tried to insert the right amount of required enthusiasm. It was not as if she had an extraordinary fondness for the distressed birds fluttering in the cage. Grouse fricandeau with red currants was one of her favorite dishes. She just preferred not to have her supper slain before her.

"On that we agree, daughter." He addressed the servant supervising the prey. "My Ellette grows impatient. Start the quarry."

"Aye, milord." Reaching into the cage, the servant withdrew a grouse and closed the lid before the others could escape.

Removing the leash, Lord Keyworth tensed with anticipation. "Ready, man?" At the servant's concurrence, he removed the leather hood. "Release the grouse."

The quarry, sensing danger, took to the sky. The advantage gained was soon lost. The hungry falcon ascended above the grouse, and then in a burst of speed plummeted toward the bird, its long narrow wings pulled inward almost like a scythe in form. The two birds collided in a breathtaking midair spectacle. Stunned or perhaps already dead, the grouse tumbled, striking the roof of the stables before hitting the ground. Claws splayed, the falcon alighted on its quarry. Bowing its slender, dark head, it ripped the grouse's throat out with its razor-sharp beak.

"What a truly gruesome display!" Piper exclaimed, joining them.

Her cousin had not yet bothered to close her mouth as

she watched with horrified fascination the falcon feast on the grouse. To the uninitiated, the scene was rather disconcerting. "Good morning, cousin. I trust you slept well."

The falcon lifted its head, watchful that no one violated its territory. It warned off its audience with an occasional, *"Kee, kee, kee."*

"Well enough, thank you." Gaining Lord Keyworth's attention, Piper curtsied. The viscount turned and offered his cheek. Piper dutifully stepped forward and gave him a kiss. "My lord, pardon my ignorance, but since the birds have been caught, would it not be kinder to have Cook wring their necks?"

He removed the gauntlet and handed it to the servant. "A practical observation, would you not say, Amara?" Lord Keyworth winked at his daughter, including her in the jest.

"Yes, Papa. Our cousin is nothing if not practical."

Miss Novell might have questioned the sincerity of the compliment if Lord Keyworth had not cordially taken both of them by the elbow and steered them away from the falcon. "The grouse was for Ellette," he explained. "Most of my birds reside in the mews at our northwestern estate, Arras Green. Still, I cannot part from my favorites. When we are in town, I usually take her to one of the commons for the hunt, but I have too many commitments this day to indulge my pleasures."

While her cousin asked various questions about falconry, Amara remained a silent companion throughout the exchange. If she felt a twinge of jealousy, she blamed it on Miss Novell's intrusion. Private moments with her father were scarce when they resided in London. Encouraged by the captivating attention Miss Novell bestowed, Lord Keyworth relinquished his hold on Amara as he gesticulated while making a point. Keeping pace with his stride, she smiled slightly at his fervor.

"Then we are in agreement?" Lord Keyworth said, a touch of his hand drawing Amara back into the conversation.

"I believe so," she replied, too stubborn to admit she had no hint to what they were discussing. Had they not been discussing falconry?

"Fine, fine. I shall send a note to Prola, notifying him that you shall be home to receive his card."

"This afternoon?" she queried, twisting the tip of one of her gloved fingers. "Heavens, it will not do."

Accustomed to his daughter's fickleness, he clenched his jaw. He was losing patience with her daily excuses. He gave them both a minute, until he trusted his ability to hold a rational dialogue with his youngest child. "I was not aware you would be out."

"Miss Novell has ruined her slippers. Mama had suggested an afternoon of shopping."

"Delay it," he ordered.

Her cousin touched him on the arm. "Naturally, we will choose another afternoon."

The charitable twit had Amara choking on her own resentment. What argument could she offer that would not be perceived as stubbornness? There was something about the conte that disturbed her. She was not the type of woman who inspired such devotion. Brock Bedegrayne's attentions only added to her confusion. What she needed was solitude, and she felt fenced in by everyone's demands.

She made a final attempt to dissuade her father. "My commitments extend beyond shopping, Papa. I promised Mallory I would pay him a visit."

Lord Keyworth's face took on a reddish hue. Almost

sputtering, he said, "Taking into account Mallory's numerous indiscretions, he must be well acquainted with false promises by way of acquisition and execution."

"He has asked me to sit for a portrait." Sensing his refusal, she added, "It is a gift for Mama—a surprise." Amara silently begged the other woman for support. "Miss Novell was present when he made his request."

Her cousin pursed her lips. "I do recall Mr. Claeg expressing a fervent desire to paint his sister."

Lord Keyworth fisted his hands in an agitated manner. "My treasure, I praise your noble intentions toward your mother. However, as always, your deeds are inopportune and hinder mine." He gave her a considering stare. "One might believe it is deliberate."

Amara clasped her hands. "No, Papa. I thought only of accepting my brother's generous offer before he was distracted by a more appealing whim."

She had not lied about her brother's mercurial temperament, and her father's grim expression revealed he concurred. "Very well."

The reprieve made her light-headed. "Oh, thank you, Papa!" She rolled onto her tiptoes and gave him several ecstatic kisses.

His annoyance gradually yielded under her delight. "You are a good daughter. Leave our conflict in my care, and all will be well. When you see your brother, remind him that he has been neglectful of his mother."

"I promise." Amara could barely contain her excitement as she watched him walk away to check on his falcon's progress with her quarry.

"Will I be joining you when you call on Mr. Claeg?"

She started at the question, forgetting her cousin had remained at her side. "I can think of no reason to insist."

"Good," Miss Novell said, sounding pleased. "While I enjoy viewing the achievements of an artist, I find the implements of the craft too odorous." Breaking off a spray of red campion, her cousin trailed down the path after Lord Keyworth.

Leaving the pair to continue their discussion on the minutiae of falconry, Amara returned to the house. A carriage would have to be readied. She grimaced, critically assessing the dress she wore. It was simply inappropriate for her purposes. Rushing up the stairs, she contemplated whether or not she should send a note ahead warning her brother of her subterfuge. In the end, she decided an unannounced visit was best. Dodging family obligations was a trait the surviving siblings shared.

CHAPTER EIGHT

Brock regarded his uninvited call to the Keyworth residence as an impulsive act, but in reality he was feeling apprehensive. Several days had passed since his visit with Wynne and Milroy. Their advice had not been helpful, and he had a slight suspicion that had been their intention. Oh, they had been friendly and sympathetic to the plight he had presented. However, they must have guessed he had not disclosed all the reasons for his interest. Even in his frustration he could not regret his silence. The truth was not his to tell.

Brock had knocked on the door and was told by the butler that the family was not at home. He had handed the man his card, but if the servant recognized the name, he showed no reaction. Resigned, Brock had been about to depart when one of the Keyworths' liveried grooms had halted an empty gig in front of the residence. One of the ladies of the house was preparing to leave. He could only hope it was the lady he sought.

Not wanting his presence to worry the servant, he approached and introduced himself as one of Miss Claeg's lovesick suitors. The young man was appreciative of Brock's predicament. He was explaining his woes relating to the courting of one of Lord Lumley's housemaids when Amara emerged from the house.

This afternoon she wore a cream round dress of thick refined India muslin with a flowing jonquil mantle. A straw bonnet was secured with a tidy bow along the right of her chin. Harried and muttering under her breath, she was almost to the street before she noticed him.

"Mr. Bedegrayne!" She glanced back at the house, probably concerned she would be caught speaking to him. Her caution always brought out the recklessness in him. If she could have read his thoughts, she would have run back into the refuge of her house.

He walked around the gig, joining her. Executing a stiff bow, he held out his hand. "I fear it is too late for discretion, Miss Claeg. I left my card with your butler." It was a declaration of sorts to the Keyworth household. He would not apologize for it.

"Then you must also be aware no one is at home this afternoon." Her movements were skittish, as she accepted his hand, allowing him to help her step up into the gig.

"We must talk."

She slid over, making room for the servant. "I agree. Regrettably, I have another appointment."

"Then we will not tarry." Climbing into the gig, he settled in the seat beside her.

"You—you cannot do this!"

Deliberately misinterpreting her protest, Brock grinned. "Jimmy will not mind sitting aft, will you, man?"

"No, sir!" Moving to the back, the servant climbed up on the small perch.

Brock and Amara both seized the reins. A childish tug-of-war ensued. "You cannot drive me. Think of the gossip!" Amara asserted.

He had underestimated her strength, but there was no doubt in his mind who would be the victor. "How can I, when all I think about is you?"

Her grip slackened at his confession. Taking up the ribbons, he paused. Their struggle had ruined her perfect coiffure. Wispy mahogany strands framed her flushed face. She looked pleasantly rumpled, although he guessed she would not appreciate the compliment.

"Where is your appointment?" There was a wealth of suspicion injected into the question. He believed she had made up the ruse so she had another excuse to avoid him.

Comprehending that nothing but force would remove him, Amara surrendered. "My brother's residence. It is on Bury Street."

His right brow lifted. "Bury Street it is." He gave an expert flick of the ribbons, and the horse commenced their short journey. "I thought Doran was the favored brother?"

Shoulders set, she seemed more interested in the horse's backside than him. Usurping her gig, he mused, had not placed him in a flattering light. Mentioning her beloved Doran had most likely doomed him to her silence.

"Doran is gone," she said simply. "His death has taught me an appreciation for the only brother I have left."

"No offense, Amara, but you and Mallory have nothing in common." Two years older than Brock, the eldest Claeg sibling had always been arrogant and wild, rejecting his father's guidance. His elopement six years ago with Lord De Lanoy's mistress had sealed his fate among the notorious.

"Mallory is painting my portrait. It will be a gift for Mama."

"You can not always be the peacemaker, little dove."

She finally looked at him. Those stormy dark blue depths ensnared him, touched his soul. "No, not always."

He could not recall when he had first given her the sobriquet. It had just seemed apt. It had probably started with her father's odd collection of predatory birds. Brock had thought the family had more in common with the birds, and Amara with the quarry. He had watched over the years as her family easily trounced her gentle nature. Nonetheless, it never deterred her from stepping between her brawling brothers, a fact he was certain neither brother had appreciated.

"Did you . . ." She let the question trail off.

"Ask. I might even tell you the truth," he lightly mocked.

Trusting him to take her to her destination, Amara focused on his profile instead of the street. "Did you send me the note and the gifts?"

He frowned, not liking his fears confirmed. "Note? Gifts? Do I have rivals for your affection, fair lady?"

"You will cease this nonsense, Mr. Bedegrayne," she warned, forgetting they were in public. "You are not courting me!"

It was then she noticed the open landau approaching them in the opposite direction. Two of the ladies were unfamiliar. But Brock recognized Mr. Wirland and the woman seated beside him as the Marquess of Holbeck's daughter, Lady Fayth. He acknowledged them with a slight bow of the head when they passed. The astonishment on the women's faces would have made him laugh aloud, but he bit his tongue at Amara's mortified groan.

"Of all the inhabitants of London, the Vining sisters

would have to be the first we encounter," she lamented. "They are dreadful prattle-boxes. Word of us together should reach everyone's ear by nightfall."

Any other day, the notion would have cheered him. It was the inconsolable expression on Amara's beautiful countenance that soured his mood. By God, forming a connection with him should not seem so appalling! " 'Tis true, you might lose a suitor or two, sullying yourself with a Bedegrayne."

"Baiting me will not improve the situation, Brock Bedegrayne," she snapped. Like an imperial princess, she serenely gestured to a location just ahead of them. "There is no need to further trouble yourself. I will disembark here and walk the remaining distance."

Her supercilious manner failed to astonish him. Despite her protests, he believed he understood the woman beneath the polished surface. "Your brother would never forgive me if I abandoned you on the street."

Nothing she could have said would counter such logic. Lips compressed, Amara visibly struggled, thinking she could punish him with her silence. She lost the battle. "Did you send me the flowers?"

A sound of disbelief vibrated in his throat. "Too ordinary. I credit myself with a bit more inspiration than conservatory posies when I set out to enchant a lady."

"Really?" He mistrusted her genial tone. "The bouquet was created from marzipan. I thought it very clever."

Had she? was his dour reflection. The ardent gentleman would regret encroaching on the lady Brock viewed as his. "Does your clever gent have a name?" He tried keeping the rush of resentment under control.

Sensing she had the advantage, Amara felt her disposition brighten. "Well, I know he is not *you*." She touched his arm, and felt the muscles jolt under her hand. "This is my brother's residence."

Disappointed their time together was ending, Brock maneuvered the horse to the right side of the street and signaled the horse to halt. The groom jumped down from his perch. Sensing Brock preferred to see to his lady, the servant moved past them and saw to the horse.

Setting the ribbons aside, he climbed down from the gig and offered Amara his hand. "I shall await your return."

His high-handedness disconcerted her; on many levels, she was unskilled in dealing with him. Exasperated, she asked, "How often do you play a groom in your leisure?"

"I cannot think of another endeavor more gratifying than seeing to your pleasure," he admitted, the double entendre sending a cascade of desire into the pit of his stomach.

He could feel her hand trembling within his own. She broke the contact once her feet met the ground. "My pleasures, withal, are not your concern. I have a servant who will see me home." Recalling her manners, she added, "Although I suspect your purpose was not so gallant, I do thank you for the escort."

"Were the box and fan favorably received?" he asked, when she turned away from him.

She halted her retreat, and paused. Returning, she stood in front of him. He watched a flurry of sentiment animate her delicate face, something he had never dared hope she would convey in words.

"I cannot recall owning anything as exquisite." She leaned forward, brushing a kiss against his cheek. "You are too generous. More than I deserve," she whispered in his ear. Before Brock could react, she pulled back and hurried toward the building.

Mallory was an obsessive tyrant. At least he was so
about his art. If she could have anticipated the trials she
would have to endure under his guidance, Amara would
never have sought him out the previous afternoon and
reminded him of his inspiration to have her sit for him.
Surprisingly, he needed little persuading. The day she had
encountered him in the museum, he had been serious
when he had expressed an interest in painting her.

As she sat there, resisting the urge to rub her cramping
muscles, it had become clear that she and the rest of the
family understood little about the demons tormenting
Mallory. His craft was both mistress and taskmaster. To
their parents, his art was a rebellious stand, and occasionally, a source of embarrassment. He possessed talent. It
would have been simpler if he had not. Until she had
placed herself into his artist's hands, she had not appreciated the preparation and deliberation Mallory poured into
his creations.

He demanded perfection. He fussed about the costume
she wore, continually manipulating the position of her
body, hands, and face. If she moved once he was satisfied
with her pose, she was sharply reprimanded. He sketched.
He cursed and sketched some more. Hundreds, it seemed,
and none pleased him. The setting seemed sparse. There
was a place for her to sit, lush draperies, greenery, and
an exotic brass incense burner. Still, there was something
in his light blue gaze that seemed fey. Whatever he saw
when he stared at her could not be viewed by mere mortals
until he painted it.

"Lines are marring your forehead," Mallory said,
adding broad strokes to his sketch. "Relax."

Amara wrinkled her face in retaliation, earning a laugh from him. Aspiring for a tranquil expression, she switched her focus to her surroundings. The building was both a showroom for his work and his home. She had been given little time to explore the house, but the studio itself smelled of turpentine, oils, and other mysterious chemicals that were appropriate for an artist's alchemy. Paintings of varying sizes covered the wall, whereas others were carefully stacked upright.

Her scrutiny returned to her brother. The studio was in better condition than her unkempt brother. Mallory's unruly shoulder-length hair hung in front of his face like the bars of an iron cage. His clothes could not have been in worse condition if he had slept in them.

She dwelled on the observation.

When she had entered the studio earlier, he had not been alone. There had been a woman. Her brother had escorted her out of the room before formal introductions could be made. His actions would have seemed odd if she had not already recognized the lady as Mrs. Carissa LeMaye. The eight-year difference in their ages had not shielded Amara from knowing the more salacious details about the woman's life. While Amara had been in the schoolroom studying Latin with her governess, the exotic raven-haired beauty had been a much sought after Cyprian. She had married well, twice, and each man had made her a widow, leaving her sizable jointures from each estate. Whatever her circumstances, her name was still discreetly linked with numerous gentlemen of the *ton,* her brother being her latest conquest. Men were corruptible twits, she bleakly brooded. In fact, there had even been rumors years ago that the young widow had once been under the protection of Brock Bedegrayne.

"Enough!" Mallory dropped the charcoal, and lifted his hands in surrender. "You will be scaring future generations if I immortalize that glower. What is wrong?"

A denial was forming on her lips, when she relented. He was watching her too closely and would recognize the lie. She stuck with the truth. "My toes are numb. I am hungry, and missed tea again. That alone will put me in ill favor with Mama." Privately enjoying his pained expression, she added, "I also have need of the convenience."

"Consider yourself unfettered." He waved her off. "Go see to your needs and I will summon the housekeeper for some tea."

Uncoiling from her position, she rubbed her lower back in a very undignified manner. "And perhaps she has a few of those little spice cakes left over from the other day. You know, the ones with the currants?"

The look he gave her was filled with brotherly stoicism. "I think we can accommodate you, dearest."

After taking care of her personal needs, Amara returned to the studio. Finding it empty, she strode to the open window. She stared down at the activity below, wondering if Brock was awaiting her return.

"Looking for anyone I know?" Mallory asked, his appearance greatly improved by her brief absence. His dark hair was combed and confined with a leather strap. He had replaced his wrinkled attire with a freshly pressed coat the color of claret and a gray waistcoat. The knot in his cravat was uninspired. Nevertheless, she acknowledged his attempt with a slight nod.

"I doubt you would believe me. I barely believe it myself."

"Oh, I have the capacity to believe the extraordinary," he retorted, apparently intrigued. "Confess all."

Amara's eyes crinkled in amusement at his protracting demand. She thought she could trust him. Besides, refusing him added more importance than it warranted.

"Mr. Brock Bedegrayne."

He was not particularly stunned by her confession. Casually dropping onto the nearest sofa, he crossed his arms over his chest. "Hmm. I had heard he had returned from abroad." Mallory gave her a considering stare. "Shall I demand grass before breakfast for your honor?"

Horrified by the possibility, she exclaimed, "Heavens, no!"

Satisfied by her answer, he settled back into his slouch. "I thought as much. In our youth, I caught Bedegrayne watching you with a less than brotherly interest. You were too young then. I might have interfered if he had acted, but he kept his distance, choosing to pursue other . . ." He made a vague gesture with his hand.

Mistresses. That was the word her brother had tactfully omitted. Old memories brought forgotten pain and anger. Once, the six years between their ages had seemed an insurmountable abyss. Now it was the least of her concerns.

"Has he made a formal declaration to our sire?"

She moved from the window. "The connection between our family and his has become strained since Doran's death. Moreover, Papa has found me an Italian conte."

His expressive face conveyed better than words what he thought of Lord Keyworth's lofty opinion. "What about Bedegrayne?"

Had she not asked herself the same question a thousand times? Since her feelings were simmering too close to the surface, she changed the subject. "You are a comely rogue, Mr. Claeg. Why have you not convinced some young lady to accept the responsibility of pestering you daily into a clean coat?"

Tipping the satinwood Pembroke table of its clutter, Mallory righted it and secured the butterfly flaps. "Probably for the same reason you resist the noble studs our father trots under your nose. I dislike being hobbled."

Amara was spared from responding to his outrageous comment. A footman entered, carrying a tray laden with a teapot, cups, plates, and a silver cake basket filled with her anticipated spice cake. After the servant departed, she joined him on the sofa.

Pouring the tea, she said, "That is a horrid thing to say."

"But apt," he countered, accepting the teacup she offered. "My marriage to Mirabella was a mistake. Not that I would ever make such an admission to our sire. Something tells me that if your Lord Homely had lived long enough to mutter his way through his wedding vows, you and I would be sharing the same point of view."

She giggled, sensing he had purposely blundered the man's name just to hear her laugh. "Lord Cornley. The horrid man's name was Cornley."

Nudging the cake basket closer, Mallory said, "Well, well, how telling. Does Bedegrayne know you have ceased grieving for your dead betrothed?"

The tea she choked on scalded her tongue. Setting her teacup down, she kept her hands busy by heeding her brother's not-so-subtle hint and served him the spice cake.

Finally, she said, "Mr. Bedegrayne, above all, understood my feelings about Lord Cornley."

Brock had never met a more nettlesome and perplexing lady than Amara Claeg. Fate had kicked him in the arse, and the lovely Miss Claeg had chalked the bloody target on his posterior. Considering his volatile mood, if she had remained, he would have throttled her and by damn, he would have enjoyed it!

"Bedegrayne, if you keep muttering and glaring at the pedestrians, someone will assume you have escaped the private asylum near the park and summon a constable."

Brock glanced up. Mallory Claeg was perched on the edge of his windowsill. From his lofty position, he must have observed the entire incident that had taken place moments earlier. Now his humiliation was complete.

"Come up," the man invited. "My neighbors will praise me for the good deed. I think it is time we renew our old friendship."

Brock almost stalked off. It was tempting, but he was not a coward. Moreover, he had a word or two for a brother who would permit his sister to drive off with a nameless Italian fop!

Claeg's aloof housekeeper led him upstairs into the drawing room. The room was designed more for pleasing the *bon ton*'s discriminating taste than for comfort. Brock assumed Claeg used the room for entertaining his high-water patrons.

"Welcome, Bedegrayne. I seem to be offering everyone tea this afternoon. I assume you prefer yours cold." Claeg held up a crystal decanter of brandy. At Brock's nod, he removed the stopper and poured two glasses. Offering one of the glasses to him, Claeg said, "What shall we toast?"

"The jade."

"Ah, right to the heart of things." He lifted his glass and imbibed. "I gather you are speaking of my sister."

For an elder brother, his host was not particularly outraged by the insult. Instead of feeling relieved that he was not apologizing his way out of a duel with Amara's only surviving brother, Brock shifted his ire onto the Claeg within his grasp.

"I would have never trusted her in your care if I had known you were so apathetic about her welfare. Has there been a moment or two in your life when you have placed someone else's concerns above your own?"

"Have a care, Bedegrayne," Mallory said, temper making his gaze flat and deadly. "I might take offense."

Brock's grip tightened on the glass in his hand. The sharp edges of the crystal pattern scored into his palm. It was astounding the glass had not shattered under the pressure. Fighting Claeg would not benefit him. After what he had witnessed this afternoon, forcing Amara to choose between him and her brother would only confirm that he was the worst villain.

Perhaps seeing more than Brock would have liked, Claeg settled into an odd-looking X-frame chair made out of serpentlike birds. He idly tapped his glass on a beak that comprised part of the arm. His expression was contemplative instead of confrontational.

"You may be correct, Bedegrayne. My family prefers bestowing love best at a distance. Even so, your interference will not be appreciated, no matter how honorable."

Since Claeg was willing to give him the information Brock craved, he could be reasonable. He chose the opposing chair. The brandy was easing the ache in his ribs. "Who was the gentleman?"

"When his servant knocked, he was introduced as Matteo Taldo, Conte Prola." He lifted a finger, silencing him. "Amara was not expecting him. If you must blame someone, blame my father. He tires of having a spinster for a daughter."

Brock took a sip of his drink, recalling the shock in Amara's turbulent blue eyes when she had noticed him. Her hand had rested on the Italian's sleeve. The guilt paling her features had him reeling with understanding. Whoever this man was, he was the reason she had been rebuffing Brock for the last two days. He had not been thinking clearly when he had advanced on the couple.

"Mr. Bedegrayne, no!" She stepped in front of her escort. "I beg of you. Please."

The Italian sniffed and drew himself up to his full height. "Miss Claeg, you are acquainted with this . . . *selvaggio,* no? Have no fear, you are under my protection."

Brock seized her roughly by the arm and hauled her closer. She did not fight him, but the gentleman took a courageous step toward him. Not caring about the consequences, he shoved the man back with his free hand, compelling him to take several quick steps back to keep his balance.

Despite his anger, he gentled his touch as he caressed Amara's cheek. "Sweet lady of perfidy. What honeyed lies will drip from your tongue?"

"No lies, Mr. Bedegrayne. Nor will I attempt convincing you with the truth." Her lips trembled, and he realized belatedly that his brutality had been a grave misstep.

"I must insist you release Miss Claeg, at once!" the incensed man demanded.

Holding her in place, he stared down at her, unprepared to release her to anyone, especially the fop. His intuition hummed, warning him that she was safe only in his care.

"Come with me," he pleaded, burying his pride. "Now!" Her trembling lips parted. For few seconds, Brock held his breath, feeling as if his heart balanced on the tip of a dagger.

"Miss Claeg!" the stranger said, pompously expecting her obedience.

Tears pooled in her eyes, damning him. He released her. She backed away from him, this time with determination rather than fear. "I must go."

Pulling back from the memory, Brock set down his brandy. She had refused him because of duty, not because she had given her heart to the Italian. He found little comfort in the thought.

"I am not in the habit of interfering in the day-by-day minutiae of my family," Claeg said, recapturing his attention. "However, when word reached me that my father had found a replacement for the tedious Lord Cornley, I grew curious."

"How curious?"

"Enough to make a few inquiries about the gent."

"And?"

Claeg shrugged. "He seems everything he claims to be and more." Meditative, he took a sip of his brandy. "Oh, I can see you are disappointed in my answer. Then again, you never did like Cornley. What will you do, Bedegrayne? You cannot challenge every man who shows interest in my sister."

"Cornley was a Machiavellian bounder who took entirely too much pleasure in hurting others. Putting a ball in him would have been too merciful." The other man thought jealousy ruled Brock's actions, but it was only a symptom.

"Luckily, Cornley spared you the awkwardness of having to leave the country by perishing in a fire. I recall Amara was despondent for months."

Either by tactful omission or ignorance, Claeg had left out several incriminating details. Six years ago, Brock had tracked down Cornley at his favorite gaming hell, the Manticore, and had challenged the drunken man to a duel. The confrontation turned deadly when knives were drawn and a brawl erupted. An oil lamp had been kicked over in the confusion, shattering against the wall. Hot oil and flame had devoured the dry wood, and soon the entire establishment had been ablaze. Brock had escaped unscathed. Three patrons had perished in the fire. One of them had been Lord Cornley. If there was justice, the man was burning eternally in hell.

"Awkward or not, Cornley would have died by my hand."

Claeg left his chair and retrieved the decanter of brandy. Returning, he refilled Brock's glass and then his own. "The man has been dead, what, five or six years and still he arouses your bitter hatred. What do you know about Cornley that my family does not?"

Brock remained silent. No one had listened to him six years ago when the match had been announced. There was nothing to be gained from discussing it now. He picked up his brandy. "Perhaps you should have your sources prod deeper into Prola's background."

"Why?"

"A posteriori. Cornley was also handpicked by your father."

CHAPTER NINE

Amara drifted somewhere between the twilight of consciousness and the cozy depths of dreams. With her eyes closed, vivid images of her day flickered in her mind like the pages of a book caught by a sudden breeze. There were glimpses of her father, the marzipan bouquet, Miss Novell, and a falcon plummeting down from the heavens for the kill.

Brushing her hair from her face, she twisted the bedding around her when she turned onto her left side. Her head was a whirlwind. She saw herself posing and teasing Mallory, spice cake, and her mother standing by the door, clearly disapproving of something she had done. She frowned, uncertain of her sins. When she approached her mother, the image blurred and changed to Brock. He was angry, so very angry. He kept pointing at her gown. Was something wrong with her gown? Glancing down, she realized she was holding the beautiful fan he had given her. Flipping it open, she gaped in horror as all the silver sequins fell like a cascade of dried petals to the floor.

Somewhere within the tangle of images, she had

slipped into dreams and from there into nightmares. Nightmares of the past.

Amara stood at the window watching the rain freeze into snow. The storm had been unexpected, but it would not ruin the festivities within Arras Green. Earlier there had been a hunt, and her mother had outdone herself with a feast worthy of a royal guest. She had heard her father boast to her mother that the Prince of Wales might attend their gathering. The house, servants, and the Claeg children had been prepared for such a contingency. Switching her attention from the scene outdoors to her faint reflection in the glass, she turned from side to side admiring her new gown. For a sixteen-year-old young lady, the cut of the bodice was the most daring she had ever worn. Judging from the various reactions she had received earlier from the male guests, her youthful figure was ripening into enticing womanly curves. Cheered by her minor and imaginary conquests, Amara leaned forward and in a feigned kiss, blew her breath against the window, making the glass fog. She wrote her initials, A. C., and drew a scrolling circle around the letters.

She gasped when strong hands covered her eyes and pulled her backward into an embrace. "Guess?" her male captor whispered against her ear.

Amara smiled, forgetting her brief fright. The warmth of his breath tickled her ear, making her shiver. Although he had tried to disguise his voice, the heart always recognized with affection. Feeling playful, she asked, "Are you one of the footmen? No, that cannot be so, for I have broken all their hearts. You must be . . ." She trailed off, drawing out the suspense. "Mr. Adler, is it you?"

There was a charged pause. "Who the devil is Mr. Adler?" The feigned outrage was almost believable.

Spinning around, she laughed and gave her captor a teasing poke on the shoulder. "Did you think you could fool me, Brock Bedegrayne? There could be a hundred men in this room and I would still recognize you, even blindfolded."

As he returned her smile, his expression told her that he did not believe her claim. "How?" he challenged, his gaze so intense, it seemed to be committing her face to memory.

She had recognized him by his scent. He had a tantalizing fragrance, which brought to mind a feeling of protection and tenderness. Since it was unseemly to admit that she sniffed every gentleman she encountered, family friend or not, she was not about to confess the truth. "It was the manner of your walk. I heard your brash swagger."

He pinched her nose in mock punishment. "Silly goose. Have you missed me?"

"Nary a moment," she lied. Once a childhood playmate, Brock Bedegrayne was now a grown man. His pursuits were no longer dictated by the whims of his family. She had once fancied herself in love with him, and the rarity of their meetings broke her woman's heart. "Have you come with your family?"

"Aye. Sir Thomas has brought my sisters, so it should please you to have other women about closer to your age."

"It does. Older brothers are so tiresome."

Not offended, he shared her amusement. "Brothers make a similar accounting for younger sisters."

She felt so comfortable around Brock Bedegrayne, regardless of the fact he had been more her brothers' friend than hers. He had always treated her like one of his sisters. He yelled when he was angry, pulled her hair when feeling provoked, and was fiercely protective. The love she felt for him was forged on a young girl's boundless fantasy, even if it was imprudent and futile. He had never sought more than friendship, nor had he offered anything overstepping the bounds of brotherly affection.

"Your home is overflowing with guests, and yet here I find you alone. Why is that?"

She had been prudently avoiding the attentions of one particular gentleman, but it seemed too cowardly to make such a confession. She wanted him to see her as a young lady old enough to be courted, not as a frightened child.

He smiled, his brows lifted with curiosity. "Do not tell me you actually believe the Prince of Wales will attend?"

His skepticism triggered a natural surge of family loyalty. "His Royal Highness has my father's support and friendship. Bestowing favor on such unwavering allegiance is not uncommon."

Unimpressed, he dismissed her defense with a grimace. Disconcerting her further, he lightly fingered one of the petite braids near her right ear. "The prince's allegiance can be as fickle as a young maid's heart."

She rushed forward, covering his mouth with her hand. "Hush! You utter the most traitorous remarks! What if someone hears you?"

Through her gloved hand, Amara could feel his grin. He replied, but it was muffled. Chagrined, she removed her hand. "I do beg your pardon."

"Nay, you wish me to the devil, Miss Claeg," he countered, unrepentant about his teasing. "The truth is in your eyes. They are as clear as a hot spring on a winter's morning. Such inviting depths tempt a gentleman to cast aside caution." Unsmiling, he moved closer, causing the tiny hairs on her arms to prickle. "Aye, they might be worth a bad scalding."

Her mouth went dry. "More like a good scolding, if you dare." He intended to kiss her. She was certain of it. Awareness rippled just beneath her flesh, making their proximity almost painful. He stared down at her, his hungry gaze fixed on her mouth. Unable to tolerate the tension a minute further, she rolled up on her tiptoes and pressed her soft mouth to his. Brock angled his head to one side, and reverently their lips touched. She closed her eyes, marveling at the perfection of the moment. Never had a kiss moved her so that she felt the ardent tingles all the way down to her knees.

Laughter coming from outside the room broke the fragile enchantment. With a mumbled apology, she jerked back and turned her head toward the door. Amara barely heard Brock's soft imprecation. She was so petrified, wondering if her mother might be with the group, that she had not released her grip on his arms. Only Brock had the presence of mind to untangle himself and put a respectable amount of distance between them.

Her brother Doran appeared at the threshold, catching sight of them. Since he had spent the last few hours liberally drinking with the other gentlemen, his youthful features took on a puckish air.

"What have we here?" He wagged a finger at them. "Naughty, naughty, dear sister. Especially since I have gone to the trouble of—" He leaned back and gave a shout to someone. The unintelligible reply had her brother doubling over with a fit of laughter. He beckoned his unseen companions to join him. "Amara, my girl, come show your betrothed a proper welcoming. We shall drink a toast in honor of your upcoming nuptials."

Amused by some prank they had played, three boisterous gentlemen came up behind her brother, who was still bracing himself up at the entryway. Ducking under her brother's arm, Lord Cornley put a companionable arm around Doran. He was a fine-looking man with gray eyes and straight blond hair that was cut to frame his face. The young earl was also quite foxed. He squinted at Brock and Amara, who seemed rooted in place. Oblivious that he was doing anything untoward, he leered at her, his expression becoming embarrassingly intimate. "Gentlemen, a'n't she a pretty one?"

Thumping Doran on the back, Lord Cornley walked toward her. He wobbled on the last step, and then seized her hand. An abrupt shriek slipped out when he dragged her into a clumsy embrace. His cohorts laughed, enjoying his audacity. She tried pulling her wrists free, but she might as well have been fettered with irons instead of muscle, tendon, and bone.

"You have been miserly in your attentions, Miss Claeg."

"It has not deterred you from finding your own amusements, my lord." Papa wanted this man to be her husband. The thought left her cold.

"As my countess, you will learn that my needs come before all. I demand a kiss from my lady."

Anticipation lit Lord Cornley's gray eyes as he dipped his face closer. The smell of spirits had her wrinkling her nose, while she turned her face away and arched her body, attempting to escape his questing lips. What feelings Brock's gentle kiss had coaxed from her congealed at the notion of Lord Cornley's touch. His friends, including her brother, thought her resistance all a jest and were clearly entertained by her efforts to thwart her betrothed's sloppy affection.

"My lord, please."

Feeling wholly inept at handling the situation, she sent a beseeching look to her only ally in the room.

Brock was gone. The room became a variegated pattern of color when Lord Cornley tired of her game, whirled them once and then jerked her closer. She closed her eyes, prepared to endure his kiss. In her mind, she envisioned years of such moments and her heart withered.

"Release her."

Amara opened her eyes at the quiet demand. Her relief was almost blinding as she met Brock's wintry stare. He had not deserted her. Sometime during her struggles, Brock had moved, positioning himself behind Lord Cornley. The merriment palled as the tension stretched between the two men. She did not take her gaze from Brock's face, but she could hear the gentlemen in the distance whispering, perhaps even wagering on the outcome.

The young earl glanced over his shoulder, summarily dismissing the threat Brock posed. "Stealing a kiss from my betrothed does not warrant your concern." The comment was nonchalant in delivery, but his fingers digging into her arms revealed his anger.

"I must insist. Miss Claeg deserves better than a clumsy pawing from a pot valiant."

"Kiss mine, you meddlesome cur." Defiant, he smashed his mouth down over hers.

Amara felt the sharp edges of his teeth when he pressed a punishing kiss to her mouth. She tasted her own blood. Cornley was proving to them all that he could do anything he desired with her and no one would oppose his actions. The kiss for all its ferocity was brief. Cursing, the earl tipped his head back at an angle that looked painful.

With no other choice than being pulled along, she realized their twosome had become a strange triumvirate. Brock had a ruthless grip on the hair at the back of Cornley's head. The unnatural angle and the impotent pain in the earl's eyes revealed that Brock finally had gained the man's attention.

"For Amara's sake, I strived for civility but I have lost interest. Let us try my forthright approach." Brock twisted his grip. "Release her and apologize."

Cornley's already pale face whitened at the increased tension Brock was applying. Growling an oath, he freed her. Amara rubbed at the stinging in her arms. She placed herself out of range of the two men.

As he watched her with a troubled gaze, Brock's light green eyes narrowed. "You have put marks on her. Apologize, and make me believe your sincerity," he threatened.

Sobering in the face of violence, her brother Doran rallied. Brock had subtly altered the balance of power in the room even though he was outnumbered. Not wanting to be the focus of an enraged friend's wrath, he hid behind excuses. "Cornley was just dallying. There was no harm intended." Shamed that he had stood by and allowed his sister to be hurt, he offered her a mute apology.

Amara was not feeling generous. Doran would have to offer more than feeble excuses for his callous behavior. He could spend his time courting her good favor instead of trying to impress her future husband. Scowling at Brock, Doran murmured something to his companions and they departed, leaving Cornley's fate in Brock's hands.

Wrenching his prize, Brock said, "Your friends have deserted you, Cornley. I can just imagine the witty tale with which they will regale the others about your sad predicament."

"You will pay dearly for this," Cornley vowed, his inflexible pose only allowing him to focus his ire on Amara.

Clutching her hand to her heart, she feared for Brock. Lord Cornley would not permit this insult to go unchallenged. They would face each other across a frost-covered field, or worse, the earl might ambush him. She could not bear for him to be hurt because she had solicited his protection. "Mr. Bedegrayne, I beg you. Release him. For your sake if not for mine."

"At once, Miss Claeg, when you have gained your apology. Cornley," he said, drawing the man up onto his toes, "you are stalling. I have heard rumors about your perversions. Do you possess a queer proclivity for pain?"

"M-Miss Claeg. I tender my ap-pologies for any embarrassment and discomfort you have endured."

"I accept them, my lord," she rushed, wanting an end to the conflict. "Please, Mr. Bedegrayne. I am satisfied."

With reluctance, Brock released the earl and shoved him toward the door. Amara sensed he hoped Lord Cornley was foolish enough to attack. His body vibrated with the need for a fight and it had more to do with his hatred for the blond gentleman than any insult he perceived toward her.

Lord Cornley must have discerned this as well. He took a moment to smooth his hair and gave his coat a straightening tug. The earl encompassed them both in his considering stare. "I concede, Mr. Bedegrayne. You wielded your advantage and can claim victory this hour. I hope it brings you pleasure." His mouth lifted in a sneer. "For within a month, I will claim what you lust for and can never have." Executing an exaggerated bow toward Amara, he touched the door for balance as he made his way out of the room.

Amara felt ill. She stared at Brock. His expression was still murderous, yet he was not running after his adversary. She blamed the earl's parting words for Brock's anger. Cornley had spoken in jealousy. He had not understood that their affection had grown from a solid foundation of years of childhood friendship. It encompassed not only Brock, but also his brother and sisters. "You humiliated him in front of his friends. For that alone, he will seek vengeance," she warned, praying she was wrong.

Flexing the hand he had used to hold the earl, he gave her an enigmatic look. Walking up to her, he gently touched each bruise on her arms. Amara was still trembling from the altercation, and Brock's concern was feeding her agitation.

"Little dove," he said, his voice roughening with emotion. "The bastard has already had his revenge."

Pressing her face deeper into the pillow, Amara murmured Brock's name. Within the foggy labyrinth of dreams, she separated from her sixteen-year-old dream image. Had she been so young and naïve? The residual fear of the dream was still pumping through her, melding nightmare and reality.

She recognized the nightmare. It had haunted her off and on for six years. Her fingers dug into the mattress. The fading images diffused into random colors and patterns as she fought her way out of the mist.

She lost the battle.

The weight of sleep pulled her down into its murky depths. The image distorted and suddenly she was sixteen again, standing in front of the window watching the rain turn into snow. It was so cold, she thought, shivering.

Turning, she walked out of the room. Instead of the outer hall, she was in the attic. A soft whisper in her head questioned the contradiction with her memory, but Amara ignored the warning. Her mother had sent her upstairs into the old nursery on an errand. Amara dared not defy her. Papa was sulking about His Royal Highness's absence and Mama was smiling so much her cheeks must have hurt.

An impromptu play had been proposed by one of the guests, and now everyone had been put to work. While the majority of the guests were playing cards, those enlisted for the play were learning their lines. Amara had been sent up to the old nursery to search for suitable costumes.

Unlocking the door, she entered the room. The glow of her candle sliced through the inky interior. The room had been closed off for years. With dust tickling her nose, she lifted the brass candlestick higher and worked her way through a maze of covered discarded furniture and trunks.

She searched the room three times before she found the trunk she needed. It had been shoved against the wall and hidden behind a black lacquered bookcase that was missing two drawers. The leather appeared black in the candlelight. The ornate brass mounts and nailing were tarnished, but the trunk was still a beautiful piece. Setting down the candlestick, she tried pulling on the handle. The trunk would not budge. Annoyed, she bent over and lifted the latch. Using her weight for leverage, she pushed the lid up and secured it. Riffling through the old costumes, she scowled at the sound behind her.

"Naturally, you arrive when I have completed all the difficult tasks. You might as well leave, else I will be tempted to lock you in this trunk when I have finished. I still have not forgiven you, Doran. Nor will I for some time," she said, her mind more on the costumes than chastising her tractable brother.

"A pity. A sister should find leniency in her brother's faults."

Her heart stuttered at the sound of the earl's voice. "I do," she said, her throat tightening. She gathered up the clothes, not caring if they were suitable for her mother's needs. "Lord Cornley, it is unseemly for you to be here. Lady Claeg would be embarrassed to learn you were in such an unkempt room."

Putting his finger to his lips, he reached back with his other hand and shut the door. "I can keep a secret if you can. Your brother was detained by your father, so I offered my assistance."

"You have my gratitude, my lord. If you will carry these garments, I will light your way."

He smiled indulgently. "There is no need for haste, Amara. I am almost your husband, so your reputation will not be ruined if you are found in my care." He took the bundle of clothing in her arms and dropped it back into the trunk.

"My lord, the others await our return."

He took her hand, and brushed his thumb in a gesture of comfort. "I think your mother has given up on the play. Most of the players are too fuddled to recall their lines. And just moments ago, while practicing a mock sword fight, one of the fools managed to pierce his opponent through the arm. The blood flowed as boundless as your father's claret, causing several of the ladies to collapse. Trust me, we will not be missed."

"Perhaps I am needed." She picked up the candlestick, uncertain how to get by the earl without insulting him.

"No more than you are here."

Lord Cornley took the candlestick from her limp grasp and placed it on the bookcase. Bracing one arm on the bookcase, he allowed his gaze to drift lower than her face. Nature had given him a lean build and an interesting face cut in sharp angles. Cast in shadows, the compelling lines segmented and hollowed his visage. With the exception of the polished gleam in his gray eyes, it appeared as if pieces were missing from him.

"I regret the manner in which I approached you earlier. You have yet forgiven your brother. Is there charity in your heart for me?"

She managed a slight smile. "Of course. It is forgotten."

"You are more generous than I deserve." He stepped closer, his size blotting the warm candlelight. She made a small, frightened noise when his hands curled around her elbows and pulled her to his chest. "No one is watching, Amara. Let me taste your generosity."

Amara tilted her chin up and accepted his kiss. His lips were smooth and cool, as he claimed hers. He tasted of spirits. She turned her face away. "The room is cold, my lord. Let us rejoin the others before we are missed."

"Innocent," he teased, leaning heavily on her for support. "Tarry a moment longer in my embrace and you shall forget all about the chill."

"Please, my lord." She stared down at the trunk. "Mama insisted I bring the costumes—"

"Confound it, forget about those damnable rags!" His weight pushed them backward against the wall. Lord Cornley was sweating despite the coolness in the room. "You were friendly enough with Bedegrayne. Doran mentioned that he caught you kissing him."

She pushed against him. "Doran lied." Clenching her teeth, she strained against him.

"I disagree. You see, I have watched Bedegrayne around you. He huffs and stomps about like a stud denied his favorite mare."

Appalled by his coarseness, she said, "You have had a cup too many if you believe such nonsense. My family has been friends with the Bedegraynes longer than I can recall. Before this evening, months have passed since I was in the company of Brock Bedegrayne. When have we been carrying on this supposed tryst? Lest you should forget, I am your betrothed!"

"Ah, the crux of my argument. Or should I say thrust?" He pressed his pelvis against hers, laughing while she tried to writhe out of his embrace.

"You are a scoundrel! When my father learns of your conduct, he will end this betrothal," she panted. His abrupt stillness had her regretting her angry words.

"I think not," he contradicted, his confidence frightening her more than his proximity. Grabbing the front of her bodice, he rended the delicate fabric. Ignoring her cry of outrage and pounding fists, the earl put his mouth on the tender flesh above her corset. He bit her, hard. The pain barely registered through the shock.

"Tell your father," he dared her, and she could see that her fear was increasing his excitement. "Lord Claeg will understand a man's impatience for his bride. The fact you may be breeding when we have finished will assure your family's backing."

Twisting in his arms, she begged, "Do not do this! I will not tell anyone! You have my word."

"A woman's word? It is not worth a farthing." Putting his arm horizontally against her throat, he added pressure until she was seeing tiny flickering white lights inches from her nose. Using his teeth to remove his glove, he discarded it. The earl reached down, and unfastened the outer buttons securing the falls on his breeches. He gave little consideration to the five inner buttons. With a savage tear, the buttons burst their thread anchors and struck the floor like a hail of pellets.

Wildly, she glanced down at the frightening shadows of linen and flesh between his hips. She repeatedly kicked his shins, but Lord Cornley was too drunk to feel any pain. In retaliation, he increased the pressure against her throat, dulling her attack so her concern was focused on drawing her next breath. Working his free hand down, his fingers caught the hem of her skirt and buried his hand underneath.

Amara screamed when his fingernails scratched her upper thigh. It was a pathetic hoarse cry. If anyone had been about, she doubted they would have heard it outside the room.

Lord Cornley, however, was prudent. Freeing his hand from her skirts, he used his full strength to lift her up and slam her body several times against the wall. Her teeth rattled together as her head ricocheted and her forehead struck his shoulder.

"Not a peep," he whispered, "unless you want me to share you with the others."

Others? It was a threat, Amara was certain. She just could not understand its meaning. The room seemed to be spinning and her head ached. "I feel poorly."

"Lying on the floor should accommodate both our needs." Catching her under the arms, he slid her between his legs onto the floor. Before she could roll away, he landed on his knees, pinning her.

Slapping his hands away from her ruined bodice, she arched her neck, preparing to scream. The earl smothered her cry with his gloved hand. The taste of wet leather made her gag. Impervious to her flailing arms, the earl reached down with his other hand and worked her skirt higher. She twisted her head.

"You will learn how to pleasure me, Miss Claeg. When your education is complete, your skills will rival those of any doxy."

Amara moaned against his palm. Tears she had no time to indulge streamed down her temples into her hair. Her struggles weakened with each passing minute. She closed her eyes and despaired when his bare fingers prodded her intimately. For violating her this night, marriage would be his reward.

"Open your eyes, and acknowledge me as your husband." He slapped her across the face when she did not comply. With her mouth free, she drew in a deep breath and screamed. He struck her again, but she was beyond caring.

"Damn you, settle down!" he commanded. Moving up her body, Lord Cornley locked her wrists together and secured them above her head with one hand. He bit her lower lip, drawing blood. Using his free hand, he tugged on her corset until her breasts spilled out of the top. He lowered his head and pressed his face into the soft flesh. Trembling, he bruised her with every touch.

The earl raised his head, and even in the dim light, she read the intent in his cold gray gaze. Shifting, he shoved the fabric of her skirt higher. Impatient, he pulled out his own shirt and cupped his rigid flesh. Stroking it, he positioned himself between her thighs.

"Scream if you like. It fires my blood," he said, ramming his flesh into her, forging a burning path into her.

Amara cried out; the pain was a thousand times worse

than she had imagined. While she struggled to get away from him, his hand tightened over her joined wrists as he pounded into her.

"So Bedegrayne did not have you, after all," Lord Cornley gloated, hellfire glittering in his savage eyes.

Amara screamed. The remnants of her nightmare had her body jackknifing on the bed.

"No! No!" she said, confused by the darkness and the past. She batted and kicked at the bedding, which trapped her legs. The frantic movements tumbled her out of the bed. She landed on her side, the impact strong enough to knock the breath out of her. As she gasped for breath, the pain in her hip brought her mind to the present.

"Not real," she murmured, pressing an unsteady hand to her hammering heart. "Just a dream." For an assurance, it was ineffective. The residual pain of her nightmare lingered with her current injuries. Curling into herself, she sobbed against her knees. It had been almost a year since she had dreamed of that terrible night. Why tonight? The answer was obvious. Brock. His return had stirred up her feelings for him again. Witnessing the earlier altercation between him and Conte Prola had merely reminded her of Lord Cornley. She pounded her fists on her knees in frustration. The earl was dead. How long would the hateful scoundrel haunt her?

A soft tap at the door had her sitting up. She held her breath, wondering if she should feign sleep.

"Miss Claeg, are you well?" her cousin queried from the other side of the door.

She could not have her cousin spinning tales at breakfast. Wiping her eyes, she sniffed. With a slight limp, she walked to the door. Amara gave her face a final scrub and opened the door, glaring expectantly at her cousin. The lateness of the hour had not diminished Miss Novell's beauty. Wearing a plain white nightshift, she had wrapped an unremarkable brown blanket around her shoulders to ward off the chill of the late hour. Her waist-length black tresses were tucked neatly within a frilly cap.

Amara, on the other hand, was feeling rather dowdy and waterlogged. "It is rather late for pleasantries, Miss Novell."

Her cousin, as she had expected, bristled at the remark. "If you do not desire visitors, then you should refrain from carrying on as if someone were murdering you in your bed. What is wrong with you?" she asked, stifling a yawn. "Did you have a nightmare?"

The worst, but she was not about to share her fears with anyone, least of all Miss Novell. If her slightly bored expression was crumbling around the edges, then it was all the more imperative that she end her cousin's curiosity. "It was the eels, you know."

"I beg your pardon?"

"I get ghastly indigestion from them. The nightmares are only part of the aftermath," she cheerfully confessed, silently willing her to go.

"What eels?" her cousin asked, clearly confused by the conversation.

Gripping the door, Amara closed the gap. "I never realized the purgative qualities of sharing one's confidences. I could go on forever."

"But—"

"However, the hour is late and you are looking pale. Sleep well, cousin," she bade her, and shut the door.

It was not until she heard the woman's departing

footfalls that she sagged in relief. If Miss Novell tattled, she would be receiving a resounding lecture from her mother concerning her rudeness. Not that she cared, she thought, padding over to the washstand. She did not bother with a candle. Her fingers touched cool porcelain before finding the water abandoned from her evening ablutions. Water trickled through her fingers as she splashed the wetness to her cheeks.

Amara picked up a towel and dried her face. Casually discarding it, she walked past her rumpled bed. She grabbed one of the blankets and wrapped it around her body as she continued on to her favorite chair near the window. Sleep had always eluded her after this particular dream. Drawing the curtains back, she opened the window and shivered at the rush of early morning air. More out of habit than thought, she pulled the pendant out from underneath her bedclothes and held it in her palm. Miss Novell's nocturnal visit and the cold air had cleared the lingering confusion of what was real and what was best buried in the past.

The young girl Lord Cornley had brutally ravished was gone. It was difficult regretting the loss. She had been too vulnerable. After that night, she had erected an impenetrable barrier around herself. She had needed time to heal. Although she doubted her family had noticed. They had been too concerned about losing Lord Cornley. Brock Bedegrayne had noticed her retreat; then again, he had been part of her nightmare.

Laid out and weakened, there was nothing she could do but endure until the earl had exhausted himself. She had lost her voice. Her screams had disintegrated into soft whimpering. Amara stared at the flickering candle on the bookcase, distancing her mind from the violence.

There was a sudden crush of weight, and then Lord Cornley was pulled off her. Scrambling backward, she pushed down her skirts. With her knees to her chest, she gathered up the flaps of her torn bodice and pressed herself against the trunk. She watched in a daze the two obscured combatants in the dark. The sickening sound of flesh connecting with flesh was too much for Amara. Covering her ears with her hands, she burrowed her face into her skirt. She rocked herself, praying the numbness settling into her bones would consume her.

"Amara."

She snapped her head up on hearing her name. Her vision blurred as the man on his hands and knees advanced slowly toward her. She was too agitated to recognize the man. A vulnerable sound vibrated in her throat, halting him.

"Dove, you are hurt. Let me help you," the man said, his own pain evident with each word.

"I—I—" She looked beyond him into the darkness.

"He cannot hurt you. I cracked his damn skull with a steel coal shovel and locked him in the night nursery. I doubt he will awaken any time soon. Regardless, it will not save him after what he has done," he promised, his anger so palpable that she cringed. He inched closer, wanting her to become comfortable with his proximity. "You know you can trust me, Amara. I just need to see how badly the bastard hurt you."

Reaching up for the candlestick, he brought the light closer. The glow of the candle warmed his harsh features. As he placed the candle on the floor, she blinked away her tears and focused on the strong, handsome face she knew so well.

"Brock?" her ruined voice rasped.

"Aye, dove." He blinked back the moisture in his own eyes. "Would you—I need to hold you. Please, Amara, I will not hurt you. I swear—"

When his voice broke, she slowly crawled into his arms. His gratitude for her trust was muffled as he pushed his face into her neck and held her too close. She clung to his chest, feeling his strength pour into her.

"I—I am sorry, I was too late." He pulled back and lightly kissed her bleeding lower lip. "Cornley is a coward. I should have known he would seek you out and use you to gain his revenge against me. When you both were unaccounted for, I feared the worst."

"Mama sent me up for the costumes." The excuse was so inane she started laughing. She could not seem to stop. Shivering, she gestured at the trunk while she tried to blank her mind of the terrifying ordeal.

Refusing to release her, Brock leaned them both to the side until he could catch the hem of one of the abandoned garments. Dragging it nearer, he draped the old mantle over her torn bodice.

"Will he die?" She could not bear speaking his name.

He glanced back. "Not yet." He subtly shifted them so Amara could not see the door barricading Cornley inside. "We have to get you out of here. You are trembling and your skin is ice." He hesitated, unsure of his next words. "A physician should be summoned. Your injuries, they need to be examined."

The thought of another man examining her intimately had her clutching Brock, a hold that must have been strangling him. "I could not bear it. No physician. Promise me!" The hysteria she had warded off during the attack surfaced now that she was safe.

His jaw tensed while she sobbed in his arms. He rubbed her back, allowing her to cry out her fears and misery. Finally, he made her look at him. Using the edge of the musky mantle, he wiped her tears from her cheeks. "You are not being sensible, Amara. When your parents learn of Cornley's treachery, they will call for a phys—"

"They must never know!" The fear of discovery dried up her tears. "You cannot tell anyone what he has done!"

"Amara—" Brock began, the argument already brewing in his eyes.

She grasped his coat and gave it a tug to make certain he was paying attention. "H-he boasted that violating me would only gain my family's backing on the marriage. My father approves of him. If there is a chance I could be breeding . . ." She trailed off, horrified by the possibility.

Rage hardened his visage. "He was still—" He visibly swallowed. Talking about it was difficult for them both. "I believe I stopped him before he could—" He cursed, unable to finish. "Christ, I will never forgive myself for not finding you before he touched you!"

"He spoke the truth. My family will marry me off to him if they learn of this." She gazed up at him, begging for his understanding. "I would rather die than yield to him again. Please. Please, Brock."

"Do you think I want you marrying this bastard? If your family supports him, I will make you a widow before your wedding night."

She could see that he meant every word. "If you kill him, you will be charged with his murder. Even if you leave the country, do you believe I would permit such a sacrifice?"

"It is my fault he hurt you."

Wearily, she shook her head and leaned against him. "He is a monster. Wedding pledges and the sanction of the church would not have altered his brutal nature."

Brock was silent. She listened to the rapid cadence of his beating heart—or was it her own? After a moment, he said, "It serves his own purpose to gloat about his deed. Denying it will not save you."

Within the comfort of his arms, Amara marveled at how clear her thoughts seemed. Even the pain had diminished. However, the tremors in her body had not relented, nor had the cold. "He was anticipating only my parents would know what had happened. They would have paid any price for his silence to avoid the scandal. Your presence has complicated things."

He nodded, immediately following her logic. "If he reveals himself, he opens himself to be challenged. For if your family will not demand retribution for his depraved actions, then I will not hesitate to do so."

"The earl's cowardice will keep him silent. I will convince my father that I find the match disagreeable. I will tell him of the rumors I have heard. Lie, if I must. Papa will not force the marriage if he believes Lord Cornley has not been truthful about his finances. Papa prides himself in being able to judge the honesty of a gentleman. I do not have the same confidence about his compliance, if he learns his daughter has been disgraced."

"Have some faith in me, Amara. Your secret is safe." His gaze grew critical. "It will be my pleasure to remove Cornley from the house. Once he awakens, the beaten cur will likely run with his tail tucked. Your bruises and bloodied scratches, however, will be more difficult to conceal."

"If I head straight for my bedchamber, I can change my gown and burn the evidence of my—my—" She felt her eyes fill with burning tears. "When the maid finds me, I will say that I fell down the stairs while carrying the costumes for the play. No one will know," she said fiercely, needing them both to believe it.

"Can you stand?" he asked, still dubious of her condition. At her shaky nod, he shifted her to the floor so he could assist her. "Here, take the candle." Even with his support, her knees collapsed under her.

"I am so weak," she complained, and then let the tears overwhelm her.

Swearing at the man who had hurt her, Brock scooped her into his arms. He backed into one of the covered chairs and sat down. "Heed me, Amara. You are not weak. I cannot think of another person who has the strength you possess."

She buried her face in the mantle. "If I fail in convincing them, I will be lost."

"With me aiding you, how can you fail?" He dug under his cravat and pulled out a long gold chain. Sliding the length over his head, he grasped the swinging oval pendant. "Do you know what this is?"

Confused by the sudden change of topic, she replied dully, "Should I?"

The pendant must have been an antique. The gold bezel was dull, almost looking like tarnished brass in the candlelight. The agate within had something, figures perhaps, carved into the surface, although it was too dark to pick out the details. She lifted the pendant for a closer inspection. The stone felt hot beneath her fingers.

He stared at her instead of the pendant. "It belonged to my mother, and her mother before her. When she died, it came to me. Since then, I have always worn it close to my heart. It reminded me of her generosity and love. It brought me comfort when I thought of what I had lost." Releasing the pendant, he worked the chain over her head. "It is yours now."

She curved her fingers around the pendant. "Brock, this is too precious. No, take this back. It belongs—"

"To you," he interjected.

To your wife, she thought, but could not bring herself to speak the words aloud.

He stood and adjusted her so she was balanced in his embrace. "Let it be your talisman, Amara," he coaxed. "Wear it, and feel my strength when yours wanes, even if we are apart." He carried her out of the room.

She despised asking, but she had to know. "What will you do with him?"

His arms tightened around her at her question. As he carried her swiftly down the stairs, they both were wary of servants and guests encountering them. She had finally given up on him, when he replied, "Have I ever broken a promise?"

"No," Amara whispered, holding the candle out so as not to ignite the old mantle. If she had closed her eyes, she would have succumbed to the exhaustion battering her.

He pressed his face against her cheek, humbled by the purity of her faith in him. "I promise you this. Cornley will never bother you again."

CHAPTER TEN

Still shaken from her restless night, Amara had fled her house and sought refuge at the Benevolent Sisterhood. The charity had once been used as a ruse to aid her brother Doran when he had found himself imprisoned in Newgate for his part in a coining operation. Their efforts to rescue him had failed miserably. Afterward, Wynne Milroy had breathed life into the illusion by officially establishing the Benevolent Sisterhood. Like most beginnings, the business had faltered; however, her friend had been determined.

What had started out as a means to feed and clothe a few more lost souls had evolved with the help of her husband into a small shelter. While the Foundling Hospital would only accept children twelve months or younger, Wynne had understood misfortune was indiscriminate of age. Her heart in particular bled for the women and children beaten down by their circumstances.

Undaunted, she had wielded her intelligence and considerable charm influencing wealthy benefactors. Amara had been enlisted long before even the Bedegrayne family had been privy to Wynne's activities. At first, she had agreed because the Bedegraynes had supported Doran even though his own family had abandoned him when faced with scandal. Later, she had been swept up in Wynne's enthusiasm. It had been during one of their misadventures that Keanan Milroy had come to their rescue. The chance meeting had altered all their lives.

"It's crooked," the six-year-old girl beside her complained, throwing her slate board on the floor.

"There, there, it is not so bad," Amara said, retrieving the board. "Your printing is improving."

One of the older boys, not to be outdone, leaned across the table and studied the girl's efforts. "Looks like maggots squirming uphill," he scoffed, which promptly launched the offended child into a fierce bout of tears.

"Nicely done, Jamie," she drawled, placing a firm hand on his neck. "It took you less than a minute to give our girl the sulks. This must be a new record for you." She gave him a nudge. "Try again."

Shifting from one foot to the other, he sent the pouting child a fuming glare. The girl retaliated by sticking her tongue out. "I beg pardon. Grand letters, really."

Amara gave him an approving squeeze. Looking to the right, she noticed Wynne had arrived and was enjoying the scene as much as she. "Keep practicing. And no fighting."

Jamie waited until he thought Amara was out of range, before he softly added, "Grand, really, for squirming maggots."

Wynne hooked her arm through Amara's, dragging them both off before they burst into laughter. "Oh, that Jamie is an imp!" she said once they were out of the room. "He reminds me of someone."

"Brock?" She tensed for no reason since her guess had been a reasonable one.

"No, Nyle. He spent most of his childhood getting his backside whacked." The delight in her face diminished. Catching herself, she gave her head a rueful shake. "Brothers. Even when they are lost to the family, one cannot cease worrying."

Amara thought of Doran, wondering if he had found happiness in his life outside England. "No, one cannot," she softly agreed.

"I was so pleased when your note arrived this morning. Our time together has been so limited." Striding to her desk, Wynne gestured toward a nearby chair.

She sat down and watched the bustling activity through the doorway. "The charity seems to run itself."

"In a way, I suppose it does. People who have come to us for assistance carry out many of the daily tasks. Too many of these people have lost more than a job or a warm bed. They need confirmation that they have something to offer to the world." Her smile brightened at the sudden appearance of a gentleman. "And I have Mr. Lyndall, who is truly the buttress of the charity. I thank Milroy daily for our introduction."

At the apex of his twenties, Mr. Lyndall had started out as a coalheaver. He had told them once that the conditions had been so harsh, the chance to pit his physical strength against an opponent in the prize ring had seemed like a way to improve the lives of his family. His powerful build and natural skill had given him some minor successes, but the life of a fighter was a brief one. When Keanan Milroy had approached him about assisting his wife with the charity, the man had eagerly embraced the opportunity.

He removed his hat and bobbed his head respectably. "You are too generous, Mrs. Milroy," he replied. "I don't mind lending a strong back when it's needed."

"A humble gentleman," she added. "After meeting my husband, I was convinced all fighters were exceptionally arrogant."

"Only second to brothers," Amara chimed in, slightly amused by the adoring expression he had when gazing at his beautiful employer. Wynne could tease a smile out of the bitterest curmudgeon. Poor Mr. Lyndall succumbed effortlessly.

He flashed Amara a quick smile and slapped his hat back on his head. "I just come to tell you. Miss Wyman arrived with her escort. I put her to work in the kitchen. She isn't pleased and you will most likely hear about it."

"Do not worry about her, Mr. Lyndall. Unlike her brother, she has never refrained from speaking her mind. I believe her little grievances result from habit more than genuine dislike. Give her time. Maddy will settle into whatever task you have given her."

"Aye, ma'am. Oh, what of the gent who come with her? He's dressed a bit fancy, but is willing to help in the unloading of the wagons."

Her gaze holding Amara's, Wynne calmly said, "It will not be the first coat my brother has ruined. Tell him I will come out later and check his progress." She lifted her brow in a conspiring manner. "That should keep him in a temper for at least half an hour."

"You have a wicked wild streak in you for someone so tiny. Milroy must have fallen for you the first time you put him in his place." He touched his hat. "It was good to see you again, Miss Claeg." Mr. Lyndall left the office.

The knowledge Brock was close sent a surge of panic through Amara. "I cannot remain for much longer. I had planned continuing on to Albemarle Street. Papa managed to get me a yearly subscription at the Royal Institute. One of the chemical professors is conducting a public experiment and I have been meaning to attend."

Closing the ledger in front of her, Wynne noted the tight grip Amara had on her reticule, and her rigid bearing, poised for flight. "We have been friends too long for you to placate me with lies, Amara. If I had known my brother's presence would send you running off, I would have never made up the excuse for him to escort Maddy here."

She sensed Wynne's hurt and despised herself for it. "You do not understand," Amara said helplessly.

"I could if you would tell me what is going on between you and Brock."

When put that way, it seemed like a reasonable request. She shifted in her seat. "What is there to explain?" Amara tried not to wince at the disappointment in Wynne's eyes. Her expression reminded her so much of Brock that the pain was almost too much to bear. "Does he know I am here?"

Wynne hesitated. "No"

Amara's relief was acute, but she kept it well hidden. "I doubt he will thank you for your efforts. The last time we spoke he was rather cross with me." She gave her friend a speculative look. "Heavens, Wynne, tell me you were not trying your hand at matchmaking?"

Wynne's mouth quirked into an unapologetic grin. "He has been very curious about you since his return. Actually, it began before he left England. He made me promise—" She stopped, realizing her confession might not be well received.

"What? He made you promise . . ." she prompted.

"It was trivial, really. He just wanted me to spend time with you. I suppose he was worried about you after Doran's death."

Surprise competed with anger, so she was more stunned than her friend when her eyes glistened with tears. "You befriended me at the request of your brother?"

"Initially, I acted on my brother's behalf," she reluctantly confessed.

Both abruptly stood. While Amara thought only of escaping, Wynne was just as determined to prevent it.

"It was a difficult time. You had buried your brother. Devona blamed herself, and your mother was—not kind." Her lips quivered, recalling the old grief. "I was thinking only of my family. Brock had the generosity of heart to think of you too. Our friendship might have started as a favor, but it continues because I care for you as if you were my sister."

Digging into her reticule, Amara pulled out her handkerchief. She dabbed at the tears. "I had always longed for a sister."

"You have one. Several, if you want to claim all the Bedegrayne women." Wynne was reaching for her own handkerchief. "Although you might want to pass on Irene. Devona and I accept her only with great sufferance."

Amara laughed. "She is not so awful."

With feigned reluctance, Wynne sighed. "I suppose not. Still, nothing short of torture will ever gain a confession from me within her presence."

They embraced. Amara pulled back first. "I must go."

Wynne walked her to the door. "Do not be nettled by Brock's actions. His approach may have seemed devious, but his concern was sincere."

"Your brother oversteps himself," Amara said, her anger renewing at the thought of his imperial manner. "He always has," she muttered under her breath as she walked away from Wynne.

She stepped outdoors. The passing of several wagons had stirred small whirlwinds of dirt in the street. Waving away the encroaching cloud of dust, she coughed into her hand. Amara hesitated. Before she could change her mind, she reentered the building. It was cowardly to avoid Brock because of nightmares that were beyond his control. Nodding at the greeting the children shouted, she strode by the office where Wynne sat diligently at the desk studying the ledger entries. She was too absorbed in her reading to notice Amara. Without stopping, she headed for the kitchen.

Harried, Maddy Wyman lifted her head from her task of splitting boiled pigs' trotters. The apron she had pinned to her gown bore several unidentifiable smears and her light brown hair was untwining from the single braid she preferred. Maddy dug her knuckles into her slender hips. "Has Mr. Lyndall banished you to the kitchen as well? The man goes too far. Next he will have Wynne in here. If you have any sense, you will slip out the front door. Otherwise, he will have you skinning and boning the eels," she said, with an exaggerated shudder.

Eyeing the sharp knife the young woman was wielding with dangerous enthusiasm, Amara maintained a prudent distance as she proceeded to the door. "I will concede to your wise judgment, Maddy." Acting as a scullery maid held no more appeal for her than it had for Maddy.

"Not that door," she cautioned. "The man himself is just beyond the door unloading provisions."

"Is Mr. Bedegrayne with him?"

Maddy skillfully cleaved several trotters on the table. For all the woman's peevishness about the task, Amara was rather impressed by her versatile talents.

"I doubt any individual with two good hands could

deflect Mr. Lyndall and his intentions." Sensing that the question went beyond polite conversation, Maddy speculatively cocked her head. "If you have need of him, pray do not worry about denying me an escort. Wynne has invited me to supper. She feels I deserve some reward for my sufferance. I have been told her cook will be preparing several of my favorite dishes."

What it revealed was that Wynne Milroy was not above using bribery. Amara wrinkled her nose. If she had spent the afternoon dismembering an animal carcass, it would have taken more than a favorite dish or two to recompense her. She shivered in distaste. "For your sake, I hope the reward is worth the undertaking. I bid you good day."

Maddy Wyman held her pleasant smile, until Amara had departed. Very odd, she thought. She would have never imagined the pairing of the reserved Amara Claeg with the rakish elder Bedegrayne. Then again, there was an inner intensity underneath his handsome face that would intrigue even the most wary maiden. Mumbling an uncharitable thought, she scowled at the growing pile of trotters. She could concoct a hundred chores superior to the one before her. Sitting outside and flirting with Brock Bedegrayne would have been an improvement in her day. Quashing the pang of envy in her breast, she heartily wished Amara luck, for the Bedegraynes were a wily clan.

Brock practically dropped the wooden crate he was carrying when he espied Amara. Sheer pride kept him on his feet. She had come to him, despite his harsh words and the confrontation with Prola. Suddenly, her appearance made him wary. Amara was a cautious soul. In all his

fevered imaginings, he could not come up with one reason why she would seek him out. At least an optimistic
one, he silently amended.

"Miss Claeg," he greeted her, with a jerk of his head.
He halted, keeping his gaze purposely impassive.

"Mr. Bedegrayne." Her hands betrayed her nerves as
she gestured at the door. "Wynne mentioned that you were
out here. It is kind of you to help."

He stared at her. The weight of the crate was straining
his already abused muscles in his arms and bound ribs,
but he loathed walking away from her until he knew why
she was deigning to speak to him. He rolled his shoulders
in a feeble attempt to ease his burden.

"Here, Bedegrayne, I will take this for you," Mr. Lyndall offered, stepping between them.

Brock transferred the crate into the man's arms. Lyndall winked at Amara. "A pretty lady always turns a
gent's brain into suet." Whistling a bawdy tune, he sauntered into the kitchen.

They stood awkwardly silent, listening to the noises
from the street and the distant laughter of the children.

"Forgive me for disturbing you," she said, glancing
back at the door behind her. He could not decide if she
was worried that their conversation would be overheard
or was simply keeping her escape route in view.

"I assumed you were here to wring those same words
out of me." He removed a handkerchief from the inner
pocket of his coat and wiped the sweat and grime from
his face.

She appeared puzzled for a moment. "For? Oh," she
said, her movements becoming more agitated. "You are
referring to the other day."

He blew out a pent-up breath. Whatever her reasons for

approaching him, they had nothing to do with the Italian fop. He tried not to dwell on the hope that she needed to see him. "I owe you an apology for my outburst. After your departure, your brother explained Prola's appearance."

"You discussed this with my brother?" she asked weakly.

"In my defense, I will admit Prola's proprietary stance took me by surprise." Given further provocation, Brock could have gleefully strangled the gentleman for assuming she belonged to him.

"The blame is mine alone. I should have warned you that my parents have grown tired of my unmarried state and have taken steps to rectify the situation." She twisted the reticule in her hands. "I lacked the courage to speak of it. Especially, since . . ." She hesitated, unable to finish her explanation.

It was not difficult to figure out the direction of her thoughts. "Especially since I despised the last man they wanted you to marry," he said, grateful she was finally willing to speak of it. "Or the fact that he died before you were bound eternally to such a ruthless miscreant."

"Brock, I beg of you—"

"Nay, do not," he said, treading over her elegant plea. He was filthy from his earlier labors and was unfit for the presence of a lady. Even so, he followed his instincts and moved closer. Tenderly, he took up her hand and pressed a kiss just above her gloved knuckles. Her bewildered expression kindled a fleeting grin. "You have never understood."

She tried matching his light delivery. "You, sir, have a very disconcerting manner."

"It heartens me that you have reflected on my character in your leisure."

A very telling flush negated any exasperated protest she could muster. "Fie, Brock Bedegrayne, I made no such confession!"

"I disagree."

Damning the consequences, he seized her by the waist and spun her. Having her in his arms even for a brief moment filled his heart to overflowing. She made a high squeaking noise when he lifted her off her feet, but she was laughing when he set her on her feet again.

"You are an incorrigible gallant. Do the ladies still swoon when you glance in their direction?"

With his hand still resting lightly on her hip, he met her teasing gaze with a brooding intensity that had the pulse at her throat fluttering. "I have never noticed. There is only one lady who ensnares my interest."

She nibbled at her lower lip, fighting not to smile. Obviously, she was pleased by his comment. "I have tarried too long. Remaining would only encourage you."

"So you sought me out to discourage me?"

"Yes. No." She huffed, trying valiantly to suppress a giggle. "Oh, cease tormenting me. I am a lady of reasonable intelligence. How do I, within minutes of your proximity, turn into a babbling scatterbrain?"

"I have that unfortunate effect on most women," he lamented, earning him an annoyed grumble. He was enjoying how little effort it took to fluster her. The notion that he could had remarkably improved his disposition. For the first time since his return, he believed he had a chance at breaching the defensive walls Amara had erected around her.

Lyndall poked his head out the door and glared at them both. "Bedegrayne, while you are courting Miss Claeg, I am enduring Miss Wyman's never-ending list of grievances under the pointed direction of a rather large knife. I am on the verge of begging for mercy. Spare us both and just kiss her!" He disappeared, uninterested in their denials.

Brock silently cursed when he saw Amara's guarded expression. The man's unexpected appearance had ruined any excuse to delay their inevitable parting.

"I am expected elsewhere."

He bleakly wondered if he would spend the rest of his life watching her walk away from him. Brock stayed her by grasping her wrist. "Amara, you never told me why you sought me out."

She shook her head. "It was nonsense."

"I doubt it. Tell me."

Amara tugged, attempting to break their link. He pulled her a step closer. Conceding to his strength, she said, "It would take too long to explain."

"Later, then," he persisted, sensing she had no intention of telling him the true reason for her impromptu visit.

"Fine." She glanced at his gloved hand on her wrist as her thoughts turned inward. "I shall be attending the theater this evening."

His grip reflexively tightened on her wrist. "Will Prola be escorting you?"

"I will be sitting with Lady Haslake and her daughters," Amara replied, her dark blue gaze gauging his reaction. "I cannot, however, overlook my family's tenacity or Conte Prola's eagerness toward securing my consent for the anticipated marriage. I expect the conte will be presented to me sometime during the evening."

She was being maneuvered into accepting this foreigner. Brock wanted to shake her for sounding resigned to her fate. "I will come for you."

She merely blinked at the vehemence in his vow. "For what purpose?" she asked, staring at him as if he were promising the impossible. "I will be well chaperoned and displayed for all of London. If you think embarrassing me will—"

Brock was not a man who fought fate. He was a healthy male in the proximity of an attractive female. When her full lips formed an inviting mulish pout, he reacted. Ignoring her gasp, he backed her up against the wall and silenced her tirade with a decisive, firm kiss.

With an involuntary shudder, he cupped her face and reveled in her taste. What a revelation! Her barbed tongue protected a wellspring of sweetness he had feared experience had made rancid.

Drawing back, he felt rather smug he had found a pleasurable means in which to silence her. "We will be doing that again, and often." He pressed a softer kiss on her slack mouth. "Leave the details to me."

"You!" She pointed at him, shaking and rigid as if she were denouncing an archfiend. "You do not have permission. Promise me—" She swallowed, blurting out, "No more kisses!"

"Amara, my delightful dove, I will not have lies standing between us. If stolen tokens warm my heart, I impatiently await the moment when I gain your *consent*."

"There is no reasoning with you." She lifted her hands in supplication. "I do not know why I bothered seeing you." Disgusted with both of them, she headed for the door.

"You pose an intriguing question, and I find myself fascinated by your answer. Why have you sought me out?" *Why now after countless years of chillingly polite aloofness?*

Amara glanced back when she reached the threshold. Somberly, she admitted, "I had a nightmare."

She was gone before he could respond.

Bracing his back against the wall, Brock sat down on his haunches. He scrubbed his face with his hands and then pressed his fingers to buffer the increasing pressure behind his eyes. She had come to him because of a nightmare. There was no need for further explanation. They both had their own lurid memories of that wretched night. The irony was not lost on him that what had driven her away from him was forcing her to face him now.

A nightmare.

"Damn."

Even rotting in his grave, Cornley was still hurting her. It was bitter hellbroth he swallowed knowing he was not blameless in the matter.

"Brock?"

He raised his head from his hands. Wynne stood several feet away from him. Maddy was behind her, still half-hidden by the doorway. Concern was etched on both their faces.

Unfolding from his crouched position, he stomped some of the stiffness from his legs. "I have work to do."

"Brock," Wynne said, approaching him. "I love you both. If I can help . . ."

"I know." He hugged her close, and accepted the comfort she offered. Pressing a kiss to her cheek, he said, "We need to muddle through this ourselves."

She squeaked when he playfully tugged her ear, promptly forgetting whatever argument she had thought to present. "You are a rotten brother!"

"I will wager Milroy snarled at any interference from the family while he was courting you."

"The situation was different."

More than she would ever understand, he mused. "Are you interested in attending the theater this evening?" Seeing Maddy, he rejected the idea. "Pardon me, I forgot you ladies have plans. Hmm, mayhap Devona?"

Too shrewd to be swayed by his change of topic, Wynne put her hands on her hips. "What are you planning?"

He had promised Amara that he would find a way to her side this evening. Dragging her off held a certain appeal, but the direct tactic would mire him in impending obstacles. His impulsiveness had caused him trouble in the past. He was learning that he savored the victories gained by his wits and not his fists.

"I am taking your advice."

"What advice?"

"That I might benefit from a little family meddling after all."

CHAPTER ELEVEN

"I propose we hold a ball heralding Brock's return. What do you think, Aunt Moll?" Irene queried, her sapphire gaze surveying the various tiers of theater boxes. At four and thirty and Lord Sutton's viscountess, she was the eldest of the Bedegrayne siblings and did not expect anyone to oppose her suggestion.

Aunt Moll perked up at the prospect. An unfortunate accident more than a year ago had limited the outings of his elderly aunt and confined her movements with a cane. Arthritis had gradually settled into the damaged limb and it appeared she would require her cane and a steady arm for the rest of her life. The news had not sent her into seclusion as it might have a passive creature. She and her Mr. Keel were too busy planning their wedding.

"It is a lovely thought, my dear," Aunt Moll said, adjusting her position in the chair slightly to keep her hip from stiffening. "Gathering the entire family together has become a challenge if not a rarity."

The coltish look Devona sent Brock said, "Did I not warn you?"

Brock was grateful his family had agreed to join him at the theater. His motives were entirely self-seeking but he was not above appreciating the twofold benefits. He had missed his family.

Regardless, he was uncomfortable with his eldest sister making such a fuss. He had never been forthright with his family about his relationship with Amara. Devona, and to a lesser extent, Tipton, knew of his interest in her. He had confided that much in securing their assistance this evening. Wynne and Devona had always been close. Whatever Wynne had deduced from his encounter with Amara this afternoon, it was certain she had shared her speculation with her youngest sibling. He dreaded the moment when the pair cornered him with their questions and suspicions.

Hoping his expression conveyed at best a vague interest, he watched on as Irene doggedly persuaded the family's agreement for holding a ball. As for Irene, he could not vividly recall a time when she had not stood apart from the other two girls. Perhaps from them all, since she was the eldest.

Almost nineteen years had passed since their mother's death, and the Bedegraynes were still feeling the loss. He had been nine when his inconsolable father had shown up at school to collect his sons. Devona had barely been freed from her back-strings, and yet no one had ever been able to dissuade her from the ridiculous notion that she had been responsible for their mother's death.

No one was really to blame for the tragic accident. While chasing after her youngest daughter, Anna Bedegrayne had been struck in the temple with a wooden board a startled workman had been holding. She had never regained consciousness.

All of them had dealt with their grief in their own fashion. No one spoke of it, but Anna's death had splintered her family. Sir Thomas had buried himself in his work and his clubs. Nyle had abandoned them long before he had ever departed England. If Irene could be accused of embracing a rigid code of rules, their younger brother had done the opposite by casting them aside along with his honor. Brock was in no position to judge. After Amara had turned away from him, he had succumbed to all kinds of vices. And while Devona tried rescuing lost friends, Wynne had aspired a rung higher by trying to save them all.

"Are we in agreement then?" Irene asked, her interruption scattering his thoughts. The white plumes sprouting from the back of her reddish-blond coiled and pinned tresses bobbed with each movement.

"Have your ball, Irene, but choose someone else to honor. I have already reacquainted myself with the individuals who were truly interested in my return. The rest can be damned."

Her lips thinned mutinously. "You are just being difficult." Anyone observing them from another box would have never guessed how close the serene Lady Sutton was to lunging and strangling her brother. "I had heard your travels had tempered your ennui. Minutes in your presence, I can see that you are as imprudent and negligent as ever."

"And you, my dear sister, are still a waspish, judgmental prig," he evenly replied, while he privately marveled at her uncanny ability to nettle him.

"Ho!" Sir Thomas said, coming up behind them. "Sutton, I daresay our arrival was well timed. Brock, my lad, you were not intent on using a fist on your sweet sister?"

By damn, tangling with Irene would ruin all he had

hoped to achieve this evening. He had never laid a hand
on any of his sisters, but the temptation grated sorely
against his restraint. Relaxing his hand, he negligently
shrugged. "I cannot deny the flat of my hand across her
backside has appeal when she persists in goading me."
Meeting her husband, Garrard Vinall, Viscount Sutton's
steady gaze, he added, "Naturally, Sutton, I yield to your
wealth of experience."

Lord Sutton braced his hands on the back of Irene's
chair. "I warrant any hand on her backside will be my
own." The protective stance made his wife seem small
and fragile in comparison to his intimidating muscular
build. Brock scoffed at the notion. Irene fragile? She was
a merciless Valkyrie when riled.

Forgetting herself, Irene rose from her seat. She turned
away from the stage and glared at both of them. "You
both will cease holding this discussion as if I am not right
in front of you. The first man who tries putting a hand on
my—backside," she said, lowering her voice in deference
to delicacy, "will lose the offensive hand."

"Steady, my gel," Sir Thomas crooned, coming around
and circling an arm around his daughter. Diffusing the
confrontation had little to do with gossip. His eldest
daughter had always taken the brunt of the ribbing in the
family. He had spent countless years stepping between
the two combatants in hopes of salvaging the spirit he
greatly admired.

"Irene, sit down before our little drama outdoes the
one below," Devona said, noticing that several people in
the next box were already angling their heads for a better
view and whispering.

Sir Thomas settled in the seat behind Irene. She was
still fuming, her lips parted, preparing to further argue her

side, but a warning glance from Sutton subdued her. Offering Brock her back, she sat down.

"There, there, Irene, tell your papa what you are so blue-deviled about," their father entreated. He scowled at Brock. "What have you done?"

Brock touched his hand to his heart, portraying mock ignorance. He was in no mood to defend himself on behalf of something he considered inconsequential.

Using her cane and hand on the armrest of the chair to adjust her position, Aunt Moll expelled her breath as a painful hiss with each movement. "Thomas, let them be. You and Sutton are always cosseting the girl. It is hardly surprising she is in high dudgeon when someone opposes her."

"Aunt Moll!" Irene exclaimed, embarrassed by the candid observation. "What is selfish about wanting to hold a ball in my brother's honor?"

"When your brother does not want to be honored," Brock retorted, his attention fixed on one of the boxes across the auditorium. A rush of elation coursed through him. Amara and her companions had arrived.

Sutton, taking the seat beside Sir Thomas, overrode Irene's scathing reply by simply caressing her shoulder. "Might I interject a suggestion before blood is shed?"

"Please do," Devona begged, seeing no end to the disagreement if Brock continued baiting Irene.

"Have your ball." The viscount lifted his hand, warding off Brock's oath. "Allow Aunt Moll and Mr. Keel to be the honored guests."

"A ball in honor of our nuptials," Aunt Moll mused, her wizened face crinkled with delight. "Oh, how I wish Mr. Keel were present so we could share the good news."

Unable to deny her aunt, Irene put aside her pride and

said, "We will tell him together if you like. I could use your assistance in the planning."

Devona beamed. "An excellent suggestion, Sutton."

"Well done," Sir Thomas praised gruffly. "My thought exactly."

Brock ignored them all. His concentration was focused on Amara. Her beauty shone across the multicolored sea of silk, beckoning him. She had yet to notice him. Whenever she started a nonchalant perusal of the crowd, one of the women at her side said something to distract her. Then the appearance of a certain swarthy gentleman had him mumbling an expletive. Brock shot up from his chair and blindly stalked to the front of the box as if he had every intention of leaping from the tier.

"Brock?" Devona queried, clearly troubled by his expression.

Raising her lorgnette to her eyes, Aunt Moll peered and said, "My dear Brock. Hasten to our Miss Claeg's side. She is in the coils of a most persistent suitor. You must bring her back so she can share the fascinating details."

He formally bowed, prepared to take his leave. Irene offered her hand, which he accepted without thought. She surprised him by digging her gloved fingers into his open palm. "Mark your temper," she counseled, "and no issuing challenges. When you are about, you represent not only yourself but the Bedegrayne family."

Instead of bristling at the remark, Brock bent closer and kissed her cheek. "Yes, mother." Being an expert at baiting, he acknowledged he deserved a little sisterly retaliation. After all, "Measure for measure" should have been the family motto.

• • •

The collective heat of so many bodies packed into the theater made the air stifling. The numerous chandeliers overhead contained hundreds of smoky candles, which only added to the problem. Almost feeling guilty, Amara opened the fan Brock had given her. She gently stirred the warm air around her, silently chastising herself for feeling uneasy about flaunting his beautiful gift. Her mother, when she had noticed it, had commented on its beauty. She had also believed the fan had been a gift from the conte. Amara had not corrected her assumption.

"What a bonny fan, Miss Claeg," Lady Haslake said. "So many young ladies do not appreciate the importance of choosing the proper accessory."

Hours earlier, she had faced the predicament of finding a suitable gown that complemented the fan. Fortunately, her maid, Corry, was resourceful and had a patient hand for sewing. She had rounded the bottom of a white satin slip with silver-embroidered trimming removed from another gown. Over the slip, Amara wore a short-sleeved pale pink net dress. Corry had replaced the gold buttons ornamenting the lace joining down the front with silver ones. A twisted fillet of pale pink satin and silver ribbon interwoven into her elegant coiffure completed her maid's inspiring results.

Lady Haslake's youngest daughter, Lady Marea, was three years younger than her sister, Lady Laurette, and Amara. She was also fiercely competitive. "May I?" the young woman asked, taking the fan from Amara for a closer examination. Tiny reflective lights from the silver sequins dotted her narrow face. "Who is the maker?"

Amara accepted the fan. "I have not a clue. It was a gift."

"A gift," Lady Laurette echoed, looking splendid in buff-colored crêpe. "Why do I sense there is more to this tale than you are admitting?"

She should have expected her friend would note the subtle evasion. Lady Laurette Omant's intelligence was remarked upon as often as her unique beauty. Lord Keyworth firmly believed in garnering advantageous friendships and the Earl of Haslake's daughters possessed the suitable pedigree. What had been conceived from duty had quickly sprung into friendship between the two eleven-year-old girls. Together they had endured dance instruction under the truculent demands of Monsieur Vipond.

"You know me so well, Rett," Amara said, affectionately using the family's nickname for her friend. "I fear my exploits of late might shock you both and I loathe jeopardizing our long friendship."

Fascinated, Lady Marea leaned closer. "Do tell us everything!"

Comfortable with her companions, Amara leaned closer, enjoying the rapt attention. Using the fan to shield her face, she wanted to ensure that her confession never went beyond her audience. "Well, since our last parting, it seems a gift from Aphrodite has been bestowed upon me."

"Remarkable," Lady Laurette said, violet eyes widened when her gaze shifted to her gullible younger sibling. "How long have you been making blood sacrifices to goddesses?"

A loud snort of disbelief from Lady Marea gained an unspoken reprimand from Lady Haslake. Appearing repentant, the younger girl whispered, "Do you have a secret place where you practice your arcane rites? What beast is worthy of sacrifice, kids or lambs?" She seized Amara's arm. "Oh, surely not human!"

Lady Laurette could not contain her merriment, and laughed. "Dolt. Amara was speaking metaphorically."

"So it is not true?" Sitting back, Lady Marea pouted, disappointment radiating from her.

Amara's lips twitched but she held her composure. "I confess, Marea, your version is more appealing than any I can invent. However, if I hear my name linked with secret cults, I promise that you will be my first blood sacrifice."

The younger sister sneered. "I am immune to threats." Having enough of their sport, she stood. "I was inoculated years ago by my haggish sister." With a swish of fabric and outrage, the youngest Omant stomped over to her mother's side.

"Are we horrid creatures to tease her so?"

"Marea deserves most of it," her friend casually admitted, unperturbed. "That head of hers is stuffed with too many fanciful stories and not enough sense. Really, Amara, you do surprise me at times." Lady Laurette tossed her dark tresses back flirtatiously, leaving Amara to wonder if the disingenuous movement was simply natural or if it was meant for an appreciative male spectator. "Evoking that Aphrodite nonsense was a calculated dissuading ploy. It is not like you to be evasive, particularly with regard to something most vapid." Her delicately arched brows lifted inquisitively. "Or is it?"

Before Amara could reply, the entrance of Conte Prola and a male companion plummeted her hopes. A confrontation would be unavoidable, she thought despairingly, forcing a welcoming smile. The Italian sought her out at once. Forgoing etiquette by not greeting his hostess first, the man set several hearts fluttering by striding purposefully toward Amara. With a gleam of appreciation in his exotic eyes, he greeted her with flamboyance only he could have managed without appearing ridiculous. She suppressed a sigh when the conte bowed and pressed a teasing kiss to her hand. If she felt a tiny chill at the contact, she preferred ignoring it.

"Signorina Claeg, your beauty, it enchants me," he said, reluctant to release her hand. As he noticed everyone's unabashed curiosity, his swarthy coloring darkened. "It is unforgivable. My manners, atrocious. All is forgotten in pursuit of my lady."

"How delightful," Lady Haslake murmured. Taking charge of the situation, she offered the conte her hand. "Miss Claeg, introduce me to your dear friend."

Amara stood, making the appropriate introductions to the countess. Conte Prola returned the favor by introducing his companion, a gentleman unknown to her, Mr. Burnes. Once formality had been satisfied, Lady Haslake placed a claiming hand on the conte's coat sleeve and introduced him to everyone in her little group.

"Amara, you have been keeping secrets from us," Lady Laurette quietly remarked. "I heartily approve of your choice."

"Not mine," she said vehemently. "He belongs to my father."

A little bewildered by all the attention he was receiving from the ladies around him, Conte Prola sent Amara an entreating glance.

"Really, Amara, have you always been so daft when it comes to gentlemen?" her friend said, her tone chiding. "He wants to be yours. A pity, really, since I adore his dark looks." Without waiting for a response, Lady Laurette joined her mother so she could be properly introduced.

She watched on as Lady Haslake introduced her eldest daughter. The exchange between the conte and Lady Laurette Omant was proper, but Amara could not help but admire her friend's playful execution. Her lack of modesty might leave a man wondering of the possibilities, but Amara was aware her friend was teeming with integrity. She would never seduce a suitor away from a friend. Perhaps, if she explained—

"Miss Claeg."

Amara had been so lost in her thoughts, she never noticed Brock's approach. So lost, she mused, that she had been staring too long at Conte Prola. At least, she must have, since Brock was glaring at her. Again.

"What are you doing here?" she asked.

His jaw was so tense, it was a wonder it had not cracked from the pressure. "If you recall, we have some unfinished business." He glanced in the direction of the conte, and his posture all but roared his displeasure.

"Mr. Bedegrayne," Lady Haslake said, disengaging herself from the circle of ongoing conversation. "You are so kind to visit us. I pray you will come to the house for a proper call when time permits."

Brock stiffly bowed. "I will endeavor to find the time, my lady."

Since Lady Haslake had two unmarried daughters, Amara could almost hear the wheels of machination turn beneath the older woman's curled coiffure. The notion of Rett turning her limpid violet gaze on Brock Bedegrayne congealed her insides.

Oblivious to the tension, the countess cheerfully continued. "I thought I noticed Sir Thomas earlier. Haslake will never believe it. For years we have begged the

stubborn man to join us. What inducement did you dangle
to secure his compliance?"

Amara nearly flinched when Brock took up her hand.
Meeting her wary gaze, he brushed a kiss against her
knuckles. There was something proprietary in his efficient movements. What brief tingle she had felt when the
conte had touched her could not compare to the quivering
avalanche of sensation that flowed across her skin.

"Like most gentlemen, my father has fallen prey to a
certain lady's charms." He schooled his features into a look
of tolerant amusement, when he glanced at Amara. "Miss
Claeg, you have been remiss in visiting my family."

Uncertain of her part, she replied, "It was never my
intention to offend. I thought your family would be
engrossed with your homecoming."

"In the hearts of the Bedegraynes, you are family and
have been missed," he softly confessed. Returning his
attention to the bemused countess, he said, "I have been
ordered to kidnap Miss Claeg or not return at all."

"Rogue!"

Tucking Amara's hand under his arm, he gave her a
smile fitting of a pirate. "Do you speak of me or my sire,
ma'am?"

The countess chuckled, her probing gaze reconsider-
ing the young woman before her. "Both. If Lady Keyworth learns of this, I will plead that the Bedegrayne men
were a formidable and most irresistible force." She looked
back, sensing her daughter's presence. Conte Prola was at
her heels. He recognized Brock immediately. The rigidity
in his gait and the insincerity of his smile belied his
friendly advance.

"Laurette, Miss Claeg is leaving the gentlemen in our
care."

Her friend curtsied. A youthful replica of her mother, she slid a curious gaze from Brock's inscrutable features to Amara's flustered one. "Mr. Bedegrayne, what plans do you have for our dear friend?"

"Nothing sinister, Lady Laurette. My family has invited Miss Claeg to join us in our box. I will return her before the play has ended."

Conte Prola pressed himself forward. "Miss Claeg, you are not obligated to leave with this—this gentleman," he jeered. "What kind of lady would allow herself to be dragged off by a scoundrel who thinks nothing of rough handling and hurling curses in the middle of the street?"

Wide-eyed Lady Marea stood beside her sister. The conte's friend Mr. Burnes had followed her, but he stood outside the circle. Bringing a fist up to his lips, he stifled a yawn.

There was temper in Brock's eyes, but there was a reckless defiance in his stance. "The forgiving kind," he tossed out, "and too good for either one of us. Shall we go, Miss Claeg?"

Upset, the conte seized Amara by the arm before she could turn away. Brock halted and stared deliberately at the man's brazen hand. "You are embarrassing yourself, sir. She may forgive. I, however, will not."

Conte Prola savagely muttered something in his native tongue. With measured care, he released her and stepped back. Amara edged closer to Brock. The conte had not hurt her. If she trembled, it was due to the fact that she had just avoided being the hapless rope in a brief, fierce battle of tug-of-war.

Mumbling a vague apology to all, she pretended Brock was not really dragging her away from a truly awkward scene.

An expert at soothing ruffled pride, Lady Haslake placed a comforting hand on the conte's arm and led him to a seat beside her. Not uttering a word, his friend followed in their wake.

Thoughtful, Marea remained at her sister's side. She gave her sister a disrespectful nudge with her elbow, earning a promise of retaliation. "A jest you both said. We just witnessed two handsome gentlemen baring their teeth over Amara. In public," she stressed, still energized from the encounter. "When she returns, I propose we pull her aside and have her retell her tale, this time without interruption. A blessing indeed!"

Laurette nodded. She had felt a twinge of envy as she watched Brock Bedegrayne visibly struggle against the urge to toss their friend over his broad shoulder and march off with her into the night. Her sister was correct. Amara Claeg was keeping secrets. When she had a chance, she intended to coax them from her.

She wrapped a companionable arm around her sister. "Come, Marea, I have lost my enthusiasm for the play. If Mrs. Siddons cannot stir my heart, let us see if flirting with Conte Prola and Mr. Burnes does not improve our evening."

Brock had anticipated a quarrel. He had looked forward to it. Stripping Amara of her polish always had some rather fascinating results. Instead, she had surprised him by leaving her friends without argument. He had wrestled with the decision of whether he should simply drag her off and damn her embarrassment, or permit himself the pleasure of smashing his fist into that condescending Italian face; it had been Amara's unrelenting little fingers digging into his coat sleeve that swayed him into doing neither.

Had she wanted to escape or was she protecting the man from his notorious temper? The uncertainty was hurling him toward acting rashly, and then everything he sought would be lost. He slowed their pace, even though there were few to hinder their journey. The orchestra had commenced, luring most of the spectators to their seats. He wanted, nay, needed this time with her.

The gown she wore shimmered with every movement. The soft swell of her breasts and hint of equally enticing hips beckoned a man to take what was being offered. There was a fire in his blood only she could assuage. He had felt it for so long, he almost hated her for it.

Noting his stare, she frowned slightly. "Is there something wrong?"

"No," he lied. He finally recognized the fan she clasped. "You are pleased with the fan?" Seeing his gift in her hand foolishly delighted him. It was a small measure, really, but for a man who had nothing, it was everything.

Sensing the mood change, Amara cocked her head. She snapped open the fan as they walked, displaying its full beauty. "How could any woman resist such a treasure?"

He halted, refusing to let her ruin it by brushing aside his generosity with playful words. "The fan was not meant for any woman. It was meant for you, Amara."

Contrite, she closed the fan. "We both know that is the problem. You should not be sending me gifts." She pivoted, so she was facing him. "And I certainly should not be accepting them. As it is, my mother thinks Conte Prola is responsible."

Without ceremony, Brock shoved her against the wall. He startled a gasp out of her, but no one could see them with a tall pedestal obstructing the view. "You bestowed the credit on that fop?"

Faintly, she said, "Well, his man had delivered a spectacular bouquet of marzipan flowers the very same morning."

The unbidden image of Prola feeding sugary petals to Amara arose in his mind. It made him want to pound the wall above her head.

Misunderstanding his fury, she tentatively touched his chest. When he remained impassive, her touch grew bolder. She stroked him as if he were some wild creature who needed soothing. "You can blame yourself for the confusion."

"You are mistaken."

"Am I? Well, neither you nor the conte added a card, so why should I correct my mother if she thinks another gentleman sent the fan? Perhaps you consider it cowardly," she argued, forgetting all about placating him, and grabbed the edge of his coat and tugged. "Nevertheless, we both know she would have thrown your box and beautiful fan onto the nearest burning grate if she had learned they had come from you."

She was not exaggerating. No matter how splendid the gift, Lady Keyworth would have understood his intent even though Amara appeared obtuse. "Fine. Your argument is sound, but I do not have to like it."

"It was a thoughtful gift. Can you blame me for wanting to protect it and—"

"Yourself?" he finished. "No. Can you forgive me and my temper?"

She sniffed, and he was grateful her eyes were clear of tears. "How can I not? What is a beast without his claws and sharp teeth?"

The lady thought nothing of provoking him. Bracing his hand against the wall, he stared down at the appealing face that had haunted his dreams. Testing them both, perhaps, the longing he had always kept banked slipped into his eyes. Her expressive blue eyes widened, and her breath became shallow as he leaned closer.

"A beast, you say," he murmured, enjoying the scent of her hair. "If I am the beast, then you must be the maiden who desires to tame me." Their lips were almost touching. A deep inhalation from either one of them would have joined them. The anticipation was a clawing need within him.

"Why would any maiden desire taming a beast?" she asked breathlessly, her gaze fixed on his mouth. "I imagine the lady envies the beast for his freedom. She hopes he will help her explore her own wild nature."

His hand above her head clenched into a fist. He felt utterly predatory, and yet he understood what she was asking of him. "Kiss me, dove. You are safe with me."

"Ow!" A stinging rap on his left ear brought him upright. He met Amara's horrified gaze briefly before he turned toward his attacker.

"Dunderhead!" Irene said, unmoved by his snarl of displeasure. "Next you will be telling me that you could not help yourself."

Amara was inching away from both of them, so he seized her hand, entwining their fingers. He had been too enthralled with Amara to notice his sister's approach. Inwardly he winced, wondering how long Irene had listened to their discourse before she had interfered. Deciding to brazen his way out of his sticky predicament, he said, "How could I, when the lady very much desires my kisses?"

"You are a beast!" Amara hissed, probably mortified he had spoken the truth.

"I thought we had already established our roles, Amara. It was our natures that deserve a closer inspection," he teased.

Irene took advantage of the distraction by rapping him on the ear again. "Christ!" he yelped, rubbing his ear. "Viscountess or not, if you try that again I will hit back, and your husband will be issuing bloody challenges, not I."

"A capuchin monkey has more sense." Irene wedged herself between them. Her eyes filled with pity when she patted Amara on the hand. "Amara, I am astounded. Why would you want to kiss a bounder such as my brother?"

Brock implored to the heavens. "Tell me why I should not toss her out the closest window and be done with it?"

Amara was unquestionably ill at ease around two squabbling siblings. "I did not want to kiss him."

"Amara, my dove," he said on a mock sigh, "I had no idea you had a proclivity for lying."

"I was not kissing you," she insisted, flustered by his stare.

He lifted a brow. "If not you, then whose heart-shaped lips were pursed under mine?"

"Leave her be," his sister ordered, pushing him away. "You deserve a swift kick for your needling and I can think of a man or two who might relish the pleasure."

Refusing to be left behind, Brock matched the pace Irene set as they headed for the box. "That is your best threat, Lady Sutton? I had expected more from a mother of four."

Irene aimed a chilling smile at him. "Ah, dearest brother, you do so love tempting me. How can I resist such a challenge? After all, you are not the only family member who can be an irritating burr on one's backside."

CHAPTER TWELVE

In hindsight, goading the paragon had not been one of his brightest notions. Irene kept her hand firmly on Amara's arm as the trio entered the box.

"Look who I found," Irene cheerfully drawled. "It appears your concerns were warranted, Aunt Moll. There were too many rogues lurking about the theater for a lady's comfort."

"You forget, Lady Sutton," Brock said, purposely using her title. "Amara was in my care."

His sister tossed a smug look over her shoulder. "I forget nothing, brother."

Brock stood impotently at the back as Amara was swept up into an enthusiastic tide of welcome. Devona hugged her friend, babbling compliments about her gown and hair. Amara greeted Tipton and Sutton with a reserved shyness he had expected, but it was his father who had him reluctantly grinning when he pulled Amara up from her curtsy and kissed both her hands. In the muted light, he could see the affectionate greeting disconcerted her. The distant thundering from the

orchestra below could not eclipse her nervous giggle.
Her unexpected response conjured memories of late
summer and childhood games. It pleased him that
instead of drawing away, she clutched his father's hand
while she answered the expected pleasantries about her
parents.

"Sit beside me, my dear," Aunt Moll invited. "It has
been too long since we have chatted."

As if sensing his frustration, Amara turned back
toward him and met his gaze. She shook her head, negat-
ing his protest before the thought was fully formed. With
an apologetic shrug, she took the seat beside his aunt.
Devona, oblivious to their silent discourse, managed to
uphold both sides of their conversation.

"Tarry not, Brock." Irene's sapphire eyes twinkled with
humor. "The play has begun without us." She slipped into
the remaining front seat beside Devona.

Confound it! Irene had succeeded in thwarting him.
Sir Thomas murmured something to Amara before he
took the seat behind her. Having witnessed their aborted
kiss in the saloon, Irene was too intelligent not to have
reasoned that he had planned the encounter with the family. She would have also deduced that he had every intention of sitting beside Amara.

Brock flinched at the hand on his shoulder. Sometime
during his dark musings, Sutton and Tipton had joined
him. There had been something in his gaze that had
warned them he was considering pitching his meddlesome sister tail over top into the pit below.

"Tweaked your nose, did she?" Sutton said, stepping
in front of him so he stood between Brock and his gloat-
ing wife. "Perhaps you should not have scorned her plans
for a ball in your honor."

He privately agreed. "What would you do if someone stood between you and Irene?"

Sutton glanced back at his wife. She had lost interest in taunting Brock, and now watched the actors treading across the proscenium. "Most likely the same thing you were planning. However, I would consider it a grand favor if you would not leave my children motherless."

"I have no intention of harming her. Overmuch," he amended.

"Miss Claeg is a gentle creature. Any confrontation at this point would only humiliate her," Tipton counseled, his expression sympathetic.

Annoyed for no more reason than that he might actually deserve their commiserating support, Brock said, "I am topped with the helpfulness from my devoted family. I doubt I could bear more."

"Come along, then." Sutton placed his hand on Brock's shoulder. This time, he accepted the companionable gesture. "You can pretend you are following the play while you plot a polite means of usurping Sir Thomas from the seat you so prize."

A rare chuckle erupted from Tipton. "By God, she is the one. I thought as much a few years ago when you carried her out of the masquerade. You should have seen him, Sutton, as he tried to soothe the ruffled feathers of his furious dove."

The night he and Tipton had dragged Amara from Lady Dodd's masquerade in a desperate attempt to find his reckless sister had been the first time in more than a year in which he had spoken to Amara. The humiliating debacle had done little to heal their breach. Shortly afterward, Brock had decided they both needed the span of an ocean between them.

"If you prefer to reminisce, I am certain we can dig up one or two incidents when you were in a coil with my sister." He gestured both men to take the seats behind their wives. Perverse as it might seem, if he could not be close to Amara, then he preferred the distance. He had always taken that stance, and perhaps it was the root of his difficulties.

"He must be in love," murmured Tipton, graciously ignoring his brother-in-law's gibe.

Brock settled in his seat. Rubbing at the pain in his brow, he quietly disagreed. He was in hell.

It took all of her restraint not to glance back at Brock. Half-listening to Aunt Moll, Amara strained to hear what Lord Sutton and Tipton were saying to him, but the singing below had dimmed the male voices into indistinct murmurs. Visiting with the Bedegraynes had always been a pleasure for her. However, she doubted that had been Brock's intention.

She risked a peek when she heard movement from behind. Instead of Brock, her restless gaze clashed with Tipton's disturbing light blue one. The corner of one side of his mouth kicked up, completely unrepentant for being caught staring. Tilting her head back, she caught a glimpse of Brock behind the two viscounts. Lord Sutton noticed her action. She could not claim a familiarity with the man, but he had the audacity to wink. Amara abruptly shifted her attention forward. Good grief, what a quandary! Had Lord Sutton believed she was flirting with him? Absently, she nibbled the fingertip of one of her white kid gloves.

"It is a pity Wynne has missed this performance. Musical farces are her particular favorite," Devona confided, unaware of her friend's misery.

Amara made a concurring sound. Appalled she was ruining yet another pair of gloves, she clasped her hands and placed them on her lap. There was a sudden surge of laughter from the pit, and she wondered if she was supposed to laugh or if the spectators below were providing their own amusements. It was shamefully apparent she was not paying attention to the situation being played out on the proscenium.

"Beg pardon, miss, are you Miss Claeg?"

Amara whirled to the left, surprised that where Sir Thomas had been seated a young woman stood. Not much older than eighteen and bearing too much weight for her short frame, the woman leaned closer when Amara nodded.

"Your brother sent me. He is waiting for you in the saloon."

Amara recognized the woman. Earlier she had stood at one end of the saloon serving refreshments. "You may tell him I shall join him shortly."

"Yes, ma'am." Using the back of the chair, the woman pushed herself upright. With an odd limp, she left the box.

With the woman's departure, Sir Thomas stepped forward and offered his hand. Amara accepted it as she stood.

Aunt Moll touched her other hand. "My dear, is all well?"

"My brother, Mallory, seeks a word with me. I shall return."

"That poor gel was as large as a brig," Sir Thomas said, not without compassion. "Has she brought you troubling news?"

"No, no, my—"

Brock blocked their way. "What is it?"

"It is nothing," she assured them both. "Mallory must have spotted me. He wishes to speak with me."

"I will take her, Father. There is no reason why you should miss the play."

"Miss what, I ask you? A lot of caterwauling and eye rolling," Sir Thomas replied, answering his own question. "I have yet to make sense of one blasted word. It makes a man wonder about his ears."

Father and son exchanged a long look. Muttering, Sir Thomas returned to his seat.

Placing a claiming hand on her back, Brock said, "I am coming with you."

"No."

There was a flare of impatience in his heated gaze. "No? I have tried my best to steal a moment alone with you and what have I gained for my troubles? Irene is laughing behind her fan, and Sutton and Tipton have been giving me pitying looks. We will address your brother, and then you will deal with me."

She was getting rather weary of the men around her and their chest-pounding ultimatums. Without a word, she continued toward the curtained doorway. Brock matched her step for step.

Amara halted before they had entered the anteroom. "*We* will not be addressing my brother. I will." She whirled, positioning herself in front of him. "There is enough speculation floating around town. Dragging me about as if I am your prisoner benefits neither one of us."

"Oh, you are bound to me, my lady," he said, lowering his voice in a way that always managed to give her chills. "The ties are silken. Unbreakable, yet they will never hurt you. *I* will never hurt you."

You already have, a voice inside her cried out. She lightly touched his cheek. "There are a thousand reasons why I should discourage you."

He leaned into her hand. "Once you might have succeeded. Now you will not turn me away."

Amara withdrew her hand. His words resounded with determination and something else she could not define. A promise? A warning? Whatever it was, she knew he had spoken the truth. "I must go. Will you wait for me?" Acquiring his agreement, she disappeared through the entryway.

Leaning against the partition, Brock broodingly crossed his arms across his chest. "Waiting. It seems I have been doing just that for almost half my life."

The saloon was occupied with more individuals than Amara had expected. Two couples and a trio of giggling young ladies barely out of the schoolroom had claimed several of the scarlet-covered sofas lining the walls. Amara padded past them toward the fireplace at the end of the room. She discreetly checked between each plaster cast depicting classical poses, quickly averting her gaze when she passed the one on her left. The couple entwined in a torrid embrace were too caught up in each other to notice her interest.

Where was Mallory?

Sensing she was on a fool's errand, she retraced her steps and headed for the stairs. A male attendant stood nearby, protecting the privacy of the subscribers. Approaching him, she asked, "Perhaps you can assist me. I was told my brother was waiting for me."

"Oh, ye must be the lady my missus was after," the man said, his assessment of her a little too intimate for her comfort. "I see no likeness between ye 'n' he."

"And the source of many of our arguments," she lied. "He has never forgiven me for benefiting from our father's comely visage." A comparison of Mallory's darker masculine looks to her own was ludicrous. He probably would bloody the nose of the first man who tried. There was definitely nothing she deemed feminine about him.

"Where might I find my brother?"

The man cocked his head. "Gone. Most gents have no patience with their *sisters*."

Her smile tightened at his knowing look. Ah, shame on her for not catching on sooner. The man was not only rude, he thought their relationship was a polite fiction.

"He said to give this to ye." Misunderstanding her crestfallen expression, he made a sympathetic noise. "A disgraceful congé, I must say. Most ladies prefer something that sparkles. Like tears," he said, pleased by the poetic analogy.

"Violets," she murmured, pressing her nose into the delicately scented petals. Someone had wrapped the small bunch with a moistened remnant of a linen cravat.

"Just disgraceful," the man muttered, seeing the glitter of tears in her eyes.

"The man." She cleared her throat. "My brother. Are you certain he is gone?"

"Aye, ma'am."

Amara rooted around in her reticule and retrieved a coin. She pushed it into the attendant's palm. "For my gratitude," she explained.

Walking away, she sniffed the violets again. The Greeks considered them the flower of Zeus. For Amara, they symbolized a token, a fragrant apology from an errant brother. In *Hamlet,* Shakespeare had written that the violet was "Forward, not permanent, sweet, not last-ing." Sadly, like the violet, her brother's remorse withered quickly once offered.

No one outside the family knew what the fragile little flowers meant to her. They had come from her brother without a doubt. Not Mallory. Doran. Once Tipton had saved her brother's life. The toll had been high, yet neces-sary. Doran had promised never to contact his family, never to return to England.

Halting abruptly, Amara realized she could not return to the box clutching the violets. Brock would never believe Mallory had given them to her. The infuriating man would assume the flowers had come from Conte Prola. The last thing she wanted was another confrontation.

Brushing a parting kiss on the blooms, she walked up to the nearest pedestal and placed the tiny bouquet at the feet of one of the statues. Without regret, she continued forward to the mahogany door that would lead her back to the Bedegraynes. The violets were a message. Doran had broken yet another of his promises.

Brock paced the small, private anteroom outside the the-ater box, resisting the urge to check on Amara. He thought it odd that Claeg had sought her out. Brother and sister had never been close. Her affection had always been for the younger brother, Doran. Perhaps their time together while Mallory painted her portrait had forged the beginnings of a friendship.

For a brief moment, he had suspected Prola of mis-chief. A cursory glance at the Haslake box confirmed his suspicions were unfounded. The Italian was still seated beside Lady Laurette Omant. The distance and the

darkness of the theater made it difficult to discern if the
play or the lady held his attention. Brock was too much of
a cynic to hope that the gentleman would aim his aspirations toward the daughter of an earl. Maybe he was not
worthy of such a lofty prize; then again, Brock did not
believe the Italian was deserving of Amara Claeg.

"You did not have to miss the play on my account,"
Amara said, finding him paused near the fireplace.

She looked harried. Even though her eyes were dry,
Brock would have wagered a hundred pounds she had
been crying. "I detest the theater. Probably more than my
father." The anteroom was cramped, barely six feet in
width. He crossed to her and tugged her down on a bench
barely large enough to hold them. "Why did Claeg summon you?"

She fiddled with the adjustment of her glove. "Nothing
dire."

He held his silence until curiosity had her meeting his
stare. Her tongue darted out, wetting her lips. Brock
watched with rapt interest. Shaking his head, he cleared
the thickness in his throat. "He went to a great amount of
effort to find you for nothing dire."

The petite bench heightened their intimacy. They sat
hip against hip, thigh to thigh. She shrugged. He felt the
subtle movement down the length of his torso. "Someone
told him I was here with your family. You know of the portrait he paints for our mother. He asked if I could sit for
him tomorrow."

"Will you?"

She stared into the glowing embers, giving him the
opportunity to study her profile at leisure. "It depends. I
have been neglecting my cousin, Miss Novell. Mama
voiced her displeasure before I departed with the

Haslakes." Amara turned toward him, something akin to humor easing the somber expression she had worn since she had entered the room. "My sin is forgivable, since befriending the earl's daughters serves the needs of my family."

"Is that what you are doing?"

She crinkled her nose. "No. I genuinely like the Haslakes. It is fortunate that what I find pleasure in and what is expected can sometimes coincide."

"And which of the two am I?" He was certainly not duty. Lord and Lady Keyworth would likely geld him if they caught him touching their precious daughter. Amara was too wary of him still to view him as someone who could give her pleasure. He was too tangled in her hurtful past. Yet the soft expression on her face gave him hope.

"The unexpected."

"A compliment, Amara," he praised, the knotted tension in him loosening into a warm liquid gush of delight. "And here I was despairing before your return that you would never succumb to my considerable magnetism."

"Lout," she said, cuffing him affectionately on the side of the head.

He snatched her hand. Turning it over within his own, he stroked her palm. She had delicate, slender hands. He found them ridiculously appealing.

"What are you doing?"

He tugged off one of her gloves and dropped it on her lap. "I hate stating the obvious." When he seized her other hand, she gave him a token resistance. He peeled the second glove off with less finesse since she was being stubborn.

"I believe in playing fair," he told her, as he removed his gloves. What he had not explained was he generally broke that particular rule every time she came near him.

Discarding his gloves, he reached out and captured both her hands.

"Do you feel it?"

Her hands felt cool. They trembled slightly within his grasp.

"W-what should I be feeling?"

"The connection between us."

Amara's eyes were wide and dilated. She was reacting as if he had stripped her bare and laid her down in front of the fire. He had an idea of her chaotic thoughts. A lady would never allow a man to touch her thus, unless he was her husband. Earlier, she had spoken of forgivable sins. Brock swallowed a chuckle, acknowledging that what he was about to do would not qualify in Lady Keyworth's rigid book of rules.

He brought her hands up to his face, inhaling the essence of her skin. "Flowers. You always smell of them."

She bowed her head. The glimpse of guilt he saw made no sense. Drawing in a shaky breath, she tried to end his exploration by pulling her hands away. "No. Someone might catch us."

"I am beyond caring, Amara. My family has weathered its share of scandal. What is the worst that could happen? Marriage? Shall I procure a special license on the morrow?" he lightly taunted, not quite understanding the anger he felt.

"Must you mock everything?"

He released her left hand, keeping the other captive. "Not everything," he murmured. Turning her hand over, he traced the slender bones just below the surface with his fingernails. The flesh on her arms prickled in reaction.

"You must stop," she insisted, her plea dissolving into a moan.

Encouraged, he nipped the inside of her wrist. "You are so sensitive. I have often imagined you in my arms, shuddering with pleasure."

His tongue flicked over the lines scored on her palm. She shifted on the bench. Brock not only understood her agitation, he craved it. Lapping his tongue down the length of her first two fingers, he slipped them into his mouth. He sucked on her tender digits. She made a faint mewling sound in her throat. The needy reverberation cleaved him in half. He felt his manhood thicken, surging with a primal response. Brock ignored his discomfort. He had no intention of assuaging his needs in a badly lit ante-room with his family just beyond the closed drapery.

"C-could I—"

She bit her lower lip and turned her face into the wall, while he scraped his teeth downward and then repeated the sensual teasing. Brock's fingers itched with curiosity. He imagined her nipples were puckered buds pressing against the restraints of her stiff corset. He longed to plunge his fingers into her bodice and cup each scented breast, lifting them to his eager mouth.

"I want to touch you," she whispered.

He pulled her fingers from his mouth and bit the flesh side of her hand with less gentleness than he would have liked. "Look me in the eye and ask."

Slowly, she met his gaze. Was it rejection she feared? By God, could she not see that he would grant her any-thing she wanted?

"Can I— Is touching permitted?"

His hands curled as he resisted lunging. With a surpris-ingly steady voice, he replied, "Always."

Amara took up his hand, comparing each side to her own. "Your skin is much darker than mine." Impulsively, she brought the back of his hand to her cheek and rubbed against him. "Hmm . . . fuzzy."

Brock choked, both amused and mildly offended. "Kittens are fuzzy."

"Woolly, then," she quipped.

Enjoying himself, he expelled a sigh full of dejection. "You are a merciless witch, Amara Claeg, comparing a man's peculiarities to kittens and lambs. What is next? A dormouse?"

Relinquishing his hand, she covered her mouth to hide her laughter. In the dim light, her mirth twinkled in her lovely blue eyes like stars reflected off a moonlit sea. Brock's heart shifted in his chest. With firelight in her hair and laughter her siren's song, he had never encountered a more alluring woman.

"Amara," he said, his voice thick with yearning. Confined by the small bench, he twisted toward her, sliding his legs under hers so that she practically sat in his lap. He silenced her laughter by framing her face with his large hands.

"Brock."

He heard regret in her inflection, but he would not heed it. "For once in your life will you forget about what is beyond the closed door!"

Her hands circled his wrists. "I cannot. What you propose is not real."

God, she was a stubborn creature! Feeling goaded, he demanded, "Is this real enough for you?"

Dragging her close, he slid his mouth over hers. Tasting her was not sufficient. He wanted to devour her. Biting her lower lip, he used his tongue, enticing her to part her lips.

Amara complied.

Moaning his approval, he brushed his tongue playfully

against hers. He showed her without words what he desired. Having gained her consent, his left hand slid down to her hip while his right threaded her hair. He bucked his body against her. Finding her own way in this passionate play, she retaliated by retreating just enough to bite his lip. Lust stewed like a heady brew in his gut. His manhood was a rigid rod beneath his breeches. His body throbbed and ached for release, while their kisses almost inflamed him to madness.

"Oh, my!"

At Aunt Moll's exclamation, Brock and Amara sprang apart. He cracked the back of his head against the wall. Poor Amara fared worse. Her leg had tangled with his, sending her crashing to the floor in an awkward heap.

Aunt Moll covered her eyes with her hand while she used the other to lean heavily on her cane. "I have been struck blind. I cannot see a blessed thing."

Brock glared at his aunt. She was not easing the indignity of the situation. He extended an impatient hand to Amara. "I will throttle you if you apologize to my aunt." He hauled her to her feet, only holding her until he was certain she would not collapse from embarrassment at his feet.

Amara was a little white around the mouth, but she was sturdier than she thought. "Oh God," she muttered, her stare fixed on the distinct bulge ruining the perfect line of his breeches.

"What, my dear?" his aunt queried, forgetting for a moment that she was supposed to be blind. Brock closed his eyes, his humiliation complete. Deducing the reason Amara was appealing for divine intervention, Aunt Moll swayed precariously, forcing Brock to surrender his remaining dignity. He caught his elderly aunt before she broke another limb.

"Not one word," he warned his aunt. "Consider adding *mute* and *deafness* to your recent affliction." He smoothly pivoted Aunt Moll away from Amara, who stood open-mouthed and seemingly incapable of speech.

Rallying, his aunt said, "I will discourage the others from retiring."

"An excellent notion," he replied, certain of his aunt's discretion. She favored Amara. And him for that matter. "We will join you soon."

Brock closed the drapery once Aunt Moll departed. He bent down and retrieved their gloves. Seeing them in his bare hands, Amara surfaced from her stolid state and snatched the gloves.

"I cannot believe I was so careless." She plunged her hand into one of her gloves, engaging in a brief vicious battle.

Brock stilled her actions. "Stop tugging. Here, allow me." He took charge of the task. "You are liable to slap yourself in the face with it if you continue."

She rested her head on his chest and shuddered. "Oh, Brock, I have never been so ashamed. How will I ever face your aunt again?"

Nestled against him, her entire body quaked. He felt like the lowest wretch. Abandoning his task, he wrapped his arms around her. Brock blamed himself. He should have predicted where the simple caresses would lead them. Every time he touched her, he tended to lose what wits he had. They had still been clothed when his aunt stumbled upon them. Still, what if Amara's inexperience encouraged her to view him as the most depraved villain, a seducer of innocents?

"It is not as terrible as you think." He was weak against her tears. "Hush now. Do not cry. I—"

She drew back so he could see her face. The suspicious glitter in her eyes made his stomach spasm, but she astounded him with her laughter. "Did you see your dear aunt's face? For a few seconds, I believed her claims that she had been struck blind!"

Brock shook his head, marveling at her fortitude. Amara had changed. There was a quiet strength within her that she had lacked years earlier. He squelched an unreasonable pang of regret. It was not because he found something lacking in her. The lack was within him. He wanted her to lean on him, but, in truth, she had stood on her own. During his absence, she had healed and continued with her life. A life without him. For the first time, Brock felt the stirrings of fear.

"Aunt Moll values your friendship and ties to our family. She will not think less of you."

Calmer, Amara worked her other glove over her hand. "You are eight and twenty. I am certain your aunt is well aware you have coaxed a kiss or two from hundreds of women." She did not sound pleased by the notion.

"Legions," he said, deliberately provoking her.

"I have no doubt," she murmured. It was a trick of the light, perhaps, and yet Brock would have sworn her eyes were more green than blue.

"Not that they meant anything," he arrogantly amended. "How could any woman when tossed amid the multitude?"

Too late, Brock recognized his error. An angry woman was not a demonstrative one. He watched her gingerly probe her coiffure for wayward curls. Capturing her chin, he confessed. "You have. One stolen kiss and you have managed to send the others into oblivion."

Amara did not exactly melt at his tender words. In fact, the expression on her face sent a cold wind through the room. "You seem disappointed, Brock. Was I supposed to swoon or throw myself into your arms in gratitude?"

He gritted his teeth. "Not precisely."

"I will not deny there is an attraction between us." She took a deep breath. "In all honesty, I wish I could consign my feelings for you into oblivion as easily as you thrust the other women out of your life."

"You are deliberately twisting my meaning."

She tossed her head back in a haughty manner. "You are pleasing to the eye and your touch is sorcery. Why should I not enjoy a dalliance?"

She pricked not only his pride, but also his temper. "The devil you will, Amara Claeg!" he roared. "You are not the sort of woman a man takes on as his fancy piece."

Her cheeks suffused with color. "I do not pretend I am a diamond of the first water, but neither am I a woman at her last prayers."

Brock tensed, prepared to pounce if she tried to leave him. Espying her fallen reticule, she stomped over to the bench and claimed it. "Furthermore, I have reconsidered our earlier debate."

"How could we debate?" he taunted, intentionally baiting her. "You were too engrossed sucking my tongue!"

She ignored his vulgarity. "I am referring to our discussion about animals." Slicing the air with her reticule she nearly struck him on the head. "I agree. You are not comparable to a kitten, lamb, or dormouse. Brock Bedegrayne, you are unquestionably a conceited, braying ass!"

He was risking his neck, but he could not help it. Brock laughed down into her gloriously furious face. She shrieked and launched herself at him. Catching her by the wrist, he spun her around and hugged her to his chest. "Such vile language. What would your mother say?"

"Go to hell!"

"Hmm, she might at that," he said with a chuckle.

Amara writhed in his arms. "Release me."

"Have a care, if you please. I develop a rather unruly response every time you rub up against me."

She ceased her struggles. Had she been so lost in her fury that she had not noticed that her enticing backside was pressed up against his turgid cock? Egad, she was an innocent.

"Heed me, my dove. Since you are apparently dense, it appears this is the time for plain speaking." When she protested, Brock intentionally ground his pelvis against her as a reminder of her tenuous position. "This is no dalliance. This is a courtship."

"A courtship?" she choked out.

"Yes. It is certain to be a difficult one since it involves the two of us."

She sniffed, and managed to exude contempt despite her predicament. "There is no need to trouble yourself. I already have one suitor I do not *want*."

It had been unwise of her to mention Prola. He felt completely unreasonable when he thought of the man. "Oh, it is no trouble at all," he purred, "since I do not intend to be your suitor. I intend to be your lover." Brock nuzzled her closer.

"Lover? Touch me and I will scratch your eyes out."

She was trembling under all that bravado. He, more than anyone, understood what he was asking. He had seen how her face had paled when she finally noticed his arousal and remembered the violence done to her. "Damn it, I am not Cornley!"

She sagged against him. "I know. I know."

"I am tired of the past standing between us."

"Cornley is dead."

Brock whirled her around, keeping her within reach. "I am not speaking of that bastard. When are you going to forgive me?"

The vivid passion he so admired faded into enigmatic coolness. "I do not understand."

"You are a liar, Amara, and a bad one at that." He let go, fearing in his present mood that he might actually hurt her.

"I should return to the Haslakes."

Now that the passion and temper had passed, she was trying to rebuild the walls he had meticulously destroyed. This was one occasion she would be walking away disappointed.

"Amara, I care little of which path we choose. The result will be the same. I can kiss you senseless or prod your cursed temper until neither of us sees reason. Either way, it will be my body covering yours, my name you cry out when the passion crests, making you wonder if a person could die from the shattering joy."

They stared at each other, both remembering the kisses they had shared, and she forgot to be angry or afraid of him. He could make her feel that way again. She must have sensed his purpose because she asked, "This is your notion of a courtship?"

"No, just a pleasurable means to end the madness. From my way of thinking, the last ten years or so have been a courtship of sorts. It is not my fault if you have not been paying attention."

CHAPTER THIRTEEN

"You are late."

Matteo scowled at his accuser as he entered the room. "It was unavoidable."

He strolled to the four gentlemen seated at the table, peering over the shoulder of the rude cur who only offered his back. It was apparent they had been playing the game of connexions for hours. Matteo silently studied the stranger to the left. His face revealed much, making him at best a mediocre gambler. The trump he played seconds later was not unexpected. Winning the trick, the man crowed his triumph.

Matteo met the sardonic gaze of the man who had scolded him. *Fat pigeon,* those pale cynical eyes seem to say. There was no doubt who was really controlling the game.

Losing interest in their card game, he strode by the table, wondering where he could place his cloak without soiling it. The room might have been private, but it was beneath his refined tastes. A scarred table and six rough-hewn chairs were the extent of the furniture. The hearth was black with soot and had not been clean in days. Utterly disgraceful. Opening a small box on the mantel, Matteo selected a brimstone match. He retrieved from the inside pocket of his coat the remnants of a cigar. Crouching down in front of the fire, he ignited the match. He suckled the cigar as impatiently as a newborn hungering for its mother's breast as he held the flame to the tobacco. Tossing the match into the hearth, he closed his eyes and savored the cigar.

With deference to Miss Claeg he had curtailed his favorite habit. He could not properly court the lady when she complained at their second meeting that the putrid odor clinging to his coat sickened her. So he suffered. A man was willing to endure any hardship as long as the prize was worthy. Miss Amara Claeg was one such treasure.

"Remove your cloak before a spark turns you into a thrashing conflagration," the dealer said, his gaze focused on the cards on the table.

Patience, Matteo counseled, when several of the gentlemen chuckled. Obeying the gruff order, he placed his cloak on an empty chair. Another man might have been angry, he mused, exhaling a cloud of smoke. What Matteo felt was pity. He deliberately leveled his gaze on his cohort. Three-quarters of the man's face and the left side of his neck gleamed like melted wax. This was an individual who understood intimately how fire ravaged tender flesh.

"How was your evening at the theater?"

"Sadly flat," he confessed, questioning the wisdom of this particular discussion in front of strangers. "The uproar from the pit fatigued my ears."

The extensive damage had left the dealer's face an impassive mask. Only his pale eyes glowed with menace. "Fortunate for you that your interests resided aloft."

"Yes." Matteo paused, waiting until the man played his card. "Miss Claeg introduced me to Lady Haslake and her enchanting daughters."

"I assume the Countess of Haslake shamelessly lapped the butter from Conte Prola's lips."

He flicked the ash from his cigar on to the floor. He smiled, recalling his discourse with the older woman. The countess was an engaging, generous woman. She was also regrettably very devoted to her earl. "The ladies, they always find pleasure in my company," he said with a careless shrug.

"And Miss Claeg?"

"Like the ripest fruit. Just out of reach," he said, feigning regret.

The man sneered. "So cut down the tree."

Matteo puffed his cigar. A man in his position would never tolerate abuse from an inferior. This crippled, pathetic devil only possessed the power he, Conte Prola, gave him. He tapped a finger against his lower lip, considering his friend's suggestion. "A wasted effort, I fear, since someone pilfered the proverbial tree."

The man crushed the cards in his hands. The game was forgotten. His companions' grumbles further agitated him. Pounding his fists on the table, he yelled, "Leave us!" He threw silver coins at their retreating backs.

Matteo smiled behind his cigar. He found it rewarding to remind a man who prided himself on his control that he lacked it when he needed it most.

With his hands braced against the table, his chest heaving, that horrible mask peered up at him. "Who?"

Although he was not pleased with the answer, he relished the role of messenger. "Bedegrayne." He held up a silencing hand. "The gentleman is infuriating, I agree."

Fists clenched, the man closed the gap between them. "He is—"

"A gadfly. Nothing more." Matteo crossed his arms, confident. "I have taken care of him."

It was almost four o'clock in the morning when Amara arrived home. She expected that her maid had fallen asleep hours earlier by the fire awaiting her return. The lateness of the hour had her staggering, but it was her encounter with Brock that had left her oddly drained and her mind hazy.

After his proclamation, he had escorted her back to her seat beside his aunt. To her credit, Aunt Moll had not told the others what she had witnessed in the anteroom. She had only smiled at Amara when she had sat down and patted her hand. Devona had distracted her by inquiring after Mallory. She had assured her friend that all was well. The mere fact that she had put the violets from her mind once Brock had begun stripping her gloves off proved how true his parting words were. It was so easy imagining them together as he had promised. Threatened, she silently revised. It worried her, although not in the manner it should.

"Amara, a moment."

Leaning over the balustrade, she watched her father cross to the bottom of the stairs. "Good evening, Papa." Tiredly, she rubbed the corner of her right eye. "Or rather, good morning," she corrected, covering a yawn.

"How was your evening with the Haslakes?"

Something in her father's inflection slithered through her weariness. "I enjoyed myself immensely. Lord Haslake joined us for a late supper after the play. He sends his regards."

They heard an indistinct thud several stories up. "The servants are waking," Lord Keyworth muttered, irritated his privacy was about to be disturbed. "Come, let us continue in my library."

Feeling the chill of the morning air, she gripped the edges of her cloak together. Amara kept silent as she followed her father. The inescapable lecture was already clearing her head. Everyone had had plans for the evening, she was certain. Her father had been at one of his clubs. Mama and Miss Novell had been expected at a card party.

"Cease your dawdling."

Amara passed through the arch into her father's realm. Set-in bookcases divided the walls of the room. A diverse assortment of subjects populated the shelves besides the mandatory parliamentary accounts and law tomes. Books on husbandry, agriculture, math, and flora and fauna resided alongside topography, military campaigns, poetry, and fiction. Fluted columns with gilded capitals supported a rectangular plasterwork ceiling design that her father claimed was faithfully copied from a Roman tomb.

Amara skirted the circular rosewood library table, which was the final repose of a baleful stuffed peregrine. The creature had been one of her father's beloved falcons. Obsidian glass eyes mirrored her movements, giving them the brief illusion of life.

Lord Keyworth lit a branch of candles near the mulberry and gold floral sofa. "Sit."

While Amara sat where she had been directed, her father grasped a painted klismos chair through its rectangular open back and dragged it closer to her. Instead of sitting as she had expected, he headed in the opposite direction. Bracing her head against her propped hand, she watched him remove a decanter from its hull-shaped leather coaster.

"I apologize for bothering you at this late hour." He poured the claret into two wineglasses. "This should warm us." Returning to her side, he offered one of the glasses.

Amara sipped the claret. The wine mixed poorly with her growing dread. "It is very good."

Bracing a hand on the back of the chair, he asked, "Do you love me, daughter?"

Perplexed, she replied, "Of course, Papa."

Lord Keyworth nodded, satisfied with her answer. "Would you say a loving father is deserving of his daughter's loyalty as well?"

She took another sip, clearing the sudden dryness in her throat. "One's duty is to the family."

"Ah." He stared down into his glass. "Then tell me, daughter, why do you shame me?"

The fevered image of her and Brock embracing, tongues mating, rose unbidden in her mind. "I—I do not understand."

"Conte Prola, girl!" he shouted, fixing his incensed gaze on her. "How long must I wait until you accept his offer of marriage?"

"The subject has never been broached, Papa," she denied.

"Bah! Why do you think he accepted my invitation? He is young, ambitious, and holds some influence in his own country. My support—"

"Your money," she interjected without thought. She regretted the hastily uttered words when he towered over her.

"A father is always gratified by his daughter's concern. Never fear, I shall profit from the arrangement."

"Marriage," she said in a stark whisper.

"I have been too indulgent with you," he said, his voice filled with recrimination. "You were so inconsolable after Lord Cornley's death, I hesitated pressuring you into another marriage."

Choking on a sob, Amara set her wineglass on the table lest she spill claret on her gown. "Your generosity has been boundless, Papa." Her stomach roiled, thinking of her grief if Cornley had lived.

"As is your selfishness!" he retorted, rankled by the edge of sarcasm he detected in her praise. "You mope around in front of Conte Prola as if the man were eighty and without a tooth in his bald head!"

"I have been courteous to him," she argued, defiant.

"Unfailingly so, it seems," he said, the bitterness of his displeasure sullying the compliment. "And what of Brock Bedegrayne? I was told you were quite accommodating to him this evening."

Comprehension lit in her blue gaze. "Prola sought you out after he left the theater." *The whining toad!* "Did he tell you the truth? Mr. Bedegrayne was simply the courier for his family. Lady Tipton, Lady Sutton, and Mrs. Bedegrayne were responsible for the invitation issued. If I had spurned their gentle request in front of Lady Haslake and her guests then I would heartily be deserving of your censure."

Amara met his anger with a mutinous stare. She cared little if her explanation was riddled with omissions and half-truths. Conte Prola had plummeted in her estimation. She had no qualms about matching his duplicity.

"Perhaps he misunderstood," her father conceded,

finishing the remains of his claret. "Nevertheless, you are not entirely blameless in the matter. You were observed leaving the box unescorted. Bedegrayne departed minutes after you."

"Papa, my leaving had nothing to do with Mr. Bedegrayne," she assured him, wearily getting to her feet.

"If you have any maggoty notions about young Bedegrayne, you will forget them. I have higher aspirations for my daughter than squandering her on a baronet's son."

"I have no intention of marrying anyone, including Conte Prola," she said recklessly. "It seems it matters not which Claeg the conte marries, so if there must be a blood sacrifice let Mallory make it!"

She had gone too far. Smashing his wineglass to the floor, Lord Keyworth rushed Amara. She yelped as he grabbed her by the arm and struck her across the face. "Disrespectful minx!" He violently shook her.

"No, I—"

He slapped her again. She flinched when he raised his fist. "Papa, please!" she begged.

Roaring his frustration, Lord Keyworth lifted her off her feet and hurled Amara away from him. She landed with a bounce on the sofa. Too frightened to feel any pain, she drew her knees up to her chin and curled into a ball.

Her father shook his fist at her. "I am tiring of your drivel." He reached down and seized her wrists. He hauled Amara to her feet. "Look at you. Hair disheveled, blotchy face, and sniveling. What man would have you?"

She yanked her arms free and swiped under her nose. "Forgive me, Papa."

" 'Forgive me, Papa,' " he mimicked. "I see nothing of myself in you, girl. I do not even believe you are mine!"

She vehemently shook her head. The cruel words were meant to wound, make her doubt. "That is not true."

"Have you spread your thighs for Bedegrayne?" he crudely speculated. "If so, you come by your whoring naturally. Mallory is the only one of you three I am convinced is from my seed."

Shivering, she pushed her hair from her face. "You are drunk. Mama would never betray you. You are only saying this to hurt me."

"Are you so certain?"

He walked over to her abandoned claret and picked up the wineglass. He twirled the stem with his fingers. "I dislike conversing business with women. However, I see an exception is called for. Nine months ago, I took some heavy losses on an ill-fated venture in Jamaica. Although Prola is unaware of my unfortunate predicament, the profits from my arrangement with him will satisfy the incurring debt and the other investors."

Amara felt as if her head were stuffed with sawdust. Her eyes stung from lack of sleep. "I do not—are you saying Conte Prola insisted I was to be part of this arrangement?"

"He was amenable to my terms after he met you." He finished her glass of claret. "Let us come to an understanding. If you refuse Prola, your defiance will be considered an ultimate betrayal to this family. From that day, you will cease to be my daughter."

Having delivered his ultimatum, Lord Keyworth set the wineglass on the table. She listened to his footfalls, the door closing behind him. Amara sank down onto the sofa. Her mien was impassive as her father's angry words reverberated in her head. She was still there several hours later when one of the servants discovered her.

. . .

"You look frightfully domesticated, *mon cher*."

Always in awe of her daring, Brock accepted Mrs. LeMaye's hand and bowed. "And you, Carissa, look quite predatory."

At twenty-nine, the widow lured more than one masculine eye with her mature beauty as she entered the room. A fortune in rubies and brilliants glittered from her neck, ears, and wrists. His gaze dipped to the tear-shaped ruby resting over her heart. The size of a nightingale's egg, it was a seductive trap, for few men could resist admiring the warm, plump swells within which it nestled. With a sigh of regret, he met her gaze.

"A compliment, Mr. Bedegrayne. You have already improved my evening," she said, her eyes inviting him to share her merriment.

"You amaze me. I would have thought a garden conversazione would be a trifle tedious for you."

Her eyes glinted, appearing as hard as the rubies she adored. "I prefer doing the unexpected," she said, sweeping the room with an assessing glance. "Besides, *mon cher*"—she lowered her voice as she moved closer— "during our brief time together, if you recall, I had better uses for my mouth than debating the twelve articles of garden theory."

As she had intended, he experienced a swift image of a naked Carissa crouched over him. Her eyes full of wicked mischief as she moved down his body and took him fully in her mouth. Christ. He ruthlessly doused the memory, even though she was the type of woman a man never completely forgot. Countless years ago, he had been drawn to the worldliness she exuded like an intoxicating perfume. Carissa had been his first lover.

Keeping her hand on his arm, she walked the perimeter of the room with him. A woman who was always seeking out potential competition, she made a cynical appraisal of a face unfamiliar to her. "Who is your young charge?" she asked, nodding to Maddy.

Brock shifted his attention to Maddy. He noted the faces of the three gentlemen surrounding her and immediately dismissed them as harmless. "Lord Tipton's sister, Miss Wyman."

"Ah, *Le Cadavre Raffiné*. A most elusive gentleman," she drawled, her ambitious mind considering the possibilities.

"And married to my sister," he reminded Carissa. There was no doubt Tipton was besotted with his wife. He would never betray her. Still, Brock understood his sister was no match for the clever, spiteful games some women liked to play. A few imprudently spoken words could hurt Devona. "Do not interfere. You will be unhappy with the consequences."

"Tut! I do not fear your threats. We both know there are peculiar delights in punishment." She took his hand and rubbed it against her cheek. "I remember your hands," she said, unruffled when he calmly took his hand back. "Why do we not leave your little rabbit with her admirers and you can show me in private how very unhappy you will make me?" She stroked his chest.

Brock stopped and stared down at her hand touching his chest. Carissa LeMaye had a beauty most women envied. Her voice caressed a man like velvet and her skills as a lover were enslaving. Nevertheless, the growing tension within him had nothing to do with desire. Beneath her fiery exterior, he had learned there was a calculating coldness. A man could perish, frozen within the chimera.

Some of his disgust must have been expressed on his face. The teasing pout she wielded like a consummate actress faded and was replaced by a belated prudence.

A soft gasp jerked Brock from his reverie. His gaze shifted from Maddy's silent disapproval to the fluid pain gleaming in the blue depths of Amara's gaze. She recognized Carissa. It was also nauseatingly apparent, she was aware of the history between them.

"Amara was able to accept my invitation, after all," Maddy said, stating the obvious. She also looked mad enough to kick him.

Deliberately, keeping her hand on Brock's coat sleeve, Carissa said, "Miss Claeg, we are encountering each other in the most unexpected places. Do not tell me you, too, have been caught up in this gardening enthusiasm that seems to have enthralled the *ton*?"

"Not particularly. I have neither the talent nor the inclination."

Carissa's fleeting smile revealed the very sharp edges of her teeth. "On this we agree. What is this fascination with groveling in the dirt like swine?"

Shaking off Carissa's grasp, Brock moved closer to Maddy. He almost hoped she would kick him. He deserved it. Silently, he tried coaxing Amara to meet his gaze. If she sensed his scrutiny, she had suppressed it along with her vivacity. To the others, she might have appeared indifferent to her surroundings. Not to Brock. He knew her too well. The greater her anguish, the deeper she tended to bury her feelings.

"*Mon cher,* now that your rabbit has her friend, we are

liberated to find other amusements, no?" Carissa asked prettily, her small retribution for his slight.

Carissa had judged her rival accurately. Her innuendo struck its mark. A spasm of pain flickered across Amara's face. Brock was torn. He wanted to soothe Amara but suspected she would spit at him if he tried.

Instead he gave Carissa the attention she craved. "You will have to find another playfellow, Mrs. LeMaye. I am discriminating when choosing good friends and amusements. You qualify for neither one."

Carissa paled, making her subtle touches of cosmetics seem garish. He had hurt her, something he had not thought possible, nor would it have changed the outcome. Sensing Amara's importance to Brock, the woman had intentionally flaunted their former association. The fact Amara believed he had chosen Carissa over her made him yearn to throttle them both!

"It appears I have arrived too late," Mallory said, joining the group. His quick perusal assessed the situation in seconds. He placed his hands on Amara's shoulders in a protective gesture. "Green-eyed, Carissa, love?"

Carissa was not fooled by his mild curiosity. Her beauty and wealth allowed her entrance into polite society, where mistresses and wives often encountered each other. Needling her lover's sister was the worst display of vulgarity.

"Simply evading the gapes. You were late," she complained, begging his understanding. "What was I to do, *mon cher*?"

"Then I am at fault." Mallory kissed Amara on the head, pretending not to notice she had shied away. "Forgive me," her brother murmured, so softly Brock wondered if he had imagined it. "You were supposed to wait for me."

"Papa improved on our plans." With her eyes she sought the room for someone. Catching sight of him, she lifted her hand. Conte Prola, without halting his conversation with two gentlemen, returned her wave.

That damnable bounder! A low growl of frustration rumbled in his throat, earning him a strange glance from Maddy. She shook her head, admonishing him. What kind of protector was he, placing her in the middle of this farce? If Tipton learned of it, he would likely autopsy critical organs from his body then and there.

"Maddy, you look parched," Brock said, his glare daring her to contradict him. "Find some lemonade."

His rudeness finally granted him Amara's attention. "Cretin," she jeered, using her ire on her friend's behalf to put voice to her own. "Maddy, permit me to join you. There is something sticking in my throat."

Something was sticking all right, Brock thought. Disgust. "I will escort you both," he curtly announced. A weaker man might have shriveled under her stare.

"Your presence is not required." She tried walking around him.

He grabbed her arm, whirling her around until she stood at her starting point. "You have it just the same."

Claeg wrapped his hands around Carissa's waist. "Your flair for spinning discord is positively Byzantine." She arched her back, gasping when he dug his fingers painfully into her sides. "Never play your games with my sister again."

Peering over his mistress's shoulder, Claeg exchanged a silent promise with Brock. Carissa's perfidy would not go unpunished. Brock dismissed the retreating couple. Whatever the woman's fate, it was well deserved. Any lingering fondness he had for her dissipated when he saw the pain in Amara's eyes.

"You are causing a scene," Amara said through a forced smile. Feeling spiteful, she deliberately stepped on his foot. He promptly released her. "Then again, you are notorious for them."

"Provoke me further and our memorable exit from the Dodds' masquerade two years ago will seem like a leisurely promenade in Hyde Park."

She raised her chin in defiance. "Touch me, and you will be meeting my brother at dawn."

"Your brother has already vanished with Carissa."

When she heard Brock utter the woman's given name, a perilous light flared in Amara's eyes.

Not certain where her loyalty lay, Maddy stood between them. "Uh, Brock?"

He gnashed his teeth at Prola's approach. He wanted the man to disappear: away from the conversazione, out of town, and most assuredly into another country.

"Your brother, he found you?" the conte inquired courteously.

Now that Carissa was gone, Amara seemed to loathe the man's presence as much as Brock did. Staring at the tips of her slippers, she replied, "Yes, thank you."

While Brock contemplated murder, it was Maddy who innocently spared the man's life. Stepping in front of Brock, she pressed Amara for an introduction. Drawing on enough feminine wiles to risk a paddling if Tipton ever caught her at it, she asked, "Conte Prola, if I may be so bold and impose on you, would you object to escorting me toward the refreshments? These stimulating discourses are so demanding on one's throat."

Brock sensed that Prola was reluctant to leave Amara alone with him. Brock completely understood the man's sentiment. Maddy brightened her smile when Prola glanced down at her. With practice, the imp would have the majority of males in London under her rule. The conte succumbed without even whimpering. Winking at Brock, Maddy led the Italian away, regaling him with her considerable knowledge of the defining qualities of a proper town garden.

"You should not encourage her. Tipton will not thank you for it."

Brock shrugged, unconcerned. "Prola wants you. He will play the gallant for Maddy because he hopes it will impress you."

"Then perhaps I should join them."

"I disagree." He turned her around, escorting her in the opposite direction. They continued down a narrow hall toward the front of the house. Brock wanted distance from Prola. By God, he wanted time with her alone. He led her down the stairs to the lobby.

"I am going back." She wrenched her arm from his grasp and dashed up the stairs.

He raced after her. When piqued, the woman had the swiftness of a gazelle. He caught her at the top. "Will you let me explain about Carissa LeMaye?"

"Explain what? That you were lovers?" She backed him down a step. "It was quite evident. I am astonished you let her wander off with Mallory. Or do you share her?"

A gentleman cleared his throat behind them. "If I may pass," he mumbled, pretending that he had not overheard Amara's insolent question. He hastened down the stairs, his brows never descending from his scalp.

"I have tolerated more than enough!" Brock marched

her up the stairs, searching for a vacant room. Lifting the door latch, he kicked open the door. The tiny room was not his first choice, but he was too furious to quibble. "A foul mouth deserves an appropriate setting."

He pushed her into the water closet.

Amara pounded on his chest. "Are you crazy?"

Brock bolted the door. "If I am, the blame is yours." He crossed his arms against his chest. Amara took three steps away from him and propped her back against the wall.

"The smell is unbearable."

"So is your opinion of me." He leaned against the door and rubbed his neck. "Amara," he entreated, "I was not much older than Maddy when I met Carissa. She was older and I had never—known a woman."

"I have heard enough."

He closed his eyes, sorting his thoughts. How could he make her understand without causing more hurt? "I suppose she chose a lowly baronet's son because I was smitten with her beauty and my inexperience amused her. The affair was brief. She left me for an older, titled gentleman who bought her a small house."

"Did you love her?" A single tear dropped from her lashes and dripped down her cheek.

Since she was calmer, he came to her. He brushed the wetness from her cheek. "No," he assured her. "Nor am I interested in renewing her acquaintance. Your brother was correct. She wanted to hurt you because she was jealous."

She shook her head in disbelief. "There is nothing enviable about me."

He flicked her chin up with his finger. "Stop belittling yourself," he rebuked, getting furious all over again.

"Carissa LeMaye was jealous. In spite of her good looks, wealth, and a multitude of lovers, she is still searching for happiness."

He linked his hands with hers. Stroking his thumb over her knuckles, he wished that instead of leather, he was touching her silky skin. "I have not been terribly discreet about my interest in you," he sheepishly confessed.

"You claimed you were courting me."

"I am. Or will if you cease avoiding me." Brock waited for her denial. She disentangled their fingers and glanced away. Patience, he reminded himself. "When Carissa learned of my interest in you, watched my face when you approached, she knew I had found my happiness. With you, Amara."

"Brock, you cannot keep saying such things."

"Her cruel machinating unintentionally proved something I have pondered for weeks." He laughed at himself. "Mayhap years."

"Do not ask me," she softly begged.

"You already answered my question." He kissed her forehead. "I am yours."

CHAPTER FOURTEEN

"Wynne, stop fretting," her husband said, keeping a reassuring hand on her lower back while Aunt Moll's butler, Aberly, guided them through a maze of halls. More than an hour had passed since the footman had delivered her aunt's nebulous summons. The note had mentioned Brock. Unable to shake her mounting alarm, Wynne had sought him out. Keanan had held her and listened. He had survived his harsh upbringing by trusting his instincts. He respected Wynne's unease; accepted her protective nature. Her family had become important to him as well.

"She is likely busy planning her wedding and needed your advice. The old woman loves issuing her commands," he said fondly, having received one or two when Aunt Moll had thought he needed advice regarding Wynne. "I doubt she considered how you might interpret it."

Wynne prayed he was correct. His sensible explanation calmed her. If his aunt or Brock were in trouble, surely the solemn butler would have mentioned it on their arrival.

Aberly brought them to the back parlor. Not bothering with ceremony, Wynne entered the room before the butler could announce them. She absently touched her heart in relief when she saw her aunt was fine.

Aunt Moll had positioned a saber-legged chair at the window. Seeing them, she reached for her cane so she could stand. "Good. You brought your man." Her aunt beamed, tilting her face upward for Wynne's kiss. She held a hand out for Keanan. He came to her side, and gently clasped it. She surprised him by holding on. "If Wynne cannot talk some sense into him, you may be needed."

"Aunt, you mentioned in your note some concern about Brock. Is he here?"

The older woman waved her hand in the direction of the window. "There. Down below. Such a stubborn lad."

Curious, Wynne and Keanan went to the window. There in the distance, they caught a glimpse of Brock's back. He had removed his coat. Some shrubbery obstructed most of their view, but he was attacking something rather ferociously with an ax.

"What is he doing? Cutting down a tree?" Wynne asked, turning to her aunt.

"Not a whole one. Just an old stump," the elderly woman explained. "He showed up quite unexpectedly. He seemed so troubled, pacing about the room and not speaking a word. I suggested a walk in the garden. Fresh air helps rid the body of ill humors." Miserable, Aunt Moll eased onto the sofa. "Then he started raving about that old stump and shiftless jobbers. Before I could utter a word, he had stalked off to the toolhouse. He returned minutes later with the ax in his hands. No argument from Aberly or myself has dissuaded him from his task. He has been out there ever since."

Wynne left the window and sat beside her aunt. Clasping her hand, she said, "Brock having a tantrum can be a magnificent display. There is nothing anyone can do but keep out of his path. Eventually, it burns itself out."

"Will you talk to him? You always did have a way with him."

Her aunt spoke of childhood confidences. The man he had become was an enigma. Not wanting to disappoint Aunt Moll, she said, "Of course. In the meantime, you need to calm yourself. When I see Aberly, I will have him send up some tea."

Keanan followed her to the door. "You are not attending him alone."

Blinking at his vehemence, Wynne said, "Brock is my brother. His temper is no fiercer than your own. While I confess he has been known to stomp about spewing his wrath, he would rather plunge a knife into his own heart than hurt anyone."

He gave her an incredulous stare. "My God, what an innocent. Even if he were King George himself, I would never leave my wife alone with a riled man holding a bloody ax!"

Habit had her parting her lips, preparing to firmly defend her brother. Sudden understanding stilled her tongue. Keanan was not really thinking of Brock. He was reliving that terrible night when he had arrived home and found a madman chasing her up the stairs with a loaded pistol in his hand. "Keanan, that is now in the past. I am taking no risk." She wrapped her arms around his waist and laid her cheek against his hammering heart.

"You will have to forgive your overbearing husband," he said, kissing the top of her head. "I have yet to recover from seeing you fight off one crazed fool. The notion of casually watching you take on another will likely put me in my bed."

Sensing his smile, Wynne pulled back. The smile was there, along with the unspoken need to protect. She knew it well, for she felt the same for this strong, generous man. "Well, if I am responsible for putting you in the bed, then I should at least join you and warm your cold feet." The last part was a lie. Keanan's body radiated like a conflagration and he knew it.

Relaxing under her gentle flirtation, he said, "Aye, my damson, at the very least. And you are still not speaking to your brother alone."

"I know," Wynne admitted, surrendering gracefully.

Brock brought the ax down, the savage collision of steel and wood vibrating up his arms. Clenching his teeth, he raised the ax high and repeated the motion as he had dozens of times. He had discarded his coat an hour earlier. The temperate weather had not prevented the linen shirt he wore from clinging to him like a second skin. He hurt. The worst of his pain, however, had nothing to do with his labor.

"Your skills clearly surpass those of your foe. I declare the stump vanquished."

His sister's facetious observation interrupted his rhythmic strokes. Brock shook off some of the stiffness in his shoulders and finished the downward stroke. From the corner of his eye, he noticed Wynne was not alone. With a derisive snort, Brock lifted the ax. He must look like a cutthroat if Milroy thought his sister needed protecting from her own brother.

"I have rung for some tea," Wynne said, managing to

keep the concern he noted in her eyes out of her voice. "I imagine you are thirsty."

"Not particularly," he replied briskly. Resting the ax handle on his shoulder, he gave her his complete attention. "Run along and have your tea, Wynne. You are better company for Aunt Moll than I."

"Something has happened," she said, certain she was correct. "If you would allow me to help—"

"No!" Despising his temper, he grimaced and flipped the ax over so the head dug into the dirt. "Let this alone. I have no need of a mother." He cringed inwardly at his harshness. If Wynne cried, Milroy would give him the bruising he well deserved. He doubted he would defend himself. Turning away, he discarded the ax in favor of a shovel. He glowered at the stump. The roots were deep and tenacious. A man armed with a surly disposition and a few garden tools was not going to conquer it, but nothing less than bloodshed would ever force him to admit it aloud.

A clod of dirt struck him on the cheek.

With the shovel still clutched in his hand, he switched his jaundiced stare on his attacker. He had decided not to be so accommodating for Milroy, after all.

Wynne glared back. Brushing the dirt off her gloves, she said, "I am not your mother. I would disown you if I was. Snarl at me again, Brock Bedegrayne, and you can expect prompt retribution."

Sisters. He had been cursed with the meddlesome three, and he was sorely tempted to pare the number. He purposely eyed the shovel. "Damn you, woman, can you not give a man his peace?" he asked.

Milroy had the indecency to laugh at his quandary. At some point, the man had deemed him harmless. It was truly insulting.

"No, I cannot!" she yelled back. "Not when you are upsetting Aunt Moll by attacking her garden."

He strove for patience. "Do not exaggerate. It is one rotten stump." Who did it hurt if he ripped it out of the ground with his bare hands? he wondered.

"You are hurting." She came closer, stilling his hand when he buried the head of the shovel in the dirt. "We are your family, Brock. Did you think we would not see your pain?"

His sister was filled with such extraordinary compassion. A part of him was tempted to bask within the warmth of her love and confide his troubles. Still, he remained silent. Wynne had faced too much strife in her young life. She would not sleep better knowing his secrets. She might not appreciate it, but he needed to protect her too.

Milroy walked over to the pile of discarded tools. Surveying his choices, he selected a shovel. "Wynne, go ahead and reassure Aunt Moll that your brother is fine. We will finish digging out this stump and join you when we are finished."

"You have dirt on your face," Brock said, deliberately marring her flawless cheek with an affectionate stroke of his soiled thumb. It was a small reprisal for her accurate aim. "Clean up, else she will think we are out here making mud cakes on a lark."

Wynne swiped at her cheek. "You will not tell me." She had not posed it as a question, just a resigned statement.

"Have you always been this stubborn?" Brock added another smudge of dirt on her chin. "I can reason this out on my own."

Unhappy with his reply, she looked at her husband. "Have you nothing to say?"

Brock held Milroy's shovel while the other man removed his coat. He handed it to his wife. "It will take two men to dig this up."

Without a word to either of them, Wynne pivoted and headed for the house. Neither the dirt on her face nor her displeasure could diminish her dignified retreat.

Brock passed Milroy the shovel. "Your wife is vexed."

Not bothered by the observation, the man stabbed the ground with his shovel. "I suppose I could have hit you on the head with the flat side of the shovel and carried you into the house, but it seemed somewhat drastic."

Eyeing Milroy's large hands, Brock figured a facer from Reckless Milroy would have been more punishing than a blow from any shovel. "I appreciate your restraint."

The men worked conjointly, exposing the roots at the base of the trunk. There was no need for meaningless banter, and Brock respected Milroy for his silence. The man threw himself into the task, heedless of his attire. He was beginning to understand why the fighter had captivated his sister.

"Step back while I use the ax on those thick roots," Milroy directed, not waiting for approval. Brock gave him the requested distance and sat down on his heels. His entire body thrummed from his exertions.

"I am not one to poke in another man's problems," Milroy said, as he adjusted his stance and raised the ax above his head. He possessed a body that was honed by hard labor. Brock grudgingly admired the man's fluid movements as he finished the stroke. A dozen strokes later, he was not even winded.

Brock rested his chin against his fist. "Why debase a perfectly sensible conviction?"

"You are family."

"You have Nevin—" Damn, he would never get his friend's new title correct. "I mean, Reckester and his mother bedeviling you. You look like a man who prefers distancing himself from family squabbles."

Milroy paused, sending him a considering look. "Once I enjoyed inciting them. Wynne has encouraged me to mend my ways."

Brock doubted anyone compelled the fighter into any decision he had not chosen on his own. "So what are you doing here? Inciting or prying?"

Wiping his face with his sleeve, Milroy gave him a cocky grin. "A little of both, perhaps." Discarding the ax, he motioned Brock closer. With the shovels they deepened the hole at the base of the stump. "I admire your discretion, but Wynne ferreted out your interest toward Miss Claeg long before you set foot on English soil."

It was his fault, he supposed. He had begged Wynne to befriend Amara in his absence. It was only natural for her to make assumptions.

"She had the advantage of knowing you both," Milroy explained, identifying with the growing frustration only a woman could engender. "Miss Claeg has feelings she never could quite hide."

"She hid them well enough when Lothbury came sniffing," Brock muttered, still displeased at Amara for encouraging the raffish marquess.

"I accept blame for that debacle." He leaned on the handle, checking the windows of the house for a glimpse of his wife. "I introduced them. Lothbury only feigned interest in Miss Claeg. He was more concerned about my meetings with your sister. I regret any pain my lack of foresight might have caused your lady."

"She is not—" He did not bother finishing the obvious lie. "Amara is generous. If she blames anyone, I assure you it is this Lothbury."

"Regardless, I am responsible and need to make reparations." Not catching sight of Wynne, Milroy resumed digging. "Maddy gave a curious account of the garden conversazione she attended with you."

He imagined she had disclosed his character as being less than honorable. Maddy considered Amara a friend. The confrontation with Carissa LeMaye had outraged the little hoyden. Barricading himself and Amara in the water closet had only lowered her estimation. Several witnesses had seen them leave the convenience together. He was certain the titillating observation had circulated the room before they retired for the evening.

He owed no one an apology except Amara. Lamentably, she was pretending he did not exist. "The evening was awkward."

"Did you really lock her in a water closet?" Milroy was fighting back his laughter.

His antics sounded ludicrous in the retelling. No wonder his family thought him daft. "I was desperate. She was not brimming with courtesy after encountering one of my former—friends."

"Oh, how prickly," the man said, a frown scouring the humor in his expression. It was easy to deduce that he was envisioning how Wynne might have handled such an incident. Not liking the ominous conclusion, he winced. "I assume Miss Claeg is upset."

Brock summoned the memory of his last moments with Amara. When he had told her that she mattered to him, he had doused all that magnificent passion her anger had set off. She had quietly thanked him as if he had complimented her on the color of her gown. Slashed to the bone by her aloofness, he had not protested when she freed the bolt. Without a parting glance, she had returned to Conte Prola's side. If the Italian had heard of their indiscretion, he ignored it. Every time their gazes crossed, the man looked triumphant.

"Upset?" Brock banished the persistent image of her almond-shaped eyes. "No. I would not describe her thus."

Giving up the pretense of their task, Milroy sat down on the stump. "Whatever she told you, she lied," he said flatly. "Maddy told Wynne that Miss Claeg was devastated to learn of your—your regrettable friendship with this Mrs. LeMaye. I saw Miss Claeg yesterday. If you have any trust in my opinion, I would conclude she is still suffering from a case of sulks."

"Was Prola with her?"

Milroy sneered. "Mingling with the lesser folk? I think not. His kind requires a whiff of hartshorn if there is a stain on his coat."

Brock agreed. He glanced down at their clothes. They were streaked with grime and they smelled no better than a dustheap. "Amara seems to enjoy his attentions."

"Oh, I am certain he makes a fair escort and his lineage keeps her parents from ranting," his companion said, his blunt reasoning sending Brock's humor tumbling. "She is also my wife's dear friend so I doubt I am wrong in thinking she finds Prola useful in tormenting you over past sins."

"I disagree." The suggestion outraged him. "Amara is not devious."

"Perhaps not," he promptly agreed. "It is interesting you have not likewise denied the existence of your past sins."

Milroy was too astute. He had purposely hindered their work, forcing Brock to face his troubles.

"Is what stands between you so insurmountable that you will let someone like Prola take the woman you want?"

Amara deserved someone better than Conte Prola. His disreputable past probably made him equally unsuitable in her opinion. Brock's grip tightened on the handle. She was not the only one who had suffered, and whether he won her by persistence or seduction, he intended to have her.

"Amara is mine."

"I never doubted it," Milroy said, standing. He clanged the edge of his shovel against the stump. "If we want this torn from the turf before we lose the light, we will need a horse and some rope."

He swallowed the reluctant smile he sensed forming. The desire to pit his strength against an inanimate foe had receded with his temper. "A sensible plan," he conceded.

"Aye, that it is." He deliberately waited until Brock had started off toward the house for a servant. "And Bedegrayne?"

Brock halted.

"Once we finish our task, we can improve upon your crude wooing style." Milroy hooted with mirth. "That is, if she will have you after you locked her in a water closet!"

Burdened with a bulky package, Amara opened her bed-chamber door with her elbow. One of the footmen had explained that the mysterious gift had been delivered during her absence. Anticipating curiosity she might not want to assuage, she opted for privacy when she unwrapped it.

She kicked the door open with her foot and entered the room. Finding her cousin preening into her dressing table mirror was a revelation. Several japanned boxes that fit in the large drawer beneath had been removed.

Clutching her package in a protective manner, Amara said, "Bored? Skulking about my room provides a meager diversion. I recommend searching my mother's chamber. She tends to be rather negligent with her jewelry."

For being caught in a delicate position, Piper was unflustered. Meeting Amara's quizzical gaze in the mirror, she said, "You hide it so well under all that bookish naïveté."

"Hide what?" Setting the package on the nearest chair, Amara untied her bonnet.

Dancing her fingers lightly over the marzipan bouquet, her cousin broke off a flower petal and placed the sweet on her tongue. "Why, your accommodating morals, Miss Claeg."

She silently congratulated herself for not crushing her bonnet. With great care, she placed it beside the package. "A lecture from a trespasser and possible thief?" Her face hardened into a mocking mask. "If my father believes you have taken advantage of his generosity, you will be bundled off on the next stagecoach. Think of your father's humiliation. Disgraced, he will likely marry you off to some poor farmer who needs a strong back rather than a pretty gewgaw."

What Amara had described seemed coldhearted, but was close enough to the truth to crack the foundation of the woman's complacency. They both were aware her beautiful cousin's fate hinged on her success in London. Hatred glinted in Piper's dark green eyes. "Who do you think Lord Keyworth will believe? This house is not so large. The servants whisper about their lord's displeasure with his rebellious daughter."

They had reached a stalemate. It rankled her that their positions were not so different. "Even so, you will acquire no favor with Papa for spouting malicious lies about me. Do not pry into something that is not your concern."

Plucking another petal, Piper sucked on the sugary delicacy. She popped up from her chair. Hands behind her back, she strolled up to Amara. "I understand more than you think." She held out a sealed missive. When Amara reached for it, her cousin purposely allowed it to slip from her fingers.

Exasperated, she retrieved the note from the floor. "You may leave."

"You should be grateful I delivered your lover's amorous tidings to you and not your father."

Amara raised her brows at her cousin's absurdity. "Such imaginative musings should be applied to pen and paper. Consider this. If your work becomes wildly popular, you could abandon your pressing quest for a husband." She walked over to the table and picked up the confectionary bouquet. "Here. With my compliments." Amara thrust the flowers at her cousin. "I was never one for sweets."

"You are undeserving of a gentleman like Conte Prola. Why he would prefer you above me is baffling."

Amara pretended the observation was not a pitiful attempt to wound her and gave her an honest response. "Prola is enamored by Lord Keyworth's wealth. For all your beauty, you are one household away from being some child's governess."

The warning was not only for Piper. It was not prudent

to misjudge the conte's beguiling sincerity. He sought more than a bride. It was on the tip of her tongue to speak her thoughts aloud, but her barb had already sunk deep.

"Wretched harpy!" Piper seethed with so much fury her body trembled. Clasping the bouquet to her bosom, she still managed to slam the door.

"Good riddance," she said, even though she regretted the animosity between them. It was upsetting to be disliked. Whenever she considered mending their relationship, her cousin usually said something impertinent and their conflict resumed. At least Piper had been too absorbed in her resentment and had forgotten about the mysterious letter.

Turning the missive over, Amara broke the seal. Out of habit she moved to the window for the favorable light. She sat in her favorite chair and read the few lines aloud.

" 'One o'clock tomorrow in Finsbury Square.' Finsbury?" She wrinkled her nose. "Why there of all places?" Merchants inhabited the square; the most notable was a bookseller.

Going to her dressing table mirror, she pushed aside the small boxes her cousin had removed. Pulling out the narrow drawer beneath the mirror, she reached her hand deep into the slot. The first note, the one she had wrongly assumed had come from Brock, was jammed into one of the cracks. She grasped the edge with two fingers and withdrew it. Pressing down the folds, she compared them. The handwriting was identical. She was such a fool. Doran had been trying to contact her all along.

By evening, Amara had devised a plan. She was not optimistic of its success. The flutter plaguing her stomach had diminished her appetite, which had won her mother's interest. If the feeling did not cease soon, she would disgrace herself at the nearest commode.

Her father had departed for a meeting, while she, her mother, and Piper had remained home. Lady Keyworth's desire for an evening of solitude had fitted nicely with her own aspirations. After an early supper, the women had retired to the formal parlor. Piper sat at a small writing desk, composing letters to her sisters. Lady Keyworth was seated near the fireplace. With her spectacles perched on her nose, she was working on some embroidery she had neglected. Amara had also decided to embroider. After stabbing her thumb five times with the needle, she set her work aside. She was too clumsy for the delicate work. Instead, she picked up Thomas Moore's translation of *Odes of Anacreon*. The words ran together like wet ink on the page. The book, nevertheless, kept her hands occupied and provided an excuse for her lapses in conversation.

After half an hour had passed, Amara placed the open book on her lap. "Mama, I received a note this afternoon."

The endless scratching from her cousin's pen halted at her bold confession. If Piper had contemplated blackmail, Amara had effectively foiled any future attempt.

"Anyone I know?" her mother asked, her attention focused on her stitches.

She fidgeted a little at using the name of a dear friend. However, she believed Brook would understand the necessity. "Yes. Lady A'Court."

Lady Keyworth paused. "She is residing in London?"

She understood her mother's surprise. Brook had fled London after her husband's death. The tragic circumstances surrounding his death and the loss of the child she carried had been too much for her friend. While most of the *ton* thought the countess was simply in mourning, Amara knew her absence was more complicated.

"A week at most. She is being very discreet. No one is aware she has returned and she insists that her presence not be revealed." Lowering her voice in a confidential inflection, she said, "There is still talk about the earl. I doubt she is prepared for all the speculation."

"Who is Lady A'Court?" her cousin interjected.

"A good friend," Amara replied, not offering Piper further explanation. She switched her attention to her mother. "Brook only has a few days left before her departure. She has invited me to visit her."

"If she has opened the family town house, no amount of discretion will keep her presence a secret," Lady Keyworth predicted.

Would her mother not be shocked if she learned the son she thought dead was prowling about town? She needed Doran's advice on how this could be accomplished without giving their mother heart failure. Or perhaps, due to their hostile parting, Doran was not yearning to see their parents at all. The depressing insight explained her brother's secretiveness.

"No, the house remains closed. I assume there were too many memories. Since her stay is short, she took some rooms." Amara hesitated. "With your permission, I would like to accept her hospitality. I had almost given up hope. She never answered any of my letters." That much was true. Neither she, Wynne, nor Devona had heard from their friend.

Her mother pushed her slipping spectacles higher and studied her efforts. "Lady A'Court will need her friends when she returns to polite society. You are fortunate the family considers you part of their intimate circle. I see no reason to deny your request."

Amara resisted the urge to wrap her mother in a zealous embrace. She was being offered more than she had hoped. Still, she could not resist pressing, "If the hour is late?"

Lady Keyworth frowned at her obtuseness. "Naturally, you will remain through the night if necessary."

The flutters in her stomach soared into her heart. They burst from her chest. Tomorrow she would be reunited with her brother. She had hours, no a day, to convince him that his family longed for his return.

CHAPTER FIFTEEN

Subterfuge rarely went unpunished. Curled around a pillow on her bed, Amara endured a restless night expecting to hear her father's fist pounding on the door. Their few conversations had been terse and weighted with commands. Needless to say, if she replied with something other than, "Yes, Papa," Lord Keyworth stared her down into silence. He viewed anything that distracted her from his private objectives as trivial, and sadly, even Doran's miraculous resurrection would not save her. Their father had disowned Doran when he had been imprisoned for his coining misdeeds. His return, if she managed to convince him to reveal his presence, might not be heralded with the enthusiasm worthy of a prodigal son. But she felt compelled to at least make the attempt.

Amara had slept later than she wanted; however, when she descended the stairs several hours later, their butler, Buckle, had told her that she was the first to awaken. She declined breakfast, not caring to linger in case her good fortune faltered. Since she had sent her maid down earlier, a carriage was already waiting. Accepting a straw-colored parasol from Buckle, she bid him adieu. One of the footmen helped her ascend the narrow steps into the carriage. She plucked at the fabric of her skirt, satisfied with her choice. She wanted to look her best for Doran without being conspicuous.

Corry had suggested a high-necked short dress of jaconet muslin. A stone-colored round mantle lined with a delicate pink covered her shoulders and flowed down to the back of her knees. Her hair had been parted down the middle and tucked under a bonnet of white-willow shavings that was adorned with pink rosebuds. Wisps of curls at her temples softened the severity of the look.

She ordered the coachman to take her to Lackington's. Once they had reached the bookseller's shop, she intended to send the carriage home. Amara required no witnesses to her perfidy. She assumed Doran had his own equipage. If not, a hackney would suffice. The details mattered little when she was minutes away from seeing the brother she had thought she would never see again.

Her trepidation increased when the multistory brick frontage of the shop came into view. High above a dome, a large flag flapped languidly from its flagpole, signaling the owner was in residence. The original proprietor, James Lackington, had retired years earlier. One of the gentleman's cousins and his partner, a Mr. Allen, ran the immense shop with its huge circular counter. Their inventory surpassed any private library. The rare and the illicit were found there.

The coachman climbed down from his perch and helped her out of the carriage. "Shall I wait out front or drive around the square until I see you?"

"You are spared from doing both, Jem," she said,

slightly distracted while she confirmed the items in her reticule. "My friend will see me home."

Jem had been in the family's employ for years. Glancing up, she could tell he was not pleased by her answer. The coachman was not watching her, but the pedestrians. It was too early in the day for the fashionable *ton* to be about; on the other hand neither was he abandoning her to roaming gangs of ruffians. She was quite safe.

"My friend is meeting me here." The instructions were a bit vague, but the bookseller's shop seemed to be a logical place. Doran probably recalled her fondness for books. "Stop scowling, Jem. I have Mama's approval. Besides, I am certain Mr. Lackington and Mr. Allen do not approve of their patrons being assaulted. Poor for business, you know."

"You will keep to the shop." He wiggled his brows in a manner that always made her smile. Since he was wearing his stern face, she doubted he was trying to be humorous so she bit down on her lower lip.

"Yes, Jem." She rushed back to the carriage. "Oh, my parasol!" Amara snatched it up and gave the man a rueful smile. "Too forgetful." She started for the shop's door.

"Miss Claeg. This friend of yours wouldn't be a gent by chance?" the coachman called out.

Amara gulped some air. "With Mama's approval? How absurd."

Climbing back onto his perch, Jem removed his tricorne and slapped the dust from it. "Lord Keyworth would sever my cods if harm came to you. Or if I let you run off to Gretna Green with some rake."

She was not positive what the man meant by his "cods," but she had tasted her father's displeasure. Summoning a smile this time was more difficult. "Jem, let us leave the fiction *inside* the shop."

The teasing comment earned a chuckle. Waving her off, the servant stayed until she had entered the shop. Once inside, Amara stood in front of one of the huge Palladian windows. She lifted a hand in farewell and watched his departure.

It was almost one o'clock. Still believing the shop was the likely choice for their meeting, Amara made a casual perusal of her surroundings. Despite the hour, the shop was filled with customers. She effortlessly picked out five women who were without an escort so any apprehension that she might call attention to herself vanished.

The shop attracted hordes of women because it carried those wildly popular novels most gentlemen detested. Lady Keyworth had discouraged her from reading them too. She feared such implausibly romantic tales might persuade her young daughter toward folly. For her, as for most young ladies with a good measure of curiosity, the forbidden was an irresistible temptation.

In secret, Amara had read those novels her mother had disparaged. The stories had been wickedly adventurous and romantic, not to mention highly improbable. She had closed each book, satisfied with the happy conclusions. What surprised her was that after the adventure had faded from her thoughts, a lingering sadness remained. Older, she now understood her mother's concern. Real life palled when compared to the excessive misery and ardent obsession printed out on those splendid pages. An ordinary husband might be viewed as a cruel substitute.

She thought of Conte Prola and sighed.

Following the walls, she roamed the shop. Thousands

of books beckoned, yet she resisted. She climbed the stairs and searched the upper floor. No Doran. The note had stated Finsbury Square. Perhaps she had gotten it wrong.

She stepped outside and opened her parasol. Strolling down the walkway, she peered into several other shops. One of the approaching gentlemen turned his head as they passed. Amara returned his admiring leer with a fixed cold stare. Contrite, he lowered his gaze and continued his ramble in the opposite direction.

Her throat worked as she swallowed her growing anger. It was just like her brother to muddle the simplest plan. Not all of her family's frustration with Doran was unfounded. Amara halted her promenade, studying the passengers in the carriages and riders on horseback. None of the faces was familiar.

Discouraged, she let her gaze travel to the grounds in the center. The contour was circular. Along the perimeter an iron railing and shrubbery enclosed the commons. She noted the gate had been left open. Two wagons were stationary near the entrance. One was stacked with water casks. The other was heaped with potted plants and garden tools. Obviously, some jobbing gardeners were tending to the maintenance of the square.

Inspired, Amara closed her parasol and stepped into the street. Pausing for a speeding carriage, she rushed forward, barely evading a man on horseback. The frightened horse shied to the left. The words the man shouted at her were hardly complimentary and disqualified him as a gentleman. She fought the urge to cover her eyes when another carriage passed close enough to ruffle her skirt. Not caring if her ankles were visible, she dashed the remaining distance.

Laying a hand across her heart, she was panting from

fear and the exertion. When she caught her breath again, she would search the common for her errant sibling. Rough hands seized her from behind and whirled her around. The shock altered her scream into a pathetic yelp.

Dimly, she recognized the stark face. It was Brock who held her in a painful grip. He hauled her up on her toes and shook her. "Of all the—" His voice gave out as his fury strangled him. "What were you doing? Do you know how many times you nearly died? I swear, you have more hair than wit." Cursing, he crushed her to his chest.

Neither the fright nor Brock's proximity was able to calm her pounding heart. Pressed tightly against him, she returned his embrace. There was nothing she could do until he was inclined to release her.

"You watched me cross the street?"

Reluctantly, he pulled back. Her bonnet was askew from his forceful handling. Brock lowered her to her feet. While he kept a hand on her, he used the other to straighten her bonnet. "I noticed a foolish woman stepping out into the street. When I realized it was you, I almost had heart failure. Can you imagine how I felt, wanting to call out and yet afraid the distraction would likely kill you?"

"I never anticipated how dangerous the street—"

Renewed anger had him yelling, "Damn it, Amara! You were not thinking at all. It is nothing short of a miracle you survived."

She was trembling. Oh, not as the result of his anger, she knew she deserved it. Her body trembled because she knew he spoke the truth. The crossing must have seemed to him wholly suicidal. "An apology for surviving seems a trifle peculiar. I offer it just the same."

He muttered something unintelligible under his breath

and hugged her again. She felt the subtle quaking of his body. "So I am being irrational. It complements your lunacy. See what a fine pair we make?"

She let him hold her, longer than was proper. He felt like the sun, and she was so cold. Remembering where they were, she was the first to pull back. "Why are you here?" An awful suspicion diminished the joy of being in his presence again. "Were you following me?"

He gave her an infuriated glare. "I thought we had already established you were the one who was touched."

Amara ignored the barb. Brock was too offended at her charge to be lying. Unless, she thought, she had been searching for the wrong man. "It is merely coincidence that brings us together on the same day, the same time."

He looked abashed by her sarcasm. The light breeze surged and played with the strands of blond hair that had escaped his queue. "Not precisely," he hedged.

She had been associating with the Bedegraynes too long not to have witnessed some of the males' under-handed practices. "Good heavens, you have had me watched. It all makes sense," she said to herself. "Brock Bedegrayne, you had no right! Who did you employ? One of the footmen, or was this task worthy of a runner?" She recalled the strange gentleman who had stared at her beyond decorum and could not prevent a shudder of repugnance.

"I have employed no one, but if anyone needs a keeper it is you!" he said, losing his temper, again. "Tipton's man was headed for the vinegar manufactory near Old Street when he caught sight of your carriage. He was not pleased that you were alone, and thought I might feel the same. Once he learned your destination, he sought me out." He scowled down at her. "So I rushed here only to see you weaving your way through a gauntlet of horses and equipages. Do you know what? Speck was correct. I am not pleased."

"That gargoyle," she seethed. Loyal to Lord Tipton, the servant had an unearthly gift for discerning trouble and took his guardian duties too seriously, much to the chagrin of the female Bedegraynes. "Are there not enough Bedegraynes in town to occupy his time?"

His lips curled into a parody of a smile. "Speck thinks fondly of you, also, for which I shall be eternally thankful. Now tell me, where are your people so I can strangle them for their incompetence?"

"I sent my coachman home."

"What?" he queried so quietly, she felt the need to rub the prickling sensation from her arms.

A thump from behind distracted her. She glanced back in time to see the wagon behind her quiver. The owner was nowhere in sight. The wheels strained forward a few inches. The horses were restless.

Brock cuffed her wrist. She forgot all about the animals when he pulled her closer. His expression frightened her. Although he leaned toward officious, he was never intentionally cruel.

"Are you meeting someone?" he demanded.

A rumble diverted her attention. She turned her head and watched in horror as the wooden pyramid of water casks shifted, straining against the rope restraints. The sickening clunk terrified the horses. The team kicked at the wagon.

Everything seemed to slow down around her. Brock shouted a warning in her ear and hoisted her off her feet as she saw several ropes snap free. The struggling horses jolted the wagon. She opened her mouth to scream. It never emerged. A final jolt and the pyramid collapsed. The first two casks rolled off the wagon and burst when they struck the ground. Amara had the sensation of flying backward. The back of her head connected with Brock's chin as they hit the ground. The rumble was deafening. He rolled them toward the gate. His body pressed her into the iron railings while the remaining casks thundered by them into the street.

The stale water seeping into her half-boots and stockings revived her. The world around her resumed its harried pace. Grasping one of the iron bars, she pulled herself up. The rolling casks had struck one carriage, overturning it. The horses had bolted, dragging the battered equipage and the occupants into a landau. She could not tell the difference between the human and animal shrieks. One horse was down and struggling to get up. She assumed its legs were broken. Ten yards away, a body was sprawled facedown in the dirt. Nearby, two gentlemen scooped up a sobbing woman and carried her off the street. The front of her gown was stained with blood. Amara looked away and gagged.

Brock surged up. Taking most of the impact must have dazed him. Cupping her face, he asked, "Are you hurt?" Not waiting for her reply, he felt her shoulders and down along her arms in search of some injury.

"You saved us," she said dully, praying she would not faint. "I was just standing there gaping at the wagon. You—"

A man rushed to them and crouched down. From his clothes, she assumed he was one of the gardeners. "Are you and the lady hurt? When I saw them hogsheads give, I figured it was dead bodies we'd be pulling out from the rubble."

Amara shivered. Brock helped her stand. "We are unharmed," he assured the upset man.

"Others—" She forced herself to look at the pandemonium in the street. "Check the people in the street."

The gardener dug his grimy fingers under his hat and scratched behind his left ear. "I don't see how this happened. Those water casks were secure, I tell you. I tied the ropes myself." Muttering reassurances, the man wandered into the street.

Brock and Amara approached the wagon. Someone had unyoked the horses and led them away from the disorder. He picked up one of the severed ropes and examined the end. Thoughtful, Brock bent down and retrieved another end.

"It was a horrible accident," she said, kicking aside a wooden rib and iron hoop to salvage her parasol. The water and mud had ruined it. She let it drop at her feet.

"So it appears." Bracing his hands on the wagon's splintered side, he abruptly said, "I will take you home."

"I cannot," Amara protested. She had lied and risked her life for this meeting. She doubted Doran would reveal himself now that Brock was with her. All of this had been for naught. The beginnings of a megrim throbbed in her right eye.

"You were meeting someone. Who? Prola?"

Somehow they had circled back to their conversation before the accident. "Not Conte Prola. In fact, I was doing my best to avoid the man!"

Her vehement reply eased the severity in his expression. "Who?"

She was not prepared to share her news of Doran's return with anyone. Tipton had risked his reputation in order to smuggle her brother out of England. Knowing

Doran had disobeyed the viscount's edict by returning divided her loyalties. She had to find her brother before he was recognized.

"No one," she told Brock. "If I return home, Mama will know I lied about Brook."

"Lady A'Court? She is responsible for this?"

His expression told Amara that mentioning the A'Court name to Brock had been a mistake. In spite of his anger, Brock was too fair to blame a helpless woman for her husband's scandalous deeds. Lord A'Court had been a sadistic fiend who hid behind his title and a thin guise of civility.

"No, Brook is not in town." She faced him. "I lied, Brock. I told my family I was visiting her. I placed myself in this outrageous predicament, so I deserve the harsh consequences. You are a sensible gentleman. What daring I have for pulling you into my deception! I accept your gracious offer. Take me home."

He escorted her away from the wagon. At some point during their discourse, the wrecked carriages had been dragged off the street and the victims had been carried off into Lackington's. Someone had summoned a surgeon. Only shrinking puddles of water and the shattered remains of the casks hinted at the tragedy.

Following the circumference of the grounds, Brock surprised her by catching her by the waist and crossing the street. They made it across without incident. He guided her toward a phaeton. A man she did not recognize nodded to them as he jumped down from the carriage. He moved on to the horses.

She could not believe Brock had been so careless as to leave his equipage in the hands of a stranger. "This is when I reprimand you for, oh, what was the phrase you used? Having more hair than wit?"

"Oh, I lost my wits completely when I met you, Amara Claeg," he said, lifting her into his phaeton. He left her alone for a few minutes while he thanked the stranger who had cared for his horses. After a brief contest of wills, the man accepted the coins Brock was offering him and departed with a wave of his hand.

Brock continued their conversation as if he had not been interrupted. "Who do you think blindly charged after you when I saw you in the middle of the street? We were both fortunate to survive your reckless impulse."

"I suppose I was not thinking at all," she miserably replied. The accident with the carriages was too fresh in her mind. She could effortlessly picture Brock's broken body under the wheels of a swift carriage.

Something in her expression must have given away her thoughts. As he climbed in beside her, he patted her thigh. "It did not happen. Put it from your mind." Taking up the reins, he signaled the horse to set off.

"You never explained why you lied to your family," Brock said, waiting until they had left the square before he engaged her in conversation again.

"Have you ever wanted to escape? Forget for a day what is expected of you? Pretend you are actually being offered choices?"

Brock gave consideration to her wistful questions. "Now and then. If you believe Irene, I quit England for the adventure. Just another Bedegrayne son shirking his birthright."

"Was she right?"

His slanting glance was enigmatic. "Partly."

If he thought she would pry, he would be disappointed. He was entitled to his privacy. Besides, it had been a difficult time. They had both spoken unkind words. She would rather not revisit the painful memories.

"When are you supposed to return from your visit with A'Court's widow?"

The sudden change of topic flustered her. In truth, she was ashamed she had revealed this unflattering side of her nature. Staring down at her mud-encrusted reticule, she said, "You must think I am a depraved creature, spinning lies like a spider on a garden wall."

She jerked her head up sharply at his spurt of laughter. "Depraved? Amara, if you are a prime example of depravity, then the rest of us are doomed to blister eternally in hellfire." The humor died on his face. "You have been raised with privilege and a heavy hand. On occasion, my family and I have noticed your fair skin has been mottled by that rigidity."

This discussion was mortifying. His words laid her bare. "Please—"

"Do not defend them," he said, his voice rising with his resentment. "Feeble excuses will never redeem them. They are unworthy of your devotion." His hard gaze had not wavered from the street. "Is it so strange their dove, like your father's cherished falcons, yearns for the freedom of the heavens? Do you expect me to admonish you? I would cut the tether myself if I thought you would not later despise me for it."

His generosity overwhelmed her. She bit down on her lip to prevent herself from telling him about Doran. Recalling his earlier question about Brook, she said, "Since most of my plans are half-baked as you so solicitously pointed out, I was rather vague with my family."

"A benevolent friend, you would remain throughout the night if asked," he mused.

Why were they discussing this? She was suffused with guilt. Amara planned to write Brook immediately and confess her sins. "It would be expected."

When they stopped for a turnpike, she finally became aware they had not deviated from their northern route. Amara looked askance at Brock. For a lost traveler, he was too relaxed. They were not headed in the direction of her family's town house. She waited until he paid the toll. "I am not confident I warrant a reprieve. However, I imagine any of your sisters would take me in if I asked."

"No."

Perhaps she had misunderstood. She wished he offered her more than his inscrutable profile. "If you are taking me home, we are heading in the wrong direction."

His mouth lifted in a faint grin. "No."

Bashing him on the skull with her reticule held a growing appeal. "You are not taking me home, nor to one of your sisters. Just what are you doing, Brock Bedegrayne?"

"Why, I am kidnapping you, Amara Claeg." With a flick of his wrists, the horses hastened their pace.

CHAPTER SIXTEEN

The view changed from town to countryside before Amara remembered to close her mouth. Brock was respectful of the unpredictability of the horses and road so he barely spared her a glance once he had assured himself she had not fainted.

Her speechlessness fascinated him. It also saved him from having to gag her, not that he was wholly convinced he could resort to such a high-handed maneuver, even though a screaming companion would hinder his plans. Amara had thought herself a devious creature. Once she found her voice, what names would she call him when she realized he was not above taking advantage of her deception?

London was behind them, when she stirred from her silence. "Jem was worried about me racing off to Gretna Green." Amara did not seem upset about her predicament, just curious.

"Who the devil is Jem?"

"Jem is our coachman, and if I had any sense I might have realized sooner that you are the devil."

Since they were alone on the road, he risked a cocky grin. "Gretna Green, you say. What are you proposing, Amara?"

There was primness to her spine, even though she was wearing a dusty gown and mangled bonnet. "Nothing," she said. "I just do not want to be responsible for Jem's severed cods."

Brock choked. "Christ, Amara, vulgarity spewing from your delectable mouth is more than I can bear. Someone should discourage your coachman from using rough language in your presence."

"He was distracted," she said apologetically. "After all, they were his cods. I am not clear on what these items exactly are, but he was distressed at the thought of losing them."

Holding his breath, he tried not to laugh. It would only encourage her. He counted to forty-five. In unison, they exploded into laughter.

"There, you see?" he said, after their merriment had ebbed into grins. "You have just proven you were in urgent need of kidnapping. It has been days since I have heard you laugh."

"We have not seen each other in days," was her dry retort.

"Not by choice. You have a nasty habit of avoiding me," he said, keeping his voice light. If he gave in to the hurt and frustration, he might yell and ruin their truce.

"Do you kidnap all the ladies who resist your charms?" she asked, still skeptical about the sincerity of his boast. "I have often wondered if the infamous gossip about you was justified."

Brock had no intention of regaling her with tales of drunken revelry and forgotten conquests. Every young man was permitted lapses in judgment. By Jove, he had been wild, living on anger and nerve. That part of his past was best forgotten.

"You are my first kidnapping. I pray you will make allowances," he implored. Brock conceded he was ill prepared for their hasty journey. However, he was not without resources. His time away from his homeland had taught him how to cope with the unforeseen.

"Fustian! This is a jest," she said, crossing her arms. "You have a myriad of flaws but you are not spiteful. You would not knowingly tarnish my reputation."

He winced at her blithe assertion of his character. "So nice of you to be so understanding of my faults. However, you have overlooked one thing."

"What?"

"Your family believes you are visiting Lady A'Court," he said, noting how her triumphant expression fell at his observation. "Alas, you are not without flaws. For instance, this propensity for dissembling. Most gentlemen would not be so indulgent."

"Indulgent," she fumed, realizing she had sprung the trap herself. "I call it knavery. You are taking advantage of my embarrassing predicament!"

"Consider it another of my lamentable failings, dove."

Amara shifted in her seat; her backside felt numb from their bone-jarring drive. Few words had been exchanged on their mysterious jaunt. She had fallen into a shrewish silence once he convinced her that nothing would discourage him from his course. He had accepted her silence with a cheery tolerance that did little to improve her mood.

From her estimation, they had been traveling for more than two hours. Brock had taken them north and slightly east. The deflection at least allayed any concern he was taking her into Scotland. They had stopped an hour into their journey when they had chanced upon a coaching inn. He had explained that the horses needed a rest. The truth was, she had needed the respite more than the agile team. She and Brock had separated, each seeing to their personal needs.

If he had been worried she might run off or announce her abduction to a sympathetic ear, he had concealed it well. Amara had not approved of his high-handedness, but she did trust him. Besides, the scoundrel had known that publicly revealing his temerity would merely gain her the tarnish she so dearly wished to avoid.

On his return, he had found her pacing the yard. The walk had improved her spirits. He had acquired a hamper during their brief parting. Once he had settled her in the phaeton, Brock moved to the rear and secured the hamper. Sensing her needs, he had satisfied her curiosity about the hamper by handing her a bean tart. Too many hours had elapsed since her last meal. She had mumbled her thanks, but it was her stomach rumbling its deepest appreciation for his thoughtfulness that earned her a chuckle and a tug on one of her curls.

More than an hour had passed since the inn. Although the tart had eased her hunger, the shaking and dipping of the carriage was not improving the budding stiffness in her shoulders from Brock's heroic tackle.

"I like a female who is not a gabbler," Brock said, smashing the wall of silence she had thrown up between them. "Makes her seem very biddable."

Very tricky, Amara thought. Brock had figured out how to goad her into speaking to him again. She surrendered to the inevitable. He had saved her life. Fed her when she was hungry. Brooding seemed mean-spirited. Besides, she had shrugged off her initial frustration long ago. Sometime during their quiet journey it had evolved into a companionable silence. She had enjoyed the quiet as much as the sprawling peaceful countryside.

"Since I am intimately acquainted with your sisters, I doubt you have ever encountered a biddable female," she countered, offering the olive branch he craved.

"It was more of a declaration than a preference," he corrected himself.

She matched his smile. "I thought as much."

The road they traveled was rutted and slowed their progress. It was not much bigger than the trails used by the occasional dairy herds she saw in the distance. Coughing on the dust they stirred, she gave in to her curiosity. "Did we miss our turn for Hyde Park or do you have a specific destination in mind?"

Brock shot her a look of disbelief. "Only you would wait hours to ask that question. Yes, Amara, I have brought you out here to see more than potato and wheat fields."

He maneuvered the horses down a long lane. The hedges outlining their path were overgrown and shapeless from neglect. Amara frowned at the imposing dwelling they were approaching. Whoever its owner, the man had neglected his property. The house was old, and in her opinion, was a step away from being considered a ruin. The four three-story octagonal towers flanking the main structure were most likely part of the original structure. The stone was crumbling in places, and the numerous windows were void of glass. A dense creeping vine was consuming the front left tower. The main part of the dwelling seemed to have been built at another time. Perhaps not recently, but someone had been restoring the dwelling. The front door appeared new and the glass in the windows gleamed in the sunlight, even though the stone needing a good cleaning.

Abruptly, the lane opened into an unremarkable rectangular gravel yard. With a brisk command to the team, Brock halted the phaeton in front of the house. When no one came rushing out to attend them, she switched her questioning gaze on Brock.

Scrutinizing the building with more appreciation than it deserved, he asked, "Amazing, is it not? During the reign of James the First all this land was a deer park."

Bemused by his enthusiasm, she watched him jump down from the carriage. He secured the horses to a hitching post. She accepted his hand, when he returned to her side. "I am amazed the house still stands. Brock, it is a derelict."

"Not quite," he said, her assessment dimming some of his initial excitement. "The towers are all that remain from the original dwelling. It belonged to the Whitmott family. A fire gutted most of the house about eighty years ago. The family rebuilt, but the lord died before the restoration was finished. His widow preferred the seaside, so the house was abandoned and eventually sold."

"Are you acquainted with the owner?"

"Well enough," he said. "About seven years ago, Will Streden bought the house and much of the original acreage. He wanted a hunting lodge when he was bored with London, and entertained the notion of restoring the red and fallow deer to Whitmott Park."

"I assume his aspirations met with failure."

"Streden is easily diverted," he said, apologetically. "After the fire in the kitchen—"

"Another fire!" Aghast, Amara wondered if all that remained of the house was a charred shell.

"Streden had not foreseen the necessity of moving the kitchen and the servants' quarters from their original subterranean level. Due to the quick actions of the servants, the fire was confined only to the lower level."

"Mr. Streden was fortunate he did not lose the entire house."

"I agree. He did, however, lose his passion for restoring Whitmott Park. Shortly after the fire, he placed the property on the auction block."

The way in which Brock stared at the house confirmed her growing suspicion. His manner was undeniably proprietary. "You bought the house," she said bluntly.

"Several years ago," he admitted, not surprised she had guessed. "And most of the land being auctioned." He escorted her to the door. "Regrettably, the purchase left my funds at low ebb. Until recently, the house remained in the state in which it had been abandoned by Streden."

"Surely, Sir Thomas—"

He agreed with a nod. "He might have, if I had asked. Nevertheless, the house is mine. Its upkeep is my responsibility."

Amara shook her head, as he opened the door for her. While other gentlemen would have raided the family's wherewithal without thought, Brock had too much pride to choose the easier path. His successes and failures were his own.

She stepped inside. The air within was not as stale as she had expected. They entered the large hall. The stone floor was barren, but someone had recently swept the dust and polished the glass in the windows. Amara pivoted when they reached the center of the hall and lifted her brows in curiosity.

"I have been out here a time or two since my return,"

he explained. "I hired some local men and women from the village to clean up the years of neglect. Until the kitchen and servants' quarters are rebuilt, I have no use for a full-time staff."

Amara strode to the chimneypiece large enough to spit a whole stag. The oak paneling was simplistic in its design. The hearth had been designed for use, not for pleasing the eye. She glanced up, taking in barren plaster walls holding up a lofty timbered ceiling. It was easy to imagine what this room might have looked like in another century. Instead of the barrenness of neglect, prized antler mountings and elaborate tapestries depicting the success of the hunt would have covered the walls. Interspersed throughout the room, swords, bows, and shields would have not only provided ornamentation but readiness if the need for arms arose.

"Where did you go?"

She was chagrined to have him catch her daydreaming; the image she had built in her mind disintegrated. The bare walls, cracked and stained by age and the elements, returned. "Considering the possibilities." She was too embarrassed to reveal the extent of her fanciful musings.

He blinked in surprise. By his spontaneous grin, she could tell her answer pleased him. "Aye," he said, rubbing his jaw. "This place does make a person dream."

"The house needs more than a dreamer. You will have to possess a vast amount of patience and a respectable fortune to restore it," she warned.

"I can claim both."

"Truly?"

She tried not to stiffen when he came up behind her. Sliding his hands over the delicate bones of her shoulders, he lightly kneaded her taut muscles. "You are proof of the first. My travels abroad ensured the second." He kissed the back of her head and released her.

"I will see to the horses."

Patience! She could think of no man who had less than Brock. He exuded his lack with every flicker of expression and the way he moved as if the people around him were only delaying him from his aspirations. The notion was absurd. Instead of laughing, Amara turned toward the door, wanting an explanation of how she proved the first.

He was out the door before she could stop him. "Have a care, if you cannot resist exploring in my absence," he called out over his shoulder. "If you fall through some rotting flooring and break your lovely neck, I doubt even I will be able to come up with a plausible explanation for your family."

Brock took his time with the horses. He had pushed the team hard, getting them to Whitmott Park. The animals deserved a little pampering. Milroy was not the only member of the family who appreciated prime horseflesh.

He also thought Amara might prefer some time apart from him. Like his horses, she seemed undaunted by their adventure. If he could convince her, Brock had every intention of pampering the lady as well.

The hall was empty when he returned. Brock shouted her name. He listened to his fading echo and then chilling silence. The front door had been left open, he had assumed from his departure. An irrational fear that she had escaped on foot danced down his spine, even as he ruthlessly discarded the thought. If Amara had been afraid of him, she'd had a dozen opportunities to call attention to her undesirable predicament before he took her out of

London. She had ignored all her chances to escape him.

Heartened by his logic, Brock retraced his steps outdoors. Following his instincts, he headed east toward the lake. It was approximately twenty acres in size, and Brock suspected one of the Whitmott heirs was responsible for its creation, although nature through the passing centuries had refined the man-made effect.

There near the shore of the lake, he found Amara. She had removed her dusty mantle and had put it to better use as a blanket. Unaware of his presence, she faced the soothing beauty of the lake. Removing her bonnet, she tossed it aside. With bare hands she reached for the back of her head. Her nimble fingers sought out each pin and captured them into the palm of her hand. Free of restraints, her dark brown tresses billowed in the slight breeze as the ends teasingly danced down her shoulders.

"You look like a water nymph."

Amara started at his voice. He was already regretting his impetuous words when she gathered up her hair and gave it an efficient twist.

"Leave it down," he entreated, sitting down beside her. He brushed away her hands and appreciatively fingered the windswept tresses that always had reminded him of polished mahogany. "Having it twisted and pinned in that fashion would give anyone a fretful headache. Besides, I like it best when you have it down."

The look she gave him through the silken curtain was coy. "You have a remarkable memory, since I was a girl the last time I was running about with my hair down."

"It was longer then," he said, deliberately drawing a horizontal line across her back. "Long enough to skim your hips." She had been a beautiful girl and he had been too old to be noticing her.

Oblivious of his uncomfortable memories, she laughed. The sound was as fluid and pure as the water lapping at their feet. She used her palm to brace herself, the action bringing her closer. "Doran liked my hair too. Do you recall the summer you and Mallory found me tied to a tree limb by my hair?"

Amara had been seven or eight that particular summer. He and Mallory had returned from hunting when they had found her hopelessly snarled. "You were crying for Doran's head, I recall. You begged me for my knife so you could sever it from his neck yourself."

She shook her head. "I was never so bloodthirsty."

"You were bloody furious," he corrected. "By the time we had cut you free, you had lost a good amount of hair."

"Mama blamed everyone," she reminisced without rancor. "Doran for tying my hair to the blasted tree. Me for allowing him to do it. You for having the knife." She sighed. "As punishment, I was not allowed to leave my bedchamber for a week."

Brock imagined being banished from the family had been difficult for the eight-year-old girl, but he kept his thoughts to himself. "Why did Doran tie your hair to that limb?"

She squinted at the sunlight, reaching inward for the memory. "I believe we were playing coachman. The limb was his perch and I was the—" She faltered.

Following the recollection to its obvious conclusion, Brock laughed. The more she scowled at him, the harder he laughed. Holding his ribs, he gasped for breath. "He made you the horse! What was he using your hair for—reins?"

"I do not remember!" she denied, her expression mutinous. "You said that I was demanding his head for the prank. What punishment does the gentleman who mocks me deserve?"

He could not recall a recent occasion when he had laughed so much. With his side aching, he fell onto his back, knocking his hat free from his head. Amara took advantage of his weakness and pounced. Rolling on top of him, she tickled him with a ruthless capability only his sisters had managed in their youth. He howled with laughter that bordered on pain.

"Cease, witch!"

Naturally, she disregarded his order. "Well, well . . . who would have guessed the handsome, arrogant Bedegrayne could be defeated by a mere woman?" She dug into his sides and was rewarded by more laughter. "I can think of a man or two who would pay dearly to learn Brock Bedegrayne is ticklish."

She was teasing. He hoped. Gazing up at her triumphant heart-shaped visage was no hardship, but enough was enough. A man had his pride. Taking advantage of a brief pause in her assault, he seized her by the waist and expertly flipped her onto her back. He straddled her hips. "You were saying?"

Amara's eyes widened, amazed by the speed with which he had neatly reversed their positions. It was hardly proper or fair, but he could not resist. Digging his fingers under her arms, he tickled her without mercy. Laughing, she arched her back, trying to bounce him off with her pelvis. "Beast. Get . . . off!"

Brock stilled as she writhed beneath him. Although her movements were not meant to entice, his body reacted. Desire bubbled through his system like white sparkling wine. Every time she rubbed her body against his, a cannonade of need punctured his restraint. Longing or something more dangerous must have shown in his eyes.

The carefree amusement that had lit her entire face earlier hardened into awareness. Blowing out her breath, she pushed at his chest. "Off," she said. The confusion and wariness clouding her eyes made him feel low enough to slither across the ground. "Get off. Now!"

He was not holding her down, so she sat up and shoved at him. Brock swung his leg clear and backed away from her. Pulling her knees to her bodice, she hugged them to her body and rocked, drawing comfort from the action.

"I—" Sickened that he had done anything to make her compare his touch to that bastard Cornley, he absently rubbed his stomach. "It was only play. I would never hurt you," he said quietly.

Amara peered at him over her knees. "I know." She sighed. "The fault is not yours. I was the one who climbed all over you. I should have realized sooner."

"What should you have realized, dove?" he prompted when she failed to finish her thought.

She looked as if she regretted speaking her thoughts aloud. Brock did not care if they sat there until sunset. She was going to tell him what put the mistrust back in her eyes. It was too late for either one of them to hide behind a wall of politeness and manners.

"Friend or not, when a woman presses herself against a man, no matter how innocently, he is likely to become encouraged. Inflamed."

Inflamed? That was one word for it. The condition seemed permanent around Amara. "You panicked because you were concerned about encouraging me?" he asked, not wanting to misunderstand her.

Indignation flared in her stormy blue eyes. "I did not panic!"

"No, you did not," he said, reviewing the encounter in his mind. "Not at first. It was not until I knocked you on your back and pinned you down that you became upset." *Just like Cornley.*

Amara laid her cheek on her knee and watched a trio of ducks gliding across the lake's glassy surface. "This is not about Cornley."

"The devil it is not," he said grimly. He crawled around to the other side, putting himself between her and the lake. "He is the reason you spent years pretending I did not exist."

She jerked her head up. "You exaggerate," she scoffed. "For goodness' sake, you have spent the last two years in India!"

Amara was deliberately being obtuse. "I speak of the years before I left," he said impatiently. "Cornley perished in that fire, but I was the one you treated like a ghost."

Her movements had become stiffer with her increasing agitation. "What are you saying?"

"You have spent so many years looking right through me, Amara, I resorted to checking my reflection in a mirror from time to time just to make certain I still existed."

"That is ridiculous."

"Is it?" He sat back on his heels. "You blamed me for your defilement."

"What? No, I—" She shook her head. "Is this why you brought me here? You want to spend the afternoon discussing pieces of my past that I have tried so hard to forget?" Her eyes glittered with unshed tears, provoked more by anger than sorrow.

"Do not feel guilty. I have spent years blaming myself," Brock said, his voice full of regret.

Amara braced a hand on the ground to help her get onto her feet. "I refuse to listen to another word."

He jumped up, and blocked her from escaping. "I never trusted Cornley. I should have guessed his intentions that night. If I had watched you with more care, been quicker in my search, he—"

"Stop!" she begged, slapping her hands over her ears. She glared at him through haunted eyes. "What do you want, Brock? Absolution? You have it. I never blamed you for Cornley's attack. Never!"

Relief flooded through him, making him light-headed. Her confession answered the question that had plagued him for too many years. Brock wanted to touch her now, but resisted. He smothered the rising guilt he felt for cornering her with the past. However, he was a desperate man. He reasoned silently that he was linked to her nightmare. Amara had coped with her violation by severing all connections that might remind her of the ordeal. The observation brought a sudden understanding.

"You do blame me," he said, reaching for her.

There was resistance with each step she took toward him. "No!"

"All these years, I had it wrong. I thought you had blamed me for not keeping Cornley from hurting you. It was not quite so simple," he said, more to himself, wondering why he had not thought of it sooner. "You blame me for being the one who found you. In all these years, you have not been able to forgive me for finding you battered and bloody, humiliated in a way I will never fully understand." His touch was gentle, as was his expression. "Have you despised me, dove, for knowing your darkest secrets?"

The tears she had done such an admirable job holding back slid down her cheeks. She choked on a sob. "I do n-not hate you. How could I? You were my salvation."

Her body was soft and warm against his. Truth shimmered in the liquid depths of her gaze. "Perhaps not," he conceded, listening to the incessant call of a sedge bird hidden somewhere in the reeds. "Even so, I still lost you."

Amara pressed her face into his chest. Her silence was damning. Although he could not be certain, he thought he felt the faint brush of her lips. Brock closed his eyes. The sunlight was abruptly too bright.

Stepping back, she brushed the tears from her cheeks. "Thank you for sharing the day with me. Your land is quite breathtaking."

He did not like the finality in her inflection. Amara's tears dripped like aqua fortis on his conscience, leaving him raw. Hurting her had not been his intention. Sometimes, he feared all he caused her was pain. "And the house?" he asked, allowing her to close the door on the past for now. He was a man who spent his life looking forward rather than back. Besides, she was about to learn the change of topic was all he was willing to surrender.

She gave him a weak smile. "It is a handbreadth from being declared a ruin. You may choose Mr. Streden's path before it is finished."

"Amara . . . Amara," he sighed. "Challenges merely whet my determination."

He strolled away, whistling a quiet tune, leaving her to ponder if he spoke only of the sorry condition of his house or of the maddening, troubled woman he had never quite exorcised from his heart.

CHAPTER SEVENTEEN

Instead of readying the phaeton as Amara had expected after her bout of tears, Brock returned carrying a fly rod and the forgotten hamper. Still whistling, he winked at her as he passed.

"Is there some trouble with the horses?"

"Not a whit."

Since he refused to halt, she was forced to trail after him. "We should start for London."

Having selected his spot on the bank, he let the hamper drop. "I prefer fishing." As he retrieved something from his coat pocket, curiosity drew Amara closer. He all but ignored her now while his concentration was focused on tying the metal lure to the braided horsehair line.

She opened her mouth, and then closed it. No one had managed to befuddle her as this man did. One minute he had her laughing like a loon, the next sobbing out old despair on his shoulder. He seemed to effortlessly wring out a spectrum of emotions from her, and still he demanded more. A part of her was tempted to capitulate, if only to repay him for the tenderness he generously offered.

"Are there actually fish in this lake?"

His brow lifted at the silliness of her query. "I thought your stomach might be appreciative of something besides another cold bean tart. Our haste has left us provision-poor." With the grace of practice, he cast the line into the water.

"If you are concerned about my perishing, we could stop at the coaching inn again," she suggested. "From the look of things, the delay will not cost us more than your diddling with your rod."

Brock threw his head back and laughed. His fly rod bobbed crazily with his merriment. "Christ, Amara! What a lovely mouth you have. I will have you know, I take rod handling quite seriously. I never diddle."

That was debatable. Since he was having too much fun misinterpreting her words, she did not bother arguing. "Even if you manage catching anything, there will be no opportunity to cook it."

He peered in her direction. "Surely there will. We are staying the night."

"Brock!" Though his gaze was fixed on the line he was handling, there was no doubt all his attention was directed at her.

The breath he expelled was weighted by weariness. "Since your temper has cooled, I am loath to remind you about the small matter of your kidnapping."

He was earnest. Brock glanced at her, attempting to judge her reaction. She had been so grateful after the accident in the square she had not considered how he might twist her awkward confession to his benefit.

"You cannot keep me here."

"You were willing to give Lady A'Court a day and a night," he calmly reasoned. "Is not the man whom you referred to earlier as your salvation worthy of the same devotion?"

Amara nipped her lower lip when she realized she was pouting. She was good and soundly trapped, thanks to her ruse. If she surrendered to his high-handedness, she forfeited only her pride. No one would learn the truth of her whereabouts. Brock had proven long ago he could be trusted with her secrets.

"If you hook a fish, your efforts will be wasted. My knowledge of cookery is limited. I was raised to be a titled gentleman's bride, not a servant," she warned.

"Cease glowering. You are frightening our supper away," he said, without looking at her. "I doubt my limited abilities will garner any praise from the *ton*, however, I can cook whatever I catch over a fire."

His boast surprised her. "I do not believe you. If you were in a kitchen, it was only long enough to charm sweets from the cook or flirt with one of the maids."

"Ah, dove, for someone who cries indifference, you must have spent a great amount of time observing me to know me so well."

She had, not that she would admit it.

"No outrage or vehement denials? Well, well . . . progress, after all." She sensed that the mockery she detected was directed at both of them. "Do not fret, Amara. Your curiosity was reciprocated."

Brock released the breath he was holding. A sideways glance revealed she had retreated to her abandoned mantle. Bending forward, she retrieved her hairpins. He felt a pang of regret while he covertly watched her coil her hair into a stylish knot and secure it. The pretense gave her comfort, he guessed. He could afford to be generous. At the moment, she was feeling vulnerable. Although he sensed no fear in her, she was no closer to understanding his actions than he was.

There was a subtle tug on the line as it moved through the water. Experience told him the resistance was aquatic grass or suchlike. He reeled in the line and cast again. The lure landed with a distinct plop and sank into the murky depths.

He glanced in Amara's direction. Only her shoes rested on her mantle. Searching the area, he noticed she had moved to the lake's edge. Not wanting to disturb his efforts, she had distanced herself from him. He was grateful she was not the type of female who moped when the fates opposed her.

Brock almost dropped his fly rod when she tantalizingly raised her skirts. She had left her stockings on, a detail he found incredibly arousing. Was she deliberately tormenting him because he had refused to return to London? He doubted it. Amara possessed genuine passion under her polite diffidence, but she was guileless. The direction of his thoughts probably would horrify her.

Wadding up a section of her skirt, she tucked the fabric between her legs. From his position, he could see glimpses of her embroidered garters. Perhaps being alone with Amara was not one of his brightest notions.

"You should have taken off your stockings!" he shouted. Hearing the odd catch in his voice, Brock cleared his throat.

"The water is cold," she replied.

Was it? The sweat trickling down his back was making his shoulder blades itch. Hungrily, he admired the way she swished her hips as she waded deeper into the water.

The appetite he needed to assuage had nothing to do with his stomach.

"Anything nibbling?"

His back jerked as if someone had taken a lash to him. "Nary a one," he said huskily, thinking like a man who wanted to nibble on his little fish. He wanted to start at her neck and work his way down to her toes.

"Hmm." She trailed the fingers of her right hand in the water and then rubbed the chilly wetness into the back of her neck. "Well, if you fail, I could always find a rock and throw it at one of those ducks. Who knows, I might actually fell one," she teased.

She moved along the shallows with her back to him, oblivious of his wicked musings. Brock had lost interest in fishing. His motions of casting and reeling were that of an automaton. If she had given him any indication that she desired his company, he would have tossed his fly rod onto the bank and joined her. He privately congratulated himself on his restraint. Amara and desire had been entwined within his heart for so long he thought the beleaguered organ might burst.

She was not entirely averse to him. He had noted a similar longing in her expression when she thought she was unobserved. Every time he touched her, she responded with the sweetness and zeal he had only experienced in his dreams. She belonged to him! He just had to convince Amara and her ambitious family before they married her off to the fop.

"Brock, your line!"

He stared down at the arcing lancewood in his hands. Feeling foolish, he tugged back and began reeling in his prize. "There is a kitchen garden in the back," he told her, his tone clipped with a mix of anger at his clumsiness and bridled yearning. "Would your limited cookery abilities recognize wild onion?"

Pride nudged her chin up so she was forced to look down her nose at him. "I suppose."

"Fine. Run along and dig some up." He cursed, feeling confined in his coat. "Christ, this one is a fighter."

"We will need a cooking pot."

"Aye. Once you have the wild onion, return to the hall and take the door on the right. You will find what we need."

"Are you certain?"

He tried not to snarl. "I have no time for you. If the task is too difficult, just wait for me in the hall. Whatever you do, keep away from the old kitchen!"

"Yes, milord," she said, adding enough sarcasm to make him wince.

A decent meal will placate her annoyance, he thought. If that did not work, he could always beg. He bared his teeth at the lowering notion and concentrated on hauling in the bloody fish.

Two hours had expired since Brock had entered the hall with a beheaded seven-pound perch. Amara had complimented his triumph over nature, and pointedly ignored his smug dismissal of her praise. Moreover, her lack of faith in his skills had offended him. She had forgotten how easily a male's pride bruised.

The tension in him puzzled her. Perhaps it was anger, though she disregarded the thought. Oh, he had thanked her politely for kindling the hearth and filling the cooking pot with water from the well she had discovered behind the house along with the wild onion he had demanded. Still, his smile never quite reached his light green eyes and he rarely engaged her in conversation unless she prodded him.

"The fish smells wonderful," she said, making another half-hearted attempt to lure him from his deliberating mood.

Brock closed the book he had been reading. Taking her comment for the hint it was, he rose from his chair and poked his knife into the boiling contents of the pot. "Hungry?" he said, his tone laced with its earlier humor.

"You would be disappointed in me if I did not appreciate your cooking skills."

"Just more for me." He gestured at the wooden bowls she had found stored with the several pots and a handful of worn utensils. "Hand me the bowls. Our surroundings may be unrefined, but the food is hot and plentiful."

Amara exchanged the bowl he offered with an empty one. They lacked a table. Most of the furniture left behind by the former owners was earmarked for kindling. They were spared from sitting on the floor because Brock had found in one of the rooms upstairs two old side chairs. The red velvet upholsteries were threadbare, but the gilded frames were solid.

Picking up her fork, Amara speared a flaky piece of fish. An approving sound rumbled in her throat. She looked over at Brock, noticing he had not tasted his food. "It is very good, Brock. Where did you learn how to cook?"

The ease with which he had prepared their basic supper amazed her. Anticipating their needs, Brock had purchased potatoes and turnips at the coaching inn. He had added them to the fish along with the wild onion for flavor. Meeting his guarded expression, she would have praised his efforts even if the food had tasted awful.

Finding what he needed in the sincerity of her words,

he visibly relaxed his shoulders. "There are wondrous sights in India, but some of them were downright primitive. You either adapt or starve," he said, shrugging. "Brogden was an excellent teacher."

Amara was acquainted with Dr. Sir Wallace Brogden only through Tipton and Devona. During the early years of the viscount's self-imposed exile from his homeland, he had served as the physician's assistant on countless voyages as they traversed the various trade routes. It was Brogden who had nurtured Tipton's interest in medicine.

She had been too distracted by Doran's imprisonment three years ago to be concerned about Tipton or his unusual houseguest. She had learned later from Devona that Brogden had been suffering the ills of an infected leg, which the delirious physician had allowed to fester. Tipton had amputated part of the gangrenous leg.

When Brogden had healed and spoke of returning to India to oversee various business interests, Brock had joined him.

"Tipton and Devona have always spoken highly of Dr. Sir Wallace Brogden. I regret he departed London before we were introduced." For a long time, she had blamed the man for taking Brock with him.

Brock looked up from his supper. "You were too busy hating me and burying your brother."

The remark struck a deathblow to their conversation. Amara conceded defeat. They finished their meal in silence.

Listening to the muffled sounds coming from the other room, Brock added more wood to the fire. He cursed his insensitivity for the thousandth time. Amara had accepted her captivity with a bemused tolerance. How had he repaid her? He had cast down her dead beloved brother between them because her implicit trust frightened him. Brock had spent the last hours of daylight contemplating how close he was edging toward proving how undeserving he was.

While she had washed their dishes, Brock had gone outside. He had brought in more wood for the hearth, checked the horses, and drawn water from the well. The hall was empty on his return. He assumed Amara was attending to her personal needs. Hooking the pot over the fire to warm, he sat down in front of the hearth and waited.

"I found this hidden in a chest." She held up a bottle of hock. "Who knows how long it has lain there. It may have turned to vinegar."

Brock held out a hand. "I will risk it, if you will." He had purchased beer for them at the inn. Amara had dutifully sipped what he had provided, although from her expression he had guessed only necessity encouraged her imbibing. "Next time I kidnap you, I will remember to bring along some tea."

Amara smiled faintly at the suggestion. Curiosity had drawn her to the hearth. Uncorking the wine, he stared at her as she peered into the pot.

"What are you cooking?"

"Your bath."

She straightened in surprise. "There was no need to bother."

Brock tipped the bottle to his lips. It was not vinegar. He presented her the bottle. "Consider it a reward for cleaning up."

Amara closed the gap between them and took the bottle from his hand. As she did so many things, she sampled the hock suspiciously. "Not vinegar," she said, wiping the wine from her lips.

With his gaze fixed on her wet lips, he rose from the chair. Clasping his hand around the neck of the bottle, he gave in to the temptation and kissed her. The tip of his tongue flicked her bottom lip before he retreated. "You are correct."

Picking up a rag, he removed the pot from the fire. "Is it too warm?" he asked, not wanting to scald her.

Amara dipped her finger quickly in the water. "Perfect. Where should I—ah—?" She broke off, uncomfortable.

It was warmest near the hearth. He discarded the thought, realizing the large hall would not satisfy her need for privacy. He set the bottle of hock on the floor. "Take the candle and follow me."

Brock led her up the stairs into one of the bedchambers. Like most of the house, the chamber was empty. The windows were shuttered from the outside so the fading twilight provided no illumination in the room. Placing the pot and rag near the unlit fireplace, he took the candle from her, and headed to a smaller adjoining room to an oversized trunk. Her soft footfalls revealed she stopped at the threshold.

"Hold this." Brock returned the candle to her and lifted the lid of the trunk. Inside, he had stored three shirts, blankets, and several feather pillows. "I prefer my comforts. Sleeping on cold stone was getting rather tiresome. One of these visits, I will get around to putting a decent bed in this house." Reaching deeper into the trunk, he retrieved a piece of soap. "Forgive me if it is not your favorite scent, but it will have to suffice." He pressed it into her hand. Grabbing one of the blankets, he escorted her back into the bedchamber.

"Will I be sleeping here?" She did not seem pleased by the prospect.

"No, I think we should remain together. Parts of this house are too unsound to risk having you walk about it at night. We will make our pallets downstairs. The large hearth in the hall will keep us warm through the night. I just thought you might enjoy some privacy."

"Thank you." She set the candle on the mantel.

"You will have to use this as a towel," Brock said apologetically. He needed to get out of the room, before he did something foolish such as asking her if he could stay. Muttering an oath, he returned to the trunk and gathered up the remaining blankets and pillows.

As he headed for the door, the glass buttons on the back of her gown glinted and caught his attention when she reached down to pick up the discarded blanket. Dropping the bundle of bedding outside the door, he approached Amara. "You are trapped."

Bewildered, she replied, "Pardon?"

"You need your maid to get yourself in and out of all that feminine equipage." Girding himself with determination, he said, "Turn around."

"Absolutely not!"

Trying to view her as one of his willful sisters, he spun her around and plucked at her buttons. "Do not be ridiculous. You can use one of my shirts as your nightdress."

"None of this is proper."

"Pretend I am your brother," he suggested, ignoring her sound of disbelief. He silently agreed. When he touched her, he was not thinking of her as a sister. The back of her gown opened, revealing a corset beneath. He set about freeing her from her whalebone cage.

Amara gritted her teeth. "Your expertise with a lady's

underclothes rivals my maid's. I would wager I am not the first female you have undressed."

He clenched and released his fingers, willing them not to tremble. "Just honing my skills for you, dove," he assured her. "Finished." He stepped away from her and swiped at the sweat forming above his upper lip. "I will leave you to your ablutions." He backed out the doorway. "Unless you require further assistance?"

Recovering from his audacity, she slammed the door.

CHAPTER EIGHTEEN

Piper was not enjoying the rout. Playing cards for endless hours at the town house of some high stickler whose name she had already forgotten was not her notion of merriment. Lady Keyworth's insistence that she lacked the proper social polish for the *haut monde* was becoming tiresome. Where was the lack? She was prettier than most of the ladies in the room. All she had to do was look at a gentleman, and soon he was begging the host for an introduction.

Her most recent conquest was awaiting her return. Mr. John Abbot was young, moderately handsome, and the owner of four breweries. He lacked the peerage so many doting mamas demanded for their homely daughters, but his wealth still opened their doors.

"Cousin, what a delightfully wicked smile. I pray it was for me."

Mallory Claeg took her hand and bowed in a manner that stated he was subservient to no one. Oh, he was a handsome devil. His light blue eyes were disturbing and intriguing. Their peculiar pale depths beckoned a person to look deeper. That, combined with his unfashionably long hair, reminded her of a sorcerer or a mystic. Realizing she was staring, she said, "You are too close."

Amusement swirled like blue mist in those enthralling orbs. "Is there such a thing?"

"Blood," she clarified. "Besides, your sister considers you too old." Piper detested agreeing with Amara, but in this instance her cousin was correct. She wanted a husband who could be swayed by her looks and unspoken promises. Call it instinct, but she doubted any woman dominated Mallory Claeg.

"Oh, by aeons," he said, too pleasantly for her liking. "Then again, I have spent most of my life flitting from one impropriety to the next."

She could well imagine. Piper had overheard Lady Keyworth's opinion to Mrs. Sheers regarding his connection with a Mrs. LeMaye. None of it was flattering. "Does it ever become tedious?"

"It?"

She made a broad gesture with her fan as she searched the room for Mr. Abbot. "Debasing the family with your notorious exploits and overblown mistresses. Considering your advanced age, you might want to settle down before it not only looks tedious but seems positively bizarre."

"Sort of like prostituting yourself for a husband, hmm?"

Her eyes flared when she found Mr. Abbot. Oh, the fickleness of the men! Instead of awaiting her return near the balcony doors, he was across the room and engaged in an absorbing conversation with Miss Vining. The enigmatic half-smile she had perfected flattened, losing its beatific softness. How could the gentleman prefer the simpering Miss Vining to her?

"I believe she has a distant connection to a marchioness," Mallory Claeg said, confirming that she had spoken the question aloud. "Her dowry is rather substantial and includes an estate in Surrey." Dismissing the couple, he returned his attention to her. "Forget about Abbot."

Her throat tightened. She did not need this blue-eyed satyr to explain why most of her admirers drifted to the Miss Vinings in the room. Piper silently cursed her father for not having an understanding for business like Lord Keyworth. All her father was good at producing was daughters. "Why, Mr. Claeg? Am I too poor?" The notion truly stung.

"No," he said gently. "Marrying a man like Abbot would never satisfy such a romantic creature as yourself. Blame your lapse on the season. It tends to muddle even the most sensible creatures. Like my sister," he added as an afterthought. "Speaking of the fair Amara, did she join you and my mother this evening?"

His kindness humbled her. She had thought him so jaded that he was beyond understanding her mortifying predicament. Not wanting him to see how moved she was by his words, Piper glanced away. "Your sister despises card parties." *Leaving me to attend these dreary functions with her indomitable mother.*

"Where might I find her?"

She hesitated, and then shrugged. Mallory Claeg did not seem to be a man who dallied in gossip. "Your sister is visiting Lord A'Court's widow."

"Lady Keyworth permitted her unmarried daughter to leave town during the season? I think not."

His cutting skepticism revived her flagging spirit. "I am not your sister's cater-cousin. She was rather mute on the details, but the young widow is discreetly in residence. Your mother and I were sworn not to tell anyone that the woman was in town."

Mallory's expression grew speculative. "Interesting."

"What?"

"Nothing, my dear," he assured her. "I was just wondering if my sister is developing a few of my bothersome tendencies."

Amara touched the soft linen of the shirt, wishing for the hundredth time that she could see her reflection. Brock had been correct. His shirt covered her as well as any nightdress. However, she still felt that wearing it was improper. It was his shirt, after all.

Squaring her shoulders, she retrieved the candle from the mantel. Amara left her clothes laid out on the floor, since she would use the room again in the morning. Before she lost her courage, she opened the door. Brock was not below as she had expected. He sat on the floor outside her door, his long legs stretched out in front of him. If he had not brought another candle, she might have tripped over him.

"You forgot your hairpins," he said, his gaze resolutely fixed on her face.

Confused by the comment, Amara touched the coil of hair at the back of her head. "Oh, yes, well, I can remove them later."

The hall seemed smaller when he stood. He circled around her, keeping his distance.

"I prepared a pallet for you near the fire. You can enjoy some of the hock you discovered while I clean up. You should have told me I smelled like perch."

"I am too intelligent to insult the man who was feeding me," she teased. "I—" She stared at his hands, trying not to remember the strength and feel of them on her as he had undressed her despite her protests. No, she had not been thinking about the fish. "I should go below."

She was halfway down the stairs when she heard the door close. Whether she desired his protection or not, Brock intended to look after her. It comforted her and left her restless at the same time.

He had prepared two pallets. The bottle of hock was set between them. In spite of the fire, the night had cooled the air in the hall. Amara chose the right pallet and slipped under the woolen blankets. She was too accustomed to the late evenings of town to be tired, so she remained seated. Reaching for the bottle, she drank. The hock was warm. She wondered if the fire or Brock's hands had heated the wine. Amara took another contemplative sip.

A muffled thud from above had her cocking her head. Moments later, she heard footfalls on the stairs. From under the blanket, she drew her knees up. Brock had been quicker bathing than she had been.

As he entered the room, she noted the changes in his attire. He had discarded his coat and cravat, and the shirt he had donned was the twin of the one she wore. He wore it loose, although with deference to modesty, he still wore breeches. Like her, his stockings and shoes had been removed.

Closing the door behind him, so the heat of their fire was contained in the hall, his brow furrowed when he saw her wrapped up in the bedding. "Are you cold? Do you need more blankets?" he asked, concerned.

She felt too awkward explaining that glimpses of her bare legs and feet had more to do with her being under the blankets than the cold. "No, I am comfortable. You are a considerate host."

"Considerate for a kidnapper, you mean," he said. The hint of derision was directed inward.

This day had developed in a way she had never anticipated. She had not found her brother. The accident at the square had frightened her. And then, there was Brock. Strong, dependable, he had offered her comfort and yelled at her for her foolishness. He was no saint. Brock blatantly had used her deceit to his own advantage. Regardless, she knew of no other who cared about her as much.

Deciding he had suffered enough, she said, "I hate dispelling any *folie de grandeur* you might have regarding your abduction capabilities, Brock, however, no one can charge you with kidnapping. Or, if someone tries, I will be forced into confessing that I was a willing captive."

"An explanation, if you please."

Wonderful. Now he was insulted.

"Brock, both of us know I could have started screaming the minute I learned you were not escorting me home." She took a fortifying sip of the wine. "Therefore, no kidnapping occurred." He looked so cross standing there with his damp hair and bare feet. Amara could not stop from giggling.

Brock's eyelids narrowed in suspicion. "Are you drunk?"

Now he was being insulting. "It takes more than a few sips of wine to get a Claeg foxed." She held the bottle up for inspection. "See for yourself, if you do not believe me."

He snatched the bottle from her hand and sat cross-legged on the pallet. Brock scrutinized the contents. Satisfied the hock had not inspired her confession, he imbibed deeply. "Before you pardon me, you should be aware that I had cheerfully planned to gag you if you had screamed."

Amara gasped. "You are jesting!"

He took another swig from the bottle. "Am I? Let us both be grateful your faith in me is untried." He passed her the bottle.

She accepted it, but did not imbibe. A piece of wood popped and shifted in the grate. There was something soothing about firelight. She was not half as concerned as she should have been. Gracious, she was sitting undressed in an empty house with a man. The situation warranted a swoon, she thought. For some reason, she could not muster any enthusiasm about propriety. Perhaps it was the company and the hock. She felt . . . safe.

"Do you plan on cuddling the bottle all night?"

Casting the shade of propriety into the netherworld, Amara stuck out her tongue. She surrendered the wine. Resting her chin on her knees, she studied her companion. Brock was a handsome man, she decided, approving of the changes the passing years and experience had etched on his visage. Conte Prola seemed almost too pretty when compared with her unshaved and brooding companion, although she doubted Brock would appreciate the compliment.

Brock wore his hair untied. The ends were slightly damp from his bath. Where she had buttoned the three shell buttons on her borrowed shirt, he had left his open, making her curious about the shadowed flesh she had glimpsed.

"Did your mother not tell you that it is impertinent to stare?"

Amara wrinkled her nose. "It is only impertinent when the individual you are admiring stares back," she blithely corrected. "Do you want to know what I was thinking?"

"No," he replied, too quickly. "Go to sleep."

Disgusted she was being dismissed, Amara slipped deeper into the bedding. "I am not sleepy."

"A pity. I am. Just close your eyes and think of—"

"What?" she demanded. "An ermine tippet, lemon ices, and ivory elephants?"

Her peevishness only made him chuckle. "So you liked my gift? You never mentioned receiving it."

"Was it from you?"

So much had happened, she had forgotten. The mysterious package she had been carrying the afternoon she had caught Piper in her bedchamber had contained the elephant. About ten inches in height, and the length of her arm, the whimsical creature was made from pieces of ivory. A net of wire and semiprecious jewels adorned its head, back, and legs.

"The workmanship is exquisite. I have never seen its equal." She rolled onto her side. "You have been so generous, Brock."

"Is this a complaint?"

Amara treasured every gift he had sent her. "No. Yes! You have to cease sending gifts to the house."

"What about the rosewood desk I have set aside for you? You will not find this kind of ivory inlay in England." He ignored her beleaguered groan. "I found it in Vizagatapatam. A—"

She stopped listening. He was probably teasing her. There was no rosewood desk, no ivory inlay. How could she explain away such an exotic gift? It was all too overwhelming. Amara closed her eyes. Papa would never permit her to marry a baronet's son who had made his fortune in trade.

"Amara?"

She turned her face toward him and opened her eyes. "Did you buy me a desk?"

"Have you not been paying attention?" he chided, any

humor he perceived in the question fading when he gazed into her eyes. "No gift should summon the misery I see in your eyes. I regret—"

"Do not apologize!" she begged. Kicking off her blankets, on all fours she crawled to his side. She rested her hands on his rigid shoulders. "I love the gifts you have selected for me. I love—"

Sometimes words were wholly inadequate. Could he not sense what she felt? Amara leaned into him and pressed her lips against his. His mouth was unmoving under her tender onslaught. Brock had initiated each kiss they had shared. She was trying to show him without words that he had taught her the pleasure of giving too.

Amara heard him whisper her name against her lips. Encouraged, she drank in his breath and nipped his lower lip lightly with her teeth. His hands settled on her waist and drew her closer. Shedding his docility, Brock parted his lips and feasted on her mouth. The man knew how to kiss a lady! A surge of dizziness assailed her. Digging her fingers into his shoulders, Amara held on. She could not match his proficiency, she mused, trying not to dwell too much on the countless women the rake had kissed before her. However, what she lacked in practice she could balance with eagerness. The notion of kissing Brock often was not repugnant at all!

With a groan, he ended the kiss. "Amara, what are you doing?" he asked, the question edged with pain.

"If you must ask," she said, holding the back of her hand to her swollen lips, "then I am more appalled by my actions than you."

He halted her retreat, adding to her humiliation. "You little fool! This has nothing to do with any lack in you.

Your kisses are potent, spellbinding, to this mere mortal," he said, furious at the realization.

"If you like—"

Brock grabbed her hand, and crudely brought it to the crotch of his breeches. She felt the rigid flesh beneath and shivered.

"Oh, I like, all right. Too much. If we had continued, I would not have been satisfied with just a sweet kiss." He shoved her away. "Go to sleep, Amara. The next time you crawl on my pallet, I will not be noble enough to send you away."

She moved back to her provisional bed, her bruised feelings resembling those of a chastised child. Therein lay their trouble. They were not children. Though if she were to judge a certain gentleman's actions, one of them was definitely acting childish. "Where are you going?"

Brock pulled on one boot and then the other. He climbed to his feet. "I need to check on the horses," he said, opening the door. "Do a good turn for us both and fall asleep before my return." He stomped out into the night.

Amara followed as far as the open door. "If you cannot bear remaining in the same room with me, why not bed down with your precious horses!" She gave the wooden door a very satisfying kick to close it. "Coward," she muttered, not knowing which one of them deserved the epithet.

She picked up the discarded wine and sipped it sullenly. Who was he to order her about like a child—or a wife! Amara gritted her teeth against the bitter derision she felt. Another swallow of wine washed away the aftertaste. Settling back down onto her pallet, she stared into the fire.

It had always been between them—this *wanting*. Once, she had been too young to recognize it. Later, she had been too wounded to appreciate it. She broodingly stared at the rumpled bedding he had hastily abandoned. Brock had always known where this attraction would lead. He had deliberately nudged them toward the abyss by stealing her from the safety of London. Still, he hesitated, though it cost him. Amara understood the next step was hers. Peering over the precipice, she realized she had never cared much for heights.

The horses had been an excuse to distance himself from Amara. Brock had checked on them anyway, using a battered old lantern to guide his way. The animals were fine.

Leaving them, he followed a rutted path to the edge of the lake. The water shone like obsidian glass in the faint moonlight. He listened to the whistle of a stone curlew while insects distracted from their nightly courtship by his lantern buzzed around him.

He had almost lost control. Without threats or calculated seduction Amara had crawled to his side and kissed him. The shock of her spontaneity had frozen him momentarily. Her generosity transcended his dreams. The shy caress of her endearing mouth against his awakened him from his enthrallment and his only thought was to take what was being offered.

He had pushed her away.

His body thrummed with a maelstrom of teeming emotion, blocking out the sounds of the night. Brock wanted Amara. He had once been willing to kill for her. Call it belated guilt, but he had orchestrated her presence at Whitmott Park once he had learned her family would not question her absence. He did not regret sharing the day with her. It was the night that tormented him. She was vulnerable. Old memories were surging with new, confusing her. Confusing him. He had resided so long in the shadows of her affection that he did not trust her invitation to bask in the light.

Brock turned his head back toward the house at the hollow sound of wood being dropped. Had the woman no sense at all? The grounds were too dangerous for her to be strolling about looking for him. Pleased he had reason to direct some of his frustration outward, he focused on the welcoming light glowing from the windows of the hall.

The door struck the wall like a crack of thunder, its reverberations echoing against the walls of the empty hall. Amara shrieked. Whirling from her seated position, she clutched the pillow to her bosom as if it provided a certain amount of protection from his perusal.

"What possessed you to leave the hall?" Brock demanded, his gaze swiftly assessing her for injury. "If you were frightened, you should have called—" Disbelief silenced his ranting as he blindly groped for the door and closed it.

Amara was sitting on his pallet.

"The next time you crawl on my pallet, I will not be noble enough to send you away."

He had warned her, had he not? Instead of being frightened off, Amara had considered his words a challenge. She was quite a lovely temptation, wearing only his shirt and wrapped up in his bedding. "If you are trying to bedevil me for snatching you from London," Brock said, his throat growing dry when she stood, revealing her bare calves and feet, "you are succeeding."

With her hands in front of her, Amara twisted the end of her first finger in an absent nervous gesture. "Dressed as I am, I have not wandered farther than the warmth of the fire."

He forgot all about the mysterious clatter that had hastened his return to her side, when she moved closer. Drawing in an unsteady breath, Amara pressed the side of her face to his chest. His arms automatically closed around her.

"Hmm," she murmured approvingly. "In the passing years, I have never forgotten the smell of you."

Baffled and pleased, he rubbed the center of her back in a coaxing manner. "Is my scent displeasing?"

"No." Already embarrassed by her admission, she nestled closer, unwilling to show her face. "It comforts me."

"An odd compliment, dove," he lightly teased, the humor he was trying to inflect having long escaped him.

She tilted her face up and would have pulled away if he had not tightened his hold. "It was heartfelt, not uttered for your amusement."

"Nor was it accepted as such," he promised. "Your words moved me." He lowered his head and kissed her. "I am so selfish, I fear of misunderstanding your intentions."

Pleasure flickered in her troubled blue eyes. Determination banked the brief respite. "You left me earlier because I needed to make a choice. I have, Brock. I chose you." Flustered, she shook her head. "Us."

Joy burst through him like an untapped wellspring. He held on to her, reeling from the sensation. "What are you saying?" He wanted her to be certain of her choice.

Leaning back in his arms, she said, "Obviously, I am lacking the practiced flattery of a seductress."

"If you speak of lies and cold cunning, we are in agreement."

A trembling smile brightened her visage. "Perhaps, if I just showed you—" She curled her arms around him and offered her mouth.

Brock hungrily accepted. Feeding on her parted lips, he moaned in astonishment when her nimble tongue pushed deeper seeking his. He happily obliged, his fingers reaching and unfastening the small buttons of her shirt. His mouth broke away from her mouth, traveled along her jaw and down to her exposed neck. He nipped it playfully. "We are too far from the fire." Taking her hand, he led her to his pallet. While she watched him shyly, he gathered up her pallet and arranged it beside his. Satisfied with his efforts, he held out his hand. "Come, dove, let me warm you."

Amara allowed herself to be pulled down on her knees.

"Your hair," he said, already searching for the pins hidden in her hair. "I want it down."

Her fingers brushed against his as she helped him take down her hair. Polished by firelight, her dark brown tresses fell and covered her shoulders.

Anticipation was headier than any wine he had ever drunk. "You are finally mine," he said with awe. The weight of responsibility squeezed his chest. "I do not want to hurt you."

"Then you will not," she assured him, though her nervous motions belied her certainty.

His knuckles grazed her knees. "I want to see all of you."

"Yes."

Brock sensed he was terrifying her. Nor did he blame

her if some part of her was quietly comparing him to Cornley. He could not change the past. It was for the future he was willing to gamble all.

Amara gripped the inner seam of the sleeve in turn and pulled each arm out. Still protected by her linen covering, she paused.

"Allow me."

Meeting her gaze, he reached for the bottom edge of the shirt. Slowly, Brock lifted the shirt. Blushing, she leaned forward, letting him pull it over her head. A glint of gold swaying between her breasts caught his attention. His hand shot out as he seized the pendant.

Reverently, his thumb brushed across his mother's intaglio. "You wear it. After all these years." Brock stared down at the maiden and her beast carved into stone.

Amara lowered her gaze. "I have never taken it off."

"Why?"

Discomforted by the question, she shifted. "That night you called it my talisman. You promised it would give me strength when mine faltered."

"Did it?"

Her lashes lifted, giving him a view of the turbulent depths of her gaze. "When the nightmares plagued me, I recalled how you held me that night and your strength. I confess in the beginning I needed it often, for my sanity was as fragile as those links of gold you grasp. Later, after our—our angry parting, I wore it as a remembrance for the treasured friend I had lost."

She had pushed him away and he had been too hurt to fight her. "You have found me again, Amara." He let go of the pendant and kissed the tears on her cheek. "I have been waiting for you to notice."

Heedless of her nakedness, she returned his kisses,

planting them along his jaw and chin. With a shaky laugh, she said, "I am so frightened!"

"So am I." Brock cupped her left breast. "We will lend each other our strength when the other falters." He brought the warm, fragrant flesh to his mouth and tasted.

"Yes," she said, her voice slightly higher than usual.

Guiding her with light touches, he coaxed her to lie down on the pallet. She raised one knee as if to shield herself from his inquisitive gaze, but he stroked her leg until she relaxed. "There are no secrets between us. No reason to hide."

He stretched beside her on his side. She giggled when he kissed the intaglio resting over her heart. Whatever their differences, she had not forgotten him. His hand traced the circumference of her navel, enjoying how her abdomen quivered.

"You are perfection."

Amara hid her expression by covering her mouth with her hand. "I am not."

"Then I will have to prove it."

He rubbed the stubble on his jaw across her nipple. She sucked in her breath and tried to sit up. Brock stilled her escape by laving the sensitive nub with his tongue. She was tense from his tender indulgence, but she settled back down.

Aroused to the point of pain, Brock adjusted his rigid cock in his breeches in order to avoid permanent damage. The demands of his body did not interest him as much as the wonder in Amara's eyes, the tiny moan she was not able to suppress. He had all night to explore her shapely body and ready her for him. When he filled her, and there was no doubt in his mind that he would, Amara would yearn for their joining as greatly as he.

• • •

Sprawled out naked on the blankets, Amara felt like a pagan goddess, and Brock was the green-eyed heathen who unashamedly worshiped her body. He used his hands and tongue, inciting an undefined need that itched beneath her skin.

He moved down her body, lavishing every inch of her with attention. She felt the sting of his teeth as he discovered a bone in her hip. She felt the sensation ripple all the way to her clenched toes.

"Liked that, did you, dove?" Even though he straddled her legs, he was careful not to put any weight on her. While she distantly appreciated his deliberate gentleness, the reckless ache he was building within her wanted something wilder and darker.

Brock continued his journey, rolling between her thighs. The soft stirring of his breath on her inner thigh made her want to wiggle away. Anticipating her reaction, he cupped her buttocks with his hands and pulled her closer.

She arched her back and cried out at the first flick of his tongue.

He raised his head and met her startled gaze. "Tasting a woman's desire is a potent aphrodisiac," he told her, the green in his eyes thinned to a ring around luminous black. Lowering his head, he tasted her again.

Feeling helpless against the tightening she felt, Amara tried to roll away. "Brock, you must stop."

"There is no shame in savoring the power you have over me." He stroked his thumb over the nub hidden within the folds of her womanly flesh, and retraced the dampness his tongue had forged. He pressed deep and found the silken flesh yielding. "Already, your body softens for mine, Amara," he murmured, nipping her thigh. "I could take you now, and all you would feel is pleasure."

The suggestion sent a lightning bolt of trepidation through her. Before she could express her panic, he kissed her down there as thoroughly as he had explored her mouth. Any thought of flight faded. Falling back into her prone position, she surrendered to his mastery over her willing body. She merely sighed when he slipped two fingers into her. The wetness of her arousal eased the escalating tempo he set while the suction of his mouth constricted the coil in her pelvis. With her hands clenched, she tensed for the unknown.

Brock jerked his head up. His eyes burned into hers. "Let go," he commanded, his fingers plunged deep.

Amara complied. She came apart in his hands. Choking out his name, she reached for him as her hips bucked with each wrenching spasm. The gentle caresses had been replaced with ruthless expertise designed to wring out her pleasure. When it finally ended, she felt hollow and aching.

Triumph gleamed in those pale green eyes. Wiping his mouth on his sleeve, he crawled up her body. Not saying a word, he pulled her into his embrace and cradled her while she wept.

CHAPTER NINETEEN

There had been other women in his life. A few before he had understood his feelings for Amara, and too many afterward, when in despair he had deemed her unattainable. He cared, yet never loved. Some might have even considered him indiscriminate, though he had given pleasure as often as he had taken it. Until now, never had he pleasured a lover until she was sobbing in his arms. It was rather humbling.

As she sniffled into the handkerchief he had handed her, her sodden gaze was rueful. "I suppose it is dreadfully uncouth crying after the seduction."

Her subtle attempt to distance herself from what they had shared irritated him. "I was loving you, not offering instruction. I will leave the rules of etiquette to your mother."

His harshness stung her. The soft look in her eyes hardened with temper. He would spend the rest of the night aroused and alone if he allowed this nonsense to continue.

"Do not think about running off. You may not like the results if I have to chase you."

Abandoning the notion of sulking exit, Amara reached for her shirt. Brock plucked it from her hands and flung the ball of linen into the fire.

The scent of scorched linen assailed their senses. Appalled, she watched the flames greedily devour her shirt. "Was that necessary?"

"It appears so. Now that I have seen you naked, I find clothing offensive."

She bit down on her lip, and he would have sworn it was to keep from laughing. "Then be prepared to be offended often, for I shall not give up wearing gowns. Not even for you, Mr. Bedegrayne."

"It is fortunate one of us can claim prudence. If any man looked upon you thus, I would be provoked to kill him."

Tugging one of the blankets around her to appease her modesty, she wrinkled her nose. "What a male thing to say!"

"My dove, a man is always earnest about his male thing," he quipped.

Laughing, she shoved him. In retaliation, he grabbed her by the waist and settled her on his lap. "You are simply dreadful," she said.

He sobered at a sudden thought. "Is that why you cried? Was I too rough?"

She waged a war between surprise and embarrassment. "No, not at all. What you did—we did . . . I found it so overwhelming. My tears, they were of joy. You did nothing."

"I respectfully disagree. It appears I was doing everything right. Want to try again?"

Instead of laughing as he had expected, Amara furrowed her brow thoughtfully. "What we did—there is more to it. You never—"

Not wanting her to dwell on her limited and horrible acquaintance with the male flesh, he distracted her by nibbling on her ear. "No, I did not," he murmured. "I want to share that part of myself with you." At the moment, his need rivaled breathing. "I can wait, if we must. If it frightens you." He was lying, of course, but he was not such a bastard he would push her into something that terrified her. Then again, he was not above engaging in a little gentle persuasion. She had admitted earlier that she had enjoyed his dedicated efforts.

"Will it hurt, Brock?"

The quake in her voice ably snuffed his mischievous machinating. "Never with me," he said quietly, willing her to believe it. "Do you recall the pleasure you felt at my touch?"

Too concerned about the answer to her own question, she ignored the absurdity of his.

At her nod, he continued. "Joining with you allows us to share that pleasure. There is no pain. Trust me in this."

"I do." She returned his kiss, prolonging the contact.

Encouraged, he gripped the edge of the blanket she had wound around her body. Amara slapped his hand and shifted away from him. So his lady wanted to play games. He was primed and quite willing. Brock lunged.

Squealing with laughter, she rolled away and struggled to her feet. She was halfway across the room before he caught her by the waist and spun her around.

"Stop, stop," she pleaded, trying to catch her breath. "I will get sick!"

"A ruse. I have never met another with a sturdier constitution than yours." He set her down anyway, but held her close. Brock groaned when her backside brushed against his erection. Within her proximity, he felt like a randy beast quivering in front of his mate just as he readied himself to enter her. The image of tearing away the blanket, pushing her against the wall and taking her chipped at his civility.

Amara must have sensed the change in him. As she turned her head, he took advantage of the tender curve between her neck and shoulder that she offered and sank his teeth into her. She leaned into him, her hand reaching back to touch his face. Last time, he had shown her gentleness. Now he would show her the passion she roused. Brock scooped her into his arms and carried her to the pallet. She fell onto the blankets, losing her hold on the one covering her.

"Do not move," he ordered while he tugged off his shirt. His hands tore at the buttons on his breeches. In his frenzy, he struggled to free them.

"If you will permit me?" The blanket fell to her waist, as she rose on her knees to assist him. Staring down at her endearingly awkward attempts to unfasten his falls, his blood pounded the beat of his heart in his ears. "There, it is done." She sat on her heels, her eyes solemnly fixed on his aggressive arousal.

"Trust me, Amara." Brock peeled his breeches down his legs and kicked them aside. "It will be like before. Only pleasure."

"I never realized there was—are you not too large?" she blurted out.

Comfortable with his nakedness, he sat down beside

her and pulled her into his lap as he had done earlier. "Stroke me," he entreated.

He thought she would refuse such a bold command. But she was braver than she realized. His cock twitched as her cool fingers petted the length of him. She pulled her hand away, faltering at his response.

"Explore me. It hurts more when you are not touching me."

"I do not understand."

"Let me show you." Putting his hand between her legs, he pressed his fingers into her nether curls. The dampness coating his fingers was enlightening. "You are so responsive, dove. Touch me again." He teased her with his fingers, making her squirm.

Amara enclosed her hand around him. Encouraged by his own questing, she measured the length of him. "Smooth, hot to the touch, and yet rigid as a sword," she marveled as if he were a specimen she was studying. "You are not wet."

She was killing him and she was not being merciful about it. "You are. You are too generous not to share." Kissing Amara, he lifted her and arranged her position so that she straddled him. He cupped her buttocks. Rubbing himself against her, the blunt head of his cock was anointed with her yielding wetness. "Take me." Crushing her to him, he filled her with one stroke.

She dug her nails into the back of his neck at his swift impalement. Her lashes fluttered open and their gazes collided. "No pain," she whispered, amazed.

"No." Not the sort that put fear in her eyes. Holding still deep within her, Brock slid his hand from her hip down the length of her leg, wrapping the limb around his waist. His fervid kiss contrasted with the restraint he had imposed on his body. "We are not limited by rules, only by our originality and endurance." He rocked within her, proving she could accommodate his loving invasion.

Her blue eyes widened at his upward thrust. "I have always considered you a clever man."

Amara clung to Brock like ivy on stone. Not that he was trying to get away, she thought smugly. From the approving noises he made, he was quite content with his situation. She followed his lead, and they moved together, slowly at first, savoring the unique joining of man and woman. Rising and falling, Brock forged into her intimate slick depths and what had shimmered just out of reach earlier coalesced into a low blossoming heat. She had always believed lovemaking was solely for a man's pleasure. Brock had helped her discover a part of herself she had never known existed.

"More," he muttered savagely, his movements losing their fluid grace. She swung a bracing hand out when he pitched forward intending to shove her on to her back. Realizing what he was about to do, Brock cursed and pulled her upright. Before she could question his indecision, he said, "This way." Lying back, he tugged her forward.

Leaning over him, Amara folded her legs while she straddled his hips. The change in their position stretched her. Brock clenched his teeth. His hands settled on her hips, coaxing her body into accepting the full measure of his manhood. He looked as if the new position pained him.

"Am I hurting you?"

The shudder began in his chest. Soon she realized he was laughing.

"Exquisitely, dove," he bit out, guiding her movements with his hands. "Promise you will never stop!"

Lowering her head so her hair hid most of her face, she shyly replied, "You are easy to please."

"Mayhap my dove thinks her beast is too tame." Mischievous delight enhanced the green hue of his eyes. "Persuading you to reverse your opinion shall bring pleasure for us both." He turned his face into her right breast and suckled her nipple. Amara moaned, enjoying the subtle tightening in her breasts.

"Brock."

"Which strokes give you the most fulfillment? This?" He teasingly kept his thrusting shallow.

Being denied the full length of him aroused and tormented her in ways she had not thought possible. When she tried to press her weight down on him, the scoundrel anticipated her reaction. Smacking her on the bottom, he grinned and held her off with incredible ease.

"Who holds the power?" she queried archly.

"Or perhaps this is more to your liking," he said, piercing the heart of her. They both cried out.

Having gained her answer, Brock was unrelenting. She might have been the one on top, but he was the one who set their reckless pace. The cords in his neck grew prominent as he drove his hips upward, plunging his thick manhood to the hilt, repeatedly, so that her entire body bucked with each battering thrust.

A sinuous warmth began intensifying in her belly, spreading and constricting every inch it consumed. Without warning, it exploded, similarly to the hammer of a pistol striking the priming pan. Her vision was a blinding flash of white as she was racked with pulse after pulse of ecstasy. As she endeavored not to collapse on him, his name erupted from her lips in a strangled gasp.

Her writhing cries severed Brock's arrogant restraint. Rearing up frantically in cadence with her fading release, he stilled, letting his head fall back, and his hips arched to meet hers. They were locked together, and his breath was a hiss between his teeth. Amara held him closer, feeling the rhythmic contraction of his manhood, the forceful gush of his seed against her womb. Brock had described their joining as a sharing of their bodies. She disagreed. It was a claiming.

Sated and sleepy, neither spoke while he absently stroked her back. His manhood had remained turgid after the release. Still, nestled within her, Brock made no attempt to disengage their tangled repose. Finally, he asked, "Have you figured out who holds the power, dove?"

He reached over and flipped the blanket over them. Pondering the answer to the riddle, she fell into a dreamless sleep.

Brock was alone on the pallet when he awoke. Stretching out the kink in his right shoulder, he searched the hall for some hint of Amara's whereabouts. The corner of his mouth twitched, fighting an indulgent grin. Poor little dove, he thought. Waking up naked beside her lover must have triggered a bout of shyness. She was probably upstairs castigating herself for her lapse of judgment while she wiggled herself back into her corset and gown. A gentleman would dress and respect her privacy, he mused, scratching the stubble under his jaw. Unfortunately, for Amara, he threw on and shed his decorum like a pair of breeches. After last night, he was looking forward to finding her and stripping her of her misgivings and whatever else she was wearing.

"Looking for me?"

She had paused at the threshold. From her expression, she must have been watching him for some time. Instead of donning her gown, she had slipped on his shirt. The sunlight beaming down from overhead gave him enticing glimpses of the naked curves beneath. A flood of possessiveness filled him, knowing only hours earlier he had feasted on the forbidden and she had let him.

Brock had been prepared to coax her from her shyness. He was unsure of the confident woman who stared brazenly at his nakedness. "Where did you go?" he asked, pulling a blanket over his hips. Seeing her rumpled and bathed in sunlight only inflamed his morning arousal.

Amara held up a bean tart. She broke off a piece and popped it in her mouth. "I was hungry."

His mouth went dry as he watched her tongue dart out, ensnaring a crumb at the corner of her mouth. "Were you planning on sharing?"

She blushed at the question. Belatedly, he recalled telling her that joining with her was a kind of sharing. It appeared she was more ill at ease with their lovemaking than she had wanted him to know. After a moment, she walked over to him. "You may have it all, if you like." She offered him the tart.

He leaned toward her and took a bite. Chewing thoughtfully, he held her gaze while he caressed her knee. His hand slid between her legs and up her inner thigh. "Are you terribly sore?" He found her silken nest, and she dampened under his skillful fondling.

"I—I am not c-certain," she stammered. The forgotten bean tart fell from her hand to the stone floor.

Reaching for her hand, he meticulously licked the crumbs from her fingers. Shivering, she closed her eyes.

"Then I will have to find out for myself."

The hackney had been her inspiration. If she had allowed Brock to have his way, he would have driven her home and brashly escorted her to the door. That would have been a fearsomely awkward scene. At the sight of her in Brock Bedegrayne's custody, her mother would have collapsed in an apoplectic fit while her father quietly started plotting Brock's murder.

She could not let that happen.

They had argued most of their journey back to London. In the end, he had conceded to her wishes and put her in the hired coach. The hard kiss he had pressed onto her tender mouth had not been half as daunting as his parting words.

"Retreat if you must, but remember well that you are mine."

How could she forget? She ached from his claiming and was likely to for days. There was no part of her that had not been marked with his mouth and hands. Even the morning had not hindered his ardor. Shameless, he had risen naked from the pallet and led her to one of the chairs near the hearth. After what they had done, she wondered if she could ever look at a chair without blushing.

Remember well.

Oh, she would indeed. Although she had washed away the evidence of their night together, his unique male scent clung to her, mingling with her own. She could close her eyes, but it was his green hungry gaze that devoured her in her mind, his guttural voice that demanded she take more of him.

Nothing could make her regret their lovemaking. Even though she had been terrified initially, he had spent the night banishing her demons one by one. She had brought him pleasure as well, she thought, a dreamy smile softening her lips. If one day was all the fates offered them, she would be content, for the memory of them together would warm her heart for a lifetime.

Lost in her thoughts, she was only vaguely aware that the hackney had stopped. The door opened and Amara looked blankly at the face of the coachman.

"'Ere ye go, lass," he said encouragingly, helping her out of the coach.

The front door of their town house swung open. Their butler, Buckle, must have noticed her arrival from one of the windows. Rushing forward, he was at her side before she had taken four steps.

"Thank you for your services," the butler said to the hired coachman. "I will return with your fee after I have seen to Miss Claeg."

"The g—"

"The good man has been paid, Buckle," she said, rushing over the man's declaration that a gentleman had paid her way in advance.

The coachman cleared his throat, understanding too well her need for discretion. "True 'nuff. A good day to you, miss." He tugged the rim of his hat and backed away.

"You look tired, Miss Claeg. Shall I call for a bath or have Cook fix you a tray?"

She absently patted her stomach. Brock had distracted

her earlier when she had been hungry. "Both. I am famished. Are my parents at home?"

"No, miss. Lord Keyworth departed with Conte Prola an hour ago. I believe they were anticipating a falconry demonstration at one of the commons."

"And my mother and Miss Novell?"

"At the dressmaker's. Lady Keyworth expressed concern that you were not available for the fitting of your new gown."

Amara winced at the reminder of the upcoming ball being held in honor of her birthday. She had deliberately skipped several of her fittings when she had begun to suspect the true reason for the festivities. Lord and Lady Keyworth intended to announce her betrothal to the conte.

"Is something troubling you, Miss Claeg?" he politely inquired, noting her pained expression.

"Nothing important. Just a loose pin," she improvised, recalling the trouble Brock had had acting as her maid. They had quickly discovered that duplicating Corry's efforts was more challenging than he had arrogantly assumed. "Anything else?"

"Just your brother."

She halted and gripped the butler's arm. Doran had tried contacting her, and once again she had missed him. "There has been a message from my brother?"

If he thought her reaction odd, his visage did not betray his opinion. "Mr. Claeg surprised the household with an unexpected visit this morning. He was rather intent on speaking with you."

"Mallory," she said cautiously.

"Yes, miss. He and Lord Keyworth briefly exchanged words and then Mr. Claeg departed."

She doubted their meeting had been a pleasant one.

"Were they arguing, Buckle?" If there was discord between father and son, the entire staff would have witnessed a thunderous display.

"I cannot say. I was not privy to their discourse."

It was too much to hope they had put aside their differences. Something was troubling her brother to rouse him out of his bed before twelve. "Very well. Thank you, Buckle." She moved toward the stairs.

"Miss Claeg?"

"Yes."

"Forgive me for any disrespect, however, I must inquire. Are you all right?" he asked, his gaze dwelling on the soiled condition of her gown.

She glanced down ruefully at the front of her skirt. "It is the gown that inspires your concern. A sorry state, I must confess. I am dreading Corry's scolding when she sees what my clumsiness has done to her fine handiwork."

Amara waved farewell to the butler and rushed up the stairs before he asked questions she was not prepared to answer.

CHAPTER TWENTY

Entering the house he had rented for the season, Brock longed for a bath, food, and a few more hours of sleep. He was not particular about the order. No one rushed out to greet him as he discarded his hat and gloves. Amara had teased him about his lack of staff at Whitmott Park. This house could use a few more servants too. Only a manservant, cook, and housemaid were looking after him. It had seemed enough a few weeks ago, but he suspected the trio fell short of a lady's expectations. After all, the household was a woman's domain.

"Good afternoon, Mr. Bedegrayne," the manservant said, struggling to put his arm into the sleeve of his coat. "Forgive my tardiness."

"I managed to open the door all on my own, Sellick." Brock could not say the same for his manservant. The man was contorted and flapping about like an outraged goose. He grabbed the servant by the scruff of his neck and forced him to stand still while he worked the man's arm into his sleeve.

"Thank you, sir." He tripped over his own foot as he picked up the hat and gloves Brock had tossed on the floor. "I suppose you will want refreshments for you and your guest."

"Entertaining whilst I am out of town, Sellick?"

The younger man's eyes rounded in horror. "Oh, no, sir! The gentleman claimed he was a close friend of yours. He assured me that you would not mind if he waited for your return."

Brock heard a suspicious sniffle. "Good God, man, are you crying?"

"The dust, sir, it tickles my nose."

He had a servant who suffered from an aversion to dust running his household. Brock liked Sellick well enough, but it was obvious the man was too inexperienced for his position. On the morrow, he would consult Wynne about finding some additional staff. As for Sellick, well, perhaps the man would be better suited as his valet.

"Get rid of whoever hoodwinked you to get into my parlor. Friend or foe, I have no interest in entertaining anyone."

"Interesting choice of words, Bedegrayne," Mallory Claeg said, striding toward them. "I was deliberating on which f-word applied to you."

Whatever brought Claeg to his door, he had come on his own. He glanced at the manservant. "Tell Cook we will need those refreshments you had mentioned." He turned on his heel and headed for the parlor he had never used. "Claeg, you surprise—"

Claeg tackled him from behind. They landed on the sofa. Clipping his chin on the wooden frame, he tasted blood. If this continued, one of them was going to get seriously hurt. Feeling he had no choice, Brock smashed the back of his head into the other man's face. Whirling on his attacker, he cocked his fist. "I prefer having you as a friend, not an enemy."

Wiping the blood from his lip with the back of his hand, he saw that Amara's brother had no intention of being reasonable. "Where have you been?" Mallory growled.

Trying for amusement, Brock lowered his fist. "It has been years since I answered to anyone." He took a few prudent steps backward and sat in a chair. "However, since you asked so politely, I will tell you. I went north to check on some property I own."

"Alone?"

"I believe that is not your concern."

Mallory stood; his long hair had become loose in their brief fight. His gaze glittered with malice. "It is, if my sister was at your side."

Having recently been in Mallory's position, he empathized with the man. "Have you spoken to your sister?"

"No," Claeg curtly replied. "Like you, Amara has spent the night elsewhere."

"Why have you deduced she was with me?"

"Several reasons. I was told my sister went to visit A'Court's widow."

"So? Are the women not friends?"

"Yes. I also know my sister lied. The dowager is not in London."

"Are you certain?"

"Yes," Claeg said succinctly. "My sister has the penchant for lies when the truth involves a Bedegrayne."

The brother suspected, but he had no proof. Brock silently contemplated his choices. "Amara is loyal to those she loves. She long ago gave up believing Lady

Keyworth's tripe about Devoña's being responsible for Doran's tragic demise."

Claeg visibly cringed at the comparison to his vitriolic mother. "Amara was with you," he said, mutinous.

The notion of facing him at dawn was unpalatable. Shooting Claeg, even if he deserved it, would not endear him to the family. "If you insist on knowing your sister's whereabouts, ask her."

"I will. If you have dishonored her, Bedegrayne, my seconds shall be pounding at your door."

Brock stretched his long legs out, appearing relaxed. "I will not fight you, Claeg, but know this. My intentions toward Amara have always been honorable. She will be my bride before the year expires."

The other man curled his hand over his fist. "Is that why you seduced her? Did you think my family would hand her over to the man who had defiled her?"

Brock jumped to his feet. The two men glared at each other with mutual dislike. "Tread carefully. I still have not forgiven you for not asking these questions when they might have been useful."

"What are you saying, or more to the point, what are you *not* saying?"

Amara trusted him with her secrets. He would not betray her, even if he could benefit from it. "Claeg, Claeg, do not ask questions for which the answers will only upset you," Brock chided.

Realizing he would not gain any further explanation, Claeg said, "Have you spoken to my father concerning your intentions, or is this blathering about marriage simply Bedegrayne arrogance?"

He planned to speak with Lord Keyworth as quickly as he could arrange it. "I can be quite convincing."

Claeg snorted. "You will have to be bloody extraordinary with the ball being days away."

The hairs on Brock's neck prickled with foreboding. He knew about the Keyworths' upcoming ball. Amara had not mentioned it, and now her silence disturbed him. "What is so important about the ball?"

"Amara did not tell you? Our father plans to use the occasion to announce her betrothal to Prola."

Sellick knocked, and entered the room carrying a tray. "I have brought the refreshments, sir."

"Not now," he growled. So, his dove thought she could fly from his arms to another's, did she? The lady might be a horrendous liar, but she had perfected the passiveness of omission with a competence that would likely get her bottom paddled the next time they met.

The manservant babbled an apology and turned to leave them. The hasty retreat slid everything on the tray to one side. Countering the shift by raising the opposite end higher, the servant gave a shout of dismay as pieces of china shattered on the floor.

Most of the anger had faded from Claeg's shrewd gaze. Surveying the wreckage created by his unexpected visit, he said, "You have much to resolve, Bedegrayne." He shook his head in pity at Sellick's sniffle. "By God, I almost hope you succeed."

The rosewood desk with its rich ivory inlay was delivered the next afternoon. The footman's announcement had Amara scurrying down the stairs, the dressmaker's protests echoing behind her. The gown she wore was held together by dozens of pins and it seemed every breath drove the sharp points into her tender flesh.

The servants had left the desk in the front hall, await-ing instructions on where it should be placed. As Brock had promised, the desk was beautiful and exotic. It was perfect.

"Amara! We have precious little time for your whims. Madame must finish her measurements, else the gown will not be ready for tomorrow evening."

Lady Keyworth had not joined her below. She stood on the upper landing, her hands clasped in agitation. Amara unconsciously placed herself in front of the desk, block-ing her mother's view.

"I was returning, Mama."

The older woman tilted her head, attempting to see what her daughter was protecting. "A gift from the conte?"

Hiding her clenched fist behind her back, the edges of her fingernails cut into her palm. What was she to do? She had begged Brock not to send the desk. He knew the magnitude of such a gift would cause her difficulty.

"Conte Prola did not send this. The desk is a gift from Mr. Bedegrayne."

Her eyes full of speculation, Lady Keyworth pursed her lips. "Why would Sir Thomas's eldest son believe you would be receptive to such an expensive offering?"

"I suppose in honor of my birthday," she explained, furious with Brock for creating this unpleasant predica-ment. "You did send invitations to the Bedegraynes?"

"Come upstairs. We will discuss the small issue of the desk later."

Her mother's evasion was telling. "How could you? These women are my friends." Realizing arguing about friendship would not soften Lady Keyworth's heart, she appealed to the older woman's self-importance. "Despite your feelings for anyone named Bedegrayne, the family holds influence in this town. Tipton and Sutton will not be pleased their wives were insulted, nor will Milroy."

"Milroy," her mother scoffed.

"Is the half brother of a duke! Do not underestimate the reach of his influence." She ruthlessly pressed on. "Papa understands the necessity of courtesy, even to one's enemy. What will he think of your oversight?"

Her mother paled, the consequences of her cruel slight finally cutting through her need for petty revenge. "Miss Novell, in my haste I have neglected several invitations. You will assist me. My daughter will continue her fitting without our guidance."

Piper stepped into view. "Yes, ma'am."

Amara was not surprised her cousin had been eavesdropping. She could almost see the wheels of calculation rotating in the woman's head as she wondered how she could benefit from the exchange she had overheard.

"Will we be sending an invitation to your friend, the mysterious dowager?"

Amara lifted her chin at the subtle cynicism she detected in the question. "Your rough edges are showing again, cousin." Piper stiffened at the insinuation. "To answer your question, the countess is still in mourning. I am certain while my mother writes her apologies to Sir Thomas and his family"—she stared sharply at her mother—"she will explain the courtesy we bestow on the dead."

"Just as you, my dear daughter, will display tomorrow evening how one goes about honoring the living."

Amara sagged against the edge of the desk. She yelped, jumping up as a dozen carefully placed pins jabbed her in the backside. Even when she was in the wrong, her mother always had a knack for lopping any advantage Amara had won.

Cloaked in colors of the night, Brock stealthily moved past the Keyworth stables and into the gardens. Within he listened to the muffled laughter of the male occupants. They were too busy with their card game to heed any noise he might make. Approaching the house, he kept his gaze on the prize. Light emanating from the window revealed his quarry was in her bedchamber and she was awake.

Good.

He wanted her alert when they had their conversation. Using the trellis as a ladder, he climbed up to one of the balconies. The next part was trickier. Unwinding the coil of rope he had slung around his neck, Brock tossed the weighted end up to the smaller balcony above. He flinched at each failure, the minutes ticking by loudly in his head as he waited for someone to become curious about the noises outside. He had padded the hook with rags but there was always a risk. His fourth attempt almost knocked him unconscious. He stifled a groan. Although his hat had cushioned the blow, the top of his head was aching. His own family would haul him in front of the magistrate if they learned of this. It was incentive enough not to fail.

The hook caught the railing on his sixth attempt.

Hand over hand, he silently pulled himself up the rope. Despite the coolness of the night, sweat beaded and coursed down his face and back. Softly grunting, he seized the top of the railing and swung a leg over. He landed in a crouch.

No one approached the window.

Brock wiped his damp forehead, giving himself a few minutes to regain his composure. Gathering the rope, he left it in a heap on the balcony. This was indeed an unusual courtship. He doubted his brothers-in-law had endured such trials when wooing his sisters. Disgusted by the madness Amara had managed to instill in him, he vowed the next time he entered the Keyworth residence, it would be through the front door.

Amara glanced up from her book for the third time and stared at the window. She should have been asleep hours ago, yet sleep eluded her. Perhaps her ennui had saved her life. She jolted at the muted thud outside her window. Setting aside her book, she quietly slid off her bed. She removed a pair of scissors from the table beside her bed. Amara slapped her hand over her mouth, containing her shriek, when Brock's face peered through the glass.

She pressed her hand to her heart. "Damn you, Brock Bedegrayne," she muttered, marching toward the window. She freed the latch and pushed open the panels. "I resisted stabbing Tipton when he tried this. You, on the other hand, tempt me over the verge of sanity!"

Brock grabbed her wrist and removed the scissors she was jabbing in his face. "Settle down. You have no intention of stabbing me."

"I am not so certain."

He placed the scissors and his hat on the table. As he recalled her words, his green gaze became mere slits. "What did you mean when you said that you resisted stabbing Tipton?"

Regretting her outburst, she said, "Nothing. I would rather discuss your nocturnal visit."

"Oh, no, dove, it is not that simple." He closed the window and the draperies. When he was finished with the task, he faced her with his arms crossed expectantly. "Explain."

She refused to cause discord between the two men. Tipton had committed no crime. "It happened years ago. Tipton—he noticed how I grieved for Doran. It was within his power to ease my torment and he chose in his own fashion to comfort me." She crossed her arms, matching his stance.

Brock's face remained expressionless. Finally, he said, "He told you about Doran."

"Yes," she hissed. "It was more than the rest of your family did. I shall always be grateful for his kindness."

He left the window, and moved so he stood in front of her. Without a word, he pulled her into his embrace. She rubbed her nose against his chest, savoring his comfort.

"Why have you come, Brock? I cannot fathom you scaling the side of the house just for a hug."

"You would be amazed by what I would risk for you," he murmured into her hair. "However, in this instance, you are correct. I am here for other reasons."

"The door!" she exclaimed, remembering that it was not locked. She broke his hold, rushing to carry out the task.

"Amara, your brother paid me a visit."

"Did he? He came to our house too."

"He thinks I lured you from town and seduced you."

It might not have been planned, but the results were the same. Concerned, she turned and met his steady gaze. "What did you tell him?"

They both spoke in whispers. Regardless, the harshness in his laughter still stung. "Not the truth. He was ready to pummel me for just his suspicions."

She had been so careful. How had Mallory seen through her deception so soon? Everything was escalating out of control. The notion of Brock and Mallory facing each other on a dew-covered common was too ghastly for contemplation.

Some of her mounting horror must have crept into her expression. A parody of a grin parted his lips. "Do not fret, dove. Your brother is safe from me. Putting a ball in him would cost me too much."

"My concern is not only for my brother, but for you as well!" she said, feeling goaded by his mockery.

"It is odd to hear you speak of caring, particularly when your brother tells me that you and Prola will be announcing your betrothal tomorrow."

The room closed in on her. "No," she said fiercely.

"Claeg learned of the good tidings from your father. Keyworth was most pleased by your consent." He seized her by the waist and hauled her up on her toes. "I could strangle you for letting me touch you!" he rasped. "What were you doing, Amara? Simply compensating the loser? Did you honestly believe I would be satisfied with one night?"

"No!" She struggled, fighting to free herself from his ruthless grip.

"If you were looking for a hot fucking, you should have explained to me my role. As you can feel"—he bumped his arousal against her—"I am always willing to oblige you, Miss Claeg."

He tangled his hands in her hair and kissed her. His tongue plundered the inner recesses of her mouth. She tasted blood, but endured the kiss. Brock had touched her, seducing her with tenderness and later with impatience. She had hurt him. In his pain, all he preferred sharing with her was his lust.

"Not here," she pleaded, fearing they would be discovered.

He responded by tearing the front of her nightgown. "Here," he said, unbuttoning the fall on his breeches. Engorged, his manhood sprang free from the matting of curls. He stalked toward her. "Now." Shoving her back to the wall, he speared his fingers into the curly nest between her legs. She gasped at his invasion. Already wet, she wiggled as his fingers sank deeper.

"You cannot fake this kind of response. You want me inside you." He lifted her high and pinned her to the wall with his thrust. "Put your legs around me."

The rough penetration stretched her almost to the point of pain. Before she could complain, he began moving inside her. Slowly, her body grew accustomed to his frenzied strokes. Trapped against the wall, she was at his mercy. The thought distressed her until she remembered this was Brock. In spite of his anger, his hold was not cruel. What might have started as punishment had spun into desire. His mouth shifted from one breast to the other, kissing and laving her nipples until she ached. Her position limited her movements, so she caressed the back of his neck.

His powerful release almost buckled his knees. Staggering to keep them upright, Brock smothered his cry of fulfillment against her breast as he emptied himself into her.

Amara made a tiny noise of discontent when he pulled out of her clinging sheath. He flinched at the sound. Gazing down at her with haunted eyes, he said, "I have no excuse for my actions. I treated you no kinder than a rutting beast, striving only for his pleasure." His hands trembled as he reached out tentatively and cupped her chin. "I would cut my heart out rather than hurt you."

She leaned into his fingers. "Oh, Brock, I knew the minute you touched me that you would never hurt me. I will confess, I was a little anxious at first. Until now, you have restrained your carnal appetites, have you not?"

"You deserve only a man's tenderness."

"Because of what Cornley did to me?" She sighed at his weary nod. "Brock, you have just proven why it will never work between us. No one can spend the rest of his or her life holding back a part of their nature just to please another. You would grow to hate me."

"Never," he vehemently denied. Shackling both her wrists, he pressed her bound hands to his heart. "Forget about your family and Prola. Marry me."

He was breaking her heart. "I did not become your lover because I thought you needed compensation. If anyone is the loser, it is me. Do you think I want to marry Conte Prola? He means nothing to me!" She blinked back the tears in her eyes.

"Refuse him!"

"Once, I thought I could." She shook her head at the futility of it all. "Papa," she said helplessly, fearing her father's wrath more than Brock's. "My family will disown me if I refuse him."

Brock was not unmoved by her anguish. He set her down, but held her close. "I can give you a family. You will not be alone."

He did not understand. Even if she summoned the courage to abandon her family, she feared how her father might execute his vengeance. "I cannot put you or your family at risk. I love you," she said passionately. "If something happened—"

"Hush." Brock placed two fingers over her lips, silencing her. "You love me?"

She nodded, letting the tears flow down her cheeks.

"I have waited most of my life to hear those three words from you," he said, hoarse from emotion. "And I have loved you longer than I can recall." He lifted her lovingly into his arms and carried her to the bed.

"I am not fragile, Brock." She slipped her legs under the blankets.

"Precious, then." He nipped her lower lip and pulled back out of reach. The last time he had not bothered removing his clothes. He felt guilty about his careless handling and had something to prove, she suspected. Wordlessly, she sat back and watched him disrobe. He had a beautiful, virile body. Just staring at him gave her a wicked thrill.

The tattered remains of her nightgown rested on her shoulders. She shrugged out of the garment while Brock kicked off his breeches. When he had shed the last of his clothing, she held the blankets up, inviting him to join her. Covering them both, he settled down beside her.

She turned on her side, and rested the palm of her hand on his stomach. Sliding lower, she wrapped her fingers around his manhood, feeling him lengthen and grow rigid at her bold contact.

He lay back and relished her petting. "Come here," he murmured, already reaching lazily for her hip.

"No. Not that way."

"Amara," he said, stunned by her rejection.

"I told you that I am not fragile. I can bear your weight. Cover me," she demanded. He had loved her in so many ways, she had not realized until later that he had determinedly avoided holding her down with his weight.

"Are you sure?"

"I assume loving each other in a bed will be rather tame after the wall," she said wryly, making his face redden.

He eased himself between her legs. "We will move slowly. You can change your mind if you become frightened."

Amara wrapped her legs around him, pulling him closer. She was slick from their previous joining, so there was no resistance when he entered her. Buried to the hilt, he held himself motionless. She arched her back, the throbbing pulse of his manhood making her crave more of him. Caging her with his arms, he stared down at her, his concern for her distracting him.

"I am going to bite you if you do not start moving this instant!"

The apprehension faded from his expression. "Promise," he whispered in her ear. He eased out of her, and pinned her hips with a forceful thrust.

Amara leaned forward and bit him on the shoulder. "Again."

His slower, controlled strokes had her squirming. She squeezed his sides with her legs, encouraging him to hasten his pace. He ignored her command.

"I cannot bear it."

"I disagree," he replied, his face taut with desire. He pushed deep, proving she accommodated every inch of him. She moaned and writhed beneath him.

They both froze at the quiet knock. Someone jiggled the latch.

"Miss Claeg, the door won't open."

"My maid," she mouthed the words silently to Brock. "Corry, I locked the door for some privacy." The wicked amusement she noted in his green eyes worried her.

With laughter twitching his lips, he resumed his devastating thrusts. The moan escaped her before she could stop it.

"Oh, you are ill. I knew something was wrong," her maid said from the other side of the door.

"No, no," she said, assuring the maid. "Stop it," she whispered to her mischievous lover. She felt overly warm and tingling just under the surface of her skin.

"You are so close," he said, biting her earlobe. "I can feel those tiny muscles milking the head of my cock. In a few more minutes, even your father's presence could not keep me from spilling my seed in you."

Her sheath constricted painfully around his manhood. The man was using her maid's presence to heighten her arousal. Curse him, it was working!

"Miss Claeg, let me into the bedchamber."

Unable to hold back the flow of her release, she turned her face into her pillow. Her hips jerked as the first wondrous wave rushed through her. The pleasure ebbed and surged with each thrust. Holding her breath, she clutched him fearing she would cry out. Brock was fighting his own limitations. The allure of her release shattered his restraint. Slanting his mouth over hers, he ground his pelvis into hers. Seconds later, the viscous pulsation of his release filled her.

"Miss Claeg!"

"Corry, there is nothing wrong. Go to bed!" she said, sounding exasperated.

"If you say so, miss."

They listened to the maid's retreat. Amara punched him in the chest. "You dolt! What were you doing?"

Unrepentant, he dealt easily with her outraged struggles. "If I must explain, then you leave me no choice. Once I have recovered from the potent wiles of your luscious body, I will endeavor to repeat my performance."

Amara lifted her brows in disbelief. "You will kill us."

"Only if it is done properly."

CHAPTER TWENTY-ONE

"You have been avoiding me."

She crossed his studio, irritated that his remark was accurate. It had taken all of her courage to face him. "Untrue. Mama has kept me occupied with various errands. You are coming to the ball?"

"That reminds me, many felicitations on your birthday, puss." Mallory leaned over and kissed her cheek. "And yes, I have received the paternal decree that by not attending the ball I will diminish my inheritance."

"That is outrageous!"

Her brother winked at her. "I thought so too. Not to worry, I had planned to attend, decree or no." He gestured at the painting in front of him. "Your portrait is nearly completed. What is your opinion?"

He had finished her face during her absence. The lady who stared back at her was striking. She wore her hair up, a riot of soft curls framing her face. Her blue eyes gleamed with intelligence and confidence. Overwhelmed, she stared blindly at the painting. "You have made me beautiful."

"No," he corrected, obviously pleased by her reaction. "This is a faithful reproduction of my model."

"Oh, Mallory."

Gruffly, he motioned toward the chair several yards away. "Sit. I can work on your hands while we talk. Do you recall the position I need?"

"Naturally. Pain imparts excellent instruction. After our first session, I could not bend my wrist without cringing."

"Have I been difficult?" he queried from behind the framed canvas.

"No less than a sister expects from her brother," she teased.

"I called on Bedegrayne recently."

"He told me." Amara closed her eyes, realizing her error.

The soft scratching of his brush halted. "Interesting. Give me one reason why I should not call him out?"

Having loved and married the wrong woman in his youth, Mallory was probably the only one in her family who would understand her situation. "I love him."

"Dear God, it is contagious," he said with brotherly disgust.

"Brock told you that he loved me?"

"Only a lovesick fool would challenge one of our father's decrees." There was a wealth of bitterness in his chuckle. "I should know."

While Mallory worked, her thoughts drifted to her night with Brock. He had spent most of the night in her bed. They had not wasted their remaining time together sleeping. Nor were there further discussions about Prola or the ball. Instead, they savored their newly proclaimed love. They cuddled, lazily exploring each other's bodies. Later, as promised, when he had recovered his vigor he had continued his seduction.

Amara's face flushed with the recollection.

She had turned discouragingly onto her stomach, pleading exhaustion. Ignoring all her protestations, he had covered her as if she were a mare and entered her from behind. The sheer wickedness of the act had prompted her immediate release. Encouraged by her sensitivity, he had driven her to completion three more times before losing himself in her softness. Only the approaching dawn and the waking servants had chased him away. She had watched his descent from the window. It was short of a miracle he had not been discovered or broken his foolish neck.

"Where did you go?"

She blinked, dissolving her last image of Brock. Repositioning her hands, she begged, "Mallory, what should I do? Papa promised that he and Mama would disown me if I refuse the conte's offer." Amara refused to tell him everything their father had said that night. Such a confession would provoke her brother into cutting his tenuous ties with their sire.

"What will you lose?"

"My family," she snapped back at his obtuseness. "Everything."

"I would not abandon you, puss."

"You might if he threatened to cut off your funds."

He clasped his heart in mock despair. "How little you think of me. What little you know." He dabbed his brush into one of the colors on his palette and the scratching strokes resumed.

"I think not only of myself. Brock could be in danger. It is ill-advised to underestimate Papa's fury. Or what if my selfishness cost Brock his family? How long before he would grow to resent me for his loss?"

Mallory cocked his left brow up at her anxious reasoning. "Since I am certain you have tried all of your arguments on Bedegrayne, what does he have to say?"

"He loves me," she said miserably. "I do not think he qualifies as rational."

He removed the brush he had clenched between his teeth. "No one in love does," he said dismissingly. "I once followed my heart and I am still living with the consequences."

"That is your lofty advice?" she asked, her voice ascending in her agitation. No longer caring about her pose, she shook out the stiffness in her hands. "What is the moral? Love destroys fools?"

"No," he countered impatiently. "Cowards never find love."

Carefully, positioning her hands again, Amara bit down on her lower lip. She found no comfort in her brother's advice.

"A little early for visiting, is it not, Bedegrayne?" Lord Keyworth inquired politely, as he skimmed the octavo in his hand. His gaze flickered over Brock. "A few extra hours in bed would have been beneficial. You have the look of a man who is suffering from overindulgence."

Brock was unable to disagree with the observation, and his cheek dimpled into an unapologetic grin. He was blissfully exhausted. His dove was a demanding creature, and he had enjoyed every hour satisfying her desires. How would Keyworth react if he learned those numerous hedonic acts had been committed with his precious daughter? Brock's lips twitched. The older man would likely swoon on his desk.

"A Bedegrayne's stamina is remarkable. Nothing will keep me from attending your ball."

Keyworth scowled, and set the octavo down. "No offense, but I was under the impression you were much like your father and detested these social frivolities?"

"What is the point of having principles, if you are not allowed to bend them on occasion?" He shrugged.

"Like sending my daughter a costly desk?"

Among other things. "I have collected many treasures during my travels. When I found the desk, I thought of Amara." Brock doubted the man would appreciate hearing that the desk had been custom made for her. "If you prefer, consider it a gift in honor of her birthday."

Even Keyworth recognized the value of the desk. Greed was a soothing balm for a bristled pride. "You are very generous. Our family is indebted."

Brock rebuffed the formal courtesy with a casual gesture. "Your approval is important. It was one of the reasons I have sought an audience with you this morning."

The older man picked up a paper knife and tested the edge. "Would it surprise you to learn I am aware of your interest in my daughter?"

"The interest is returned, Lord Keyworth."

"Civilization was not built on the whims of a young lady. Nor are fortunes." He tapped the blade idly on his finger.

The stirrings of temper burned in his gut. Brock was not expecting the man to embrace him, but he would not tolerate being patronized. "I can offer Amara a name she can bear proudly and my successes abroad will put jewels around her neck and silk on her back."

"I respect Sir Thomas. Our association, both personal and business, can be traced back to long before you were born. The loss of that friendship had troubled me." Keyworth bowed his head, weighted with regret. "For the sake of Sir Thomas, I will be forthright. There are several reasons I find you unsuitable. You lack the proper peerage I seek for my daughter. Until recently, your prospects were, at best, dismal. Even if I amended my opinion, Lady Keyworth will never accept a connection between our two families. Simply put, you are unworthy of my Amara."

The tempest simmering in his stomach boiled over. He tasted acid in his throat. Unworthy? The devil he was! What kind of man preferred brutal rapists and unctuous foreigners for his daughter? Shaking with rage, Brock stood.

Pulling out his pocket watch, Lord Keyworth checked the time. "You must forgive me, our chat took longer than I had expected. You are still welcome to attend the ball. Conte Prola and Amara are planning to announce their betrothal this evening. Being Sir Thomas's son, you will concede defeat graciously, I know, and offer the couple your compliments."

The image of Prola sharing Amara's bed was intolerable. "The hell I will," Brock growled, bracing his palms on the desk. "For Amara's sake, I approached you in a manner deserving of your position. Having failed, I will use the candor you favor. Amara belongs to me. Marry her off to Prola and she will be a widow by her wedding night." Having issued his warning, Brock turned to leave.

"Mr. Bedegrayne!" Lord Keyworth roared. "Prola is not the only man who would be in jeopardy on his wedding night."

The gauntlet of war had been cast to the ground.

• • •

Matteo found Lord Keyworth near the aviary. All around them, servants went about their tasks preparing for the ball. Instead of doting on one of his winged predators, the man was stroking the sleek plumage of a ringdove.

"I sent for you hours ago."

It was the arrogance of his summons that had cost the man his hours. The conte was not his servant. "An unavoidable delay, I confess," he said soothingly.

"Brock Bedegrayne was here earlier."

"This was upsetting to your lady, no?"

The bird shrilled in protest at the viscount's fierce grip. "*I* am upset. The man will ruin everything if we do not stop him."

Recently, he had come to a similar conclusion. "Forgive me. I do not understand. What has the man done?"

"The bounder intends to marry my daughter. I have reason to believe she has encouraged him."

"How is this?" he demanded, puffing with indignation. "You assured me your daughter was a virgin!"

The insinuation his daughter was despoiled had Keyworth sputtering. The older man's face was mottled with an unflattering red hue. "I have not dishonored our agreement with lies. My daughter is untouched," he said, although he did not sound convinced.

Matteo frowned down at the agitated bird. "Why have you summoned me?"

"I do not trust Bedegrayne. He might try kidnapping my daughter."

It was a possibility. "Where is Miss Claeg?"

Keyworth glanced up at one of the upper-story

windows. "I ordered her to remain in her bedchamber until the ball. She will not defy me."

"I have confidence you will protect her, even from herself. What do you require of me?"

"Find Bedegrayne. Give him an excuse not to be present this evening. Is the chore too unsavory?"

He knew one or two gentlemen who enjoyed such work. "No, no." The image of Bedegrayne broken and bleeding brought a gentle smile to his lips.

"Good!" Keyworth said, letting the ringdove drop to the ground. "If you get missish, just remember, the man will not hesitate strolling over your rotting corpse to reach my Amara."

Matteo nudged the bird with his toe. The ringdove did not move. Its fragile kohl-lined head rested limply in the grass at an awkward angle. Blood welled in its blind dark eyes. Lord Keyworth in his fury had strangled the poor creature.

Above them, Amara paced the width of her room. The chaos of preparation resounded through the entire house. Instead of assisting her mother as expected, she had been ordered to her bedchamber. Even her mother had been surprised by her father's vehement adamancy. Her parents had been still arguing when she left the parlor.

Papa's surliness had not distressed her. The source of her unease had been hidden in her reticule, when she had entered the house. She had discovered the note on the floor of the carriage after she had said farewell to her brother.

Amara looked at the crumpled note she had clenched

in her fist. Shaking out the paper, she smoothed the creases out with her fingers. There was a single word.

"Tonight."

Doran was coming home.

CHAPTER
TWENTY-TWO

Catching sight of her brother coming up the stairs, Wynne groaned, "I have no time for you." With one of her daughters sleeping comfortably on her shoulder, she continued down the hall to the nursery. Brock followed in her industrious wake.

She greeted the nurse, who was dressing the infant's twin. Obviously, he had interrupted his nieces' bath.

"Wynne, your brother is here!" Milroy shouted from below.

His thunderous announcement woke up the sleeping infant. With a voice rivaling her sire's, she cried out her displeasure.

Wynne gave her brother a caustic glare.

He spread his arms in supplication. "You are not the only one in a rush."

Making soothing noises, she rubbed her daughter's tiny back. "I was so tempted to ignore Lady Keyworth's belated invitation. The audacity of that woman! If not for Amara, I would have tossed her note into the fire."

"Amara had no role in the affair. Her anger matched yours when she learned of her mother's deception."

"You are quick to defend her. Does she know you have taken up the sword on her behalf, my gallant knight?"

Wynne waited until the nurse had placed the infant she was caring for into the crib. "Come, Aideen, give a kiss to your annoying uncle."

Brock dutifully leaned over and pressed a kiss on the top of his niece's head. Affectionately, he stroked the child's head, hoping someday that he and Amara would be blessed with children. He was willing to dedicate day and night to the endeavor.

"You are grinning like a simpleton," his sister observed disrespectfully. Bestowing a kiss on Aideen's chubby cheek, Wynne handed her daughter to the nurse.

Rubbing the aches out of her arms, she said, "Why have you come? I had assumed we would see you later at the ball." Satisfied the girls were settled, she headed back downstairs.

"You will," he promised, his long legs equalizing her head start. "However, you have something I must claim first. Father told me Mother's sapphire ring is in your temporary custody."

"It is." Hooking her arm around Milroy's waist, she said, "You should be getting dressed, not playing in the stables."

"Why would I be playing with my horses, when I could be playing with you in the bath?" Milroy teased her.

Wynne peeked at Brock, clearly embarrassed that her brother was listening to her husband's ribald suggestion. Straightening with dignity, she ignored her husband and asked, "What do you want with Mother's ring?"

"It is for Amara." He took a deep breath. It amazed him that his sister's approval meant so much. "As soon as I can obtain a special license, I intend to marry her."

His sister was stunned, her green eyes glittering with moisture. "Oh, Brock!" She threw herself into his arms and hugged him fiercely.

"Does this mean you approve?" Brock asked, looking at Milroy for guidance.

Wynne pulled back, smiling. "Of course. I love Amara. Marrying you will make her my true sister."

Delighted by her response, he scooped her up and spun her once. "Glad I can be so accommodating, dear sister!"

His brother-in-law pounded him on the back. "Let me be the second to congratulate you on your good fortune. Miss Claeg is an admirable lady."

"I cannot fathom how you convinced Lord and Lady Keyworth to accept your offer of marriage," Wynne said, awed and pleased. Some of her pleasure dimmed at his evasive shrug. "You have gained their consent?"

"Amara is old enough to marry without it," he muttered defiantly.

Wynne folded her arms across her breasts. "What else? There is more that you are not telling us."

The truth would be known to all in a matter of hours. "Keyworth plans to announce Amara's betrothal to Conte Prola this evening."

Milroy's indigo gaze hardened subtly as he stared over his wife's head. "How serious is the trouble you are facing?"

Whether or not he asked for it, he had the man's support. "Keyworth and I exchanged threats. If Amara chooses me, her family will disown her." Or worse, he added silently.

"Poor Amara must be terrified!" Wynne wailed, concerned for her friend.

"She knows I love her."

Brock, too, was battling his personal share of fear, but he did not voice his worries aloud. Keyworth's threats did not bother him half as much as the prospect that his lovely dove might choose family duty over love.

"Where is he?"

Anticipation and irritation had prompted the question, Matteo decided. "Soon, friend, soon."

He had had someone discreetly watching Bedegrayne's residence all afternoon. The man's tardiness was unexpected. Guests were already arriving at the Keyworths' residence. If Bedegrayne was to attend the ball, he would return home eventually to dress.

"What of the servants?" the gruff voice persisted.

"Burnes observed the old cook and a housemaid departing earlier. I believe there is a manservant, but he will be no match for us if he is foolish enough to interfere."

"I want to deliver the deathblow."

"You may have your fun, but later," the conte assured him. "I cannot be late for the ball."

Entering the house, Brock thought it odd that one of the servants had left a burning oil lamp on the front hall tile.

"Sellick!"

There was a scuffling sound coming from upstairs. The asinine man had probably locked himself in the linen closet again. Before Brock could take a step forward, the constricting strength of a man's arm looped under his chin. Brock dug his fingers into that intractable muscle while his attacker dragged him back a few feet. He heard the door close behind him.

"Signor Bedegrayne," Prola greeted him, circling around so they stood face to face. "Good, you have not dressed. I would despair over ruining your favorite coat."

"Keyworth thought you were capable of delivering his message," Brock sneered, his tone ripe with disbelief. "At mealtime, you probably have one of the footmen carve up the meat on your plate."

The man threatening to crush his windpipe chuckled.

"Amusing, yes. That is why I have brought my friends. Have you met Burnes, Signor Bedegrayne?" the Italian asked, motioning to the man who stood near the parlor door.

Brock recognized the gentleman. He had been the Italian's companion the evening he had collected Amara from the Haslakes' theater box. Counting the immaculately dressed Prola, it was three against one. The odds were not to his liking, but he had endured worse.

"Why do we not continue our introductions in the formal parlor? If you have not murdered poor Sellick, we can summon him for the brandy."

Prola drove his gloved fist into Brock's stomach.

"You can do better. Amara has punched me harder than that."

Paling at the insult, the fop demonstrated how respectable his punch could be when properly inspired. The air in his lungs exploded from his chest as Brock doubled over. The painful spasms rippled all the way down to his balls.

There was more laughter from the towering tree trunk

behind him. Finding joy in one's work had its own rewards.

"Naturally, your absence will dishearten Miss Claeg," Prola said, adjusting the fit of his glove. "I can do no less than offer her your humble regrets. Burnes, once you have discouraged the signor, bind him." The conte's visage gleamed with malevolence. "I have another friend who desires an introduction. Now you must forgive me. I must leave. My lady, she awaits." The finality of the door shutting filled the house with silence.

The odds had improved, two against one. Encouraged, Brock gripped the arm around his throat and kicked out with both legs. The blow struck Burnes in the chest, sending him crashing into the wall. Twisting for his freedom, he and the laughing assailant turned in circles. Outweighing him by three stones, the man tightened his hold waiting for him to tire or pass out from the lack of breath.

"Hold him!" Burnes ordered. He landed two quick punches into Brock's ribs. "This is for the bloody kick." Using his booted foot, he struck the outside of Brock's right knee.

Brock's legs collapsed under him. His vision grayed as the full weight of the man behind him pressed him into the marble tile. At least his attacker was no longer laughing. Staggering to his feet, the man pulled Brock upright. Burnes was trying to dislocate his patella, perhaps both of them. Grunting against the pain, he deliberately put his weight on his injured leg and kicked the bastard in the crotch.

Direct hit.

Sucking air, Burnes clutched his wounded cock and fell to his knees. Brock hoped the unyielding tile ground his patellae into powder. Cursing, the other man rammed him into the wall. Dazed, he reached back for his unseen assailant's eyes. His fingernails scraped deep furrows into his attacker's cheeks. The man screamed. He forced Brock's head down, so that his next collision with the wall would be headlong.

The sickening thud made both men flinch. The arm around his throat loosened and fell away. Brock whirled around in time to see the large man collapse in an unconscious heap.

Smiling, with a fireplace poker in his hands, Sellick stepped over the body. "Am I too late, sir? It took longer than I had anticipated to escape my bindings."

Bracing his palm against the wall, Brock took the fire poker from his manservant's hands. "Sellick, remind me tomorrow that I am increasing your wages." Limping forward, he proceeded to give Burnes a complimentary lesson on discouragement.

Amara stood next to her parents as they greeted the late arrivals. She wore the gown the dressmaker had delivered in the late afternoon. It was a white crêpe train dress. The sleeves and round bottom were scalloped with amethyst satin ribbon. A wide band of black velvet confined the waist with a clasp encrusted with diamonds and amethysts. For the special occasion, Lady Keyworth had loaned her one of the Claeg necklace and earring sets that best complemented her gown.

All she needed was Brock.

Her gaze drifted to the front door each time Buckle opened it. Brock had yet to appear. By now, she had welcomed most of the Bedegrayne clan. As late as an hour ago, Wynne and Milroy had arrived. Her friend had embraced her warmly and kissed her on the cheek. She even complimented Lady Keyworth on her gown. The wary viscountess had returned the flattery and directed Miss Novell to escort the couple upstairs.

Where was he?

Her afternoon sojourn in her bedchamber had given her the opportunity to sort through her confusion about Doran. Amara had decided to tell Brock about her brother's return. He was a gentleman whom she could trust with all her secrets.

"Ladies, it is time we proceed along to the ballroom," her father said. "Buckle will contend with the laggards."

Giving the closed door a final glance, Amara followed behind her parents. She halted at the threshold, letting her parents disappear into the silken throng. Standing on her toes, she craned her head searching for anyone related to the Bedegraynes. Undoubtedly, one of them knew of Brock's whereabouts.

"Signorina Claeg!"

The man glided toward her with a silent swiftness worthy of her father's peregrine Ellette. She curtsied and extended her hand. "Are you enjoying yourself, my lord?"

He kissed her fingers lightly. "*Sí,* your presence enchants all."

The gentleman had a lovely way of speaking. It was a pity she could never love him. "The dancing is about to commence. Would you grant me a small favor and invite Miss Novell to join you in the first set? There are several hostess duties I must attend to before I am allowed to enjoy the festivities." If she did not want him, there was no reason her cousin might not find him a suitable candidate for a husband.

His expression revealed that he wanted to refuse, but

good manners prevailed. "For you, signorina, anything. A small favor for you," he said, staring eloquently into her eyes. "Later, a grand one for me."

The reminder of her duty made her stomach roil. She walked away from him trying to keep from retching. Blindly, she ran straight into Tipton. "I beg your pardon, my lord."

"You seem unwell." He beckoned to someone in the distance. "Can I get you something?"

"Someone," she amended. "I need to speak with your wife or Wynne."

The man wielded mysterious powers, for the two ladies appeared.

Wynne held her hand. "What is wrong?" she asked quietly.

"I will get her something to drink," Devona volunteered, slipping back into the crowd.

"Where is Brock? He promised to be here."

Wynne glanced questioningly at Tipton. The surgeon shook his head. "He will come. My brother does not break his promises. Besides . . ." She trailed off, reluctant to disclose the rest.

Amara squeezed her hand, encouraging her to continue. "You know something more. What?"

The other woman wrinkled her nose. "I will incur Brock's wrath for telling you this, but he called on us this afternoon."

"I assume this was more than a family visit?" Tipton mused.

"He wanted Mother's sapphire ring." Wynne hugged Amara, barely containing her excitement. "He told us that he intends to marry you. We truly will be sisters!"

The surgeon granted Amara one of his rare smiles. "So

Bedegrayne has finally caught his dove," he said, his usually enigmatic eyes glowing with approval. "Welcome to
the family, little sister."

Dazed by the affection, she accepted the cup of punch
Devona pushed into her hand. It took Wynne seconds to
whisper the good news in her sister's ear. Shrieking, the
youngest Bedegrayne embraced her. Tipton's quick
reflexes seized the cup before his wife spilled the punch
down the front of Amara's dress.

"Brock's declaration is a bit premature," Amara cautioned, dampening everyone's enthusiasm.

Wynne sobered first. "The conte."

"Who the devil is he?" Tipton asked.

"My sanctioned betrothed," she admitted forlornly.

No one wanted to alarm Amara, so the sisters waited until
she was distracted by one of the footmen. Devona and
Wynne with Tipton's assistance gathered up the Bedegrayne
clan. An impromptu meeting was discreetly held outdoors
in the garden.

Perplexed by all the tension she saw on everyone's
faces, Maddy said, "The room is so crowded, I could not
reach Irene and Sutton. Where is Sir Thomas?"

"I noticed a short fairy with silver hair had him cornered," Milroy said with a lilt of amusement. "For once,
he seemed merry in his predicament."

"Then we shall not interrupt them," Tipton decided.
"We can turn Sir Thomas and his blustery temper loose
on the Keyworths once we know all the details."

Milroy idly massaged his fingers on his left hand. "Is
this about Brock?"

"What about Brock?" Maddy chimed in, anxious.

Devona comforted her younger sister-in-law. "We will tell you everything later." She addressed the men. "Perhaps both of you should check his house?"

They would raise questions leaving en masse. "He will not thank us for overreacting," Wynne said.

Tipton agreed. "I will go."

"No," Milroy contradicted. "Stay and watch over the family. I'll check Bedegrayne's house. I've more experience with this kind of trouble."

Amara did not recognize the footman who had summoned her. This was not particularly strange since extra staff had been hired for the ball. "Repeat the message."

"Just one word, Miss Claeg," the servant dutifully repeated for the third time. "I was to say the word *tonight*, and tell you to slip out unnoticed. He is waiting for you on the street."

"Tell no one," she ordered, dismissing the footman.

"Yes, miss."

She bridled at the servant's sly grin. The man most likely thought she was running off to a clandestine meeting with her lover. Avoiding her parents and Buckle, Amara was on the stairs when Prola called out to her.

"My lady!" He rushed forward and clasped her hand. "We must speak."

"It will have to be later, my lord. I—" How could she think of a plausible lie when Doran was waiting for her just beyond the door!

"No, signorina, now," he imperiously commanded. "I must know your heart. You accept my offer, yes?" His grip was fierce as they stood on the stairs. He was attempting to tug her up and she desired the opposite direction. If she remained at his side, they would spend the rest of their days at cross-purposes.

Her answer was unequivocal.

Amara used her other hand to gently free herself from his grip. "I must refuse you, my lord. You offer me everything but the one thing I need—love."

"It is this Bedegrayne!" Prola seethed, muttering oaths in his native tongue. "Your papa, he will not permit this refusal!"

"No. Anything precious is costly." She was forfeiting her family. After this night, she was as lost as her brother Doran.

Amara hurried down the stairs.

"You are nothing but Bedegrayne's whore!" he shouted. "You are not worthy of my spittle!"

Carriages congested the street. Leaving the protection of the house, she headed east. Doran did not reveal himself. Turning around, she followed the street past her house, her frantic gaze searching the shadows between the carriages.

"Amara."

The soft masculine whisper floated on the evening air. She paused, almost afraid she had imagined it.

"Amara."

Slipping behind one of the parked carriages, she followed the voice. Horses nickered greetings as she moved down the street, losing sight of her house.

"Amara."

This time the pitch had gained strength. "Doran?"

"Here," the voice invited.

She stepped closer. A hand was clapped over her mouth, cutting off her cry of surprise. Another hand held her arm. She struggled vainly in her captor's embrace. A man emerged from the shadows. The lamp he grasped was positioned low to the ground, keeping his face in shadow. Only when he reached her did he raise it to his scarred face.

"Remember me?" the man rasped.

Not even the hand over her mouth stopped her screams.

CHAPTER
TWENTY-THREE

Brock and Milroy entered the Keyworth ballroom together. Cleaned up and attired in black breeches and matching stylish silk coat, Brock looked no different from any other gentleman. Until one noticed his bleeding lower lip—and the limp.

Sir Thomas ambled over to the men. "Brock, my boy, you have moved beyond fashionable into rudeness. What—" His feathery brows furrowed as he noted his son's numerous injuries. "Were you ambushed by a footpad?"

"No. Where is Amara?" He turned to Milroy. "Do you see her?"

His companion shook his head. "Here comes Tipton."

The viscount's pale eyes gravely studied him. More surgeon than aristocrat, Tipton grabbed Brock's jaw with one hand. Ignoring his brother-in-law's impatience, he silently evaluated the bruise blooming on Brock's throat.

"Three men were waiting for him," Milroy explained. "Prola was counting on the advantage of strength and surprise to outweigh any fighting skills Bedegrayne might possess." There was cold satisfaction in his gaze.

"Obviously, they gravely misjudged Bedegrayne's fondness for his neck."

Brock pulled his face away from Tipton's hand. "I can speak for myself."

"What's this?" Sir Thomas challenged. "By damn, I will call this Prola scoundrel out myself!"

"Quiet," he said to his father. "Milroy, search the room for Amara."

"Aye." He disappeared from their view.

"How badly are you injured?"

Brock returned his attention to Tipton. "Just a minor collection of bruises. One of the bastards tried to break my leg." His grin was ferocious. "He failed." Burnes and his companion were not dead, although when they regained their senses they might wish they were. "The pair will be in front of the magistrate come morning."

"Good. They are one less problem we will have to settle later."

"Lad," his father interjected, "Prola has been present most of the evening. Where does he fit in this mischief?"

"He punched me first. I intend to return the favor." Accepting his father's handkerchief, he dabbed at the blood on his lip. The stinging cut alone had put him in a nasty mood.

Mallory Claeg clapped a hand on his shoulder. "Bedegrayne, are you trespassing or did my father actually let you through the door?" Finally noticing Brock's battered condition, he was visibly shocked. "Dear Lord, how many footmen did you pummel into the dirt?"

"None," he snapped, exasperated he was wasting time with further explanations. "Where is your sister?"

Claeg snorted, obviously soaring on something stronger than punch. "I can barely find myself in this mob."

Brock gripped the other man by his coat. "Listen. Keyworth sent Prola and a few of his friends to my house. If not for my manservant, my corpse would have been tossed in the Thames."

"Sell-lick?" he slurred, not believing a word of it. "The man couldn't hold a tray. What'd he do, trip the assailants?"

He had no time for this. Brock shook him. "Sober up, Claeg." The man's teeth rattled quite nicely. "If we do not find Amara, your father will marry her off to a promising murderer."

"I will kill him."

Brock had no idea if the man was referring to Prola or his father. "Find your sister first. The brawling will come later." He released Claeg and watched him stagger away.

"Brock!"

Wynne, Maddy, and Devona moved toward the men. Clenching against the painful impact, Brock groaned when his sisters collectively embraced him.

"Ladies, he has sore ribs and a lame leg. You are torturing him with affection," Tipton admonished.

The women sprang back so quickly that at any other time their antics might have made him laugh. "Amara. Have you seen her?"

"Milroy found us and explained," Wynne said, despising that her words were additional blows. "Brock, an hour has lapsed since anyone last spoke to her."

Fifteen minutes later, Claeg returned looking grimmer and less inebriated than he had during their previous encounter. "Prola is missing."

Recovering from her faint, Amara slowly opened her eyes. The street and carriages were gone. While she was unconscious, they had moved her to a tiny room. The crude walls and the coolness hinted that she was below-ground, perhaps in a wine cellar. Three men sat around the table playing cards. Lying on her side, she twisted the bindings at her wrists. The loops of rope were so taut, she whimpered.

"Ah, the sleeping queen awakens."

The snide announcement had all three men turning to stare at her. The man she recognized and feared the most stood and came closer. "Miss Claeg, the passing years have enhanced your beauty."

Glancing down at her bare hands, she realized they had stolen her jewelry. Amara awkwardly brought her bound hands up to her chest, ignoring the burning conse-quences of her questing fingers. Her talisman was gone! She swallowed her growing panic. "Where is my brother?"

The question distracted her captor. "Mallory? Still at the ball or whoring. It hardly matters."

"Doran. Where is my brother Doran?"

That horribly scarred face grinned down at her. "Dead, Miss Claeg. You know he died in the Gate."

She brought her knees up, curling into herself. Doran was never there. It had all been a ruse to lure her away from her family. The disappointment she felt was choking the breath out of her. "What do you want? Money?"

"I want what was denied me six years ago—money and marriage," Lord Cornley rasped, reaching down for her.

Out of respect for his host, Brock had intended his chat with Keyworth to be private. Then he thought of Amara. She was alone and at Prola's mercy. He blamed Keyworth.

Unerringly, he limped toward his quarry. Seizing the man
by his cravat, Brock hauled him out of the card room.
Squawking like one of his prized falcons, the man sputtered for his release. There was a flurry of protests and
feminine shrieks as they moved down the hall and into
the viscount's study. Brock threw him against a table. The
menacing stuffed peregrine perched on the polished surface crashed to the floor.

Keeping his hand down on Keyworth's neck, he lifted
his head at the patter of a dozen footfalls. His family and
some of the more daring guests had followed. "None of
you have any part in this." Brock wished them all to
leave, especially his sisters. He did not want them to witness the burgeoning violence within him.

"Damn you, Tipton. Get the women out of here."

Devona shook off her husband's restraining hand.
"Brock," she pleaded. "He is her father."

Keyworth stirred at their voices. "Someone get him off
me. He intends to kill me!"

"Odd, you mention killing. Were Prola and his men
following your instructions when they tried to kill me?"

The older man kicked out, striking Brock's uninjured
leg. Angered, he raised the viscount's head and smacked
it on the table.

Lady Keyworth screamed. Pushing her way through
the crowd, she said, "The watch has been summoned. Mr.
Bedegrayne, you will spend the rest of your miserable
life in prison if you do not free my husband!"

He glared at the woman. If he was going to prison, he
might as well be deserving of the crime. Brock squeezed
the neck in his ruthless grasp. "I am not the only man in
this room setting off to prison. Tell her about Prola."

"Madam, I am innocent. I—I only asked the conte to

speak with B-Bedegrayne before the ball. He was upset when I rejected his offer to marry our daughter. I was afraid he might h-hurt her." The viscount winced, preparing for punishment.

"Pitiful," Sir Thomas muttered, dismayed by his old friend's babbling excuses.

"Talk?" Brock mocked, letting his gaze slide over to Lady Keyworth's bloodless cheeks. "The man broke into my house and left me at the mercy of his two friends, the type who do not ask too many questions and are built like oaks. I was fortunate I survived!" The viscountess started crying.

"Brock," Tipton said, bringing him back to the present. "Amara."

"My lord, where is my sister?" Claeg asked, standing behind his mother.

She sniffled into her handkerchief. "What of our daughter?"

"Your husband sold her to Prola."

"I did no such thing," the man wailed. "Ask him. He must be somewhere in the house."

Strangely, Brock believed him. There was a chance Prola had confronted Amara about the marriage and she had refused. Acting on his own, he had kidnapped her. He leaned over, close to the man's ear. What he had to say was for this man alone.

"You accused me of being unworthy. Unworthy is selling your daughter six years past to the highest drunken bidder in order to satisfy your greed. It is inviting that man into your country house and being so careless, the villain beats and defiles the daughter you should have treasured. I despise you. When I find her, I am taking her away from you. Pray, Keyworth, that Amara is unhurt, because the next time we meet, I will do more than wrinkle your cravat."

Releasing the older man, Brock limped toward his family. Claeg walked away, obviously determined to continue the search for his sister, leaving his mother to comfort her husband. Behind him, Brock could hear Lady Keyworth sobbing. Tipton put his arm around him and took some of the burden off his injured leg. Everyone parted for them. Some of the guests seemed as if they wanted to applaud his vulgar display, others were simply horrified.

"I am not leaving the house until we locate someone who noticed Amara leaving," Brock said.

"We will find her, my dear," Aunt Moll promised. She patted his arm. Blinking back tears, his sister Irene nodded. She moved on, watching over their elderly aunt.

Twenty minutes later, the Keyworths' butler, Buckle, dragged a terrified footman in front of Brock. His accounting of Amara's final moments in the house was baffling until the quaking man described the gentleman who had paid him one pound to deliver his message. It was Prola.

The coach swiftly barreled across town. Brock's knuckles still stung from the brief, yet enlightening chat he had had with Prola's cohort, Burnes. It seemed the Italian kept two houses in London: one for appearances, and one that Burnes had said was for discreet nocturnal encounters. If Prola had Amara, he would have taken her to that house.

Tipton and Milroy had joined Brock. Fortunately, they had convinced Sir Thomas that he was needed at home to guard the ladies. Digging out a rusty old pistol that he had stored under the coach's seat, his sire was seeing rogues in every corner. Brock needed Prola alive. He was not so confident he could keep the elder Bedegrayne from putting a hole in the Italian's heart before the man revealed Amara's whereabouts. Or anyone else, including himself! Everyone was too hot-blooded.

Tipton competently wrapped strips of linen to bind Brock's right leg. The night air was stiffening his muscles. He could barely put his full weight on it. The tight wrapping provided some extra support.

"You should have stayed with your wives."

Milroy sat forward, his arms resting between his legs in an attempt to diminish his large size. It did not help. "Prola might not be alone."

"Burnes and the laughing strangler are sleeping in a cell. How many friends does one man hire?" Brock wondered aloud.

Claeg, who had buried his face in the crook of his arm, snickered. "Obviously, they did not pound the humor out of you, Bedegrayne."

"'Ey, I resisted reenacting my ambush with your father, though I was tempted when I noticed him running about and demanding my arrest."

"You showed remarkable restraint," Claeg praised. "If anyone had actually listened, I would have held him down for you."

The thought made him chuckle. This was the first time he had laughed since he had left Amara. Swearing, Brock groaned and held his gut. "The next man who makes me laugh will get my foot."

Tipton closed his medical case. "What did you whisper in Keyworth's ear?"

"Your words troubled him," Milroy observed.

He leaned back in the seat and closed his eyes. Brock

regretted losing his temper. He had wanted Keyworth to understand that Brock's hatred stemmed from what had been done to Amara, not to himself. If there was justice, the knowledge would torment him, consuming his sanity as greed had feasted on his rotten soul.

Amara was forced to stand beside Lord Cornley while he played cards. His obsession with the game allowed her to peek at his profile. His once handsome face was ruined. The flesh not disfigured by the fire, age, and overindulgence had softened. Only his eyes appeared the same. They were still hard, brimming with malice and selfish ambition.

"Everyone stares," he murmured, not glancing up from his hand. "You cannot help it. The scars ensnare."

"How did you survive the fire?"

"Providence. The fire caused such an uproar, no one noticed my brother had dragged me out. Of course, there were pieces of me he could not save." He bobbed his hairless brow at her.

Like his wits? She did not express her opinion aloud.

Sounds from above had everyone glancing up. The footfalls traveled the length of the room and then faded. None of the men seemed worried about their late caller. A door creaked somewhere in the house.

She shivered. "You never mentioned you had a brother." Amara twisted the ropes at her wrists.

Cornley sipped his beer. "Why would I? He was poor, titleless, and lacked my good looks. Most women ignored him."

The door swung open. Amara had not perceived she

was inching backward until one of the men grabbed her bindings and pulled her closer to the table.

Conte Prola laughed at her surprised expression. "John," he ordered Cornley in crisp English, "get our lady a chair. She looks as if she is about to swoon."

"May I present to you my brother, Matthew Fenner," the earl said, using a falsetto voice.

Amara let herself be pushed into the chair one of the men procured. "Brother. You fooled everyone. My father—my—everyone!"

The man named Matthew Fenner bowed. "Thank you, Miss Claeg."

She persisted, trying to find the conte in this gentleman. "Are you even from Genova?"

He shook his head apologetically. "We have traveled extensively over the years, but England is my homeland. Conte Prola is merely a useful character. He opens doors that are now closed to Lord Cornley."

Cornley muttered under his breath.

"After I rejected your proposal of marriage, you could have left town. Your—the conte could have continued on somewhere else."

"There is no need to move on once we are married," Matthew assured her.

It suddenly occurred to her why she had resisted Conte Prola. It was his eyes. Those gorgeous orbs were always so eloquent, their bluish depths filled with a liquid sincerity she never quite believed. Now he watched her, his gaze sharp and filled with a touch of arrogance. The determination gleaming from within absolutely terrified her.

Her hands concealed under the table, Amara diligently plucked at the knot with her fingers. She wet her parched lips with the tip of her tongue. "My father is ambitious. Even so, he does have his principles. A foreign count is acceptable for his daughter, a swindler is not," she said, allowing the derision she felt to reflect in both her expression and voice.

Lord Cornley pounded his fist on the table, causing her to flinch. His body shook with mirth instead of the anger she had expected. "She is correct. Keyworth would choose a monkey over you!"

"Silence, you grotesque monstrosity!" Prola shouted over his brother's laughter. Walking around the table, he grabbed Amara's upper arm and pulled her up. "Your father will not contest a consummated elopement." He pinched her arm so hard the muscles grated against bone. "Are you breeding, Miss Claeg? Keyworth will be pleased you have settled so quickly into marriage."

Amara parted her lips.

"Yes," he said, seeing her sudden comprehension. "I am aware how close you were with Bedegrayne. I followed you both out of London. Your activities that night were most shocking."

Cornley slammed his cards down on the table. "It is unfair! You cooed and sighed for Bedegrayne. When I had you, all you did was whine and scratch."

The scoundrel! His attack had almost destroyed her sanity. She wanted to kill him for what he had done. Using her bound hands as a weapon, she struck Prola in the face.

The unexpected blow stunned him. He staggered backward, landing on the lap of one of the other men. The chair tipped over.

Amara did not hesitate.

Baring her teeth, she dashed by Cornley and through the open door before anyone recovered from her bold escape. She ran through the connecting chilly corridor. Someone had lit the lamps suspended from the arched stone ceiling, chasing the darkest shadows away, although the bleak light did little to quell her fear of the unfamiliarity of her surroundings or the ambitious men behind her. With her heart pounding in her ears, she moved as fast as her skirts permitted, half convinced phantom fingers were brushing her nape.

The corridor widened. This room was unlit, the only hint of its dangers provided by the distant corridor lamps. Amara cried out as she collided into something solid. Using her bound hands to feel her way around the obstacle, she dropped into a crouch. The rough fragrant wood of the oak casks confirmed her earlier suspicion that they had indeed stashed her in a cellar. She flinched when one of the men shouted that he had glimpsed her. Since he was on the opposite side of the subterranean chamber, she guessed the befuddled man was pursuing rats. *Rats,* she thought with a squeamish shudder. Forsaking modesty, she hitched up her skirts so she could crawl forward to the closest rack of wine bottles. Her fingers closed around the neck of one of the bottles and silently removed it from its dusty berth. Wielding it like a club, she stood and moved stealthily in what she hoped was the direction of the stairs. The sound of scuffling feet had her pressing herself against the wooden frame of one of the numerous racks.

"Amara," Cornley rasped, his voice the embodiment of all her nightmares. "If marrying Matthew is disagreeable, you could have me." She counted the approaching footfalls.

"Never," she vowed. Aiming high, she swung out and shattered the bottle into his horrified visage. Dropping the severed neck of glass, she ran straight to the stairs. More bottles shattered as Cornley blindly thrashed into the racks. His eerie howls had her panting in terror. Halfway up the unlit stairs, she blindly slammed into one of her captors.

His arms circled around, binding her to his chest while she kicked and screamed.

"Amara!" the man shouted, dragging her the remaining distance up the stairs and into the light. She fell onto the floor, striking out at real and imaginary foes.

"Dove, dove," Brock said, dropping to the floor and pulling her into his arms. He repeated the word over and over until the world around her came into focus. She finally recognized the three formidable men standing above her: Mallory, Tipton, and Wynne's Milroy. They had formed a protective circle around her and the man who held her so fiercely that she could barely draw a breath.

Shaking, she squeezed him tighter. She choked on a bubble of laughter at his groan. "Brock," she cried for her friend and her lover. "Cornley is alive."

The news was met with grim silence. The sounds of breaking glass and rage-filled shrieks still echoed from below.

"Prola saved him from the fire. I—I hit him in the face with a bottle. They are brothers, you know," she chattered, not certain she was making any sense.

Mallory bent over and kissed the top of her head. Then he met Brock's livid pale green gaze, and the two men conversed without speaking. With a nod, her brother straightened and headed down the stairs. Tipton and Milroy followed. Cornley would not escape justice this time.

Overwhelmed by the ordeal, she leaned into Brock. "Once again, you rescued me from Cornley."

Trying to shield her with his body, he rocked her. She

felt his denial long before he quietly said, "No, Amara, this time you were strong enough to rescue yourself."

The nightmare had ended. Amara barely felt anything as she watched Prola and a mewling Cornley with blood and gore on his ruined face being turned over to the police. Perhaps the brandy Brock forced down her was to blame, but she thought she would feel something, anything.

Mallory appeared before her and with sweet gentleness took up her hand. "You have hurt yourself, puss. Let the surgeon tend it."

She glanced helplessly at the three-inch cut across her right palm. Until her brother had brought it to her attention, she had not even noticed she had been hurt. Still bleeding, the laceration pulsed and burned. She must have cut her hand when she hit Cornley with the bottle.

"I've got her," Brock said, using the linen strips bandaging his own leg to wrap around her hand. His gaze heated with something darker than anger when he said to Mallory, "Follow after them, and make certain Cornley and Prola remain under guard. I do not trust myself if justice fails us."

"You are not alone in this," her brother said, the softness he had shown her vanishing at the mention of her captors. "Take care of her, Bedegrayne."

Amara wanted to call her brother back for fear he might try something foolish. Milroy, perceiving her distress, gave her a reassuring nod and trailed after her departing brother.

"You both need tending and this place is unsuitable. I have already sent word home to expect our arrival," Tipton said with his usual peremptory aplomb.

Amara was too tired to argue. Besides, she was not certain her father would accept her into his household again. She allowed Brock to assist her to stand. "Tipton, once you came to me in my bedchamber and eased my grief by telling me that Doran was alive." Brock tensed; his grip on her arm bordered on painful. Ignoring him, she begged, "I need the truth, my lord. Does my brother Doran still live?"

"Tipton." Brock managed to infuse both a command and a warning in the one word.

Regret washed over the surgeon's austere features. "No."

The edges of her vision started to gray and close in on her. Amara did not realize she was falling until Brock caught her in his arms and lowered her to the floor.

"Damn you, Tipton!" Brock seethed. "Has she not suffered enough for one evening? Why did you have to tell her the truth now?"

She never heard Tipton's calm reply. Her last thought before she succumbed to the darkness was that Brock had always known of Doran's true fate and had let her believe the lie.

Brock carried Amara into the bedchamber his sister had prepared earlier and placed her on the bed. She had not said one word since she had revived from her faint. That had not deterred him from holding her while they traveled to Tipton's town house. She had not resisted his embrace, nor had she clung to him. Tipton, in his dispassionate manner, explained the circumstances that had led to her brother's murder. Expressionless, she had stared out the carriage window. Brock was not even certain she had heard Tipton.

His teeth snapped together in frustration. They had gone through so much for him to lose her now. At first, he had wanted to break Tipton's neck for his revelation. Tipton had quickly cooled his ire by pointing out that Amara had fallen for Prola's ruse because of their deception. She whimpered now as Tipton unwound the linen around her hand to examine her wound. The ropes that had bound her wrists had cut into her tender flesh as she had struggled to escape. Holding her close, he closed his eyes in pain; the knowledge boiled in his gut that he was once again responsible for Cornley's harming her.

"I regret so much, Amara," he said wearily. "My actions in the past have not always been respectable or redeemable." He laughed softly at himself. "Loving you tempered the wickedness that threatened to consume me in my reckless youth. I need you to believe in me again."

Amara sealed his lips with just the light touch of her fingertips. He kissed her fingers, accepting her silent forgiveness. Ignoring the tears that were threatening to unman him, Brock held her while Tipton stitched the deep three-inch gash in her palm. He distracted her with a slightly embellished tale about his ambush and his clumsy manservant's heroics. There was no point in confessing how perilous the situation had become. He could not help the omission. Whether she accepted him in her life or not, he intended to spend the rest of his life protecting her. She and Tipton laughed with him. Then the horror of the night sank beneath her icy veil. She turned her face into his chest and began to sob. Tipton finished stitching her wound, then silently departed, leaving Brock to the healing of her heart.

Unable to bear her wild grief, he pulled her into his

lap. "I will not tell you not to cry," he said, rubbing her back as if she were a child. "You have experienced enough pain in your young life not to shed a tear about the past." She clung to him and cried. He preferred the tears, believing they were more healing than the icy walls she had tried to build to protect herself. Brock did not speak again until her gulping sobs had quieted to an occasional shiver. "I was never the kind of man who looked farther than a few days ahead. Loving you gave me a future to dream about. Do you know what I see?"

Amara sniffed into a handkerchief and cuddled closer. He tolerated the physical pain her movements caused him because he preferred having her close when he spoke of his dreams.

"Do I not have a say in this grand future you have planned for us?"

Since he heard the amusement in her tone, he relaxed and smiled. "I see us married, Amara, and soon, since I need you snuggled by my side at night." His hand slipped down to her stomach and rested there, wondering if their child already slept in her womb. "I see us with a house filled with children because a love like ours was meant to be shared."

"And because you look forward to such an endeavor," she added, blushing prettily at her boldness.

"I confess that I intend to concentrate all my energies toward the task as soon as possible," he teased, and then sobered. "Your mother and father will most likely disown you if you marry me, dove. You will have Mallory, of course. Their disapproval has not bothered him in the past. And I can offer you my family. They have loved you almost as long as I have. Who knows, maybe someday, if Lord and Lady Keyworth can forgive me for stealing you away, I can figure out a way in which to give your family back to you."

"You offer me so much, Brock. What can I offer you?"

His lips quirked into a sinful grin as he eased her onto the pillows and caged her with his body. "You can fill my days with joy and my nights with wicked carnal delights. Allow me to demonstrate," he coaxed, dipping closer for a kiss.

"Finished?" Tipton asked, interrupting Brock's seduction. "You both need sleep. Acting as your physician, I recommend postponing those carnal delights for a few nights. Amara might hurt you." He winked, and set off to find his wife.

Brock sat up in bed and removed his coat and cravat. In deference to his countless bruises, he did not remove his breeches and shirt. Amara was going to be rather upset with him when she saw his injuries and he preferred having her in his arms. He settled back down on the bed beside her.

Covering her eyes with her undamaged hand, Amara suddenly moaned.

"Should I summon Tipton?"

"No, no," she said, looking miserable. "I forgot. Brock, they took my jewelry."

The tension eased from his shoulders. "Let us worry about the Claeg family jewels tomorrow."

"I do not care about my mother's jewelry!" she said fiercely. They both ignored her tiny lie. "Brock! Your mother's intaglio is gone."

"Not quite." Digging several fingers under his shirt, he revealed the gold chain. Claeg had found all the jewelry stolen from Amara in Cornley's coat pocket. Wincing, he pulled the chain over his head.

"You have it," she sighed, clutching her treasure to her heart. She slipped the intaglio over her head and sank back into the pillows.

Brock smiled down at the intaglio, the maiden and beast forever bound together in stone. "Rest, your talisman will protect you."

Surprised, Amara looked up, her stormy blue eyes filling with tears. Lovingly, she laid her hand against his cheek. "He always has."